A Study in Sherlock

A Study in Sherlock

Stories Inspired by the Holmes Canon

Editors

Laurie R. King and Leslie S. Klinger

Stories by

Alan Bradley • Tony Broadbent • Jan Burke •
Lionel Chetwynd • Lee Child • Colin Cotterill •
Neil Gaiman • Laura Lippman • Gayle Lynds and
John Sheldon • Phillip Margolin and Jerry Margolin •
Margaret Maron • Thomas Perry • S. J. Rozan •
Dana Stabenow • Charles Todd • Jacqueline Winspear

Poisoned Pen Press

First Edition 2011

10 9 8 7 6 5 4 3 2 1

Library of Congress Catalog Card Number: 2011934771

ISBN: 9781590585498   Hardcover

Poisoned Pen Press
6962 E. First Ave., Ste. 103
Scottsdale, AZ 85251
www.poisonedpenpress.com
info@poisonedpenpress.com

Printed in the United States of America

Contents

An Introduction

Laurie R. King and Leslie S. Klinger

Only true genius can produce an invention, or a hero, that fills a gaping hole in our lives we never knew—never even *suspected*—was there. For millennia, we were perfectly content with pen and paper; then e-mail was introduced and now no one can live without it. Paintings and lithographs held all the rich vocabulary of visual creation—until photography became our native tongue. And we had a whole raft of heroes to tell stories about: why on earth would we need a self-described "consulting detective" with misanthropic attitudes and unsavory habits?

But one day in 1887, Arthur Conan Doyle sat down to write a tale of an odd young man with peculiar skills and changed the world. *A Study in Scarlet* is indeed a young man's story, packed to overflowing with Romantic Adventure and startling ideas, with thrilling lines (lines a modern editor might blue-pencil as melodramatic) such as "There's the scarlet thread of murder running through the colourless skein of life, and our duty is to unravel it, and isolate it, and expose every inch of it."

In no time at all, an entire industry of homages and satires, pastiches and parodies sprang up around Sherlock Holmes. Holmes was imagined in a thousand non-Doylean manifestations: married; in exotic climes; paired with historical and literary figures; made younger, older, taller, shorter, more robotic, more emotional, nearly every variation conceivable. Conan Doyle himself wrote non-Holmes stories that were yet openly patterned on the character. That previously unsuspected gaping hole in our lives (the size and import of which Sir Arthur refused to acknowledge) proved to bear the shape of nothing short of an archetype: a modern-day knight errant; a man whose passion for righting wrongs is mistaken for a cold intellectual curiosity; a tortured hero with but a single friend; a man who never lived "and so can never die," who is more alive today than any other resident of the Victorian Age, including Victoria herself.

The tales in this volume show eighteen top writers exploring the contours and boundaries of that archetype, playing with the ideas of how this Platonic ideal of a detecting hero might look in different situations, wearing a variety of faces. Some recount untold adventures of the Master Detective; others look at him from fresh perspectives; still others listen to the echoes of his passing.

All are stories inspired by Sir Arthur Conan Doyle and his first study in Sherlock.

Laurie R. King is the award-winning (Edgar, Creasey, Agatha, Nero, Lambda, Macavity) and bestselling author of a score of crime novels, half of them featuring "the world's greatest detective—and her husband, Sherlock Holmes." Mary Russell (*The Beekeeper's Apprentice; Pirate King*) has been described as a young, female, twentieth-century Holmes, a gent whom she finds wandering through 1915 Sussex looking for bees and promptly insults. King's temerity was rewarded by induction into the Baker Street Irregulars, where she was put to work editing Holmes-related books, both fiction and non-, by her Irregular betters, in a thinly disguised attempt to keep her from writing more Russellian novels. Her books and a whole lot of somewhat related academic material can be found at www.LaurieRKing.com.

Leslie S. Klinger is the Edgar-winning editor of *The New Annotated Sherlock Holmes,* a collection of the entire Sherlock Holmes Canon with an almost endless quantity of footnotes and appendices. He also edited the highly regarded *The New Annotated Dracula* and numerous anthologies of Victorian detective and vampire fiction and criticism. Working with Neil Gaiman, he is currently editing *The Annotated Sandman* for DC

Comics. Klinger is a member of the Baker Street Irregulars and teaches for UCLA Extension on Holmes, Dracula, and the Victorian world. A lawyer by day, Klinger lives in Los Angeles with his wife, dog, and three cats. He first met Sherlock Holmes and his world in 1968, while attending law school, through the pages of William S. Baring-Gould's 1967 classic *The Annotated Sherlock Holmes,* and was hooked for life. This anthology is the result of discovering that many of his seemingly normal writer-friends shared his passion for the Holmes stories.

A Study in Sherlock

You'd Better Go in Disguise

Alan Bradley

How long had he been watching me? I wondered.

I had been standing for perhaps a quarter of an hour, gazing idly at the little boys in sailor suits and their sisters in pinafores, all of whom, watched over by a small army of nannies and a handful of mothers, waded like diminutive giants among their toy sailing boats in the Serpentine.

A sudden breeze had sprung up, scattering the fallen leaves and bringing the slightest of chills to an otherwise idyllic autumn afternoon. I shivered and turned up my collar, the hairs at the back of my neck bristling against my jacket.

To be precise, the pressure of my collar put a *stop* to the bristling which, since I had not noticed it until that moment, made the feeling all that much more peculiar.

Perhaps it was because I had, the previous week, attended Professor Malabar's demonstration at the Palladium. His uncanny experiments in the world of the unseen were sufficient to give pause to even the greatest of sceptics, among whom, most assuredly, I do not count myself.

I must admit at the outset to an unshakeable belief in the theory that there is a force which emanates from the eye of a watcher that is detectable by some as-yet-undiscovered sensor at the back of the neck of the person being watched; a phenomenon which, I am furthermore convinced, is caused by a specialized realm of magnetism whose principles are not yet fully understood by science.

In short, I knew that I was being stared at, a fact which, in itself, is not necessarily without pleasure. What, for example, if one of those nattily uniformed nannies had her eye upon me? Even though I was presently more conservative than I once had been, I was keenly aware that I still cut rather a remarkable figure. At least, when I chose to.

I turned slowly, taking care to pitch my gaze above the heads of the governesses, but by the time I had turned through a casual half circle they were every one engaged again in gossip or absorbed in the pages of a book.

I studied them intently, paying close attention to all but one, who sat primly on a park bench, her head bowed, as if in silent prayer.

It was then that I spotted him: just beyond the swans; just beyond a tin toy *Unterseeboot.*

He was sitting quietly on a bench, his hands folded in his lap, his polished boots forming a carpenter's square upon the gravelled path. A solicitor's clerk, I should have thought, although his ascetic gauntness did not without contradiction suggest one who laboured in the law.

Even though he wanted not to be seen (a fact which, as a master of that art myself, I recognized at once), his eye, paradoxically all-seeing, was the eye of an eagle: hard, cold, and objective.

To my horror, I realized that my legs were propelling me inexorably towards the stranger and his bench, as if he had summoned me by means of some occult wireless device.

I found myself standing before him.

"A fine day," he said, in a voice which might have been at home on the Shakespearean stage, and yet which, for all its resonance, struck a false note.

"One smells the city after the rain," he went on, "for better or for worse."

I smiled politely, my instincts pleading with me not to strike up a conversation with an over-chatty stranger.

He shifted himself sideways on the bench, touching the wooden seat with long fingers.

"Please sit," he said, and I obeyed.

I pulled out a cigarette case, selected one, and patted my pockets for a match. As if by magic a Lucifer appeared at his fingertips, and, solicitously, he lit me up.

I offered him the open case, but he brushed it away with a swift gesture of polite refusal. My exhaled smoke hung heavily in the autumn air.

"I perceive you are attempting to give up the noxious weed."

I must have looked taken aback.

"The smell of bergamot," he said, "is a dead giveaway. Oswego tea, they call it in America, where they drink an infusion of the stuff for no other reason than pleasure. Have you been to America?"

"Not in some time," I said.

"Ah." He nodded. "Just as I thought."

"You seem to be a very observant person," I ventured.

"I try to keep my hand in," he said, "although it doesn't come as easily as it did in my salad days. Odd, isn't it, how, as they gain experience, the senses become blunted. One must keep them up by making a game of it, like the boy, Kim, in Kipling. Do you enjoy Kipling?"

I was tempted to reply with that exhausted old wheeze, *I don't know, I've never kippled,* but something told me (that strange sense again) to keep it to myself.

"I haven't read him for years," I said.

"A singular person, Kipling. Remarkable, is it not, that a man with such weakened eyes should write so much about the sense of sight?"

"Compensation, perhaps," I suggested.

"Ha! An alienist! You are a follower of Freud."

Damn the fellow. Next thing I knew he'd be asking me to pick a card and telling me my auntie's telephone number.

I gave him half a nod.

"Just so," he said. "I perceived by your boots that you have been in Vienna. The soles of Herr Stockinger are unmistakable."

I turned and, for the first time, sized the man up. He wore a tight-fitting jacket and ragged trousers, an open collar with a red scarf at his throat, and on his head, a tram conductor's cap with the number 309 engraved on a brass badge.

Not a workman—no, too old for that, but someone who wanted to be taken for a workman. An insurance investigator, perhaps, and with that thought my heart ran suddenly cold.

"You must come here often," I said, giving him back a taste of his own, "to guess out the occupations of strangers. Bit of a game with you, is it?"

His brow wrinkled.

"Game? There are no games on the battlefield of life, Mr. —"

"De Voors," I said, blurting out the first thing that came to mind.

"Ah! De Voors. Dutch, then."

It was not so much a question as a statement—as if he were ticking off an internal checklist.

"Yes," I said. "Originally."

"Do you speak the language?"

"No."

"As I suspected. The labials are not formed in that direction."

"See here, Mister—"

"Montague," he said, seizing my hand and giving it a hearty shake.

Why did I have the feeling he was simultaneously using his forefinger to gauge my pulse?

"...Samuel Montague. I am happy to meet you. Undeniably happy."

He gave his cap a subservient tip, ending with a two-fingered salute at its brim.

"You have not answered my question, Mr. Montague," I said. "Do you come here often to observe?"

"The parks of our great city are conducive to reflection," he said. "I find that a great expanse of grass gives free rein to the mind."

"Free rein is not always desirable," I said, "in a mind accustomed to running in its own tram tracks."

"Excellent!" he exclaimed. "A touch of metaphor. It is a characteristic not always to be found among the Dutch!"

"See here, Mr. Montague," I said. "I don't know that I like—"

But already his hand was on my arm.

"No offence, my dear fellow. No offence at all. In any case, I see that your British hedgehog outbristles your Dutch beech marten."

"What the devil do you mean by that?" I said, leaping to my feet.

"Nothing at all. It was an attempted joke on my part that failed to jell—an impertinence. Please forgive me."

He seized my sleeve and pulled me down beside him on the bench.

"That fellow over there," he said in a low voice. "Don't look at him directly—the one loitering beneath the lime. What do you make of him?"

"He is a doctor," I replied quickly, eager to shift the focus from myself. The unexpected widening of my acquaintance's eyes told me that I had scored a lucky hit.

"How can you tell?" he demanded.

"He has the slightly hunched shoulders of a man who has sat by many a sickbed."

"And?"

"And the tips of his fingers are stained with silver nitrate from the treating of warts."

Montague laughed.

"How can you be sure he's not a cigarette smoker and an apothecary?"

"He's not smoking and apothecaries do not generally carry black bags."

"Wonderful," exclaimed Montague. "Add to that the pin of Bart's Hospital in his lapel, the seal of the Royal College of Surgeons on his keychain, and the unmistakable outline of a stethoscope in his jacket pocket."

I found myself grinning at him like a Cheshire cat.

I had fallen into the game.

"And the park keeper?"

I sized up the old man, who was picking up scraps of paper and lobbing them with precision into a wheeled refuse bin.

"An old soldier. He limps. He was wounded. His large body is mounted upon spindly legs. Probably spent a great deal of time in a military hospital recovering from his wounds. Not an officer—he doesn't have the bearing. Infantry, I should say. Served in France."

Montague bit the corner of his lip and gave me half a wink.

"Splendid!" he said.

"Now then," he went on, pointing with his chin towards the woman sitting alone on the park bench closest to the water. "Over there is a person who seems quite ordinary—quite plain. No superabundance of clues to be had. I'll bet you a shilling you can't supply me with three solid facts about her."

As he spoke, the woman leaped to her feet and called out to a child who was knee-deep in the water.

"Heinrich! Come here, my sweet little toad!"

"She is German," I said.

"Quite so," said Montague. "And can you venture more? Pray, do go on."

"She's German," I said with finality, hoping to bring to an end this unwanted exercise. "And that's an end of it."

"Is it?" he asked, looking at me closely.

I did not condescend to reply.

"Let me see, then, if I may succeed in taking up where you have left off. As you have observed, she is German. We shall begin with that. Next, we shall note that she is married: the rings on the usual finger of the left hand make that quite clear, an opinion which is bolstered by the fact that young Heinrich, who has lost his stick in the water, is the very image of his pretty little mother.

"She is widowed—and very recently, if I am any judge. Her black dress is fresh from Peter Robinson's Mourning Warehouse. Indeed, the tag is still affixed at the nape of her neck, which tells us, among many other things, that regardless of her apparent poise, she is greatly distracted and no longer has a maid.

"In spite of having overlooked the tag, she possesses excellent eyesight, evinced by the fact that she is able to read the excruciatingly small type of the book which is resting in her lap, and without more than an upward glance, keep an eye upon her child who is now nearly halfway across the basin. What do you suppose would bring such a woman to a public park?"

"Really, Montague," I said. "You have no right—"

"Tut, my dear fellow. I am merely exercising the possibilities. In truth, I have barely scratched the surface. Where were we? Oh, yes. German. Indubitably German. But from which region in particular?

"Let us begin with young master Heinrich. What was it she called him? 'My sweet toad,' wasn't it? An expression which, although not restricted to Baden, is nevertheless much more commonly to be heard there than in other parts of the country.

"Very well, then let us for the moment hypothesize that the young widow is from Baden. How may we test that rather broad assumption?

"Let us dwell for a moment upon her teeth. Surely you noticed, as I did when she called out to her child, that she showed a very fine, strong set of teeth, remarkable however, not for their completeness or their pleasing alignment, but rather for the fact that they are pinkish: a rare, but nonetheless documented phenomenon which arises only in those who have been accustomed to drink, from birth, the iron-rich waters of certain spas.

"As I know from my own remarkable cure in those waters, one of those with the highest content of ferric matter is at Mergentheim. Yes, I should say we could not go far astray if we pegged the lady as a Swabian from Baden. That and her accent, of course."

I couldn't restrain a laugh.

"Altogether far-fetched," I told him. "Your hypotheses, as you call them, leave no elbow room for reality. What if, for instance, she is mourning her father? Or her mother? Or her great-grandmother, for that matter?"

"Then her name would not have been splashed all over the front pages of this morning's newspapers as the wife of a murder victim."

"What?"

"Tragic, but nevertheless quite true, I assure you."

He reached with two fingers into his vest pocket and extracted a double-columned clipping which he proceeded to unfold and flatten on his knee.

"*Shocking death in Buncombe Place,*" he read aloud. "*Police were called at an early hour this morning to Number Six, Buncombe Place by Mrs. Frieda Barnett, who had, moments before, found her husband, Welland Barnett, aged fifty, of the same address, dead in the drawing room in a pool of his own blood. The victim had received a number of stab wounds to the back of his neck, any one of which might have proved fatal, according to the police surgeon at the scene…*"

"They oughtn't really to put that in," he interrupted himself. "Not until autopsy and inquest are complete. I'm quite sure that heads will roll—if it is not indelicate to express such an opinion."

I couldn't find words to respond, and Montague went on with his reading.

"*The deceased was described as a man of regular habits, and had no known enemies, according to Mrs. Barnett, who is left to mourn with her only child, Heinrich, aged four years…*"

"They always go for the heart, don't they, these scandal sheets—like the bullets at a military execution. Where were we—oh, yes, her child…"

Montague paused to look out at the little boy who had now fished his stick from the water and was giving the surface a good wet thrashing by way of repayment.

"*...her only child, Heinrich, aged four years,*" he went on. "*Inspector Gregson of Scotland Yard has given it as his opinion that robbery may have been a motive, inasmuch as a small silver key of peculiar design was missing from its customary place upon the victim's waistcoat chain, according to Ellen Dimity, the Barnetts' cook. Inspector Gregson declined to give further information until investigations are complete, although he has requested that any person or persons who might have further information bearing upon this crime,* et cetera, et cetera, et cetera. Would you like to read it?"

He offered the paper, but I shook my head.

"No thank you. I find such things upsetting."

"Indeed," he said, "as do I. Which is precisely why I made my way to Number Six, Buncombe Place, and begged my old friend Gregson to let me have a look round."

"Inspector Gregson? You know him?"

Montague chuckled, a surprisingly shrill cackle that ended in a suppressed cough.

"Old lags have friends, too," he said. "Surprising, isn't it, the people you meet in a park?"

I said nothing because there was nothing to say.

"The thing of it was," he went on, as if I had asked him to, "the position of the wounds, which were high on the back of the neck. Welland Barnett was an exceedingly tall individual, over six feet in height—as much as six foot three or four, by my own measurement of his prostrate body. Am I upsetting you?"

"Not at all," I said. "It's just that I've not yet eaten today, and I'm afraid it's telling."

"Ah, then. Presently we shall step round to the Hart and Hurdy-Gurdy for a pig's knuckle and a pint of Burton. Then we shall be fit for whatever lies ahead."

I gave him a weak smile.

"And then there was the widow," he said, glancing at the woman in black who sat, again motionless, upon the bench, her gaze fixed firmly upon the ground.

"How peculiar, don't you think, that she should leave the house under circumstances in which drawn drapes and smelling salts are most often the order of the day?

"But perhaps it was the child—perhaps she wanted to get young Heinrich as quickly as possible away from that house of death. But no, the good Gregson assured me that the child had put up quite a fuss—what you might call a scene, in fact—over being dragged into the street and involving, in the end, more of the neighbors than it ought.

"Gregson could not detain her, of course. She had given her account of finding her husband's body; her words had been taken down in the prescribed form; the house had been searched; the body was in the process of being removed.

"Why, then, would she leave?"

I shrugged.

"Who could know?" I said. "There are as many reasons as stars in the heavens. It is pointless to guess."

"Guess?" Montague's voice and his eyebrows shot up. "Where murder's afoot the guess is disallowed. The facts must be driven home one by one like nails into the shoe of a horse. *Tap! Tap! Tap! Tap! Tap!* Do you hear them, Mr. De Voors?"

"No," I replied, "but then I've never been given over greatly to imagination."

"Then I shall help you," he said. "Imagine this: imagine that on a fine day in autumn a woman leaves the house in which her husband has just been brutally murdered, and sets out with her only child, for a park that is somewhat more than a mile away.

"Why not the park that is directly across the street from where she lives? Why not the one in the next block—or the next?

"The child has no sailboat, but only a stick which he picked up near the gate. I saw it with my own eyes. So it is not the water which is the attraction. It is, in the second place, distance. She did not wish to be observed. She came here, as I knew she must have done. Where else may one with a child become invisible but in the city's largest park?"

"The second place, you say? Then what is the first?"

"I should have thought it obvious," Montague said. "She came here to meet someone."

"Good heavens!" I exclaimed. "Who?"

"You," said Montague, folding the clipping and returning it to his pocket. "Before you arrived, I watched the lady fiddling with the key. She fished it from her bag a half-dozen times to make sure she still had it. When you finally appeared—you were late, by the way, judging by the number of times she consulted her watch—she made a point of not looking at you. More to the point, you did not look at her. Quite astonishing, when you come to think of it: such a fine figure of a woman seldom remains unogled by a gentleman of your…ah…"

"This is preposterous," I said.

"Is it?" he asked, his voice as level as a gaming table. "In spite of the evidence to the contrary?"

"What evidence?" I could not resist asking. The fellow was trying to rack up a score against me.

"Your height, of course," he said. "You would be quite capable of stabbing in the neck someone as tall as Welland Barnett—not that that means anything in itself. But then we come to your behaviour: you circled any number of times round the bench upon which the lady is sitting, but you did not approach. At first, it was because of the nanny—that one with the curly red hair who was begging to borrow her pencil to fill in one of those new-fangled crosswords that are becoming all the rage. Then it was the retired tea broker who perched beside her for a maddeningly long time as he fed the pigeons. After that, the two police constables who strolled by. No, sir, she has simply not had the opportunity to hand over the promised key, a key which quite clearly, even at this distance and with my no-longer-perfect vision, is one of those used to unlock a box at the National Safe Deposit Company in Victoria Street.

"As to your relationship to her, it is best not to enquire, except that it ended in a pretty little plot involving a worthwhile amount of money and, if I am not mistaken, a life insurance policy. It is an old story: the Freudian practitioner; the female patient who is trapped in a loveless marriage; the sympathetic talk ('transference,' I believe you call it); the temptation; the fall…"

"This is outrageous," I said, my voice rising. The governesses were by now staring at us openly.

"And then," Montague said, almost as an afterthought, "there is the blood upon the instep of your right shoe. I saw it when you crossed your legs."

I leaped to my feet and looked round wildly. There sat Frieda, still staring at the ground as if in a trance. Had she even noticed my predicament?

"Watson," he said in an altogether different voice, "I believe this is where you come in. Pick up his rolled newspaper. Be careful of the knife."

The doctor, who had been standing all the while casually under one of the limes, came forward, and there was suddenly in his hand an ancient but no less dangerous looking military pistol. He held it shielded by his black bag in such a way that it could be seen only by Montague and myself.

"Keep quite still," Montague said. "My medical friend is somewhat out of practice in the small-arms department. The thing has a hair trigger, and we don't want any nasty accidents, do we?"

"Ah, constables!" he said, as the strolling policemen made their appearance. "Right on the second, as usual. We've been expecting you. There's someone here your superiors will doubtless be pleased to see. Who knows? There might even be a promotion in it."

"You devil," I spat. "You're no more Samuel Montague than the man in the moon. You're Sherlock Holmes!"

As the constables, one on each side, seized me by the arms, he stood up, put one heel to the instep of his opposite foot, and made a little bow.

"By the way," he told them, "the lady on the second bench is Mrs. Barnett. Inspector Gregson will be forever in your debt if you should mention to him the curious silver key which you will undoubtedly find in her handbag.

"Come, Watson," he said to the doctor, "the incomparable Evelyn Laye is at the Gaiety and we have just time enough to fortify ourselves with roast beef at Simpson's. The thespian art is one which does not always receive sufficiently hearty applause."

As they dragged me away, I couldn't resist taunting him over my shoulder.

"What will you do, Holmes, when you've brought to book the last criminal in London? You'll have no more excuse to dress up in your fancy disguises!"

I'll admit my fury had got rather the better of me. As we passed in front of her, Frieda—poor, dear, weak Frieda, with the now-that-you-mention-it pinkish teeth—didn't give me even so much as an upward glance.

"Elementary," I heard him call out as we passed beneath the limes and walked towards the iron gates. "Elementary, my dear fellow. I have my eye on a cottage in St. Mary Mead."

Alan Bradley's Flavia de Luce mysteries have been translated into thirty-one languages. Bradley has retreated to a Mediterranean island, taking with him only his wife, his books, and two cat assistants. As a boy, he was introduced to the Holmes tales by a favorite uncle, who faithfully reread them every fifth year. He is also the coauthor (with the late Dr. William A. S. Sarjeant) of the controversial *Ms. Holmes of Baker Street*, in which the authors prove that Sherlock Holmes was a woman. Bradley may have changed his view since.

The last official record of Holmes's life is the story "His Last Bow," published in 1917 in the collection of the same name. It tells of Holmes's war service as an undercover agent and is written by an unknown author (although it appeared under the byline of Sir Arthur Conan Doyle).

As to "An Exact Knowledge of London"

Tony Broadbent

It was a crisp morning and quite bracing even for that time of year, the fog of yesterday thankfully consigned as if to distant memory, and certainly cold enough for my breath to steam in front of me and linger for a moment before it disappeared into the ether. I remember staring up at Isambard Kingdom Brunel's magnificent iron-and-glass canopies, a sequence of all-encompassing spans that dwarfed everything beneath. And maybe it was the hour or my heightened sense of place, but I couldn't help but notice that the diffused light from above reduced shadow and perspective to such a degree that people below were rendered as tiny indistinct figures in a landscape. It struck me then that the many diverse aspects that presented themselves to my gaze resembled nothing so much as a series of huge painted backcloths in some newly got-in production at Drury Lane or Covent Garden. But, as the immortal Bard once wrote, *all the world's a stage.*

Indeed, the noise and bustle of the great terminus sounded for all the world like an orchestra tuning up and awaiting its conductor; all at once cacophonous, discordant, and deafening and yet even to my untutored ears, oddly comforting; a sonic harbinger of a symphony newly composed to celebrate a mighty capital city in constant reinvention of itself.

Maintaining British-army time, I stood there, fully five minutes early, both feet firmly planted, as wave after wave of blank-faced commuters streamed past me toward the exits and the entrances to the Underground. I took several deep breaths so as to help gather myself for the day ahead. I may have also rubbed my arms with my gloved hands and even stamped my feet, though I'm sure that was more from a simple desire for additional warmth than any undue display of impatience. But then as I've so often observed when in London, the very act of waiting, be it for taxi, Tube train, omnibus, or policeman, is a necessary part of one's visit, and to fight against the inevitability of lost minutes or indeed lost hours would be as if to try and hold back the very times and tides, which is to say quite impossible. Not that that has ever stopped people from trying. I do remember I pulled back the cuff of my leather glove to glance at my wristwatch. "Times and tides, indeed," I muttered.

"Er...you wanting a cab, are you, sir?"

"Well, yes, I have been waiting...I mean, yes, I do want a cab, thank you."

"Very good, sir, where is it you'd like to go; that all your luggage, is it?"

"Ah...Baker Street, please, number 221B. And, yes, it is."

"Need help with it, sir? Only, I couldn't help but notice the walking stick."

"Well, perhaps a hand with the suiter; it is a little heavy. I'll keep my shoulder bag with me."

"Right, you are, sir. Nice Brady bag, that. Got one myself and very handy they are, too. Going hunting, shooting, and fishing, are you, sir?"

"Yes, I rather suppose I am," I said good-humouredly.

Suddenly there was a tremendous bang, in all probability nothing more than a luggage trolley or parcels van hitting a barrier, but it startled me no end and I may have uttered a cry of alarm, I can't recall. For it was then I took a single step forward and stumbled over my ballistic nylon garment bag, lost my balance and went sprawling, dropping my walking stick and sending myself and everything flying. "Blasted leg!" I cursed aloud. "It'll be the death of me yet."

"Here, you okay down there, are you, sir?" the taxi driver called out.

It's as much the embarrassment as the shock you have to contend with when you suffer an unexpected fall, and it took me a moment or two to gather my wits. "Thank you, I'm fine," I shouted back, quickly waving away a passerby who'd stopped to enquire whether I needed help. "Just me being clumsy," I offered by way of explanation. "Perhaps, Mr. Taxi Driver, if you'd be so kind as to store my suiter up front, with you?" I called out to the cabby.

"Righto," he shouted, and I heard him exit the cab and saw him fully for the first time as he came round to where I was still lying on the cold concrete. I slowly got to my feet, holding on to the side of the taxi for balance, and bent down and after a little scrambling around managed to retrieve my tweed cap, my walking stick, and my shoulder bag. As I brushed myself down, the cabby shook his head in sympathy. "You took a right tumble, but as long as you're alright?" I nodded and waved a hand as if to wipe away the whole incident. "Very good, sir. I'll get this garment bag of yours stowed up front. Need help getting in? Only, I've got a ramp I can pull out if you can't manage the step?"

I shook my head, thanked him profusely for his concern, opened the passenger door, and climbed gingerly into the back of the taxi. The cabby nodded and returned to the driver's seat. I have to admit I was a little shaken by the incident and I took no small comfort in hearing the door-locks engage as the cab drove off, up towards Praed Street. And I settled back in my seat, let out an audible sigh of relief, and then reached for my mobile telephone.

"Stop! Please stop! Please pull over," I called out. "I think I dropped my phone, back there, when I fell over. If I can possibly get out and take a look?"

"Blimey. Righto. Hold on."

The taxi skidded to a halt and the moment I heard the doors unlock I grabbed the door handle and was out and onto the pavement and off like the proverbial rabbit. "Thank you," I called over my shoulder. But I hadn't gone ten feet when I stopped dead and spun slowly around. "No, no, wait a minute. Fool me." I returned to the taxi and bent down to be at eye-level with the driver. He lowered the window. "Sorry to be such a bother, but could you open up so I can take a quick look inside my garment bag before I go scuttling off like an idiot? As now I come to think of it, I'm sure I put the damn thing in one of the pockets."

The cabby smiled, but I noticed his eyes were a tad wary, out of long habit, no doubt, but he nodded and opened the door to the front luggage area. I pulled the door fully open, nodded my thanks, and began feverishly unzipping the outer pockets of my garment bag, in my haste all but upending it and sending everything flying again: paperback, Moleskine notebook, spectacles case, tin of peppermints, ballpoint pen; there seemed no end to the contents of those deep pockets, but alas there was no mobile phone. I stuffed everything back, without regard to order or placement, zipping up the pockets and refastening the straps as fast as I could, although I'm sure I must've still appeared unduly clumsy. "I was so certain I put it in here," I said. "Not at all my usual place for it, though; silly of me really." Then I had a sudden thought and felt along an upper seam of the bag and pulled open the hidden pocket. "Here it is, of course, in the so-called handy secret pocket. Thank heaven for that; I'd so hate to have lost another iPhone. Don't seem to know where my head is these days."

The cabby nodded in seeming sympathy and gave me another look. "Right then, sir, now we've got that...er...sorted, Baker Street, you said?"

"Ah, no, look, on second thought, I think I better head straight over to St. Bartholomew's Hospital, Giltspur Street."

"Barts? Right you are, sir." He paused, and I'd swear that for a brief moment a shadow flickered across his face. "That new Cancer Centre, is it, sir?"

I shook my head and gave him a reassuring smile. "No, no, nothing so serious; just a visit to the museum, the north wing; the Henry VIII gate will do."

"With the one-way, I'd best drop you on West Smithfield Road, if that'd be okay?" I nodded. "Right you are, then, sir. If you'd just hop back in."

So off we set again, my mobile phone now safely in my hand, my canvas shoulder bag by my side. London sped by at what a good and dear friend of mine had deduced was no faster than ever it'd been in the time of horse-drawn hansom cabs. I shook my head. Times and tides, indeed. I have to admit I felt not a little silly about the whole wretched incident and I could only imagine what the cab driver must've thought about it all. I took more deep breaths to help calm myself and looked around the interior of the cab. It was bright, airy, and clean, everything one expects of a London taxi, but there was something else besides.

"Excuse me, is this one of those new-style London cabs?" I asked, in a voice loud enough to attract the taxi driver's attention.

"Yes, very well spotted," he shouted over his shoulder. "Haven't had it long, coming up on three or four weeks, now; the LTX4, top of the line, all mod cons, lovely little job; still got that lovely new cab smell."

"Can't quite put my finger on it," I offered, by way of obser-vation, "but it seems so much nicer, all round, somehow."

"The makers would love to hear you say that," he chortled. "Take this intercom we're speaking over, most people don't even realize the plexiglass partition isn't open between them and me and they just start talking, normal like. You just press the button back there or I do in here; works a treat. So there's no need for any more of that looking-back-over-my-shoulder-and-shouting-my-head-off malarkey. Even with a full complement of five passengers, every-one can clearly be heard. There's even an induction loop for the hard of hearing."

"How very thoughtful," I said, surreptitiously checking my iPhone for any e-mails or text messages.

"It is," he said. "On top of which the cab's specially designed to accommodate a wheelchair if need be. Add individual head restraints, a child harness, air-conditioning with separate climate controls for the passengers, plus directional spotlights if anyone wants to read a newspaper or catch up on office work, and it's a real step up in creature comforts. Same goes for me: lumbar support, coil-spring suspension, power-assisted steering, anti-lock braking, the lot. I can even hook my MP3 player in for a bit of music if I want. It's got a computer and a navigation system, too, should ever I have need."

He chatted on, amiably, about his new pride and joy and before I knew it we'd arrived at Barts. "How fascinating," I said, "the continuing evolution of the London taxicab; always the same, only different." I paused. "Look, I say, I only need ten minutes or so, to take some photographs. Would it be possible for you to wait for me while I go inside?"

He wrinkled his nose. "Yes, I don't see why not. I'll just keep the meter running; you take all the time you want. It's all the same to me."

"Thank you," I said. Then, clutching my canvas shoulder bag, I got out of the cab, crossed over the pedestrian divide, slipping between the bollards as I did so, and went to stand in front of the archway. I took photographs of the statue of Henry VIII, turned and waved at the taxi driver, and pointed through the arch. I held up a hand with fingers splayed. "Five minutes," I mouthed. He nodded back, pulled out a newspaper, and began reading. I, meanwhile, went in through the archway, changed camera lenses, peered at the digital display, and took some more photos. Then I sent a quick three-word text message. After a few more minutes I glanced at my watch. Time enough. I stepped out from beneath the archway and walked back across the median to where the taxi was parked. I got in again and expressed my thanks.

"I've had the heater on, so it's nice and toasty for you," the cabby said over the intercom. "Off to Baker Street, now, is it?"

"Look, I know I said 221B Baker Street was my ultimate destination, but there are a few other places I'd really like to visit before that. I have a list."

"A list of points of interest? And I suppose you'd like me to wait for you at each one?" I nodded and he tapped his chin with a finger, as the meter ticked on in the background. "Yes, I suppose I could do that, sir," he said, nodding. "It still being kipper season and things a bit slack on account of winter weather."

"It'd really be most helpful," I said, hurriedly turning to the appropriate page in my Moleskine notebook and holding it up for the cabby to see. He opened the tiny window in the glass partition and I pushed the little black notebook through to the driver's compartment and he took it and glanced at the list, then he looked at it again even more closely. He turned and looked at me, with eyes narrowed, an inquisitive smile pulling at the corners of his mouth.

"If I'm not mistaken, sir, all these points you've got listed feature in stories by Conan Doyle; specifically the adventures of one Sherlock Holmes?" He paused. "Would I be right in presuming you're one of them 'Holmesians'; 'the game's afoot!' and all that malarkey?" He smiled openly, then. "Although of course it was you wanting to go to 221B Baker Street that really gave the game away. You're not the first, you know; I've had lots of people like you in the cab—Yanks mostly or 'Sherlockians' as they call themselves over there. Though you'd be surprised at the number of people who come all the way from Japan just to say they've trodden in the footsteps of Mr. Sherlock Holmes. In full regalia, some of them: deerstalker and Inverness cape; magnifying lens; meerschaum calabash pipe; the whole blinking kit and caboodle; even had a person bring a violin along with them, once, although I couldn't say whether it was a Stradivarius or not."

I marshaled my case. "I was thinking, I know the meter's running, and I can settle that with you now, but could I perhaps hire the cab for the entire morning? Certainly be much more relaxing for me, possibly a little more profitable for you. At whatever rate you think would be appropriate, of course."

He tapped his chin again. "Bit unusual, but not unheard of. Happens from time to time. Americans, again, mostly, especially when the City was growing with a bang. Before that it was the Japanese, and before them the Arabs, all of them buying up the best properties as fast as they could. Now, of course, it's as likely to be a Russian businessman or Chinese entrepreneur."

I continued to press my case. "As you can see, all the destinations are in central London; there's nothing farther west than Chiswick, north of St. John's Wood, or east of Aldgate Underground, and the only place I've got listed south of the river is Waterloo Station." I paused and it was then I played my trump card. "Of course, if you don't happen to own your cab?"

He slowly slid his eyes in my direction. "I do, as a matter of fact, sir, and always have done, just like me dad and me grandad, and his dad and grandad before him. So, me being a musher, an owner-driver, I can do what I like." He chuckled. "I take it you're not a Yank or a Russian oligarch, are you, sir?"

It was my turn to chuckle then. "Nothing so exotic; English, through and through. I'm simply indulging in a little hobby of mine and hoping to use the photographs I get to illustrate a book I intend to write."

"And that'd be a book about Sherlock Holmes, would it, sir?"

"Hope so, although I don't have a publisher lined up for it yet."

"Well, I couldn't possibly stand in the way of literary endeavor or artistic merit. Alright then, clear what's on the meter and we can go from there. I can do credit card, debit card, chip-and-pin, whatever you prefer." I shook my head and handed through a twenty-pound note to cover the journey thus far and what I thought would be a suitably appropriate tip. He nodded. "Cash, is it? The poor man's credit card, as it was once so described. Thank you much, sir, very generous of you. As for the next two-three hours, I reckon I'd normally do anything up to fifty miles, all told, so let's call it two hundred quid, even."

"Agreed," I said. "And I'll add a twenty-pound tip. And I'll pay you now."

"Again, very generous of you, sir."

I opened my wallet again and extracted another crisp, new twenty-pound note, together with four crisp, new fifty-pound notes.

His eyes didn't miss a thing. "No need to go to Cox and Co., near Charing Cross, then? Or Lloyds TSB, as it is now, of course."

"I always prefer to pay cash, if I can," I offered without any further explanation. "And, again, you're sure it's no bother?"

"As I said, sir, no bother. All in a day's work." He nodded and smiled and slid the banknotes inside his own commodious wallet. "Thank you."

"Good," I said, removing my overcoat as it was now rather warm inside the taxi. "Glad that's settled. Now we can truly say: 'The game's afoot!'"

"And very appropriate, too, if I may say so, but before we step into the unknown, so to speak, would you mind if I ask you something by way of a personal question? Nothing intrusive, just me indulging a little hobby of my own, you could say, founded as it is upon the observance of trifles."

"Yes, I see no harm," I said, immediately putting up my guard. "I have rather imposed myself on you, after all. What would you like to know?"

"Are you a doctor, by any chance, sir, and more to the point, ex-military?"

"Well, yes, I am, as a matter of fact. I studied at Barts. Simply wanted to take another look at the old place before it's changed out of all recognition."

"After which you were a houseman, possibly a GP? Forgoing private practice until you joined the Royal Army Medical Corps; the old Linseed Lancers, *In Arduis Fidelis,* 'Steadfast in Adversity,' and all that? With whom you completed a couple tours of duty in Afghanistan? And from whom you've only very recently been demobbed—in all probability due to that leg wound of yours?"

"Well, yes, I was, I mean I did, but how on earth did you deduce all that?"

"Easy enough, sir. And please don't mind me saying, but if *clothes doth oft proclaim the man,* then it's highly unlikely you were ever in private practice. Tattersall-check brushed-cotton Viyella shirt, frayed at the cuffs; Harris Tweed jacket, leather patches at the elbows; cavalry twill trousers, well used; highly polished pair of tan brogues, recently reheeled and resoled; everything courtesy of Messrs. Aquascutum and Church's, ergo Regent Street not Jermyn Street; all standard issue 'home counties,' not-so-well-off officers, for the use of. Then, of course, there's the little matter of your regimental tie; alternate maroon and yellow, broad diagonal stripes against a dark blue field; not to mention your lapel pin featuring the RAMC's rod and serpent cap badge, in miniature."

I found myself fiddling unconsciously with my tie. I swallowed and endeavored to remain calm. One doesn't come across such displays every day.

But the taxi driver hadn't finished with me yet. "Then of course there's what's left of that suntan of yours, which incidentally is so engrained a child could see it never came from just ten days in Torremolinos. Add the sweat-stained NATO watchband on your rather, if I may say so, somewhat worse for wear Rolex Oyster Perpetual. Add to that the limp when you walk. And I'd say you got yourself banged about a bit, maybe as the result of coming into too close a proximity with an IED, and subsequently you had a couple of months' hospital and physiotherapy, before finally being invalided out back into civvy street? That's about it, though, given no more than a cursory look."

"But that's extraordinary," I spluttered. "How on earth… how could you deduce so much from so little, the improvised explosive device and everything?"

"As I said, it's just a little hobby of mine, sir, seeing as how I come into contact with so many strangers during my working day. And what with one thing and another, I've found it pays not just to look, but to try to really see."

"You most definitely have a touch of the detective about you," I said.

"Comes from being blessed with a ceaselessly inquisitive nature and an eye for the telling detail. Take that posh new

Cancer Centre at Barts. I've heard rumour people there are embarking on stem cell research. Yet another attempt to further the brave new world that began some fifteen and more years ago when the very first mammal, Dolly the sheep, was cloned in a laboratory up near Edinburgh. Now, according to the BBC, over in Japan they're going to try and get some poor elephant to give birth to a prehistoric giant woolly mammoth. You ask me, they'll be cloning people next, the most dangerous bloody mammal of all. After which, there'll be no telling who they'll try bringing back to life. I tell you, there's always been a lot more goes on than they'll ever let on to the likes of you and me. So it wouldn't surprise me if secret experiments had been going on for years and the scientists were just waiting for the right time to tell the public the truth of it: that they've already got real live human clones ready and raring to go."

"What an outlandish thought," I said, but there was little stopping him after that, as we'd obviously touched upon a hot button of some kind. It happens, of course; social barriers become lowered because of some unexpected shared experience, there's a precipitous lessening of reserve, and for a time perfect strangers are suddenly conversing together like old friends. Even though it is true that, in our case, he did most of the talking while I did most of the listening.

After Barts, we fairly flew round to Aldersgate, the Stock Exchange, Liverpool Street Station, and Aldgate Underground station, with me exiting the cab at each stop so as to snap off some digital photographs. And we were on our way to the next point of interest on my list when the taxi driver asked me over the intercom whether I'd like some coffee when we reached the Tower of London. "Got a whole thermos flask full here, up front; black, no sugar, good-quality beans that I ground myself. Got a spare clean cup, too."

"How very kind," I said, and within minutes he'd pulled over close by the main entrance to the Tower and had poured the coffee and handed me a tiny cup through the equally tiny opening in the plexiglass partition and we sat there, very contentedly, for a good five minutes and more, he up front, me in back.

"Had them all at one time or another," he said, sipping his coffee.

"I beg your pardon?" I said, desperately trying not to spill mine.

"Holmes and Watson—we've had almost all of them, over the years; by which I mean, me great-great-grandfather, me great-grandfather, me grandad, me dad, or me; we've had nearly all the actors in the cabs at one time or another. Great-great-grandad had William Gillette, a real gent by all accounts. Great-grandad had Eille Norwood and that Yank with the famous profile, John Barrymore. Grandad had Clive Brook and Arthur Wontner and once even conveyed the inimitable Basil Rathbone around town." There really seemed to be no stopping him and, all reserve now dispensed with, he continued to rattle off name after name, a veritable *Who's Who* of the acting profession, from the dawn of the twentieth century through to the present day. "Then of course Dad went and did him one better by picking up Orson Welles, who did Holmes on the radio, over in America; huge, he was, almost filled the entire backseat."

I thought it only polite to show interest so I took a chance and interrupted the flow and offered up my one and only Wellesian quote. "Orson Welles said of Sherlock Holmes, 'that he was a gentleman who has never lived and yet who will never die,' which was really rather clever of him, don't you think?"

The taxi driver threw me a rather disdainful look. "An all too memorable utterance whose very theatricality only serves to misdirect, if not utterly confuse. If only he knew the half of it." He paused to sip his coffee. "Who else, now? Carlton Hobbs. Douglas Wilmer. Oh, yes, Peter Cushing. He was a very good Holmes, who oddly enough also once played Conan Doyle himself. As for Watsons, we've had Robert Stephens and his Watson, Colin Blakely; Christopher Plummer and *his* Watson, James Mason; and Mr. Jeremy Brett, of course, God bless him, with his two dedicated Dr. Watsons, Messrs. Burke and Hardwicke.

We thought Granada Television really nailed it, Brett especially. Tell the truth, we thought we'd nailed him, himself, he was that good. Who else? Well, Dad had Michael Caine and Ben Kingsley, but so have I since they've been knighted." I nodded, encouragingly, so as not to distract him. "I've had that Yank, Robert Downey Jr., as a fare twice now; in town, for films one and two; mad sod, but pleasant with it; nothing like the real Holmes, of course, but great fun; lots of adrenaline and all that indefinable star power the tabloids are always going on about. That last time, he even had his Watson with him, our very own crumpet catcher, Jude Law. Girls chasing them both down the street, grown women, too, like they were a pop group or something, remarkable to watch, it was. My most recent Holmes was from the Beeb's *Sherlock,* their modern take on it all, starring that bloke Benedict Cumberbatch. Odd bloody name for an actor, if you ask me, but it seems to stick in the mind, even if people can't ever pronounce it properly. I also liked his Watson: Freeman, Martin Freeman; very believable and very down to earth, and a Hobbit now, so they tell me. Anyway, add it all up and there've been hundreds and hundreds of films. And dozens and dozens who've played Holmes on celluloid and TV, on radio and on the stage. And all over the world, too, even Russia and Japan. It fair boggles the mind, it does."

"Who would've ever thought there'd been so many?" I agreed.

"All roads lead to Rome and all Sherlocks to London," he said.

If you only knew the half of it, I thought, but I said: "You're so right, the BBC's *Sherlock* series is excellent and produced with real affection, I thought."

"Yes, very clever, although, as you can well imagine, I didn't much fancy all that business in the first episode about the barking-mad taxi driver as played by Phil Davis, an otherwise excellent actor. I ask you, why on earth tar the noble fraternal order of London taxicab drivers with such a nasty brush? London cabbies as murderous villains, I should cocoa. Where would visitors to London be, or Londoners themselves for that matter, without the honest, upstanding, supremely knowledgeable

London cabby at their constant beck and call? Nowhere, that's where. They'd have to lump it on the buses and Tube or put up with all the nonsense and malarkey of dealing with all those unlicensed mini-cab drivers, none of whom are required to have an exact knowledge of anything, let alone London. No, that whole rotten business spoiled it for me. I blame the writers, myself: character assassination of a respected hardworking guild, for easy plot gain, showed real lack of imagination on their part."

Of course, I had to speak to that. "I didn't at all take it as an *ad hominem* attack on all London taxi drivers; merely the portrayal of a single, terminally ill individual with a sick and twisted mind who just happened to drive a black cab. I'm sure the writers didn't intend that it reflect on the entire profession."

"Nevertheless, the damage is already done, isn't it? Our reputation's been scarred. Simply putting the thought in people's minds is bad enough. And I tell you, it's not easy being a cab driver; it's hard work having to recall all twenty-five thousand streets within a six-mile radius of Charing Cross Station. And it's not just about having an exact knowledge of London, and a green badge to show for it; with me it's about having an exact knowledge of the Canon, as well."

"The Canon? You mean, all fifty-six short stories and all four novels of the adventures and exploits of Sherlock Holmes as recorded by Dr. John Watson?"

"Of course, what else could I mean? I'm certainly not referring to all that fake Holmes nonsense that gets cobbled together on a depressingly regular basis by all them would-be authors. No, there's nothing compares to Conan Doyle's original stories. 'Ere, I'll show you. You cop hold of this list of points of interest you want to visit." He opened the tiny window in the plexiglass partition and pushed my notebook through to me. "Now you just shout out places on your list, in any old order, any which way around."

"Very well," I said, sitting back in my seat, "if it's the complete Canon that you claim to have knowledge of, where does Cannon Street station figure?"

"Very funny," he said, "but I can assure you Cannon Street railway station looms large in 'The Man with the Twisted Lip.'"

"What about Euston Station?" I asked.

"'The Priory School.' Am I right, sir?"

"Very probably," I said. "Very well, then, where do Liverpool Street, Charing Cross, Victoria, and Waterloo stations all figure?"

"'The Dancing Men,' 'The Abbey Grange,' 'Silver Blaze,' and 'The Crooked Man.' And while you appear to be blowing smoke, sir, Paddington Station, where I picked you up earlier this morning, figures in 'The Boscombe Valley Mystery,' as well as in *The Hound of the Baskervilles.*"

"Alright, then, where we just were: Aldgate Underground station?"

"Again, easy-peasy, 'The Bruce-Partington Plans.' Blimey, I'm really racking up the points here; you're going to have to try harder than that, sir."

"Bentinck Street, Bow Street, and Brook Street?"

"That'd take us to 'The Final Problem,' 'The Man with the Twisted Lip,' and 'The Resident Patient.'"

"And Conduit Street, Covent Garden Market, and Church Street—Stepney, not Paddington?"

"ABCs, is it? Very well, then, in order: 'The Empty House,' 'The Blue Carbuncle,' and 'The Six Napoleons.' What next, D for Downing Street and 'The Naval Treaty'? I'm telling you, I know every single point on your list to a T, so even if you were to throw the Temple, the Tower of London, and Trafalgar Square at me, you still wouldn't catch me out."

"Very well," I said, trying not to show how truly impressed I was, for it was now all too clear he really knew the Canon and was a veritable Leslie S. Klinger, Esq., in the guise of a licensed London cabby, "do pray tell."

"The Temple, the Tower of London, and Trafalgar Square will take you, respectively, to 'A Scandal in Bohemia,' *The Sign of the Four,* and *The Hound of the Baskervilles,* again. Had enough? Have I made my case?"

"Most excellent, I must say," I said, but I wasn't going to give up so easily. "Let me try another track, take me to that 'vile alley lurking behind the high wharves which line the north side of the river to the east of London Bridge.'"

He simply chuckled. "Very well remembered on your part; you're of course referring to Upper Swandam Lane and 'The Man with the Twisted Lip'? I should cocoa. It doesn't even exist and never did. I'd give him a twisted lip as soon as look at him, if I only had half the chance. He should've known better, a man of his intellect; I mean to say, he could just as easily have written Lower Thames Street and it would've been spot on, so to speak."

"Sir Arthur Conan Doyle, you mean?"

"No, Dr. J. H. Watson, who do you think? And as for him writing about Paul's Wharf, again in TMWTTL, well it exists, of course, only not at all where he says it is…I mean was."

"On purpose, do you think? To throw people off the trail?" I said.

"Wouldn't put it past any of them, Holmes in the deducing, Dr. Watson in the writing, or Conan Doyle, himself, as agent, *nom de plume,* or whatever his preferred style of address. It's always wheels within wheels with them three, mysteries and enigmas and riddles, always and forever in plain sight to catch you unawares. 'The Politician, the Lighthouse, and the Trained Cormorant'? Do me a favour; it was never published. So who's to say there ever was such a case? And what about his so-called monographs: 'The Typewriter and Its Relation to Crime,' 'Upon the Tracing of Footsteps,' or 'Upon Secret Writing'? They're all of them just titles as tittle-tattle, nothing but springes to catch woodcocks."

"I must say your knowledge of the Canon is truly astonishing," I said. "I'm sure it must be the perfect complement to The Knowledge—the official examination you had to undergo to become a licensed London taxi driver."

"Yes, three years' hard slog that was, but a Knowledge of Holmes is the work of a lifetime; several of them, truth be told. And it's funny you should put the two together like that, as there are many cabbies reckon the term originated with Sherlock Holmes and not, as some would have it, some nameless Victorian-era Commissioner of Police. Stands to reason, really; Holmes said it was a hobby of his to have an exact knowledge of London and an exact knowledge of London is the *sine qua non,* so to speak, of the London Hackney Carriage Act, which, I think, proves my point all the more. After all, who better to give it name than one who employed so many hansom cabs in the prosecution of so many of his famous cases? That's why so many of us always have a well-thumbed copy of the Canon in the cab, along with a *London A to Z* and the latest edition of *Time Out.*"

"All the necessary tools of the trade," I said, handing back my empty cup. "Thanks for the coffee and food for thought." And with that we resumed our clockwise traverse of London, visiting all the remaining Holmesian points of interest as itemized in my little Moleskine notebook. As I'd done throughout the morning, I sent a short text message to confirm each point visited. And within two and a half hours we'd completed the tour and arrived at my final destination.

"Right, then, here we are, 221B Baker Street, not that any of the so-called experts even agree to this day exactly where it is or was."

"Just here, at the corner of George Street, will do fine," I said, quickly looking around me to ensure I wasn't inadvertently about to leave anything of mine behind. I gathered my overcoat, tweed cap, woolen scarf, and canvas bag and even double-checked to see that I had my mobile phone with me. "Thank you for a most illuminating ride," I called out. "I learned a great deal."

"You're welcome," he said. Then to my surprise he exited his cab and came round to retrieve my garment bag himself. As I stood there on the pavement, he looked me in the face and shook my hand. "Very pleased to have made your acquaintance," he said. "You be sure to go safe, now."

I nodded my thanks and stood there as he returned to his cab and drove off, soon to be lost in the steady flow of traffic down Baker Street. I turned and quickly walked back up Baker

Street and within minutes had come to my lodgings. I let myself in with my key. I closed the front door, locked and bolted it, dropped the walking stick in the rack in the hallway, the garment bag on the floor, and raced up the stairs, removing my leather gloves as I did so.

My companion hardly glanced up as I entered and all I received by way of a greeting was a single nod of acknowledgement and a long bony finger that pointed toward the much-abused, oversized partners' desk, covered as it was with stacks of produced and yet-to-be produced screenplays and TV adaptations; piles of books, book proposals, and uncorrected proofs; and boxes galore of graphic novels and video games; even the latest action figures of Downey and Law as they appear in *Sherlock Holmes: A Game of Shadows.* Transmedia to the max, as the trade papers would have it. I let slip my overcoat and dropped my shoulder bag onto a chair, hurriedly retrieving my Canon EOS 600D digital SLR camera and attaching it to the USB cable already plugged into the iMac, so that all the photos and video clips I'd taken of the taxi driver could upload while I was attending to everything else. As I sat down, the iMac computer's twenty-seven-inch display had already refreshed the IMDb page devoted to Jared Harris, the actor cast as dastardly Professor Moriarty in the new Warner Brothers film. I closed it, quickly scrolled down to the appropriate application in the Dock, launched it, selected "Audio" from the drop-down menu and immediately heard the now all too familiar voice coming from the external loudspeakers. One odd thing, though: the accent seemed to have undergone a remarkable change, with all traces of "Mockney" now fully expunged.

"Of course, I had him picked out in a trice, what with his off-the-rack British warm, ghastly tweed flat cap, cheap brown leather gloves. On sartorial grounds alone, I think we can definitely discount this one; the very idea of him being the real thing is just too fanciful by half. Not sure where you got your intelligence about him, but to my eye he's a rank amateur who doesn't know his Conan Doyle, his Sherlock, or his Shakespeare. And limp or no limp, you'd

have thought his walking stick was made of rubber; as clumsy a person as ever I've met; dropping things, simply everywhere. I tell you, the quality of target candidates has most definitely gone down."

I took the proffered glass of sherry and continued to listen in as the cab driver reported the day's events back to his lord and master. The sound quality was rather good, even if I say so myself, and despite the slight static it was clear I'd managed to get all the miniature microphones positioned to optimum effect. My colleague leaned forward and tapped the desk with a long finger to attract my attention. "He deduced you were RAMC?" he asked, quietly.

I nodded. "The regimental tie, of course. He also identified the rod and serpent on the lapel pin. And as for the carefully contrived mufti, the badly scratched Rolex, and the suntan you had me work on these past many weeks, they all proved inspired."

"So very cooperative of him to have seen what we wanted him to see."

"Yes, and as you can hear, he's rather pleased with himself about it. But as you've always said, 'Blood will out.'"

My colleague nodded and I opened a second application that brought up a detailed map of London onto the screen. The red dot moving slowly across the display, as if directed by some unseen force, told us that the tiny Hitachi satellite navigation transponder I'd managed to get positioned up under the rear wheel arch was functioning properly. It remained to be seen just how effective the dozen or so specially colour-matched RFID tags of various sizes I'd secreted around the cab would prove to be, especially in conjunction with the Real-Time Location System we'd only recently acquired, but that was work for another day. Meanwhile, our once-friendly cab driver continued to vent his spleen.

"Why on earth the constant need to push Holmes onto an ever-gullible public? You'd have thought everyone would be sick to death of him by now, but there's a never-ending stream of it and it's only gotten worse of late. Every damn Tom, Dick, and Harry is dreaming up some new madcap scheme or other to do with Holmes

and Watson. There are those dreadful big-budget Hollywood films, the damn TV series, seemingly multiple one-offs; books and audio books and bloody e-books, all coming out of our bloody ears; and that's not counting those violent bloody video games and all those weird comic books intended for illiterate adults. For the life of me, I can't imagine what it is everyone hopes to achieve with it all. And I absolutely dread to think where it's all going to end. They should just bloody well leave well enough alone and stick with the Canon, plain and simple; surely that should be good enough? I know none of it's still in copyright, but is that any reason for everyone to keep on taking a bite out of the old beekeeping bugger?"

There was a long pause and but for the continued background noise I would've thought there'd been a break in transmission. I held my breath, hoping against hope that the "cabby" hadn't spotted any of the microphones I'd hidden inside his taxi. Thankfully, though, my worries proved groundless, as it soon became very clear he'd simply been gathering his thoughts.

"And you know what really gets my goat, it's the fact that it's us who've actually done the most to keep his reputation alive. I mean, where would the name of Sherlock Holmes be without your own particular brand of genius? He'd be a mere footnote to detective fiction, nothing more. The plain truth is, whenever his name is mentioned, people always remember you in the same breath; it's you they remain most in awe of. So if, as they say, a man is truly defined by his enemies, then it's you that's most clearly defined him and that should rightfully take the lion's share of any glory that's going."

It was then we heard the voice that once heard can never be forgotten. I glanced over at my companion, who nodded and removed the long cherrywood pipe from his mouth, his eyes suddenly as hard and as black as obsidian.

"My dear young Sebastian," said the silken voice of the Napoleon of Crime, for it was he, undoubtedly, who was now speaking. *"You should not judge by outward appearances alone. Our fiendish would-be nemesis is the very wiliest of adversaries, as too is his seemingly clumsy and bumbling partner-in-crime. Always remember that what is on the outside is always on the inside, but what is on the*

inside is not necessarily always revealed on the outside. We have no earthly idea when or where the real Holmes will return or in what guise. It could be as bookseller, ornithologist, apiarist, pathologist, or priest, or any one of a thousand disguises. That is why we must remain ever vigilant and seek out and examine each and every one who would play the role of consulting detective and each and every one who would then act as his fawning amanuensis. We must establish who is really who and then determine whether they might prove a future hindrance to our purpose and, if such be the case, to deal with them in the most severe, most expeditious manner possible."

It was very apparent that a particular hot button had just been pressed again and pressed particularly hard. And I admit I was moved to lower the volume somewhat.

"Fiend is right, the wily, scheming bastard should up, up and play the game and come out and fight like a real man. 'Steel true, blade straight'? What utter tosh. He's the one who ruined my family's good name and brought us all so low, damn him to hell. All I've ever asked for, all any of us have ever asked for, is the chance to get a good, clear shot at Holmes's head, which as you well know is all I really live for. As for the rest of it, as always, dear Uncle Morrie, when you hit the nail on the head, you hit it so very good and hard. And I hear you, I do. I know we have no choice but to continue searching for the cunning swine and I give you my word I'll keep on doing that. I'm only sorry the day turned out such an utter waste, but there it is. We'll get him, eventually, though, we will. Anyway, look, I'll get the taxi garaged and the garb of London cabby put away in the props cupboard until next time. I'll also make good and sure the VH-V2 air gun, telescopic sight, and hollow-point ammunition are all safely tucked away. After which, of course, I'll take the usual precautions to ensure I'm not followed. One can never be too careful, as you're always so very fond of telling me. I'll report in again in an hour when I'm en route to my club. For now, Sebastian Moran, Holmes hunter, over and out."

All we could hear then was the white noise of London as amplified from inside the taxicab. And the very last we heard that day was the latest in the long line of Moran progeny humming tunelessly to himself. I couldn't for the life of me make out what it was, but then a long, thin finger reached out across the desk and, with a double click of the mouse, the sounds from the Harman/Kardon SoundSticks, sited either side of the computer, were eclipsed.

I turned to face the extraordinary man I'd known for what seemed several lifetimes, as his eyes flashed in triumph. "Know your enemies, my dear fellow. Know them with an exactness that renders them, their habits, their subterfuges, their weaknesses, and their strengths, as clearly as if they were life-sized pieces arrayed before you on a giant chessboard."

I nodded and reached for the sherry decanter as my closest-ever male companion and dearest friend reached for his violin case.

"A good day's work on your part, old friend," he said. "Well done."

I raised my glass. "Yes, cheerio. But, as you've always said, the only possible place to hide a secret is in plain sight."

He paused before raising his beloved Stradivarius to his chin. "As Professor Moriarty is ever vigilant for our return, it behooves us to promote ourselves and our likenesses in any and every way possible. We needs must give continuous form, substance, and exercise to his worst imaginings; that we, his two most implacable foes, have risen, yet again, Lazarus-like, from the dead."

"Give a dog a bone, Holmes?"

"Indeed, my dear Watson. And not just cupboards full of skeletons, but whole battalions, entire multitudes, if need be. All to ensure that Moriarty and his wretched gang simply cannot see the wood for the trees. For as elementary as the ruse undoubtedly is, the one indisputable fact in our case is that there truly is safety in numbers."

I raised my glass again and sat there—with not a single thought of putting pen to paper—and sipped at my sherry and listened contentedly as the notes of Mendelssohn's "*Lieder ohne Worte*" once again worked their very particular magic upon me and brought the day's work to a more than agreeable close.

Tony Broadbent is the author of a series of mystery novels about a roguish Cockney cat burglar in postwar, austerity-ridden, black-market-riddled London who gets blackmailed into working for MI5 and is then trained by Ian Fleming. His first, *The Smoke,* received starred reviews. The follow-up, *Spectres in the Smoke,* was awarded the Bruce Alexander Historical Mystery Award in 2006 and was proclaimed by *Booklist* as one of the best spy novels of the year. The third, *Shadows in the Smoke,* is soon to be published. Broadbent was born in England, a short train ride away from Baker Street, and now lives in Mill Valley, California, with his beautiful American wife and a real cat burglar of a cat. He was introduced to the Sherlock Holmes Canon on the very Christmas Day he'd deduced for himself that Santa Claus was indeed his own father in disguise.

The Men with the Twisted Lips

S. J. Rozan

"The Lascar," said Chan Ho, cradling his delicate porcelain teacup in his hands, "is a dangerous man."

Not a word of disagreement was uttered by any of the three guests gathered in Chan Ho's carpeted upstairs parlor. The day being hot, the windows stood open, but even the afternoon Limehouse ruckus of creaking carts and hawkers' shouts did not distract the men from the issue they had been brought together to consider. No more did the sweet scent of opium smoke rising faintly from below, to which all four men were inured; for Chan, and his guests also, as well as the Lascar whose transgressions were at issue, owned and managed houses for the enjoyment of that drug.

Portly Wing Lin-Wei, leaning forward to pluck a second candied plum from the silver bowl, replied, "Indeed, Chan, his flagrant contempt for the authorities only grows. He appears to have no respect for the customs of the land in which we find ourselves, nor any understanding of his position here. His attitude, his actions, they endanger us all."

"In which he differs from you, Wing," murmured Zhang Peng-Da, a skeletally thin and sour man who had not touched his tea. "You with your gifts of silver coin, your fawning attentions on the constabulary. Your pathetic attempts at spoken English! It is humiliating."

A tight smile creased Wing's full cheeks. "Perhaps, Zhang, my willingness to make efforts to adjust to our new home accounts for the difference in our clientele."

"If there is an advantage in having the cost of an opium pipe borne by a duke rather than a dustman, I do not see it," Zhang sneered. "In fact, if dustmen, not dukes, were our only patrons, perhaps there would be no need of this discussion."

"Zhang is correct." Chan spoke in mild rebuke to Wing, who was both the younger man and the more recent arrival to London. "If we accommodated only those whose habits did not draw the attention of the newspapers, not to speak of that of the ladies' groups, it is possible we would have none of these difficulties. Yet we are hardly in a position to inquire into our customers' social standing or employment before we render our service, or, for that matter, to turn any away. Nor have we ever needed to, as long as we take pains to be discreet. The smoking of opium is in England a legal pastime, the efforts of some civic groups to the contrary notwithstanding. May I remind you all, that is why we came here."

Chan paused and looked about him at the men seated on the heavy wooden armchairs. Zhang wore his usual sneer and Lu Yang, the youngest of them, radiated impatience. Only Wing sat placidly, with the patience of an egret waiting to stab a fish. Chan sighed. Had the choice not been dictated by the requirements of the scheme as he set them out to himself, he might have selected other confederates to join him in accomplishing his ends. Restraining the more flamboyant activities of the Lascar proprietor of the Bar of Gold would be to the advantage of every man who owned an opium establishment in Limehouse, and Chan might easily have found more compatible allies. However, as things stood, each of these men brought with him an element indispensable to the successful prosecution of Chan's idea.

"Our profession is not thought respectable," Chan went on, "but we are largely ignored by those with whom we have no traffic. We *all*"—he emphasized the word, to remind the men of their common interests and of the necessity to put aside rivalries and work together on the task before them—"depend upon this relative obscurity to allow us to prosper." Satisfied that he had made his point, Chan allowed himself a sip of tea. "Our ability to carry on our commerce in peace is threatened of late, however, by the scandalous behavior of this Lascar. His haughty disregard of the need for discretion, especially in his more questionable activities, has brought undesirable notice to the Bar of Gold. Thus unwanted attention has recently been directed at the Limehouse district, more than once. You especially, Zhang, as your establishment abuts his, are, I am sure, particularly concerned."

Zhang glared but did not contradict.

"The current situation involving Mr. Neville St. Clair," Chan came to the point, "is, I think you will all agree, untenable. What we have discovered, the authorities will eventually discover also. There will be an outcry against the Lascar that will encompass the entire district. It will be opium that is blamed, it will be our business establishments that are held up to scrutiny, it will be we who pay the price. Zhang's concern that high-society patrons of our establishments draw excessive notice will be borne out with full force, when Mr. Neville St. Clair is discovered to be perpetrating this outrageous fraud from his quarters at the Lascar's, here in Limehouse."

"Mr. Neville St. Clair does not smoke opium," Wing stated mildly, licking syrup from the end of his thumb.

"Nevertheless!" Zhang snapped. "Chan is correct. Mr. Neville St. Clair's begging, in the person of the repulsive Hugh Boone, for which he has already been taken up a dozen times, is dependent on his rooms in our streets. His discovery will have repercussions here; worse still will be the shock when his identity is revealed to the citizens of Lee, where he lives his respectable life."

Chan could not miss the disdain with which Zhang said "respectable," but he let it pass. "My point exactly," he confirmed. "That Mr. Neville St. Clair is perpetrating this fraud upon not only the kindhearted gentlemen of the City, who feel moved by his seeming plight to give him alms, but also upon his own wife, his children, his neighbors, will be too much for many people. Some will use the disgust of the moment to point the finger of accusation at us all. I believe in English the phrase is 'tarring with the same brush.'" This was addressed as mollification to Wing, who nodded, acknowledging the honor. "Also, may I remind you, this is not the Lascar's first offense against the calm order of the Limehouse district. It is time he is taught a lesson."

"I do not understand, really I do not!" This outburst, finally, came from Lu Yang, who had not yet spoken. Chan knew Lu to be hot-blooded—the result of unbalanced *qi*—and was impressed that, from respect for his elders, the young man had managed to keep himself in check this long. "This Lascar has been a thorn in our sides since I came to London."

Zhang snorted.

"Since long before that, Lu," said Chan.

"Yes, I know that! So why do we hesitate? I can send a man to eliminate our difficulties as soon as night falls. The Lascar will not trouble us again." Lu sat back in his chair, crossing one leg over the other. Unlike the three elder men, who wore long blue silk merchant's robes as they had in their hometowns in China, Lu had adopted the wool trousers, jacket, and collared shirt of his new city. Chan wondered idly what such clothing felt like; perhaps he should try it.

"No, Lu," Chan said. "Your man might eliminate the Lascar—"

"Might? He will, without question!"

"He will not, as skilled as he may be, because you will not send him. The Lascar has men also. We are attempting to lessen the amount of attention paid to Limehouse, Lu, not to increase it. A blood feud declared upon any of us by the Lascar's men will have to be answered by all of us. The ensuing mayhem will bring a storm upon our heads. No, this situation must be handled with discretion. The Lascar must be spoken to in language only he will understand."

Lu fixed his eyes on Chan, then relaxed and smiled. "Are you proposing we eliminate Mr. Neville St. Clair? That is an excellent idea! The Lascar will feel our displeasure—"

"Absolutely not!" Chan could see the young hothead would bear watching. "Or," he allowed himself a smile, also, "in a way, I suppose I am. We must cause Mr. Neville St. Clair to vanish from our midst permanently, yes, but without violence. If we proceed as I am recommending, the Lascar, having lost the income he receives from his lodger, will also be required to fend off a certain amount of attention from the constabulary. Once this occurs, a discreet visit from one or more of us will be all that is needed to open the Lascar's eyes to our displeasure with his behavior. We will have shown the lengths to which we are willing to go—to which we are capable of going—to protect our livelihoods. This will be a simple warning. Not particularly costly, to be sure, but the only one of its type. He will understand."

"And if he does not?" Wing asked.

"He will also understand that there are further steps we can take." Chan nodded pointedly at Lu, who returned both smile and nod.

"I think," said Zhang, whose tea had by now grown cold from inattention, "we are all prepared to hear your scheme, Chan. We will decide how to proceed after the particulars have been explained."

As senior man after Chan himself, it was Zhang's privilege to speak for the others. "Very well," Chan assented. He poured more tea for those who had drunk, refilling his own cup also. Lifting it, he said, "We must rid ourselves of the threat posed by the presence of Mr. Neville St. Clair by exposing his fraudulent practice, in a way so subtle as to cause him—healthily whole—to disappear, never to return. We must also, by this same stroke, lead the Lascar to understand he remains under the most vigilant watch. Although it is essential the authorities be involved, they must be restrained. Agreed?"

"Just how do you intend to achieve all of this, Chan?" Zhang inquired testily.

"There is one man in London capable of accomplishing our purposes with as much zeal as discretion." Chan looked about him once again. "I propose we employ Mr. Sherlock Holmes."

"Oh, really!" Zhang snapped. "Have you had resort to your own pipes? We, the men of Limehouse, will hire London's great consulting detective—this is your grand plan?"

"I have not said," Chan responded, smiling, "that we will hire him. I am merely suggesting we employ him."

As Chan explained his scheme to them all, the edge of hostility in his parlor gradually melted into the nodding of heads and the tranquillity of considered discussion.

"I had discreet inquiries made," Chan told the men, "into not only Mr. Neville St. Clair, but others in his circle. I searched not specifically for further evildoing, but only to find something we might use to our advantage in this affair. I was, therefore, open to all information that came my way, not only that which might be obviously valuable at first glance." He doubted if any man there would take a lesson from this; still, it was his duty to instruct. "After some time, a most interesting fact was presented to one of my agents, by a clerk at the Aberdeen Shipping Company."

"They with offices in Fresno Street?" inquired Zhang.

"Precisely. Mrs. Neville St. Clair, I am told, awaits a parcel, to arrive on the SS *Harding* on Thursday next. The unloading of the ship's cargo will be concluded by the Saturday evening. The following day being the Christian Sabbath, Mrs. Neville St. Clair will be notified by telegram on the Monday morning of the safe arrival of her parcel. She will be invited to gather it from the Aberdeen offices."

"Will she come herself?" Lu asked with calculation in his voice.

"According to the clerk, a sharp-eyed young man, past experience indicates that she will. Thus, gentlemen, we will have a rare opportunity on the day she chooses to come to London. I propose we use it thus."

The men being, after discussion and debate, in agreement with the plan as Chan Ho elucidated it, each was dispatched to his assigned task.

Zhang would designate three men to remain in the doorway of his own establishment, hard by the street-facing window of the rooms Mr. Neville St. Clair took at the Lascar's. These men would be given a simple task, the successful accomplishment of which would demand much patience, but little effort.

"My men's duties being successfully performed," Zhang said skeptically, "I still see no guarantee we will achieve the result we desire."

"We will achieve it," Chan responded. "I have set a watch upon Mr. Neville St. Clair these few weeks past. He is a man of punctilious habits, to be depended upon. Taking leave of Hugh Boone, Mr. Neville St. Clair spends a quarter of an hour at the open window, reliably each day. Perhaps, to make the transition, he requires the fresh air." The men all laughed, for, with the wharves, the gutters, and the opium houses, the air of Upper Swandam Lane was generally agreed to be the worst in all London.

Zhang having been satisfied as to that point, Wing prepared to go off to speak to his friends among the constabulary—Chan noted a small, superior smile in Zhang's direction when he made this promise—to get their agreement to be in place at the required moment. Wing also would be instructing the officers as to advice to be given to Mrs. Neville St. Clair at the proper time.

Lu, the most audacious of them, was known by Chan (but not, until that afternoon, by the others) to have a man of his own in service at the Lascar's. "A Dane," Lu told them, "a young and ambitious man, more loyal to my gold than to his master." This man would be charged with preventing the admission of Mrs. Neville St. Clair to the Lascar's establishment, if possible.

"If he cannot?" inquired Wing. "If, perhaps, the Lascar is prepared to allow the lady access to the rooms upstairs rather than suffer officers of the law to invade his establishment?"

"From our point of view, that would not be ideal," Chan admitted, "but it would not be disastrous, either. Possibly, the hideous aspect of the beggar Hugh Boone will so startle her that she will inquire no further. If so, we can continue as planned. If, in the event, Mr. Neville St. Clair, having already dispensed for the day with Hugh Boone, cannot recover him fast enough, his duplicity will be revealed to his wife. This, as I say, is not ideal, for if her horror of the situation is sufficient she might be inclined to make it public, exactly the circumstance we are attempting to avoid. I rather think not, however. I believe we can depend upon Mrs. Neville St. Clair's discretion, if not for the sake of her husband, whom by all accounts she holds very dear, then for that of her young children."

The role of Chan himself in the scheme was to give instructions to the clerk at the Aberdeen offices through his agent, and then to keep abreast of developments there, so that the four men would be able to identify the precise moment at which to set their plan into motion.

As the men were departing, each to play his part, Wing spoke in sudden afterthought. "I have heard," he said, "from my friends among the constabulary"—Chan heard Zhang softly snort, but Wing continued, unperturbed—"that the brilliance of Mr. Sherlock Holmes shines even more brightly in the company of his chronicler, Dr. John Watson. If Mr. Sherlock Holmes is consulted by Mrs. Neville St. Clair upon this matter, will it be possible to ensure Dr. John Watson's involvement as well?"

Chan smiled. "It will, Wing. That, too, has been arranged."

The moment for which the men had been waiting came the Monday following the docking of the SS *Harding*. The telegram alerting Mrs. Neville St. Clair to the arrival of her parcel was dispatched by the sharp-eyed clerk early that morning, requesting the lady to inform the shipping line concerning her intentions to collect it. Mrs. Neville St. Clair replied by return telegram that she would come that very afternoon. The train schedule from Lee to London having been carefully studied by Chan, it was ascertained that should Mrs. Neville St. Clair hurry directly to the Aberdeen offices it would be a simple matter to delay her departure from them—mislaid paperwork, a fee to be paid—until a time convenient for the men's scheme. As it happened, however, the lady went about some errands, and presented herself in the shipping offices at a perfect hour. Her parcel was delivered into her hands by the sharp-eyed clerk.

As the clerk, collecting his wages later, related to Chan, he followed his instructions to the letter, telling her while she signed the register that, as a lady such as herself would find the nearby streets distasteful, he would advise making the turn into Swandam Lane where a hansom cab might be found. Mrs. Neville St. Clair thanked him for his consideration and left. A few moments later the clerk, muttering to his office mates about a task with which he had been charged, left his desk and followed her. He was close behind, careful to hide himself, when the lady reached Swandam Lane. As she neared the Lascar's establishment, the clerk signaled to the men in Zhang's doorway, gesturing from a few steps back at the lady so that Zhang's men, who had been waiting for this sign, would know that this figure was indeed Mrs. Neville St. Clair.

Zhang's men then went into action, moving as a group into the street, boisterously disputing some point as though continuing an argument. They stopped on the muddy cobblestones so as to loudly make their points with each other. This had the requisite double effect of slowing the progress of Mrs. Neville St. Clair, and causing heads to turn in their direction—including, as intended, the head of Mr. Neville St. Clair in his window at the Bar of Gold. From that window issued a loud but inarticulate cry. Zhang's three men immediately ceased their argument as heads turned once again, people in Swandam Lane seeking, instinctively, the source of the piteous noise. Among those glancing up was Mrs. Neville St. Clair. From the confused and horrified expression that swept the lady's features, both the clerk and Zhang's men understood that she had seen, in that window of the Lascar's establishment, what she had been intended to see.

From there events continued to unfold as the men had planned them. The Lascar's assistant, the Dane secretly in Lu's service, forbade the entrance of Mrs. Neville St. Clair to the Bar of Gold, turning her away though she was desperate to the point of distraction. Just after that moment, alerted by the shipping clerk, an inspector and two constables of Wing's acquaintance who had been biding their time in Fresno Street presented themselves at the corner with Swandam Lane. The lady hastened to them, and together they rushed back to the Bar of Gold, where the inspector demanded to be admitted. The small group then hurried up the stairs to the front room on the second floor, there to find Hugh Boone, a well-known redheaded beggar of singular repulsiveness. What had become of Mrs. Neville St. Clair's husband, whom she had seen peering from the window of that very room, could not be ascertained. However, as the Dane related later, blood decorated the windowsill, certain items of Mr. Neville St. Clair's clothing hung in a closet, and, most damning of all, a gift the gentleman had promised to bring his small son was discovered in a box on a table. The beggar Hugh Boone was taken into custody, but there the case remained. No sign of Mr. Neville St. Clair himself having been found, Scotland Yard was without charges to level against the beggar, although the fear of foul play was very strong in the heart of the unfortunate man's wife.

The following Wednesday evening, as fog was beginning to swirl through the streets of London, the small group of opium-house owners gathered again in Chan's parlor.

"It appears," Zhang said, settling his gaunt frame upon a carved armchair, "that your plan has met with some success thus far, Chan." This inarguable fact seemed to lighten Zhang's perennially dark countenance not at all, though Chan noted that this time he did sip a cup of tea.

"The next steps are all in place," Chan assured them all, pouring tea for the other two men as well. "Mrs. Neville St. Clair, having received no satisfaction as to her husband's fate from the assiduous but fruitless efforts of Scotland Yard, has chosen to follow the advice of the good Inspector Barton." Chan saw Wing smile, which indulgence Chan did not begrudge him, as the inspector had been instructed in that advice by Wing himself. "This afternoon, Mrs. Neville St. Clair was received at the Baker Street rooms of Mr. Sherlock Holmes."

"Was she indeed?" Wing lowered his teacup, licking his full lips. "Well done. What do you expect will happen now?"

"As Mr. Sherlock Holmes can be relied upon to be resourceful," Chan replied, "I am confident he will call at the Lascar's soon, in an excellent disguise. He will request a pipe, settling himself upon pillows in a secluded spot from which he will be able to observe the other patrons. He will hope thus to find, in the mutterings of those sots, a clue to the disappearance of Mr. Neville St. Clair. Being a patient man, he will continue in these efforts for two days, or more. Of course, he will learn nothing by this."

"Then what is the point?"

"The subtlety of the mind of Mr. Sherlock Holmes—" Chan smiled. "—could lead one to believe he is not an Englishman at all, but one of us. The fact that he learns nothing by his stay at the Bar of Gold will be, in fact, what he learns. It will become the knot at which he will chew, eventually to unravel the problem before him."

Wing and Zhang considered this. Lu, with his flare for the dramatic, put down his teacup and took up the story. "The attendance of Mr. Sherlock Holmes upon the Lascar's opium rooms," he said, "will be useful to us in another way, also."

"How so?" asked Wing.

"As soon as it became known that Mrs. Neville St. Clair had presented herself at 221B Baker Street, the young Dane in my employ at the Lascar's made his way to the home of one Mr. Isa Whitney. There he invited that gentleman, as a regular patron of the Lascar's establishment, to come to Swandam Lane to sample, with the proprietor's compliments, a pipeful of the latest shipment of goods received. Mr. Isa Whitney, being much addicted to opium, appears to have found the invitation compelling, so much so that he accompanied the young man without delay. The Dane has been instructed to continue to ply Mr. Isa Whitney with a fresh supply of pipes, for which I will bear the cost." He waved a hand to indicate that this was a mere trifle, not to be discussed. The others nodded to acknowledge his generosity, though Chan reflected that the cost of a pipeful of opium in London was not so great that Lu's fortune was likely to be noticeably diminished by it. "By these means," Lu continued, "the attendance of that gentleman at the Lascar's establishment has been assured for the near future."

Chan observed Wing and Zhang exchanging a rare glance of sympathetic concordance. It was Zhang who expressed their mutual thought: "I fail to understand, Lu, what involvement Mr. Isa Whitney has in this affair."

Lu smiled. "He has none. However, it is the practice of Mr. Isa Whitney's wife, when trouble comes upon her, to consult an old friend, a school companion. This excellent woman is one Mary Watson, whose husband, Dr. John Watson—that surgeon known to his wife affectionately as 'James'—serves with great forbearance as Mr. Isa Whitney's medical adviser. More than once, Dr. John Watson has been called upon to untangle Mr. Isa Whitney from the clasp of the opium pipe. It is Mr. Isa Whitney's sojourn at the Bar of Gold that will bring Dr. John Watson there, thus making him available to attend Mr. Sherlock Holmes."

"Can we depend upon his discovering the detective," Wing asked mildly, "if Mr. Sherlock Holmes will be wearing so excellent a disguise?"

"Certainly not," Chan responded. "He will not discover Mr. Sherlock Holmes. London's most brilliant consulting detective will discover him."

As Chan had predicted it, so it transpired. Lu's Dane having returned to the Lascar's establishment, he sent word upon the Friday evening that Dr. John Watson had called at the Bar of Gold demanding to speak to Mr. Isa Whitney. That gentleman being found in a sorry state, Dr. John Watson paid his debt and put him in a cab for home. The doctor did not, however, accompany him, but rather lingered in Swandam Lane for some few minutes, until one of the other opium smokers emerged from the establishment. The bent old man who stumbled into the street exchanged words with the doctor, who accompanied him for a time—the Dane stealing silently behind them—until suddenly the old man straightened out and burst into a hearty fit of laughter. The Dane observed the two men as they spoke. The old and decrepit opium addict, having miraculously recovered both his vigor and his wits, whistled for their carriage. As it rolled away, the Dane returned to his position at the Lascar's door.

The following afternoon, final confirmation as to the success of the plan was received from one of Wing's allies in the police, a constable who provided Wing with information from time to time. Mr. Sherlock Holmes and Dr. John Watson had called very early in the morning at the Bow Street gaol. They had spoken in private with Inspector Bradstreet; what precisely had transpired in Bradstreet's office was not known to Wing's informant, but the two had been taken by the inspector downstairs to the cells. There they remained for some time. Shortly after they returned to the street, to drive away in a carriage, a gentleman was escorted from the area of the cells whom the constable had not previously seen. That gentleman summoned a cab and was overheard to request delivery to the train station with all speed. The enterprising constable, thinking to learn something of what had transpired in the cells, took himself down the winding stair to the whitewashed corridor lined with doors. To his surprise, the beggar Hugh Boone was gone, his cell empty though the constable had not seen him brought up the stairs.

"Mr. Sherlock Holmes was overheard to mention breakfast to Dr. John Watson in a most jovial manner as they left the gaol," said Chan to the guests gathered for one final cup of tea in his parlor. "I think he will be reflecting no further upon this matter."

"That's rather a shame," said Wing, "as we might therefore be thought to be intruding if we were to express our appreciation for his help. No, Zhang, you needn't glower, that was merely levity."

"Indeed," said Chan, anxious to get the issue disposed of once and for all. "In any case, I believe that will be an end to this matter of Hugh Boone, or Mr. Neville St. Clair, renting rooms at the Bar of Gold. All that remains is for the Lascar, in the most delicate but firmest of terms, to be made to understand that it was we who engineered these events. Once it is clear we are prepared to proceed with an equal measure of subtlety, but nothing approaching this level of restraint, should we be provoked again, I think we will be able to count on the Lascar's cooperation. Yes, I believe a discretion previously unknown will suddenly begin to show itself in the behavior of our Lascar colleague. Would you all be prepared to accompany me right now to the Bar of Gold?"

"I am," Lu responded instantly.

"I also," Wing agreed, finishing his tea.

The three turned to Zhang, who, after a silent moment, shocked them all when he permitted his lips to twist into a smile. Answering smiles were received from the others. "I have no objection," Zhang said, and so, still smiling, the four men of Limehouse made their way to the street.

S. J. Rozan, a lifelong New Yorker, first encountered and devoured the adventures of Sherlock Holmes at the age of twelve during the same convalescence as when she discovered Edgar Allan Poe. S.J. is the author of thirteen novels and three dozen short stories. She's won the Edgar, Shamus, Anthony, Nero, and Macavity Awards, and other honors, including the Japanese Maltese Falcon. However, none of these have been enough to entice Mr. Holmes to give her a call. She will keep trying.

For Dr. Watson's perspective on the events narrated in this story, see "The Man with the Twisted Lip" by Arthur Conan Doyle, first published in the *Strand* (1892) and collected in *The Adventures of Sherlock Holmes*.

The Adventure of
the Purloined Paget

Phillip Margolin and Jerry Margolin

Everything about the moor made Ronald Adair uneasy. He had lived his whole life in Manhattan and he felt that there was something inherently wrong with places where you could actually see the horizon and the silence wasn't annihilated by honking horns and pounding jackhammers. There were no Michelin-star restaurants in this wasteland, but there were bogs that could swallow a man in minutes. Ronald shivered as he imagined being sucked down into the ooze, struggling helplessly until the slime choked off his last terrified scream.

A year ago, Ronald had flown to Hollywood to talk to a studio head who wanted to buy the movie rights to *Death's Head,* the video game that had made him a multimillionaire. He'd brought his girlfriend along and she had insisted that they visit the La Brea Tar Pits. The place had given him the willies. Sixteen-foot-high mammoths had disappeared into that darkness. At his last physical, Ronald had measured exactly five foot eleven inches tall. If he was sucked into one of those pits he wouldn't stand a chance. He wondered if he would even recognize a tar pit or a bog should he wander out upon the moor. At least the manholes in Manhattan had covers you could see.

And then there was the Hound! Ronald knew *The Hound of the Baskervilles* was fiction but he was a fanatic Sherlockian—an investitured member of the Baker Street Irregulars with a complete set of Conan Doyle first editions in his library—so he also knew that Arthur Conan Doyle's tale had been inspired by the legend of the seventeenth-century squire Richard Cabell, a monstrously evil man who had allegedly sold his soul to the devil. Cabell was buried on the moor and his ghost was said to lead a pack of baying phantom hounds across them on the anniversary of his death. Intellectually, Ronald knew there was no Hound prowling the "craggy cairns and tors" Conan Doyle had described in his story, but somewhere in the lizard part of his brain lurked the fear that an unearthly, slavering beast with glowing red eyes might roam a godforsaken place like this.

Ronald scanned the eerie countryside through the window of the jet black SUV that had been waiting for his private plane at Heathrow. The moor was shrouded in a thick, impenetrable mist that would cloak any ravenous fiend lurking near the dark pools of liquid peat. He pulled his gaze away and checked his cell phone. There were still no bars. They had disappeared as soon as the SUV passed through a small village which, the driver informed him, would be the last sign of civilization he would see before they arrived at Hilton Cubitt's estate.

There were two other SUVs and a chauffeured limousine in the caravan that was headed toward Cubitt's manor house. Ronald had seen the passengers in the other SUVs at Heathrow when they walked to the vehicles from their private jets. He had one thing in common with them: an outstanding Holmes collection. The limousine had joined the convoy as it left the airport and Ronald had no idea who was riding in it.

In the SUV directly behind Ronald was William Escott, a heavyset, dissipated Texas oilman who had inherited his wealth from his father. Ronald had disliked the collector the first time their paths had crossed at an auction. His low opinion of the man had never changed. Escott was a foul-mouthed slob who drank too much and talked too loudly. He had actually gotten into a fistfight during the Baker Street Irregulars' annual meeting in New York in a dispute over the date of the action in "The Musgrave Ritual." Escott did not limit his collecting to Holmes. He had an ownership interest in the Houston Astros and one of the best collections of baseball memorabilia outside of Cooperstown.

Robert Altamont was in the SUV that was following Escott. He was a chubby five-ten with a ruddy complexion, straw-colored hair, and bright blue eyes. The inventor had grown up on a farm in Oregon and had made his fortune after graduating from Boise State, but he dressed like a Boston WASP, affected a Haavaad accent and tried to create the impression that he'd been educated at places like Andover, Princeton, and MIT. The veil was easy to penetrate. Ronald had seen him use the wrong fork more than once at the BSI banquet and had caught numerous grammatical errors when Altamont tried to throw French phrases into a conversation.

Altamont had never confirmed the gossip about the source of his wealth but it was rumored that he had invented an electric car that really did what it was supposed to do and had sold the technology to a consortium of car manufacturers who now held the patent and the design in a vault in a secret location. The deal had supposedly made him a fortune.

Altamont was as avid a Sherlockian as Ronald. He had been turned on to Holmes by his older brother when he was ten years old and had started collecting on a small scale when he was still poor and in college. After he became rich Altamont not only built one of the world's best Holmes collections but expanded his interests to Shakespeare First Folio, signed first editions of famous literary works, and French Impressionist paintings.

The caravan rounded a curve in the road and a pair of wrought-iron gates attached to weather-worn stone pillars suddenly appeared out of the fog. The gates and the house they protected looked familiar and Ronald had no trouble figuring out why. Hilton Cubitt had chosen this desolate stretch of the moor for his manor house because he wanted to model it after

Baskerville Hall but the description in Doyle's story did not provide enough detail, so he'd had the architect study the plans for Cromer Hall, which had inspired Doyle's fictional architectural creation. Cubitt's manor house was a variant of Tudor Gothic. There was a central three-story section with two-story wings on each side. The manor was gray stone. Octagonal stone chimneys rose at several points along the slate roof. The gray stone blended into the sullen surroundings and looked rather foreboding. For a brief moment, Ronald imagined that the high windows at the front of the house were watching him arrive.

The SUVs and the limousine stopped in front of a high, carved door fashioned from weather-worn oak. The driver opened Ronald's door and he stepped out. The chill wind that swept across the desolate landscape stung his cheeks and he turned up the collar of the motorcycle jacket he wore over a black turtleneck and worn jeans. Ronald knew he was underdressed for a stay at a British manor house, but one nice thing about being filthy rich was that he could dress any damn way he pleased.

The limousine parked next to Ronald's SUV. When the chauffeur opened the rear door, Ronald was surprised to see Peter Burns work his way out of the rear seat and limp around the front of the vehicle, leaning heavily on his cane. Burns was a dealer in rare books and the owner of London's Great Mystery bookshop. Ronald had met him on a few occasions and he'd had many transatlantic dealings with him by phone or e-mail. Burns had a thin, aristocratic face with high cheekbones, a nose as sharp as a knife, and a narrow, pointed jaw. A pleasant smile and a head of curly gray hair softened his features. He was slightly taller than Ronald but the two men were eye to eye because he was forced to bend forward slightly due to the height of his cane.

"So Hilton invited you, too," Ronald said.

"Didn't you know I was coming?" Burns asked.

"Hilton told me there would be other guests, but he didn't tell me who they were. Do you know why he summoned us?" Ronald asked.

"That's what I want to know," said William Escott, who had no compunction about butting into the conversation. Ronald and Peter Burns looked down at the five foot four interloper who seemed to be almost as wide as he was tall.

"I'm also curious, chaps," chimed in Robert Altamont. "All Hilton told me was that my visit would be one of the most memorable events of my life."

"I'm afraid I've been sworn to secrecy," Burns said. "But Hilton will explain why you're here soon enough."

Before anyone could ask any more questions the front door was opened by Phillip Lester, Cubitt's butler, a dignified and superbly fit ex-SAS sergeant whose military service records were shrouded in mystery. Lester was flanked by two men who looked like bodybuilders and had the hard eyes of people who have seen the dark side of life. The visitors were beckoned into a cavernous entryway. A massive stone staircase led up to the second floor and suits of armor stood at attention on either side of the bottom step.

"Welcome to Cubitt Hall," Lester said as the drivers brought in Ronald's stewardess case, Burns's golf-club-size duffle bag, Escott's valises, and Altamont's monogrammed luggage. "Before I can show you to your rooms I'm afraid the security staff will have to go through your belongings and search you."

"This is outrageous," Escott shouted. "No one is going to lay a hand on me."

"Mr. Escott," Peter Burns interceded. "Take my word for it, you will think nothing of this search when you discover why you are here."

Escott looked like he was about to say something else but he snapped his jaws shut.

"Very well," he said as he raised his hands above his head and let one of the security men pat him down while the other went through his suitcases.

"I'll show you to your rooms so you may freshen up," the butler said as soon as the men and their luggage had been searched. "Mr. Cubitt would like you to meet him in the library for drinks before dinner at five."

"A drink sounds mighty good to me," Escott said.

Hilton Cubitt was an average-looking man who had made an above average fortune in the stock market, but he had just been through a costly divorce from his fourth wife and Ronald had heard whispers about severe financial reversals. Had Cubitt invested heavily with Bernie Madoff? Was his fortune depleted by the failure of several banks? If so, Cubitt did not show it. He strode into his library dressed in a hand-tailored suit sporting a confident smile.

Cubitt was five-nine with the compact build of the rugby player he'd been at Oxford. He'd parlayed a degree in finance into a fortune as a hedge fund manager and he'd used some of that fortune to build collections that were the envy of everyone who collected in his fields of interest. Cubitt was rumored to own the thirty-fifth Vermeer and he had an antique car museum that housed some of the rarest vehicles ever created, but he had two favorite collections.

Cubitt had spent a year in the States as a graduate student at Columbia. During that year, he had become a fan of American baseball and his favorite team was the New York Yankees. He had an impressive collection of Yankee memorabilia, which was said to include a World Series uniform worn and signed by Babe Ruth and the bat Mickey Mantle used when he hit his longest home run plus the uniform he wore when he hit it. The originals of these items were supposed to be in the Baseball Hall of Fame but there were rumors that Cubitt would neither confirm nor deny that the items in Cooperstown were copies.

Cubitt's other pride and joy was the world's largest collection of artwork pertaining to Sherlock Holmes, some two to three thousand pieces.

Cubitt's guests were seated in his library in upholstered high-back chairs set up in a semicircle in front of a massive stone fireplace. A roaring fire radiated enough heat to counteract the chill and drinks had been provided by the butler. Every inch of wall space on either side of the fireplace was taken up with ornately carved floor-to-ceiling wooden bookshelves. Ronald had inspected some of the spines while waiting for Cubitt to appear and had been impressed by the quality of the collection.

"Thank you for coming, gentlemen," Cubitt said as he strode to a spot in front of the fireplace. "I am certain that you will find your journey worthwhile."

"And why is that, Hilton?" Escott asked. "Why did you drag us out here?"

Cubitt smiled. "I'm going to keep you in suspense a little longer, Bill. Please follow me."

"Any chance I can see your Yankees memorabilia?" Escott asked.

"Perhaps, but I'm reluctant to do so since I hear that you're a Red Sox fan."

Cubitt led them down a long hall and stopped in front of a carved wood door while the butler unlocked it. When the door swung open, Ronald could see that the wood covered a thick steel inner door. The guests entered a pitch-black room. When Cubitt threw the light switch Ronald, Altamont, and Escott gasped. Only Peter Burns showed no reaction. He had been guiding Hilton Cubitt since the millionaire began collecting and he had been in this room on many occasions.

The gallery was massive and every square inch was covered by artwork related to Sherlock Holmes. What drew Ronald's eye was a wall covered by Sidney Paget drawings. Paget was the original illustrator of the Holmes stories in *The Strand Magazine*, where the stories first appeared. There were only supposed to be thirty-five existing originals out of the hundreds of drawings Paget had completed. The most famous Paget was from "The Final Problem." It showed the fight at Reichenbach Falls between the detective and his archenemy, Professor Moriarty, and had sold for more than $200,000 at auction.

"Are these…?" Ronald asked.

Cubitt nodded. "All originals."

"My God," Ronald said. On the wall were more than twenty Pagets that were not supposed to exist.

Cubitt gestured to four chairs that had been placed in front of the wall with the Pagets.

"Please sit down."

Ronald could not tear his eyes away from the Pagets as he lowered himself onto his chair. When the men were seated, Cubitt walked in front of them and put his back to the wall.

"Bear with me while I tell you a story. Queen Victoria was born in 1819 and she ruled England from 1837 until her death in 1901. It is not widely known, but the queen was a huge fan of the Holmes stories and she was devastated when Doyle, who had grown tired of his creation, killed him off in 'The Final Problem' in 1893.

"On June 20, 1897, England held the Diamond Jubilee to celebrate the fact that Victoria had surpassed King George III as England's longest-reigning monarch. It is not clear who, but someone close to the queen had the brilliant idea of asking Doyle to write a Holmes story solely for Her Majesty. Paget was asked to illustrate the tale."

"Everyone knows that never happened," Escott scoffed. "It's a legend like the Loch Ness monster, with about as much truth to it."

Cubitt smiled. "That is the majority opinion."

"You're not saying it really happened, are you?" Altamont asked with raised eyebrows and a smirk that broadcast his opinion of the tale.

"Why don't you let me finish. Then you can draw your own conclusions," Cubitt answered. "Those of us familiar with this so-called legend know that the story and the illustrations were alleged to have been individually bound in leather and presented to the queen. That is where the story usually ends, but some years ago Peter went to an estate on the North Shore of Long Island, New York, and bought a collection from Chester Doran, a distant relative of John Jacob Astor. Over dinner the conversation turned to Holmes. Doran asked Peter if he was aware that Astor had once owned the only copy of a short story Doyle had written for Queen Victoria and the original artwork Paget had created for it."

Ronald turned toward Burns but the dealer's face showed no emotion.

"Peter told Doran that the story in question was not believed to have actually existed, but his dinner partner assured him it was real. According to Doran, Astor heard the rumor while visiting England in 1912. Using contacts in the royal family he learned that the story was still in Buckingham Palace.

"Doran grew reluctant to continue his tale at this point but Peter persuaded him to complete it. Doran told Peter that Astor paid a huge sum to a servant to steal the story and the artwork, which he received the day before he was to sail back to the States."

"Didn't Astor go down with the *Titanic*?" Ronald asked.

Cubitt nodded. "He was one of the poor souls who sailed on that doomed ship in April 1912. Those scholars who heard the rumor that Astor possessed the story and artwork believe that they joined him at the bottom of the sea. But Doran claimed that he had discovered a Paget drawing in a leather case in a trunk belonging to John Jacob Astor that had been mistakenly left behind in England when the *Titanic* sailed and was shipped to Astor's estate a month after the ship sank."

"You're saying you have the Paget?" Ronald asked incredulously.

Cubitt walked to the wall on the far side of the room and took down a painting that concealed a wall safe. He spun the dial, opened the steel door, and took out a framed fifteen-by-twenty-inch drawing. Escott leapt to his feet but Altamont and Ronald were too stunned to move. Cubitt placed the drawing on an easel that had been set up in front of the safe.

"Gentlemen," Cubitt said.

Ronald and Altamont stood slowly and stared at the drawing like men in a trance. The three collectors edged forward with the same reverence priests would show if they were approaching the Holy Grail. Ronald's heart beat furiously. The drawing was a full-length portrait of Holmes in a long coat and his famous deerstalker hat smoking a pipe in front of the fire at 221B Baker Street. It was signed SP, as Paget always signed his drawings, and dated June 20, 1897. There was no known Paget this large and the date under the signature was something no Sherlockian collector had ever seen on a Paget drawing.

"My God," Altamont gasped. "How much did you pay for this?"

"I'm afraid I'll have to keep that information confidential."

Escott snorted. "Whatever you paid was money down the drain. This has got to be a forgery."

"Peter vetted it thoroughly," Cubitt said. "Before I bought it he had the paper tested, the ink tested. He had it examined by Paget experts. I've seen the documents. It is authentic."

Escott tore his eyes away from the drawing and cast a sly glance at his host.

"Why are we here, Hilton? I reckon there's more to this than an art show."

"There's no fooling you, Bill," Cubitt answered. "With the acquisition of this Paget I have completed my collection of Holmes memorabilia and I've decided to sell it off. Collecting Holmes has no interest for me now that I have the whole set. I'm going to have Peter handle the sale of my collection but I wanted to give you three a chance to bid for the most important piece of Holmes memorabilia ever discovered because you are the only Holmes collectors with the financial resources to buy it. Tomorrow morning I will hold an auction for the Queen Victoria Paget."

◇◇◇

Hilton Cubitt's personal chef produced a dinner worthy of the best French restaurant but Ronald and Altamont were too distracted to do more than pick at their food. William Escott devoured his meal with gusto and drank with even greater enthusiasm. Ronald was exhausted from the flight, the long drive, and the excitement caused by Cubitt's startling surprise. As soon as it was socially acceptable, he called it a night and went to his room, but he found that he was too excited to sleep. He was also troubled by a question of ethics.

If the Paget was genuine, it was in truth the most important discovery in the history of Holmes collecting. But it was also stolen goods. If the existence of the Paget was made known, along with the manner in which it was acquired, the British government would demand its return. Neither he nor Altamont nor Escott had brought this up to Cubitt.

Robert Altamont was a genius and Ronald was certain he had considered the moral and legal conundrums the owner of the Paget would face. Ronald would not have been surprised if Escott had failed to think through the problem presented by the drawing's provenance. The Texan wasn't very bright. His morals were also suspect. If he did realize that the owner of the Paget would be in possession of stolen property, Ronald doubted that it would spoil his sleep.

Ronald had always prided himself on being an honest man. If he bought the Paget he would have to keep it hidden. If he hoarded his treasure so the British government didn't learn of the Paget's existence would he be able to look himself in the eye whenever he looked in a mirror?

Ronald's bedroom was large and dominated by a king-size canopy bed in which he tossed and turned while visions of the Paget kept sleep away. A little after midnight, he finally gave up any idea of getting a good night's sleep and got out of bed. Ronald had started a legal thriller on the plane ride from New York to London and he fished his e-book reader out of his traveling bag, hoping that reading would tire him out. There was a comfortable armchair next to a high window with a view of the moor. Ronald settled in and turned on the lamp on the side table.

Forty-five minutes later, the words were swimming in front of his eyes and he turned off the light. The reflection from the lamp had made it difficult to see through the window. The moment the light went off Ronald saw another light bobbing up and down on the moor. The fear he felt when he read *The Hound* flooded him and he took an involuntary step away from the window. Then he caught his breath and leaned forward.

The quarter moon provided little illumination and thick, fast-moving clouds frequently blocked even those feeble rays. For a second, Ronald thought he could make out a silhouette moving across the moor, whether man or woman he could not be sure. Then the light disappeared and he guessed that the person had moved behind a hummock or rock formation that was blocking the light.

What would possess someone to venture out on the moor in the cold and dark? Ronald could not imagine anything that would send him out into that trackless, merciless waste with its quicksand bogs and God knew what else. But the puzzle intrigued him and he decided to sit again and keep a vigil in hopes that the phantom would return and he could discover its identity.

◇◇◇

Ronald jerked awake. At first, he had no idea where he was. Then he realized that he had fallen asleep in the chair by the window. The sun was just rising over the moor and he could make out stunted trees, barren ground, low hills, and rocky prominences. Nothing about the place in daylight changed his mind about his desire to avoid it.

Ronald's Franck Muller wristwatch was on his nightstand. It was just shy of seven a.m. He showered and shaved before dressing in pressed jeans, a tight black T-shirt, and a Harvard sweatshirt. Unlike Robert Altamont, he had actually gone to Harvard for two years before dropping out to work full-time developing *Death's Head*.

The table where they had eaten dinner was set. Silver serving dishes had been laid out on a long credenza. Phillip Lester asked him if he'd like some coffee. While Ronald poured a glass of orange juice and filled his plate with bacon, scrambled eggs, and a scone, the butler brought him a cup of the best black coffee he'd ever tasted. Ronald asked where it was from and Lester told him that the blend had been specially created for Mr. Cubitt but that was all he was at liberty to say.

"Did you sleep?" Robert Altamont asked from the doorway soon after Ronald had dug into his eggs. He was wearing gray slacks, a white silk shirt, and a blazer.

"Not until the wee hours. I was too wound up. What about you?"

"I caught a few winks but thinking about the Paget kept me up most of the night. I've been collecting forever but I've never been in a position to own something like this."

William Escott walked in before Ronald could reply and made straight for the food. He stacked his plate so high that Ronald waited for it to collapse like a building brought down by a demolition expert.

"When's the auction?" Escott asked the butler, though it was difficult to understand what the Texan had said because his mouth was stuffed with food.

"Mr. Cubitt should descend shortly."

"Can we see the Paget again or do we have to wait for Hilton?" Ronald asked.

"Last night, Mr. Cubitt instructed me to take you to the gallery if you requested a viewing."

"Well, I certainly do," Escott said. He pulled a magnifying glass out of his pocket. "I'm not buying unless I get a chance to inspect the damn thing. Personally, I think this picture is just too good to be true." He snorted. "Queen Victoria, the *Titanic,* John Jacob Astor. The whole thing sounds like a plot for a comic book."

After everyone had eaten, Lester led them to the gallery. The door was closed but there was a key jutting out from the lock.

"That's odd," Lester said. He tried the door and it opened. The butler stepped into the pitch-black room. As soon as the light went on he tensed. Ronald looked over Lester's shoulder to see what had prompted the reaction. His eyes widened.

Hilton Cubitt was sprawled on the floor, staring at the ceiling with dead eyes. There was a bullet hole in his forehead. Ronald stared, transfixed by the grisly scene. Then William Escott's shout jerked him out of his trance.

"It's gone!"

Ronald followed Escott's pointing finger and found himself staring at an empty easel. The Paget was missing.

◇◇◇

Ronald was shaken by the sight of Cubitt's corpse. While Phillip Lester called the police, he returned to his room and collapsed in the chair by the window. Ronald had confronted death every day while he was developing *Death's Head*. His digital victims had been stabbed, decapitated by chain saws, riddled with machine gun bullets, and fed to sharks. His game contained a copious amount of animated blood that flowed and spouted from hundreds of grisly wounds, but nothing he'd dealt with in the world of his video game had prepared him for the sight and smell of real death.

Ronald wanted nothing more than to be allowed to run home to the safety of his penthouse, but he knew he was going nowhere until he had spoken to the police. That prospect was unnerving, but not nearly as unnerving as the realization that the person who had murdered Hilton Cubitt was probably near enough to kill again.

◇◇◇

Inspector Andrew Baynes had been dispatched to Cubitt Hall as soon as Hilton Cubitt's death had been reported by Phillip Lester. He was six feet tall with thinning black hair and a wiry build. After organizing the crime scene and making certain that his forensic experts were hard at work in the gallery, Baynes had Ronald Adair, Peter Burns, Robert Altamont, William Escott, and Phillip Lester escorted into the library.

The inspector studied them as they filed into the room. Baynes was an exercise fanatic and something about the short, fat Texan repulsed him. Maybe it was the smirk on Escott's face or his nonchalance in the middle of a murder investigation or the fact that he had not shaved and was dressed in a maroon track suit, but Baynes was certain he would not like the man.

The butler was all business. He was dressed in a suit and tie and had been extremely helpful from the beginning.

Peter Burns was also dressed in business attire and limped in using an elegant cane. It was clear that walking was a chore for him. The rare book dealer being the tallest of the five men, the inspector could look him straight in the eye. Burns didn't flinch under Baynes's intense scrutiny, but returned the inspector's stare without blinking.

Ronald Adair looked impossibly young to be as rich as he was rumored to be but he also looked very nervous.

Finally, there was Robert Altamont, who entered the room cautiously and looked ill at ease.

After having the men sit in the seats they had taken the night before, Baynes asked them to explain why they were at Cubitt's manor house. Then he asked Phillip Lester to tell him about the discovery of the body.

"And no one heard a shot?" the inspector asked when Lester was through.

"That's not surprising, sir," the butler said. "Mr. Cubitt's art collection is very valuable and the gallery was constructed like a vault. The doors are thick steel and the walls are also steel lined. The room is quite soundproof."

"Did any of you hear anything that might be useful?" the inspector asked.

Ronald hesitated. Then he raised his hand timidly.

"Yes, Mr. Adair?" Baynes prompted.

"I didn't hear anything, but…Well, I was so wound up by Mr. Cubitt's revelation that I couldn't sleep. So I read in a chair by the window in my bedroom in hopes that I would grow tired. At some point I started to yawn so I closed my book and turned out the lamp. That's when I saw something on the moor."

"Some*thing*?"

"I couldn't make it out. Whoever it was had a light of some sort because that's what attracted me."

"What time was this?" the inspector asked.

"I can't say with certainty but I began reading a little after midnight and probably continued for half an hour to forty-five minutes. I never looked at my watch."

"So sometime around one in the morning?"

"That would be a good guess."

"We'll see what the medical examiner has to say about time of death but you may have seen our murderer if he puts it in that neighborhood."

"Unless Adair is making up this ghostly apparition on the moor," Escott said. "It sounds like something out of *The Hound of the Baskervilles.*"

"I assure you this is no fabrication," Ronald snapped, "and you've some nerve to suggest that it is."

"Take it easy, Adair," Escott answered. "No need to get excited unless you have a guilty conscience."

"Call me a liar again and you'll see how excited I can get."

"Gentlemen," Baynes cautioned sternly. "I insist that you calm down."

Ronald and Escott glared at each other but they held their tongues.

"Can someone explain why this stolen drawing is so important?" Baynes asked. Then he listened intently while Peter Burns related the background of the missing Paget.

"And it's valuable?" the inspector asked when Burns was through.

"Very," Burns answered.

"What does that mean?"

"The Paget is the rarest piece of Holmes memorabilia in existence and would fetch several million dollars at auction."

Baynes whistled. "Now that's a motive for murder. But I have a question for you, Mr. Burns. If this painting—"

"Drawing, Inspector," Burns corrected.

"Right, drawing is so unique, why was Mr. Cubitt selling it?"

"He said he had collected everything he could of Holmes and wasn't interested anymore," Altamont said.

"Actually," Burns said, "Mr. Cubitt wasn't completely honest about his motive. His fortune had taken quite a hit lately and he was forced to sell off his collection. I tried to talk him out of it but his back was to the wall."

"What are you doing to find the Paget?" Escott demanded. "I'm still ready to bid if the thing is real."

"Can't you wait for Hilton to be buried?" Altamont asked with disgust.

"No one will be able to do a thing with Cubitt's estate until it's probated," Ronald said.

"You should search the help. One of the servants probably took it," Escott said.

"That may not be the case," Inspector Baynes said. "Mr. Lester has informed me that the cook, maids, and serving staff were dismissed after dinner. They all live in the village and were gone long before Mr. Cubitt was murdered. The security men room together in a cottage behind the house and they say that neither of them left the cottage last night. The drivers who brought you from Heathrow are rooming above the garage and they alibi one another. They also say that none of their cars left the house last night and no one saw a car leave after the last of the staff drove off."

"Are you looking for the drawing?" Altamont asked the inspector.

"I've got my men searching the house. If we find the Paget we may find the murderer."

"The drawing may not be in the house," Ronald said. "If no one drove away after the murder then the Paget must be close at hand, which means it is either in the house…"

"Or somewhere on the moor where your phantom stashed it," Baynes said.

Ronald's brow furrowed. "I've just had a very troubling thought," he said. "If the staff, the drivers, and the security men are accounted for, the killer has to be one of us."

Baynes nodded. "My thought exactly. Do any of you have alibis?"

The men looked at one another. Then all of them shook their heads.

"Something just occurred to me, Inspector," Robert Altamont said.

"Yes, Mr. Altamont," Baynes said.

"Peter, Bill, Ronald, and I may not have alibis but none of us could have committed the murder."

"Why do you say that?"

"Hilton was shot to death."

Baynes nodded.

"Then we couldn't have killed him. When we arrived, Hilton's security men searched us and our luggage. None of us had a gun on him or in his bags."

"An interesting point," Baynes conceded.

He turned to the butler. "Mr. Lester, are guns kept in the manor house?"

"Yes, sir. I have a pistol and so do the members of the security team. Then there are hunting rifles."

Baynes sighed. "All right, I'll have one of the boys from the lab go with you. I want every gun accounted for and tested. And I guess I'd better send a search party onto the moor. Will someone please describe the drawing?"

◇◇◇

Phillip Lester had set out tea and snacks in the dining room and Inspector Baynes and Ronald bumped into each other there.

"Have you found anything?" Ronald asked. The inspector shook his head.

"We've searched all over Cubitt Hall and the moor and we haven't found the Paget or the murder weapon. And none of the guns Mr. Lester turned over could have fired the shot that killed Mr. Cubitt. Unfortunately, there are a number of bogs and sinkholes on the moor into which the murder weapon and the drawing could have been dropped. If the murderer disposed of them there we have no chance of recovering them."

"The killer may have disposed of his weapon on the moor," Ronald said, "but he'd never leave the Paget there."

"What makes you say that?" Baynes asked.

"Sequestering the Paget on the moor would risk exposure to the elements and damage to the drawing. *I* would never take that gamble."

"You might if discovery of the drawing could lead to your incarceration for life for murder."

"You're not a collector, are you?"

"No, sir."

"Then it will be impossible for you to understand the reverence we collectors have for objects we desire. Trust me, Inspector, that drawing is not on the moor. It is somewhere in this house, unless..."

Ronald's brow furrowed. Then his eyes widened and he whispered, "Oh, my God!"

"What are you thinking?" Baynes asked.

Ronald turned to the inspector. "Have you recovered the bullet that killed Hilton?"

"Yes."

"Is it a soft-nosed revolver bullet that mushroomed on impact?" Ronald asked.

Baynes's mouth gaped open. "How did you know that?"

"Elementary, my dear Baynes," Ronald answered with a wide smile.

"Huh?"

"Sorry, I couldn't resist. I need one more piece of information and I'll be able to tell you who killed Hilton Cubitt and the location of the Paget."

Altamont and Escott protested at having to spend another day at Cubitt Hall but Inspector Baynes insisted. He had phoned an urgent request to police contacts in the States. Baynes received the information he needed just after dinner and gave it to Ronald Adair. Half an hour later, Baynes had Escott, Lester, Burns, and

Altamont rounded up and brought to the library where they took their places, once again.

"I wish I could take credit for cracking this case," Baynes said, "but the honor belongs to Mr. Adair. So I'm going to let him tell you what he figured out."

The others cast suspicious glances at Ronald as he stood and took his place next to the inspector.

"It was the bullet that killed Mr. Cubitt that led me to the solution to this puzzling mystery. Hilton was killed with a revolver bullet. I asked the inspector if it was soft nosed and had mushroomed on impact. He confirmed this fact."

Ronald noticed that Altamont's brow furrowed first and Escott's a moment later.

"Does that description sound familiar, gentlemen?" Ronald asked his fellow Baker Street Irregulars.

"'The Adventure of the Empty House,'" Escott blurted out.

"Exactly, Bill. In that story, Colonel Sebastian Moran tries to assassinate Sherlock Holmes with an air gun. The weapon was constructed for Professor Moriarty, Holmes's archenemy, by Von Herder, a blind German mechanic. In the story, Doyle writes that 'the revolver bullet had mushroomed out as soft-nosed bullets will.'"

"You're saying Cubitt was killed with an air gun?" Altamont asked incredulously.

"Something like it," Ronald answered.

"But you were all searched," Lester said. "How was the gun brought into the house?"

"No one searched you," Escott said.

Ronald laughed. "No, no, Bill. The butler didn't do it. The weapon used to kill Hilton Cubitt was concealed in Peter Burns's cane."

Burns looked astonished. "I don't know whether to laugh or get angry, Ronald." He held out his cane. "Feel free to inspect this as much as you wish. I assure you it's quite solid."

"Oh, I don't doubt that. What I do doubt is that the cane you are using is the same one you carried on the evening we arrived at Cubitt Hall. I am exactly five foot eleven and you are taller, but when we met outside the front door I looked directly into your eyes because you had to bend down to lean on your cane."

Burns looked puzzled. "Where is this going?"

"Inspector Baynes is six feet tall, Peter. When we were first questioned in the library I noticed that you were eye-to-eye with the inspector, but it didn't dawn on me that this might be important until I realized that Hilton Cubitt was murdered with a variant of an air gun. That's when I realized that there had to be two canes and the one with the concealed gun was shorter. I'm guessing that the real cane was concealed in the lining of your duffel bag."

Burns looked completely befuddled. "I don't know what to say. If the gun was in a phony cane I brought here, where is it now?"

"Buried in a bog in the moor along with the Paget," Ronald answered.

"My God, Ronald, are you insane? I would never destroy that drawing."

"You would if it was a fake. Bill, Robert, and I have more than enough money to have bought the Paget if it was real. We would have no reason to steal it. And if we did, we would know that our luggage would be searched when we left so we couldn't get it out of the house. And we would never leave it outside on the moor where it would be prey to some of the world's most foul weather.

"But none of us would have any compunction about destroying a fake Paget. And that is what you sold to Hilton. He depended on you to verify its authenticity before paying millions to your accomplice, Chester Doran.

"You and Doran assumed that Hilton would keep the Paget in his collection and that he wouldn't tell anyone about it. If the British government learned that Hilton had a Paget that was stolen from Buckingham Palace, it would demand its return. Cubitt assumed we would ignore the moral implications of obtaining stolen goods in our desire to obtain the most important and rare piece of Holmes memorabilia that ever existed, but you couldn't take the chance that we would make the existence of the Paget public.

"Hilton suffered huge financial losses and needed large sums of money fast. You must have been terrified when he told you he planned to sell the Paget. Even if the buyer decided to keep its existence secret you knew he would insist on independent verification of an object that valuable and you would be exposed. You didn't steal the Paget to possess it. You stole it to destroy it."

"Well, this is an interesting theory but you don't have this so-called air gun or the Paget so all you do have is a theory."

"Not quite," Inspector Baynes chimed in. "The New York police have Chester Doran in custody and he has been granted immunity as part of a plea bargain. When he heard he could be an accomplice to murder it wasn't hard to get him to cooperate. He's told us everything.

"Mr. Burns, I am placing you under arrest for the murder of Hilton Cubitt."

◇◇◇

William Escott and Robert Altamont drove back to London as soon as Inspector Baynes released them but Baynes asked Ronald to walk with him on the moor. Ronald explained his reluctance to go anywhere near the treacherous bogs but the inspector assured him it was perfectly safe.

Ronald and the inspector set off along a marked path. As they walked Ronald began to see that the moor could be scary but there was also a tranquil beauty in the lush vegetation and a sense of awe that was evoked by the cold, gray, mist-shrouded, low-hanging sky.

"Before you left, I wanted a chance to tell you how impressed I was by your deductions," the inspector said. "You'll probably have to testify at Burns's trial. When you return to England, perhaps you'll assist the Yard in solving another case."

Ronald gave a self-deprecating laugh. "I doubt I'd be much use unless the case was connected to Sherlock Holmes. If Doyle hadn't had Colonel Sebastian Moran use an air gun in 'The Adventure of the Empty House,' I'd never have tumbled to Burns's scheme."

"Then I'll keep an eye out for a case with a Doyle connection."

A stiff wind slashed Ronald's cheeks. He hunched his shoulders and looked nervously at his fog-shrouded, bog-infested surroundings.

"I'll think about it, but don't call me if the case involves a bloodthirsty beast and the moor."

Jerry Margolin is the owner of the world's largest collection of original cartoon art and illustrations dealing strictly with Mr. Sherlock Holmes. Jerry lives in Portland, Oregon, with his wife of forty years and a cat named Paget. He has been a member of the Baker Street Irregulars since 1977. His brother and coauthor, Phillip Margolin, introduced him to Sherlock Holmes at age ten.

Phillip Margolin has been a Peace Corps Volunteer, a schoolteacher, and is the author of fifteen *New York Times* bestsellers. Phil spent a quarter century as a criminal defense attorney, during which time he handled thirty homicide cases, including twelve death penalty cases, and argued before the United States Supreme Court. He lives in Portland, Oregon, and is proud to be a cofounder of Chess for Success, a nonprofit that uses chess to teach elementary school children study skills. When asked to contribute to this anthology, Phil jumped at the chance to collaborate on a Holmes story with his brother.

The resemblance of any of the characters in this story to any living or dead Sherlockians is probably intentional.

The Bone-Headed League

Lee Child

For once the FBI did the right thing: it sent the Anglophile to England. To London, more specifically, for a three-year posting at the embassy in Grosvenor Square. Pleasures there were extensive, and duties there were light. Most agents ran background checks on visa applicants and would-be immigrants and kept their ears to the ground on international matters, but I liaised with London's Metropolitan Police when American nationals were involved in local crimes, either as victims or witnesses or perpetrators.

I loved every minute of it, as I knew I would. I love that kind of work, I love London, I love the British way of life, I love the theater, the culture, the pubs, the pastimes, the people, the buildings, the Thames, the fog, the rain. Even the soccer. I was expecting it to be all good, and it was all good.

Until.

I had spent a damp Wednesday morning in February helping out, as I often did, by rubber-stamping immigration paperwork, and then I was saved by a call from a sergeant at Scotland Yard, asking on behalf of his inspector that I attend a crime scene north of Wigmore Street and south of Regent's Park. On the 200 block of Baker Street, more specifically, which was enough to send a little jolt through my Anglophile heart, because every Anglophile knows that Sherlock Holmes's fictional address was 221B Baker Street. It was quite possible I would be working right underneath the great detective's fictional window.

And I was, as well as underneath many other windows, because the Met's crime scenes are always fantastically elaborate. We have *CSI* on television, where they solve everything in forty-three minutes with DNA, and the Met has scene-of-crime officers, who spend forty-three minutes closing roads and diverting pedestrians, before spending forty-three minutes shrugging themselves into Tyvek bodysuits and Tyvek booties and Tyvek hoods, before spending forty-three minutes stringing KEEP OUT tape between lampposts and fence railings, before spending forty-three minutes erecting white tents and shrouds over anything of any interest whatsoever. The result was that I found a passable imitation of a traveling circus already in situ when I got there.

There was a cordon, of course, several layers deep, and I got through them all by showing my Department of Justice credentials and by mentioning the inspector's name, which was Bradley Rose. I found the man himself stumping around on the damp sidewalk some yards south of the largest white tent. He was a short man, but substantial, with no tie and snappy eyeglasses and a shaved head. He was an old-fashioned London thief-taker, softly spoken but at the same time impatient with bullshit, which his own department provided in exasperating quantity.

He jerked his thumb at the tent and said, "Dead man."

I nodded. Obviously I wasn't surprised. Not even the Met uses tents and Tyvek for purse snatching.

He jerked his thumb again and said, "American."

I nodded again. I knew Rose was quite capable of working that out from dentistry or clothing or shoes or hairstyle or body shape, but equally I knew he would not have involved me officially without some more definitive indicator. And as if answering the unasked question he pulled two plastic evidence bags from his pocket. One contained an opened-out blue U.S. passport, and the other contained a white business card. He handed both bags to me and jerked his thumb again and said, "From his pockets."

I knew better than to touch the evidence itself. I turned the bags this way and that and examined both items through the plastic. The passport photograph showed a sullen man, pale of skin, with hooded eyes that looked both evasive and challenging. I glanced up and Rose said, "It's probably him. The boat matches the photo, near enough."

Boat was a contraction of *boat race,* which was Cockney rhyming slang for face. Apples and pears, stairs; trouble and strife, wife; plates of meat, feet; and so on. I asked, "What killed him?"

"Knife under the ribs," Rose said.

The name on the passport was Ezekiah Hopkins.

Rose said, "Did you ever hear of a name like that before?"

"Hopkins?" I said.

"No, Ezekiah."

I looked up at the windows above me and said, "Yes, I did."

The place of birth was recorded as Pennsylvania, USA.

I gave the bagged passport back to Rose and looked at the business card. It was impossible to be certain without handling it, but it seemed to be a cheap item. Thin stock, no texture, plain print, no embossing. It was the kind of thing anyone can order online for a few pounds a thousand. The legend said HOPKINS, ROSS, & SPAULDING, as if there were some kind of partnership of that name. There was no indication of what business they were supposed to be in. There was a phone number on the card, with a 610 area code. Eastern Pennsylvania, but not Philly. The address on the card said simply LEBANON, PA. East of Harrisburg, as I recalled. Correct for the 610 code. I had never been there.

"Did you call the number?" I asked.

"That's your job," Rose said.

"No one will answer," I said. "A buck gets ten it's phony."

Rose gave me a long look and took out his phone. He said, "It better be phony. I don't have an international calling plan. If someone answers in America it'll cost me an arm and a leg."

He pressed 001, then 610, then the next seven digits. From six feet away I heard the triumphant little phone company triplet that announced a number that didn't work. Rose clicked off and gave me the look again.

"How did you know?" he asked.

I said, "*Omne ignotum pro magnifico.*"

"What's that?"

"Latin."

"For what?"

"Every unexplained thing seems magnificent. In other words, a good magician doesn't reveal his tricks."

"You're a magician now?"

"I'm an FBI special agent," I said. I looked up at the windows again. Rose followed my gaze and said, "Yes, I know. Sherlock Holmes lived here."

"No, he didn't," I said. "He didn't exist. He was made up. So were these buildings. In Arthur Conan Doyle's day Baker Street only went up to about number eighty. Or one hundred, perhaps. The rest of it was a country road. Marylebone was a separate little village a mile away."

"I was born in Brixton," Rose said. "I wouldn't know anything about that."

"Conan Doyle made up the number two twenty-one," I said. "Like movies and TV make up the phone numbers you see on the screen. And the license plates on the cars. So they don't cause trouble for real people."

"What's your point?"

"I'm not sure," I said. "But you're going to have to let me have the passport. When you're done with it, I mean. Because it's probably phony, too."

"What's going on here?"

"Where do you live?"

"Hammersmith," he said.

"Does Hammersmith have a library?"

"Probably."

"Go borrow a book. *The Adventures of Sherlock Holmes.* The second story. It's called 'The Red-Headed League.' Read it tonight, and I'll come see you in the morning."

◇◇◇

Visiting Scotland Yard is always a pleasure. It's a slice of history. It's a slice of the future, too. Scotland Yard is a very modern place these days. Plenty of information technology. Plenty of people using it.

I found Rose in his office, which was nothing more than open space defended by furniture. Like a kid's fort. He said, "I got the book but I haven't read it yet. I'm going to read it now."

He pointed to a fat paperback volume on the desk. So to give him time I took Ezekiah Hopkins's passport back to the embassy and had it tested. It was a fake, but very good, except for some blunders so obvious they had to be deliberate. Like taunts, or provocations. I got back to Scotland Yard and Rose said, "I read the story."

"And?"

"All those names were in it. Ezekiah Hopkins, and Ross, and Spaulding. And Lebanon, Pennsylvania, too. And Sherlock Holmes said the same Latin you did. He was an educated man, apparently."

"And what was the story about?"

"Decoy," Rose said. "A ruse was developed whereby a certain Mr. Wilson was regularly decoyed away from his legitimate place of business for a predictable period of time, so that an ongoing illegal task of some sensitivity could be accomplished in his absence."

"Very good," I said. "And what does the story tell us?"

"Nothing," Rose said. "Nothing at all. No one was decoying me away from my legitimate place of business. That *was* my legitimate place of business. I go wherever dead people go."

"And?"

"And if they *were* trying to decoy me away, they wouldn't leave clues beforehand, would they? They wouldn't spell it out for me in advance. I mean, what would be the point of that?"

"There might be a point," I said.

"What kind?"

I asked, "If this was just some foreigner stabbed to death on Baker Street, what would you do next?"

"Not very much, to be honest."

"Exactly. Just one of those things. But *now* what are you going to do next?"

"I'm going to find out who's yanking my chain. First step, I'm going back on scene to make sure we didn't miss any other clues."

"*Quod erat demonstrandum,*" I said.

"What's that?"

"Latin."

"For what?"

"They're decoying you out. They've succeeded in what they set out to do."

"Decoying me out from what? I don't do anything important in the office."

He insisted on going. We headed back to Baker Street. The tents were still there. The tape was still fluttering. We found no more clues. So we studied the context instead, physically, looking for the kind of serious crimes that could occur if law enforcement was distracted. We didn't find anything. That part of Baker Street had the official Sherlock Holmes museum, and the waxworks, and a bunch of stores of no real consequence, and a few banks, but the banks were all bust anyway. Blowing one up would be doing it a considerable favor.

Then Rose wanted a book that explained the various Sherlock Holmes references in greater detail, so I took him to the British Library in Bloomsbury. He spent an hour with an annotated compendium. He got sidetracked by the geographic errors Conan Doyle had made. He started to think the story he had read could be approached obliquely, as if it were written in code.

Altogether we spent the rest of the week on it. The Wednesday, the Thursday, and the Friday. Easily thirty hours. We got nowhere. We made no progress. But nothing happened. None of

Rose's other cases unraveled, and London's crime did not spike. There were no consequences. None at all.

So as the weeks passed both Rose and I forgot all about the matter. And Rose never thought about it again, as far as I know. I did, of course. Because three months later it became clear that it was I who had been decoyed. My interest had been piqued, and I had spent thirty hours doing fun Anglophile things. They knew that would happen, naturally. They had planned well. They knew I would be called out to the dead American, and they knew how to stage the kinds of things that would set me off like the Energizer Bunny. Three days. Thirty hours. Out of the building, unable to offer help with the rubber-stamping, not there to notice them paying for their kids' college educations by rubber-stamping visas that should have been rejected instantly. Which is how four particular individuals made it to the States, and which is why three hundred people died in Denver, and which is why I—unable, in the cold light of day, to prove my naive innocence—sit alone in Leavenworth in Kansas, where by chance one of the few books the prison allows is *The Adventures of Sherlock Holmes.*

Previously a television director, union organizer, theater technician, and law student, Lee Child is the worldwide number one bestselling author of the Jack Reacher series. Born in England, Child now divides his time between New York and the south of France. He clearly remembers his interest in the matter at hand being sparked by reading in his grandmother's *Reader's Digest* an article about Joseph Bell, Arthur Conan Doyle's medical school professor, often supposed to be the model for the character and therefore in Child's opinion the "real" Sherlock Holmes.

"The Red-Headed League" appeared in 1892 and was collected as part of *The Adventures of Sherlock Holmes.*

The Startling Events in the Electrified City

(A manuscript signed "John Watson,"
in the collection of Thomas Perry)

During the many years while I was privileged to know the consulting detective Sherlock Holmes and, I fancy, serve as his closest confidant, he often permitted me to make a record of the events in which we played some part, and have it printed in the periodicals of the day. It would be false modesty to deny that the publication of these cases, beginning in 1887, added something to his already wide reputation.

There were a number of cases presented to him by people responding to the new, larger reputation my amateurish scribbles brought upon him. There were others on which I accompanied him that I have never intended to submit for publication during my lifetime or his. The event in Buffalo is a bit of both. It is a case that came to him from across the Atlantic because his reputation had been carried past the borders of this kingdom between the covers of *The Strand Magazine*. And yet it is a case deserving of such discretion and secrecy that when I finish this narrative, I will place the manuscript in a locked box with several others that I do not intend to be seen by the public until time and mortality have cured them of their power to harm.

It was the twenty-fifth of August in 1901, the year of Queen Victoria's death. I was with Holmes that afternoon in the rooms that he and I had shared at 221B Baker Street since Holmes returned to London in 1894. I was glad I had closed my medical office early that day, because he seemed to be at a loss, in a bout of melancholy, which I silently diagnosed as a result of inactivity. It was a day of unusually fine late summer weather after a week of dismal rainstorms, and at last I managed to get him to extinguish the tobacco in his pipe and agree to stroll with me and take the air. We had already picked up our hats and canes from the rack and begun to descend the stairs, when there came a loud ringing of the bell.

Holmes called out, "Hold, Mrs. Hudson. I'm on sentry duty. I'll see who goes there." He rapidly descended the seventeen steps to the door and opened it. I heard a man say, "My name is Frederick Allen. Am I speaking to Mr. Holmes?"

"Come in, sir," said Holmes. "You have come a long way."

"Thank you," the man said, and followed Holmes up the stairs to Holmes's sitting room. He looked around and I could see his eyes taking in the studied disorder of Holmes's life. His eyes lingered particularly on the papers spread crazily on the desk, and the very important few papers that were pinned to the mantel by a dagger.

"This is my good friend, Dr. John Watson."

The stranger shook my hand heartily. "I've heard of you, Doctor, and read some of your writings."

"Pardon, Mr. Allen," Holmes said at this juncture. "But I wish to use this moment for an experiment. Watson, what would you say is our guest's profession?"

"I'd guess he was a military man," I said. "He has the physique and the bearing, the neatly trimmed hair and mustache. And I saw the way he looked at the manner in which you've arranged your rooms. He's a commissioned officer who has inspected quarters before."

"Excellent, my friend. Any further conjecture?"

"He's American, of course. Probably late of the conflict with Spain. American army, then, judging from his age and excellent manners, with a rank of captain or above."

Mr. Allen said, "Remarkable, Dr. Watson. You have missed in only one particular."

"Yes," said Holmes. "The branch of service. Mr. Allen is a naval officer. When I heard his accent, I too knew he was American, and said he'd come a long way, implying he'd just come off a trans-Atlantic voyage. He didn't deny it. And we all know that the weather the past week has been positively vile. Yet he didn't think it worth a mention, because he's spent half his life at sea." He nodded to Allen. "I'm sorry to waste your time, sir. Watson and I play these games. What brings you to us, Captain Allen?"

"I'm afraid it's a matter of the utmost urgency and secrecy, gentlemen."

Holmes strolled to the window and looked down at the street. "I assure you that I have been engaged in matters of trust many times before. And Dr. Watson has been with me every step in most of these affairs. He is not only an accomplished Royal Medical Officer who has been through the Afghan campaigns, he is also a man of the utmost discretion."

"I believe you, Mr. Holmes. I have permission from the highest levels to include Dr. Watson in what I'm about to impart."

"Excellent."

"No doubt you know that in my country, in the city of Buffalo, New York, the Pan-American Exposition opened on the first of May. It's been a highly publicized affair."

"Yes, of course," Holmes said. "A celebration of the future, really, wouldn't you say? Calling the world together to witness the wonders of electricity."

"That's certainly one of the aspects that have made us most proud. It was hoped that President McKinley would visit in June, but he had to postpone because of Mrs. McKinley's ill health. At least that was the public story."

"If there's a public story, then there must be a private story," said Holmes.

"Yes. There were indications that there might be a plot on the president's life."

"Good heavens," I said.

"I know how shocking it must be to you. Your country is renowned for its stability. Not since Charles the First in 1649 has there been the violent death of a head of state, and when your late, beloved Queen Victoria's reign ended a few months ago, it had lasted nearly sixty-four years. In my country, during just the past forty years, as you know, there have been a civil war that killed six hundred thousand men, and two presidents assassinated."

"It's not a record that would instill complacency," I admitted, but Holmes seemed to be lost in thought.

He said, "Who is suspected of plotting to kill President McKinley?"

"I'm afraid that I've reached the limit of what I'm authorized to say on that topic at present," Captain Allen said.

I felt the same frustration I often have at official obfuscation in my own military experience, where a doctor is outside the chain of command. "If your business is a secret from Holmes, then how can you expect him to help you?"

"I spoke as freely as my orders allowed. My mission is to deliver a request that you two gentlemen come for a personal and private meeting with the President of the United States, who will tell you the rest." He reached into his coat and produced a thin folder. "I have purchased a pair of tickets on the SS *Deutschland* of the Hamburg Amerika line. The ship is less than a year old, a four-stack steamship capable of twenty-two knots that has already set a record crossing the Atlantic in just over five days."

"Very fast indeed," I conceded.

Holmes lit his pipe and puffed out a couple of times to produce curlicues of bluish smoke. "How did the President of the United States come to think of me, when he can have many capable men at his command within minutes?"

"President McKinley is an avid reader. I gather he's read of your accomplishments in *The Strand Magazine*."

I confess that when I heard those words, I found that my ears were hot and my collar suddenly seemed to have tightened around my neck. Vanity is a powerful drug, able to strengthen the heartbeat and circulation extraordinarily.

Holmes said, "I can answer *for* myself, because I only have to answer *to* myself. I shall be happy to meet with the president. When does the *Deutschland* weigh anchor?"

"High tide is tomorrow at nineteen hundred."

Holmes turned to me. "And you, Watson?" It was not the first time when I thought I detected in Holmes a slight resentment of my relationship with the lovely creature who was, within the year, to become my second wife. It seemed to me a tease, almost a challenge, an implication that I was no longer my own man and able to have adventures.

I did not take the bait and say something foolish in an attempt to save face. "I must speak with a dear friend of mine before I give you my word. But I'm almost certain I will join you."

Allen smiled and nodded. "I thank you both, gentlemen. I'll leave the tickets with you. Once again, I must bring up the uncomfortable issue of secrecy. I must adjure you both to absolute silence about the nature of your voyage."

"Of course," I said, since the request was clearly addressed to me. Holmes could never have been prevailed upon to reveal anything he didn't wish to. I, on the other hand, was about to go to Queen Anne Street to speak to a beautiful and loving woman, and get her to agree I should go to another continent without being able to tell her which one or why.

What was said during that night's discussions, and what inducements were offered to break my oath of silence I leave to the reader's own experience. I did present myself on the London docks at nineteen hundred the next evening with my steamer trunk packed. Holmes, upon seeing me arrive in a carriage, merely looked up and said, "Ah, Watson. Prompt as always."

We sailed on the tide. The steamship *Deutschland* was a marvel of modern design, but also of modern impatience. The powerful engines in the stern below decks could be heard and felt without difficulty anywhere on board at any hour of the twenty-four, despite the fact that the bow was more than six hundred feet from them. I had been accustomed after several tours in India to long voyages under sail. The old, graceful, and soothing push of wind, where the only sound is the creaking of boards and ropes as they stand up to the sea is disappearing rapidly. Even HMT *Orontes,* which brought me back to Portsmouth after my last tour of duty, had its three masts of sails supplemented by steam power below deck. Some day, no doubt, travel by sail will be a pleasure reserved for the leisured rich, the only ones who will be able to afford the time for it.

Our enormous steamship pushed on at full tilt, regardless of the weather. Holmes and I walked the deck and speculated on the true nature of our enigmatic invitation. Rather, I speculated, but Holmes maintained the irritating silence into which he often retreated when a case began. It was something between a boxer's silent meditation before a match—among Holmes's several skills was a mastery of the pugilist's art—and a scientist's cogitation on a natural phenomenon. Long before the ship steamed its way into New York harbor, I was grateful that its soulless speed would deliver me of the need to be with a man who neither spoke nor listened.

It was late afternoon when the crew tied the bow and stern to cleats, and stevedores hauled our steamer trunks from our cabin. We were on the main deck prepared to step down the gangplank to the new world. Captain Allen joined us, and he engaged a closed carriage to take us to a different dock. "Have either of you been to the United States before?" Allen asked.

"I have," Holmes said. "In 1879 I traveled here with a Shakespeare company as Hamlet. I hope to play a less tragic part on this visit."

When we arrived at the new jetty, we found that all the sailors there were in military uniform. They rapidly loaded our trunks aboard a much smaller craft, a Coast Guard vessel of some fifty feet in length, with a steam engine. Once we were aboard, the vessel was pushed from the dock, oriented itself due north, and began to move across the harbor. The air was hot and humid that afternoon, and I was grateful when the vessel began to lay on some speed. I came to understand from one of the crew that the purpose of the vessel was to outrun the craft of smugglers and other miscreants and bring them to a halt, so its speed was considerable. Before long we were out of the congested waters of the harbor and heading up the majestic Hudson River.

Much of the land along the river was wooded, but here and there on the shore we could see charming villages, most of them apparently supported by a combination of agriculture and light manufacturing. I could see growing fields of maize and other vegetables on the distant hillsides, but nearer the water were smokestacks and railroad tracks.

As I explored the Coast Guard cutter, I happened upon Allen and Holmes at the bow. "Excellent means of travel," Holmes said, and Allen replied, "It's not the usual way, but it was determined that a government vessel would not be suspected to be smuggling two Englishmen to Buffalo."

"Is the secrecy warranted?" Holmes asked.

Allen said, "If all goes well, we may never know."

"Indeed."

We disembarked at a city called Albany. I found all of the names of British places in America—York, Albany, Rochester—disturbing in some fundamental way. It was like emerging from a wilderness trail and hearing that I had arrived at Charing Cross. But I said nothing. At Albany we were transferred to a railroad train, and moved on at still greater speed. We followed roughly the course of a narrow, straight waterway called the Erie Canal, which had for the past seventy years or so brought the natural resources and products of the western parts—lumber, produce, and so on—back to the ports like New York. I found the vastness of the place a bit unnerving. By the time we reached Buffalo we had gone more than the distance between London and Edinburgh, and not left the state of New York, one of forty-five states, and by no means the largest.

The next day at four in the afternoon, we arrived at the train station in Buffalo. It was an imposing piece of architecture for such a distant and provincial place, with patterned marble floors and high stone galleries like a church. There I received my introduction to the peculiarity of the American mind. In the center of the large marble floor was a statue of an American bison covered in a layer of what I believe to be polished brass. Although this beast is commonly called a "buffalo," it is nothing of the sort, not at all like either the Asian buffalo or the African. The Americans simply like to call it a buffalo, as they like to grant the name "robin" to a native migratory thrush that is not a near relative of a British robin. Further, although the bison posing as a buffalo is the informal mascot of the city, the city's name has nothing to do with animals. It seems that Buffalo is a corruption of the seventeenth-century French name for the place, "*Beau fleuve*," beautiful river, an accurate description of the Niagara, on whose banks the city is situated. The logic was all virtually incomprehensible, but even the dimmest visitor could see that the inhabitants of the place had built themselves what looked like a golden calf and placed it in the station. As I was soon to learn, this was a city that worshipped industry, technological progress, and prosperity as fervently as the biblical sinners worshipped their own false deities. Holmes and I were about to happen upon one of their greatest pagan celebrations: the Pan-American Exposition was a festival of electrical power.

We were rushed from the station to a carriage and taken to the Genesee Hotel at Main and Genesee Streets. The Genesee was one of several large and thriving hotels in the central part of the city, with more under construction. The hotel served to seal my impression of the city, which was full of people from elsewhere, there to sell or buy or negotiate or merely gawk, as a place that grew and changed so rapidly that one had better write down his address because the next time he saw the location it might look different.

Captain Allen waited while we checked in and let the bellmen take our trunks to our suite. Then he took his leave. "I shall call upon you gentlemen at ten this evening on the matter of which we spoke," he said, turned on his heel, and went out the door. The carriage took him away.

Holmes and I went upstairs to our quarters. "We shall be here for at least a week," he said. "We may as well do some unpacking."

I took his advice, and watched out of the corner of my eye as he did the same. He had an array of unexpected items with him that I had not noticed during the six days at sea or the two days of travel into the interior. In addition to the clothing and accessories that he wore in London, there were some clothes and shoes that looked like those of a workman, some firearms and ammunition, an actor's makeup kit, and wooden boxes that were plain and unlabeled, which he left unopened in the trunk.

We took the opportunity to bathe and dress appropriately for our evening appointment. Holmes was a tall, trim man who looked positively elegant when he chose to, and a visit to the President of the United States was one occasion he considered worthy of some effort. In all modesty I must assert that my somewhat broader body was also suitably dressed. The elegant and tasteful lady I had been courting had, long before the voyage, insisted on going with me to a fine tailor on Savile Row where I was outfitted with several suits I could barely afford.

At exactly ten there was a knock on the door of our suite. Captain Frederick Allen was there to escort us. He conducted us to a waiting cabriolet, and we went down a broad and nicely paved street called Delaware Avenue. On both sides there were stately, well-kept homes of three stories, made of wood or brick or both, and surrounded by impressive lawns and gardens. We stopped at number 1168. When the cabriolet pulled out of earshot to wait, Captain Allen said, "This is the home of a local attorney, Mr. John Milburn, who is serving as president of the Exposition."

We mounted the steps and a pair of American soldiers in dress blues opened the doors for us, then stood outside for a few moments to be sure that we had not been followed. Then they stepped back inside and resumed their posts. Mr. Allen led us across a broad foyer to a large set of oak doors. He knocked, and the man who opened the door surprised me.

I had seen photographs of William McKinley during the election of 1900, and there was no mistaking him. He was tall, about sixty years old, with hair that had not yet gone gray. His brow was knitted in an expression of alertness that made him look more stern than he proved to be. His face broadened into a smile instantly, and he said, "Ah, gentlemen. Please come in. I must thank you for coming halfway around the world to speak with me."

"It's a pleasure, sir," Holmes said, and shook his hand.

I said, "I'm honored to meet you."

We were inside the library in a moment, and then someone, presumably Allen, closed the door behind us. Holmes said, "I don't mind if our friend Captain Allen hears what we say."

The president shook his head. "He knows what I'm about to tell you, and some day in the future having been here might make him subject to unwanted inquiry."

The president went to the far end of the library and sat in a leather armchair. I noticed he had a glass on the table beside him that appeared to be some local whiskey-like spirit mixed with water. "Would you care to join me in a drink?"

I saw that there were a decanter of the amber liquid and a pitcher of water on a sideboard, and a supply of glasses. In the interest of politeness, I poured myself three fingers of the distillate. Holmes said, "Water for me, Watson, at least until I'm sure I won't need a clear head."

I brought him the water and we each sat in armchairs facing the president. Holmes leaned back, crossed his legs at the knee, and said confidently, "You're a president who has learned of recent plots against his life. You are about to appear in public at an international exposition. I assume that what you want is for me to take charge of your personal security to ensure that you are not assassinated."

"Why no, sir," President McKinley said. "I called you all this way because I want you to ensure that I *am* assassinated."

"What?" I said. "Perhaps I—"

"Your surprise proves you heard the president correctly," Holmes said. Then he looked at President McKinley judiciously. "Dr. Watson will agree you appear to be in perfect health, so you're not avoiding the pain of a fatal illness. I can see from the lack of broken vessels in your facial skin that the alcohol you're drinking now is not your habitual beverage, but an amenity for guests. You were only recently reelected by a nation grateful for your service. Unless there's some curious delay in the delivery of bad news in this country, I don't think there's a scandal. And if you wanted to kill yourself, you're fully capable of obtaining and operating a firearm, since you fought in your Civil War. Why would a leader at the apex of his career wish to be murdered?"

"I don't wish to be murdered. I wish to appear to have been murdered."

"But why? Your life seems to be a series of victories."

"I've become a captive of those victories," he said.

"How so?"

"Five years ago, with the help of my friend the party boss Mark Hanna, I assembled a coalition of businessmen and merchants, and ran for president on a platform of building prosperity by giving every benefit to business. Using protective tariffs and supporting a currency based on the gold standard, I helped lift the country out of the depression that had started in 1893, and made her an industrial power."

"Then what can be the matter?"

"I'm a man who got everything he wanted, and has only now discovered that his wishes weren't the best things for his country."

"Why not?"

"Unintended consequences. Mark Hanna got me elected, but in doing so he spent three and a half million dollars. I'm afraid we have irrevocably tied political success to money, and that the connection, once made, will be disastrous for this country. The men with the most money will buy the government they want. I got us out of a depression by favoring business. I believed men of wealth and power would be fair to their workers because it was the right thing to do. Instead, the giant companies I helped act like rapacious criminals. They employ children in inhuman conditions in factories and mines, murder union spokesmen, keep wages so low that their workers live like slaves. Their own workmen can't buy the products they make, and the farmers live in debt and poverty. Since my reelection, I have been trying to bring sane and moderate regulation to business, but I have had no success. My allies, led by my friend Senator Hanna, won't hear of such a thing. My opponents don't trust me because I was champion of their oppressors. I wanted a second term to fix all the mistakes of the first term, but I find I can't fix any of them. I am clearly not the man for this job."

"Your people reelected you."

"I should not have run. I am a man of the nineteenth century. I understood the challenges of the time—bringing an end to slavery, building the railroads, settling the western portions of the country. But my time is now over. We have moved into the twentieth century, and I have overstayed history's welcome."

I said, "Mr. President, if you were to be assassinated, what would become of your nation?"

He smiled. "That is one of the few things that don't worry me. I selected a special man to be my vice presidential running mate. His name is Theodore Roosevelt. He's what I can never be—a man of the twentieth century."

"I'm afraid I know little about him," said Holmes. "I remember reading that he led a cavalry charge up San Juan Hill."

McKinley nodded. "He was running the U.S. Navy when war was declared. He resigned his Washington job and then organized his own troop of cavalry, fought alongside his men, and was recognized for his bravery. He is a genuine hero. And that should help when the country has to accept him as president. He is as well educated as a man in this country can be, is a respected historian, but also spent years running cattle in the Dakota Territory. He is only forty-two years old. He is fearless, intelligent, and utterly incorruptible. He is a man who sees these times so clearly that to a nineteenth-century man like myself, he seems clairvoyant. He is the man for the challenging times that are coming."

"What challenges do you mean?" I asked.

"The ethnic and linguistic groups of Europe have been forging themselves into nations and joining alliances for decades now—Germany and Italy have risen, and Germany defeated France in 1870. The pan-Slav movement has united Russia with the Balkans. The strength of Russia places it at odds with the Turks and the Japanese. Now all of these nations, and dozens more, are in the process of arming themselves. They're galloping toward a conflagration."

"And what can Mr. Roosevelt do?"

"In a few days, he can begin by showing the world that once again, there will be an orderly succession here. When one American leader dies, another stronger and better leader will immediately step up into his place. And then Mr. Roosevelt will show the world that the United States has might. Knowing him, I believe he will begin with the navy, which he knows best. He has already suggested sending a Great White Fleet around the world to show the flag. Germany has been working to build a fleet stronger than the British navy. Maybe if the kaiser becomes aware that he would need to defeat two strong navies, he will hesitate to attack anyone for a time."

"So you see Roosevelt as buying time?"

"Yes. I believe that if he does the job right, he can delay a general war by ten years. If he's better than that, he can delay it by fifteen years. America is on the rise. Each day that our leaders can keep the peace makes the country richer, stronger, and less vulnerable. Keeping the peace will also give him the time to begin conserving the country's wild places for posterity, and to begin curtailing and breaking up the trusts that have sprung up in industry to strangle competition and impoverish farmers and workers. I don't know what else he'll do. He is the man of the future, and I'm only a man of the past. I just know the time has come to get out of his way."

"And what would become of you?"

"That, sir, will be up to you. I would like to have you arrange my assassination within the next few days. Then I want you to help me with my afterlife. My wife, Ida, and I want to go off somewhere to live the years allotted to us in anonymity and privacy. I love my country and I've done my best for it all my life. But now I would be content to watch it from a distance." As he looked at Holmes, the president's brows knitted in that stern way he had.

Holmes sat in silence for a moment. "Sir, I accept your charge. Tonight, I believe, is the third of September. We must move quickly and keep the number of conspirators very small. I believe we'll be ready to move on the sixth." He stood.

McKinley smiled and stood with him, so I had little choice but to do the same, although I felt a bit confused by their haste. I too took my leave, and Holmes and I went outside to find Captain Allen waiting by our cabriolet. We got in, and Allen said to the driver, "The Genesee Hotel," and then stepped aside and let the cab go by.

On the way up Delaware, Holmes told the driver to stop at the telegraph office. There was one on Main Street, which was not far from our quarters. He went inside and wrote out a message he covered with his hand so I couldn't accidentally glance at it, handed it to the telegraph operator, and paid him a sum of three dollars.

When we were back in the cabriolet, he said, "Take us to the Exposition grounds, please."

"The buildings will be closed, sir," said the driver. "It's nearly midnight."

"Exactly," said Holmes.

The cab took us north along the deserted Delaware Avenue. The clopping of the horse's hooves on the cobblestone pavement was the only sound. All of the great houses were closed and darkened.

After no more than ten minutes, we reached a section of the avenue that curved, and as we came around, the Pan-American Exposition rose before us. From this distance it was a strange and ghostly sight. It was 350 acres of buildings constructed on the site of the city's principal park. Because the Exposition was, above all, a celebration of progress exemplified by electrical power, all of the principal buildings were decorated and outlined with lightbulbs, and all of them were lit, so the place looked like the capital of fairyland.

The countless bulbs glowed with a warm pink hue which never glared or fatigued the eyes, so a spectator's attention was drawn to every detail, every color. I was dumbstruck at the sights. The Exposition grounds were bisected by a grand promenade running from the Triumphal Bridge at the south end to the Electric Tower at the north end. There were canals, lakes, and fountains surrounding all the buildings, so these large, compli-cated, and beautiful constructions with heavily ornamented walls were not only illuminated and outlined by the magical light-ing, but the glow was repeated in lakes and canals that served as reflecting pools. As we approached, the impression was of a city, with domes and towers and spires everywhere.

The architecture was indescribable—a fanciful mixture of neoclassical, Spanish Renaissance baroque, and pure whimsy all placed side by side along the midway in every direction. There were some constructions that reminded me of the more ornate Hindu temples I'd seen, with their red and yellow paint and green panels.

Whenever I thought I had perceived the organizing principle of the Exposition, I saw my guess was inadequate and partial. The colors of the buildings at the south end were bright and vivid. The Temple of Music was a garish red, with green panels in its dome and a liberal use of gold and blue-green. Nearer the north end, by the Electric Tower, the colors had grown to be subtler, gentler, and more subdued, as though they represented a change from barbaric splendor to modern sophistication. I also saw monu-mental sculptures, like frozen plays, that purported to represent the Rise of Man, the Subjugation of Nature, the Achievements of Man. Another series was labeled the Age of Savagery, the Age of Despotism, the Age of Enlightenment. Perhaps if there was an organizing principle, it was that these were people who worshipped progress and pointed it out wherever they could detect it.

From time to time Holmes would jump down from our carriage and look closely at some building or press his face against the windows to see inside. Or he would stand on the raised edge of a fountain and stare along a prospect as though aiming a rifle at a distant target. He craned his neck to look along the tops of parapets, as though he were looking for imaginary snipers.

At length I got out and walked with him. "What are we doing?" I asked.

"The Exposition has been open all summer, and it's now enjoying advertising by word of mouth. Current estimates are that it will have been visited by eight million people by its closing next month. If we came to do our examination tomorrow morning, not only would we draw attention to ourselves, but we would be trampled by the crowds."

"But what are we examining it for?"

"Vulnerabilities and opportunities, my friend. Not only must we find the best means, time, and place to conduct our feigned murder of the president, we must also make sure that we retain a monopoly on presidential murders for the day."

"What?"

"You recall that President McKinley managed to give Spain a crushing defeat in 1898. That must make him seem to many European powers a dangerous upstart. He also has let the unscrupulous owners and operators of large U.S. companies and their political minions know that he intends to rescind many of their privileges and powers. I can hardly imagine a person with worse enemies than he has."

"Is what you're saying that we must keep Mr. McKinley alive in order to assassinate him?"

"Precisely. Our little charade can only flourish in the absence of genuine tragedy." He walked along a bit farther. "That is why I told him we would move on the sixth. Giving ourselves until the tenth or twelfth might expose him to unacceptable risk."

I remained silent, for I had finally realized what he was looking for. He showed special interest in the Acetylene Building, examining it from all sides and shaking his head. "The danger of explosion is too obvious," he said. "We can avoid the hazard by keeping him away."

We got out again at the Stadium in the northeast corner of the Exposition. It was a formidable place, considering it was built only for this summer, and like the other buildings, would be torn down at the end of it. The place could hold twelve thousand spectators. "This spot is tempting," he said. "The marvel of large open spaces like this is that we could have him stand at a podium in the center, and assemble twelve thousand witnesses in the seats. They would all later swear that they saw the president killed, but none of them would have been close enough to really see anything but a man fall over."

"It's something to keep in mind," I said. "We could contrive a rifle shot from up high—maybe on the Electric Tower—and pretend he'd been hit."

"Let's see what else is available." We returned to our cab and Holmes directed the driver farther down the main thoroughfare.

We moved south to the ornate Temple of Music. It was about 150 feet on a side, with truncated corners so its square shape looked rounded. It had a domed roof, and every exposed surface was plastered with ornate decorations and painted garish colors, primarily red, and surrounded by statuary representing some sort of allegory that no living man could decipher—kinds of music, I supposed.

Holmes showed particular interest in this building. He walked around it from every side, looked in the windows, and, finally, picked the lock on the door and went inside. It was a large auditorium with a stage at the far end and removable seats in the center. "I believe we may have found what we were looking for," he said. When we went out, he took a moment to relock the door.

We took our cab back to the Genesee Hotel and paid our tired driver handsomely for the long evening he'd had.

The next morning, as Holmes and I were having breakfast in our room, there was a quiet knock on the door. I got up to open it, expecting it to be Captain Allen. But there, standing in front of me, was an elderly man. Judging from his snow-white hair, his clothing, worn and a bit discolored from many washings, and the positively ancient shoes he was wearing, I thought him to be a tradesman who had gotten too old to pursue his trade. As kindly as I could, I said, "May I help you, sir?"

"Yes, my friend," said the old man in a cracked voice. "Is this the suite of Mr. Holmes?"

"Why, yes it is. Would you like to come in?"

As he stepped into the sitting room, Holmes emerged from his bedroom and grinned. "Ah, Mr. Booth. I'm very glad to see you could come so quickly." He added, "And thank you for hiding your identity so effectively."

The elderly gentleman immediately straightened, stepped athletically to Holmes, and shook his hand with a smile. "The journey was by night, and very quick," he said. "I came as soon as my final show was over. We're due to begin rehearsals for the next one in New York in a month, and if I'm not back, my understudy will stand in for me." He looked at each of us in turn. "Do you mind if I make myself at ease?" he said, as he pulled off the white hair, then carefully removed the mustache and put them in the pocket of his oversized coat. He had become a young man, perhaps twenty-one to twenty-five, as tall and healthy-looking as before he had been bent and weak.

"This is my friend Watson," said Holmes. "He has my utmost confidence and trust. Watson, this is Mr. Sydney Barton Booth, a member of the premier family of actors in this country."

I pulled him aside and whispered. "Booth?" I said. "But Holmes—"

"Yes." He spoke loudly and happily. "The same."

The young man said, "I'm twenty-three years old. My uncle John Wilkes Booth's terrible deed took place twelve years before I was born. He was the only one of my father, grandfather, and nine aunts and uncles who sympathized with the Confederacy.

The others were staunch Union people and supporters of President Lincoln."

"The Booth family have long ago outlived any suspicion," Holmes said. "In the interim, they have continued their tradition of fine acting, and particularly in the realistic portrayal of human emotion. Mr. Sydney Booth is considered the finest of his generation. I had deduced from our invitation that we would need the services of an excellent American actor. A friend of mine from the British stage whom I contacted before we left informed me that the Booths have always searched for a way to make up for the mad actions of Mr. Booth's uncle. He also gave me his professional opinion that the present Mr. Booth was likely to be our man. We need him more than I had predicted, although in a performance with a very different ending."

"But have you warned Mr. Booth of the delicacy and danger of the role he would be playing?"

Holmes turned to Booth. "Mr. Booth, our scheme is dangerous in the extreme, and will earn you little thanks if you are successful. The only reward is that it is a patriotic task that I am persuaded will strengthen your country—and with it, ours, at least for a time."

Booth said, "I can think of nothing that would make me happier."

Holmes said, "There will be only a handful who are invited to join in our conspiracy. In addition to us there will be the president, of course; his trusted secretary, Mr. Cortelyou; the chief of police of Buffalo, Mr. William Bull; the head of the military contingent, whom I hope will be our friend Captain Allen; and Dr. Roswell Park, the most respected physician in the city. Each of them may have a trusted ally or two who will need to be told some part of the plan, but not all."

"That reminds me," I said. "I must be on my way. I'm meeting with Dr. Park this morning." I took my hat and cane and left the suite.

I found that my American medical counterpart, Dr. Roswell Park, was a man of great learning and a citizen of some standing in the medical community. He and I toured the University of Buffalo medical school facilities, the county morgue, and three of the local hospitals, as well as the field hospital that had been established at the edge of the grounds of the Pan-American Exposition. Everywhere we went, all doors opened and he was welcomed, something between a visiting potentate and a fatherly benefactor.

He and I examined the X-ray machine that was on display at the Exposition, which made it possible to see inside the body to detect a break in a bone or identify dangerous lesions. There was also an infant incubator on the midway, which I found particularly promising.

In many of our moments we were in places where the only possible eavesdroppers were the dead—the cadavers used for dissection by medical students, or the fresh bodies of transients found near the docks off Canal Street. During these times we discussed the difficulties of the assignment that the president and Holmes had given us, but we found a number of solutions in accepted medical protocols and in the simple matter of being prepared in advance to make sure events unfolded in certain ways and not others. Dr. Park was a man of such thoroughness that he thought of some things I had not—making sure that certain interns and nurses would be the ones on duty the afternoon and evening of September 6, because they would unhesitatingly follow his every order, and arranging to have horse-drawn ambulances prepared to make certain clandestine deliveries during the nights that followed. By the end of that day I was ready to entrust my life to Dr. Park. It was a sentiment that went unexpressed, because that was precisely what I was doing, as he was entrusting his life to me.

I returned to the Genesee Hotel in the evening, and found Holmes and Booth still in earnest conference. Holmes had brought out the makeup kit that I'd sometimes seen him use in London. It was a mixed collection of substances he had borrowed from the art of the theater, but even more liberally borrowed from the more subtle paints and powders employed by fashionable ladies in the interest of beauty. He had often gained information in the past by posing as a longshoreman or a gypsy or an old bookseller, and this kit had helped transform his face. It seemed from the change in his appearance that the young actor Mr. Booth was as expert as Holmes. He had changed once more. He now appeared to be a rough sort of fellow of thirty years who worked outdoors with his hands. His skin and hair had darkened a bit so he seemed to be from somewhere in continental Europe.

They had also laid out a series of maps of the Pan-American Exposition grounds that Holmes appeared to have drawn from memory. Booth was studying one of them.

"You'll have to wait long enough so the first hundred or so get through the doors and meet the president," Holmes said. "By then the line will be moving in an orderly way, and the guards will be getting overconfident and bored. Remember that the first move is mine. You will act only after I do."

"I understand," said Mr. Booth. "And then I'll make some hasty attempt at departure."

"Certainly, but be careful not to succeed. You must remain embroiled with the guards and police officers. If you make it into the open, one of them will surely get a shot off."

"I'll be sure to be overwhelmed promptly," said Booth.

And on they went. Since my presence was not required I retired to my bedchamber and settled my mind with a nap, which helped me to digest the many details I would need to remember two days hence. It was a few hours later before Mr. Booth stood and shook Holmes's hand. By then, I noticed, he had once again become the old white-haired man.

"I won't see you again until the afternoon of the sixth, Mr. Holmes. I'm sure we agree on all of the essentials of the performance. If you learn of any changes, please let me know. I'm staying at the boardinghouse at Main and Chippewa Streets."

"I will, Mr. Booth. In the meantime, know that we have great confidence in you, and we salute you for your patriotism."

"Good-bye. And good-bye to you, Dr. Watson. I'll see you in a couple of days."

"Good-bye, Mr. Booth."

And he was gone. Holmes quickly put away his disguise kit and some other items he and Booth had studied, and said, "I'm hungry, Watson. It's time for a late supper."

We left the hotel and walked around the block to a small establishment that had many of the qualities of a London public house. Sitting at a table in the rear of the house was a large man in a blue police uniform. His hat was on the table next to an empty beer glass, and as we came in the door, I saw him move it to the seat beside him.

"Mr. Bull," said Holmes.

"Sit down," said the policeman.

Holmes and I took a pair of seats across the table from him, and he raised his hand and beckoned, and the bartender arrived. Mr. Bull said, "Have you had dinner?"

"Well, no," I said.

"These two gentlemen will have dinner, please. And a pitcher of beer. Put it on my tab."

"Thank you," said Holmes. "Do you happen to know what dinner consists of this evening?"

"Roast beef on kummelweck, pickled hard-boiled eggs, beer, sauerkraut, and pickles," said the barman. "All you want."

"Excellent," Holmes said, with what appeared to be sincerity.

I was surprised at the eagerness with which Holmes and the police chief attacked the strange food, but I joined in with little hesitation, and found that the bar fare was exactly what I needed after a long day with my medical colleague. I particularly liked incidentals that had been judged not worth mentioning—short lengths of sausage and small pieces of chicken, primarily thighs and wings. I have often found that in exotic countries the native diet is exactly what is required for the maintenance of health and vigor.

Holmes stood and looked up the hallway behind the barroom to be sure there were no eavesdroppers, then opened the conversation almost immediately. "Chief Bull, do you know why I asked for a chance to meet with you?"

"I do," he said. "When Captain Allen came to me on your behalf, I made inquiries with the president's secretary, Mr. Cortelyou. I'll confess I was feeling insulted that they would hire a private citizen from another country to do my job of protecting important guests in my home city."

"And did Mr. Cortelyou settle your mind on that score?"

"He did," said Bull, then leaned closer to us and kept his voice low. "Now I'm not insulted. I'm afraid for everyone involved. If this goes wrong, it will be difficult for anyone to believe that we weren't joined in a murderous conspiracy. Once the name 'Booth' is mentioned…" He shuddered.

"We must be certain that there are no mistakes," said Holmes. "The fact that you are with us has helped to settle my mind considerably."

"And what will you need from me?"

"First," said Holmes, "we must request that you maintain the utmost secrecy. This is not a hoax that can later be revealed. We mean to establish a historical event that will remain enshrined in public knowledge for centuries. The men who know of it are the three of us, the president, Mr. Cortelyou, Dr. Roswell Park, Mr. Booth, and Captain Allen. I believe we can keep it within a small circle of honorable men, only those who must know."

Chief Bull sipped his beer thoughtfully. "Agreed. Any of my men will do as I say because I say it. They don't need to know why I say it."

"Exactly," said Holmes. "The portions for which we most need your help are the arrangement and disposition of the audience, the immediate aftermath of the performance, and then, just as important, the events of the following two weeks."

"You have my cooperation," he said. "We'll need to go over exactly what you want to happen, and what you don't want to happen."

"I propose to do that as soon as we have finished this sumptuous repast," said Holmes.

And he did. It took only about an hour spent pleasantly in the American pub for Holmes to choreograph exactly what he wanted—where each officer was to stand, how the citizens would be lined up to meet the president, what would happen as soon as Mr. Booth discharged his part, and so on. Chief Bull, I must say, proved to be a canny and intelligent strategist, picking up every detail and foreseeing more than a few that came from his professional knowledge of the behavior of crowds. By the end of the hour, when he stood and retrieved his policeman's hat, he and Holmes had a clear understanding.

Holmes was extremely thorough by habit and temperament, and in the time that followed he made sure that each member of the group knew something of the role of each of the others, so that none would mistakenly impede the execution of another's part. At his urging, each went to the Exposition alone and studied the areas he would need to know during the fateful day, like an actor blocking his part in a play.

And then, before I was even prepared for the day to come, it was the sixth of September. The moment I awoke I knew that the day was going to be hot. The sun had barely risen on the slightly overcast morning when it began to exert a power over the city. The humidity reminded me of those days in Delhi just before the government would decamp each year to the higher, cooler climate of Simla.

At 7:15 a.m. the president awoke at 1168 Delaware Avenue, the home of Mr. Milburn. He took a walk along the avenue, where he met another solitary figure, a tall, trim gentleman equipped as a peddler on the way to the Exposition with a tray of souvenirs to sell. I'm told they walked together for only a couple of blocks, but in that time, a great deal of information was conveyed in both directions. Then the mysterious salesman parted with the president, and they went their separate ways.

Later in the morning Holmes and I were at the railway station to board a train which was to take us to Niagara Falls. I noticed that there seemed to be a large number of prosperous-looking and well-dressed gentlemen waiting on the platform, even after Holmes and I had climbed aboard. The train was held up at the last moment, to take on a particular passenger. The president and his party arrived by coach and were ushered to a special car. The local dignitaries were far too numerous to be admitted to the car, but they filled in on the nearest alternative cars as well as they could, with little jostling.

I whispered to Holmes, "Where is Mrs. McKinley?"

He whispered back, "She's still at the Milburn house. Her husband fears this heat would be too much for her." He paused, significantly. "And she has a great many preparations to make. She will have a large role to play in the next few weeks."

The train took us along the Niagara River, which I judged to be a half-mile wide with a current of three to five knots for most of its length. It was pleasant to ride along at a brisk pace in the heat. But Holmes insisted on standing and walking the length of the train. I said, "What are we doing?"

"Looking," he said. "Look for faces that are familiar, faces that don't belong here, faces that don't want to meet our gaze, faces that look at us with too much interest."

We walked from one car to another, with a leisurely gait, looking at the many passengers. At times Holmes would stop and speak to someone in a seat. "A wonderful day to visit the falls, isn't it?" he would say. Or "Do you have any idea when this train reaches the falls?" Or even, "Is this seat taken?" The person would reply, he would nod and touch the brim of his hat, and then go on. I can be sure that nobody who was in the public sections of the train escaped his scrutiny. At the end, when we were standing at the back railing of the front car, staring ahead at the coal car and the engine, I said, "Well, we've looked. What have we seen?"

"Not enough," he said. "But we'll see more on the way back."

"What do you expect to see?"

"You and I have a plan. But what if someone else has a plan of his own? This is a fine day for it. The Exposition is a fine place for it. But an even better place might be the falls."

"You mean—"

"I mean nothing more than that. Search the faces, Watson." He opened the door and went up the aisle. This time we were facing the passengers, and had a better opportunity to stare at each one.

At the end of the last carriage before the president's, he whispered, "We shall have to be vigilant today. There are three on this train who are not what they seem."

"Which ones?"

"There is a man in a coal black suit in the third car up. He is thin, with long elegant fingers that play idly along the length of his walking stick. He has on the floor between his feet a hard-sided case. I wondered at it because he didn't put it in the luggage rack."

"Do you suspect it holds a weapon?" I asked. "Perhaps something silent like the air gun that the blind craftsman Von Herder made and Colonel Moran used in his crime some years ago?"

"The same idea crossed my mind when I saw it, but then I noticed that the clasp on the case bears the emblem of Bergmann-Bayer, a maker of military firearms for the Spanish army," he said. "The weapon needn't be silent if he intends to fire it after we reach the falls. I'm told that the roar of the water is so loud that you could fire a field piece and the report would seem no more than a pop. No, I think with him, we have time."

"An angry Spaniard, trying to get revenge for the war. Who are the other two?"

"One is the middle-aged lady, quite small, wearing the brown dress with green trim in the front car."

"A lady? Surely you can't be serious."

"She's an unusual lady. She has a very slight but fresh cut, half an inch and nearly vertical, along her jaw line on the left side. I noticed from her movements that she is right-handed. And that is why she cut herself on the left side while shaving. It's harder to reach with her razor."

"So it's a man."

"And one who shaved extra closely this morning. The makeup powder she must have applied after it happened has run in this heat."

"Incredible," I said. "She...he could be carrying anything under those skirts. A brace of pistols. A cavalry sword. Even a rifle." I thought for a moment. "If we'd only had time, we could have devised a way of ensuring safety."

"Oh?" said Holmes.

"A device of some kind—perhaps an archway that each passenger had to walk through that had powerful magnets hanging from strings. They would detect the iron and steel of a weapon, swing right to it, and stick."

"We may consider the idea another time, perhaps," he said. "I believe we must get close to the third man before the train arrives. He is the one who seems to offer us the most imminent competition."

"Who is he?"

"Think about this. We bought a ticket. We got on the train. We walked from back to front, then from front to back. We've stopped to talk. I just saw a sign that said we were entering La Salle, which is the last place before Niagara Falls. Has the conductor punched your ticket?"

"Why, no."

"He hasn't checked anyone else's either. When I looked at him he avoided my eyes and stared ahead as though he were driving the train. The conductors I've observed can practically feel where they are on a line without looking. They have an almost miraculous sense of the exact duration of the journey. I would guess that in a moment he will be making his way to the back of the train looking very conductorly, if you'll permit me to coin a term. But what he'll be doing is using his uniform to be admitted to the car where the president sits."

And within minutes, there he was. As we were reaching the outskirts of a larger city that could only be Niagara Falls, the false conductor suddenly came down the aisle, taking tickets and punching them. He punched them without looking closely at them, which made him seem very experienced, but he was actually too engrossed in judging the distance to his destination, the door of the last car.

Holmes sat in the aisle seat on the right of the car, and I sat in the seat across the aisle from him as we watched the man's progress. I waited for Holmes to make a move, but he allowed the conductor to continue his advance. I looked at Holmes repeatedly, but saw no sign in his expression that he had even noticed. He actually was gazing out the window at passing glimpses of the river between the quaint buildings of the City of Niagara Falls. The conductor continued his approach. He was ten feet from the door, then five, but Holmes never moved. Finally I could stand it no more. I had my cane across my lap, and as he stepped to the door of the presidential car, I jabbed it between his ankles, tripped him up so he sprawled on the floor, swung the stout ivory handle across the back of his skull, and then threw myself on top of him. I could tell he was dazed, half-conscious, and somewhat deprived of wind. Holmes rather casually reached into his waistcoat pocket and handed me a pair of handcuffs without even standing up. The sight irritated me, but I could see I had only a single choice to make—accept them or reject them, and either must be without comment. I chose to accept them because the conductor was a man of some size and probable strength, and I pulled his arms behind his back and clasped the irons on his wrists quickly before his senses fully returned.

Holmes helped me roll him to his side, and patted his blue uniform tunic. He pulled from the man's uniform a loaded .45 caliber Colt revolver, a quite sizable weapon for concealment. Holmes slipped it under his coat, and looked up at the nearby passengers, who were all members of the group of local dignitaries not important enough to sit with the president. He fanned the fallen culprit with his conductor's hat and said to the others, "This heat can make a man faint with just light exercise."

The man had planned his crime rather well. The train was already pulling up to the platform at Niagara Falls. He had clearly intended to go in, shoot the president, then jump from the last car as the train slowed while approaching the platform. He could have thrown away the conductor's hat and coat in a second and looked like anyone else in the crowd gathering at the station to see the president's arrival.

The train stopped, and we waited for the other passengers to make their exit. Then Holmes knocked on the president's car, and a young soldier opened the door. We could see four other soldiers behind him. "This man was attempting to get in and shoot the president," Holmes said. "Be sure he is locked up in the Niagara Falls police station right away. Take no chances. You are dealing with a murderer." He handed the soldier the gun, helped the failed assassin to his feet, and walked down the aisle toward the exit at the front of the car.

Seeing that we were alone, I said, "Why did you do nothing while I fought an armed assassin?"

"Untrue, Watson. I cheered you on—silently, for reasons of security."

I straightened my clothing as we walked out onto the platform and soon caught up with the American president and his party. They made their way down a broad street lined with trees to a series of staircases that led down to the very brink of Niagara Falls. The blue, wide river narrows at this point into the brink of a semicircular cliff, then drops 170 feet to a churning white cauldron below. The sheer volume of water pouring over the falls was astonishing. It threw a white cloud of mist hundreds of feet into the firmament that was visible for miles. The roar of the water was constant, unchanging, hypnotic. It didn't matter that the falls were so loud, because their immensity and beauty rendered all sensible men mute, and made all commentary inadequate. Whatever we might have said would have seemed irrelevant.

I noticed as we approached the giant falls and the sight and sound overwhelmed all else, Holmes's visage seemed to cloud and then freeze in a stoic expression. He walked along, and for a moment, his eyes lost their focus.

"Steady, Holmes," I said. "I know what you're remembering, but right now, I need you here and on duty."

Holmes patted my arm. "Good point, my friend. Reichenbach Falls is a good ten years behind us. It is uncanny how sounds and smells can bring back moments from the past. But we linger in them at our peril."

We walked along about three hundred feet behind the presidential party, and I could see that Holmes was not watching them, but studying the faces of the people in the crowd. Seeing so many well-dressed men and women in a single group on a promenade along the railing that separated them from the chasm made an impression on all the strangers who were there on holiday. It was difficult for me to tell whether the average American citizen recognized William McKinley, but it was also often difficult for me to tell whether any individual was an American or not. I heard speech that was French, German, Spanish, and several kinds of central European Slavic. There were several Asian voices also, including some speaking Hindi or Punjab. We were, after all, at one of the seven wonders of the modern world, and people had come from all the continents to see it. Very few took their eyes off the water except to watch their steps to keep from falling into it. Presidents, kings, or emperors were tiny, paltry sights compared with nature's titanic spectacle.

But suddenly Holmes picked up the pace. He walked straight away from the group along the railing, then ran up the stairs toward the street level. I followed him at a distance, not wanting to draw attention to myself, and consequently, to him.

As soon as I was up at the level of the street, I could see that he was watching a man in a dark suit. He followed him to the south, along the river above the falls. He went two blocks, and I could not quite imagine what harm the man could cause going away from the president's party at the brink of the falls. But then I saw what Holmes must have perceived instantly: the man was making his way along the path to the footbridge to the largest of the islands above the falls, which I later learned was called Goat Island. His approach was rendered nearly invisible by the many trees growing on the island, shading the paths. From there, he moved along the shore of Goat Island to a second footbridge that led to a much smaller island called Luna Island, a tiny wedge of land right at the edge of the falls.

Holmes was moving at a terrific pace now, running along, hat and cane in hand, jumping over low bushes, always staying out of the man's sight by taking a longer way around. I felt that because he was circling the man, I should walk along in a more leisurely and direct way on the well-marked footpath, so we could capture him in a pincer maneuver, if necessary.

As I came to a straight stretch of pathway, I feared the man would turn around and see me, so I too moved onto a more verdant route, walking along beyond a row of rather large trees. As it happened, I had the man in clear sight when Holmes came into view again. The man was the tall, thin man with the black suit from the train, and I saw he was still carrying his hard-sided case. He stood at the edge of the falls, looking over. Then he looked to his right along the jagged rim of the falls toward the observation point. From his vantage he could see President McKinley and his party clearly.

The dark-suited man went to a spot in the nearby bushes within a yard of the brink, where water amounting to millions of gallons was propelling itself at some thirty miles an hour off a cliff. He knelt, opened his box, pulled out what looked like the tripod of a surveyor's transom, opened it, and extended the legs. He placed a small brass scope on the top and sighted along it, making a few adjustments. He was clearly looking in the direction of the president and his hosts. Then he knelt again and worked to assemble several pieces of gleaming metal. As he rose to his feet, I could see that what he had was a metal tube a bit thicker than the barrel of a rifle, and at the butt end of it, a mechanism that looked like the receiver of a pistol. From a distance it looked like a telescope. He attached the device to the top of the tripod, adjusting a set of thumbscrews, and Holmes began to run.

I ran too, and as I did, I realized that what the assassin had was a specially designed rifle with a smaller telescopic sight mounted independently to the tripod. He had spotted his prey and aimed the gunsight before attaching the rifle. Holmes and I came close, then stopped and began to approach him silently from two directions. We walked toward him, watching him peer into the scope at the president. Then he knelt and reached into his carrying case, pulled out a box magazine, and inserted it into the now-assembled rifle.

As the assassin's eye reached the eyepiece of the telescopic sight, Holmes and I surged forward like two rugby players lunging into a scrum. I crashed into the man's shoulder, throwing him against the railing, while Holmes hit the tripod and pushed it over the railing, where it fell, turning over and over, toward the churning water below.

"Oh, excuse me, please, gentlemen," said Holmes to both of us. "I tripped on that protruding rock along the path. I hope neither of you is injured." He helped me up first, and then took the arm of the man in the black suit and began to brush the dust off him, roughly.

"I'm terribly sorry about your telescope," he said to the man. "Or was it a camera? Either way, I insist on paying you its full value."

"You—" The man suddenly contained his rage, like a man turning off a faucet. "You haven't hurt me at all," he said. Now I could hear the Spanish accent that I was expecting. "And the telescope, it was just a trifle, a toy that I bought in New York."

"I insist," Holmes said. He took out his billfold and produced a sheaf of American money. It looked to be a great deal, but since American money consisted of identically colored, sized, and shaped currency, I couldn't tell how much at a glance. When the man wouldn't reach out for it, Holmes stuffed it in the breast pocket of the black suit. "Please, sir. I've already ruined your day. It's all I can do."

And then Holmes turned and walked off quickly, leaving me with the frustrated murderer. It occurred to me that with his weapon being churned about underwater far below, the man was relatively harmless. Nonetheless I tipped my hat as a pretext for backing away, then turned and went after Holmes. Just before the pathway took a turn to the pedestrian bridge off Luna Island I looked back to see him throw the hard-sided gun case over the railing into the chasm.

As I reached the main walkway above the falls I saw that the president's party, having observed the cataract from nearly every prospect, and seen the electrical power plant invented by Mr. Tesla on the shore below, was now walking toward the nearest city street. Holmes left the group and joined me. "They're going to lunch, Watson."

I was ravenous, not having eaten since my hasty breakfast of tea and toast in the hotel. "Shall we join them?"

"In a manner of speaking, yes. But I believe we must feed our eyes and noses today, and not our bellies." He broke into a brisk walk, and I noted that instead of the front door to one of the row of restaurants, Holmes headed up a narrow alley and stopped at an open door.

Hearing the noises coming from inside, I said, "The kitchen?"

He nodded. "Your medical education and experience make you the ideal man to ensure that no poison made of a medical derivative is introduced to the food—opiates, for instance—or any of the biological toxins like botulism. And I have some familiarity with most of the common substances like arsenic and strychnine, as well as a few that have seldom been heard of outside a shaman's hut. Come, my friend. Anything that doesn't look or smell right must be discarded."

We entered the kitchen. Outside it was a hot, humid day, but inside it was like the engine room of a ship steaming through hell. The *sous-chefs* were working stripped to the waist, their bodies glistening with sweat as they labored over their bubbling soups and sauces, braised their meats, and baked their fish. Holmes and I threw off our coats and waistcoats and joined the staff, examining every dish that went out through the swinging doors to the dining room, sniffing each uncooked carcass, tasting a pinch of every spice, and inquiring into the freshness and provenance of every comestible. We found no poisons and only one dish of elderly oysters, but the work lasted nearly two hours, and when we went outside to join the president's party on its walk to the train, I felt as though I had been catapulted out of Hades into paradise.

At one the train loaded and left for Buffalo, and I stood outside the car on the small area above the rear coupling where there was a railing, enjoyed the wind moving over me, and watched the passengers through the glass from there. Holmes joined me after a time. He said, "When we reach Buffalo the president will rest for an hour in his room at Mr. Milburn's home on Delaware Avenue. At four o'clock they'll bring him to the Exposition, and he will greet his constituents at the Temple of Music. That's our hour and I must prepare for it. After this, you and I will not see each other for a day or two. I trust that you and Dr. Park have made all the preparations you'll need?"

"I'm certain of it," I said. "He's a brilliant doctor with a scientist's mind, and he took to conspiracy quickly."

"Good," said Holmes. "Then I wish all of us the favor of fortune." He turned, walked off into the next car toward the rear of the train, and disappeared from my sight.

The train arrived in the station in Buffalo at one thirty, and the president and his party left in carriages, but I didn't spot Holmes among the throng. Nor did I see him anywhere else. It was as though he had crumbled into dust and blown away in the breeze.

I took a carriage directly to the Exposition grounds. I walked to the hospital that had been set up on the site, introduced myself as Dr. Mann, and indicated that I was to be the physician in charge for the shift that began at five p.m. As we had anticipated, the administrative nurse, a formidable woman of about fifty years, sent a messenger to Dr. Park to verify my credentials, even though she had seen him give me a tour of the facilities only two days earlier. The delay gave me an opportunity to leave, so I went off on the pretense of inspecting the ambulances stationed on the midway in case of emergency. Actually I made my way to the Temple of Music and introduced myself to the policeman at the door as Dr. Mann. He called for Chief Bull to come to the door, and Chief Bull greeted me warmly and admitted me. Through the windows I could see that there were already large crowds of people who had been arranged into an orderly queue waiting outside for the president. I pitied them, and fancied that before long I would be catering to cases of heat exhaustion.

During the next minutes I stood in the building inspecting the arrangements for the president's visit. Many chairs had been removed, to make way for the president's receiving line. He was to be standing approximately in the center of the auditorium with some of his entourage and the soldiers. People would be permitted inside, and each would shake hands with him, and then be turned and sent out.

I heard a murmur outside. It grew into a commotion. The doors opened, and President McKinley entered. He took his place flanked by Mr. John Milburn and Mr. Cortelyou. There were eleven soldiers and four police officers in the building, including Chief Bull. The president gave the order at four o'clock, and the soldiers opened the doors.

The orderly line of citizens advanced into the building. There were men, women, and a fair number of children. When I saw the children I shuddered, but then I saw that their parents were keeping them in close order, so I worried less. The president met each person with a smile and a greeting, and then the policemen moved each person out of the way so others would get their turns. I conjectured that the soldiers and police officers had agreed to move the crowd along smartly so more of them could get inside into the shade.

And then there was trouble. I could see it developing as the crowd inched forward. There came a tall, thin, swarthy man with a handlebar mustache and black curly hair. He was muttering angrily to himself as he stood in the queue, in a language which after a moment I realized was Italian.

He began to draw glances from the onlookers, and then from the guardsmen. Three of the policemen sidled along up the row of people, apparently straightening the line and narrowing it strictly to single file as it got close to the president. When they reached the Italian, one of them spoke to him in a low voice and took his arm like an usher to move him a pace to the left. He reacted like a madman. He punched the policeman, and turned to charge the other two. They were taken by surprise, so he bowled them over into a pair of ladies, who were thrown roughly backward onto the carpet.

That part of the line became a battle royal, with eight or nine soldiers and all the policemen diving onto the pile and delivering blows with less judiciousness than fervor. When the sudden motion froze into a contest of tugging and resisting, I recognized that the swarthy Italian had a profile very familiar to me. I also noticed that he had one of the women in an apparently unbreakable embrace. After a second I realized the offended woman was the disguised man Holmes had recognized on the train.

Just then, as the crowd ahead of the Italian swept forward, partly to meet the president and partly to get out of the way of the fighting, one of their number, a man who looked Central European—perhaps a Serb or a Croatian, with dark skin, hair, and mustache—stepped into the vanguard. He had a white handkerchief in his hand, as several others did, to wipe away the perspiration before shaking the president's hand. I saw that nearly all of the policemen and soldiers were occupied with the disorderly Italian and the ones still near the president were watching the fray, mesmerized. So when the man aimed a revolver he'd hidden under the handkerchief at the president, there was no one there in time to prevent it.

He fired once, and a brass button on the president's coat threw sparks. His second shot was not deflected. The president gripped his belly and fell. As the president fell, the soldiers and policemen let go of the unruly Italian. Some went to the president's side, and the others surrounded the assassin. Fortunately, a tall man of African descent had been behind the shooter in the line. He batted the gun from the man's hand and kept him from escaping. If he had not done that, the soldiers almost certainly would have shot the culprit. Instead, they dragged him to the floor and delivered a series of kicks and punches.

The president, lying on the carpet in the arms of his secretary and Mr. Milburn, called out, "Don't hurt him, boys!" The calm, wise words seemed to bring the men to their senses. They subdued the culprit and took him out to a police van that was parked near the building.

Meanwhile, I pushed my way to the president's side. "I'm a doctor," I called out, and the guards made room. I opened his coat as I leaned close to listen to his breathing. As I did, I surreptitiously produced a small vial of fresh chicken blood from my waistcoat and spilled it on the white shirt just above the belt. "He's wounded, but alive," I said. "Lift the president to his carriage," I ordered. "We'll take him to the field hospital on the Exposition grounds."

The strong young soldiers nearby lifted the president and placed him in the carriage. I joined him and Captain Allen jumped into the driver's seat and whipped the horses to such a gallop that I feared the president would die in a carriage accident and take me with him. I managed to speak with him a bit in a low voice. "How are you, sir?" I asked.

"Excellent, Dr. Watson," he said. "Seldom better."

"Good. We'll try to keep you that way. Now put on this coat and hat." It was a rather dull brown coat that looked very different from his tailored black one, and a bowler hat like the ones many men wore that day. When we were near the Indian Congress, Captain Allen drove the coach into a horse barn. Allen and I got into a second coach that was waiting there. Our horses had easily outrun word of the attack on the president, and as we pulled away, I could see that none of the visitors touring the Exposition noticed Mr. McKinley in his new garb entering the Indian Congress.

Captain Allen whipped the new set of horses, and I went to work on the substitute patient already waiting on the seat, a cadaver that Dr. Park and I had selected at the medical school the previous day. I covered his torso with Mr. McKinley's black coat, and his face with my handkerchief, as though keeping the sun out of his eyes. When we reached the field hospital, I jumped out, and Captain Allen and I put the corpse on a stretcher. Two orderlies loitering outside rushed to carry it in. "To the operating room immediately," I shouted. We took the stretcher inside and locked the door.

After a few minutes, Dr. Roswell Park arrived at the door with several of his assistants and nurses, and made the little hospital look as though it were being run with great professional skill. With him to assist, I began the operation. I had removed bullets from a number of soldiers while on duty in India, so I was extremely familiar with the procedure and the many ways in which it can succeed or fail. As I worked on the cadaver to make it look as though it had been opened to search for the bullet, he complimented my technique several times.

We had only the open part of the abdomen uncovered by sheets, and the deceased man who was supposed to be the president lay on his back with a face mask over his mouth and nose and a surgical cap on his head. Nonetheless, it occurred to me that we were fortunate that while millions of lightbulbs were displayed everywhere throughout the Exposition, nobody had thought to install a single bulb in the hospital.

Through Dr. Park's nurses and assistants, we slowly fed our fiction to the outside world. We said the president was a healthy specimen, and he had been lucky. The first bullet had hit a brass button and ricocheted, leaving a shallow gash along his side. The second shot entered the abdomen at close range, but the pistol had been a small caliber, and most likely Dr. Mann would find and remove the bullet in the present surgery. Once that happened, McKinley could be expected to recover fully. But after more than four hours of surgery, we changed the news slightly. Dr. Mann had not found the bullet, which must have fragmented in the body.

This was the story all that evening. It was still the story when we moved the cadaver to Mr. Milburn's house to recover. At various times during the next few days we issued reports that the president was recovering nicely, that his spirits were high, and that we expected an early return to health.

Meanwhile, as Holmes told me later, the rest of the deception went tolerably well. The assassin captured at the Temple of Music was taken to the police station. He, of course, was Mr. Booth. He identified himself as Leon Czolgosz, the son of

Polish immigrants, who had been struck by the inequality in the way the president was treated compared with an ordinary man. Because of Chief Bull's fears of public emotion aroused by his crime, Czolgosz was kept apart from other prisoners.

The president had made his way into the Indian village, where he met Holmes, no longer an Italian madman. Holmes was waiting for the president with three Iroquois Indians he had met while they were studying at the University of London years before—two Senecas and a Mohawk. Holmes applied some of the makeup he had brought, and within a few minutes he and the president were the fourth and fifth Iroquois Indians. After nightfall, the five men left the Exposition in the midst of a growing crowd, and rowed across the Niagara River into Canada.

With the help of his Iroquois friends, Holmes conveyed Mr. McKinley to Montreal, where he put him on the steamship *Arcturus,* which sailed on September 9 for London. I'm told he was an impressive figure, registered in the ship's manifest as Selim Bey, first cousin to the third wife of the Sultan of Turkey. He wore some makeup, a large turban, and a sash with a curved dagger in it. After he reached London he took another ship for Tangiers as the Reverend Dr. Oliver McEachern, a Methodist missionary.

Five days after the *Arcturus* sailed, on September 14, I was forced to declare President William McKinley dead. He had been said to be recovering, but a few days later he succumbed to blood poisoning. There was some speculation, especially in the papers in New York City and Washington, that Dr. Mann had botched the surgery. There was even some lamentation that on the grounds of the Exposition had been an experimental X-ray machine, which could easily have found even fragments of a bullet. That was precisely why I, or Dr Mann, had forbidden its use.

Nine days later, on the testimony of eyewitnesses, Leon Czolgosz, the young man who had shot the president, was convicted of murder. He was taken from the court to Auburn Penitentiary, where he was executed in an electric chair, another application of the marvels of electricity celebrated by the Pan-American Exposition in Buffalo. The one flaw of the modern method in comparison to hanging was that when a single wire was loosened, an electric chair became simply a chair. A fine actor can perform a set of death throes that would make a gravedigger faint.

Holmes and Dr. Mann were among the dignitaries who attended the very small funeral held at the penitentiary for the murderer. The casket had been nailed shut because the face of the killer Czolgosz had been disfigured by sulfuric acid poured on the corpse by persons unknown. Presiding over the funeral was a young clergyman who gave an extremely impressive elegy, inspiring all listeners with the notion that even the worst sinner can be forgiven and admitted to the kingdom of heaven. Afterward we took him to the nearest railway station and bought him a ticket, not to heaven, but only to New York, where he was in time to begin rehearsals for a Broadway play called *Life,* which opened the following March to appreciative notices.

After the state funeral of the president in Washington, it was popularly supposed that Mrs. Ida McKinley returned to Ohio where she was to live with her sister. I often thought of her during the next seven years, knowing that she was living happily by turns as the wife of Selim Bey or of the Reverend Dr. McEachern—a veiled Moslem to the Christians, and a Christian to the Moslems, a person who pretended never to speak the language of those around her, and never had to explain herself. When she died after seven years, her body was secretly shipped back to Ohio and then buried by her sister, as though she had lived as a reclusive widow all along.

On the fourteenth of September, 1901, when it was first announced that President McKinley was dying, a number of notables rushed to Buffalo. One of them was his old friend Senator Mark Hanna, and another was the young vice president, Theodore Roosevelt. He stayed at the Ansley Wilcox mansion at 641 Delaware Avenue, where he was sworn in late that night as the twenty-sixth president of the United States. Whether in later years Roosevelt lived up to his predecessor's hopes, I cannot say. As Selim Bey or Dr. McEachern, the former president declared himself to be happy in retirement and never gave another political opinion. But the Great War he had feared did not begin until 1914, did not involve America until 1917, and ended a year later as he had hoped it would, with his country victorious and growing stronger.

Curator's Note: Although Dr. Watson's claims cannot be verified, the circumstances of the manuscript's discovery in a locked metal box hidden in his great-grandson's home in London with several other, equally startling manuscripts might add credibility for some readers. Many personalities in Dr. Watson's story were real people, e.g. Mark Hanna, Ida and William McKinley, Dr. Roswell Park, Mr. John Milburn, George Cortelyou, Chief William Bull, "Dr. Mann," Leon Czolgosz, Theodore Roosevelt, Ansley Wilcox, and Sherlock Holmes. Watson's description of the assassination appears to agree with descriptions by eyewitnesses, even in the particular of the distraction of the guards by the unidentified Italian. Czolgosz's body actually was rendered unrecognizable because of sulfuric acid poured on it by persons unknown after his execution. The actor Sydney Barton Booth really was a descendant of Edwin Booth, a pro-Lincoln member of the acting family, and he had a fine career that lasted long enough for him to appear in several successful motion pictures. As for timing, we do know that the whereabouts of Holmes and Watson are unknown between Thursday, May 16, 1901, when the "Priory School" events took place, and Tuesday, November 19, 1901, when they were seen during the "Sussex Vampire" case.

Thomas Perry is the author of nineteen novels, including the Edgar-winning *The Butcher's Boy,* the *New York Times* bestseller *Nightlife,* and the ongoing Jane Whitefield series. *Metzger's Dog,* a *New York Times* Notable Book of the Year, was recently selected by National Public Radio listeners as one of the one hundred best thrillers ever. His novel *Strip* was a *New York Times* Notable Crime Book for 2010. His next book, *The Informant,* will be published in spring 2011. Perry lives in Southern California. He has always loved the Sherlock Holmes stories and saw this anthology as a chance to add one more story that Sir Arthur Conan Doyle might have written if he'd gotten around to it.

MYSTERIOS

THE CASE OF THE UNWRITTEN SHORT STORY

By Sticky Cotterill.

It all began in October 2010 when I got an e-mail from Laurie King asking me if I'd be interested in writing a short story with a Sherlock Holmes theme.

I'd always liked Laurie. He was force-ful but never rude. And I was pleased he'd found a new inter-est to take his mind off of leaving CNN.

So I said yes.

Tell you the truth, I've never actu-ally read any Sherlock Holmes and I walked out of the Guy Ritchie movie after fifteen minutes.

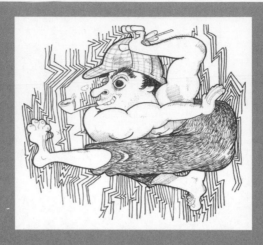

It was
the
kung
fu
thing.

It was like that X-rated version of <u>Pride and Prejudice</u> I had to sit through for two hours.

All right. Let's be 'avin' ya. Who's next fer me youngest?

We British just don't do things like that.

It was obvious Laurie still had friends in high places 'cause he got us a contract with Random House even before anyone had written anything.

And I imagine the CNN investigatory team still owed him a favour or two because out of nowhere all these giants of crime fiction suddenly signed up.

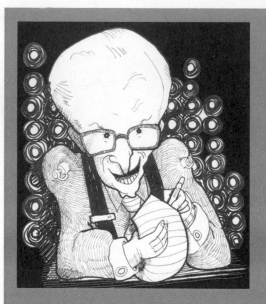

Even old Laurie himself was taking a shot at writing. Had to admire his spunk.

So I lied that I was a huge fan of Sherlock Holmes. "Loved his books, especially that one...you know... the one with the thing? Yeah, that one. Loved it." And I decided to show off and do a graphic story. Despite my advanced years I still have a dream that one day I'll be discovered and asked to do an entire graphic novel. A lot of graphic novels are banal and lacking in common sense.

I can do that.

But therein lies the rub.
(Whatever the heck that
means.) You see, Sherlock
Holmes is a period drama
and consequently you're
supposed to be historically
accurate, i.e., do research.
Not my strong point.

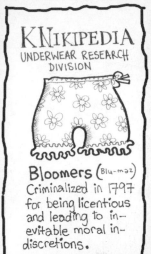

KNIKIPEDIA
UNDERWEAR RESEARCH
DIVISION

Bloomers (Blu-məz)
Criminalized in 1797
for being licentious
and leading to in-
evitable moral in-
discretions.

   If you just write, you
can pretty much leave it
up to the reader's imagination
to fill in the gaps. But when
you draw it, you can't get away with gaffes.

They're out there, you see. The Lost People of Amazon ...
lurking...waiting for you to make a mistake.

★☆☆☆☆ **Some "writers" just don't deserve to live.** Take Colin Cotterill for example. This pathetic excuse for a historian has managed to remove what little enjoyment there might have been in this pathetic book by not doing his <u>homework</u>. Any four-year-old knows that the six-spoked hansom cab wheel was not introduced in London until March 1890, two weeks AFTER his story ends. I'd like to give this rubbish NO stars but I can't. Have I said PATHETIC yet? <u>**Read more**</u>

Published one day ago by Realbooklover

And if that wasn't enough pressure, I was already at page eight and I hadn't started the bloody story yet.

I needed a gimmick. I knew all those real writers would mine the shafts of Holmes connections: Auntie, next door neighbour, cat. So I decided to make my protagonist a common man of nineteenth-century England who had never heard of Sherlock Holmes and had no interest in him at all.

I would call my hero George Groombridge because that's the name of my mum's boyfriend and she'll get a thrill out of it. (He might not be so chuffed.)

I'd been working on that illustration for two days, common man George screwing up the metal Baker Street sign, when my current wife, Gogo, leaned over my shoulder and said...

Of course they... Wait!

BRIKIPEDIA

Damn. Ceramic. They had to dig a groove out of the bricks and cement the... Cement?

STIKIPEDIA   Invented 1867. Safe.

But now you're getting the idea of how hard this is.

So, you see? I was getting into it. George, with his professional integrity on the line, had no choice but to go back to Baker Street in the dead of night to prove to himself that the toffee-nosed git was wrong.

There was just one problem. I'd spent as much time on research as on drawing the gosh-darn pictures. And I ask you, exactly how much money were we likely to make out of a Sherlock Holmes book? Even if the timing was perfect and it came out at the same time as the movie sequel, it wouldn't make a lot of difference. Moviegoers wouldn't know a book if it dropped on their heads. So with twenty "odd" writers we'd clear about $4.20 after tax. With that in mind, I decided that was as good a time as any to give up research.

At this point I was distracted by two things. Firstly, boredom. Nothing exactly "exciting" had happened. This might explain why Guy had introduced kung fu and sex into the story.

I decided I might cause some levity by giving the characters funny names, such as Erstwissel, the maker of George's spirit level. You may notice a lot of characters in olde England had very silly names. It makes you wonder where their ancestors are. Not too many prime ministers or Britain's Got Talent winners called Bumble or Crackit. Well, here's the reason.

See how easily my mind wanders? But a more serious distraction at that moment was the arrival of the monsoons. I had a garden to protect from global warming. Sherlock lost me for a month.

When I got around to mopping silt out of the studio I saw George was already at Erstwissel's (tee hee). Manufacturer of quality equipment by appointment to Her Majesty the Queen.

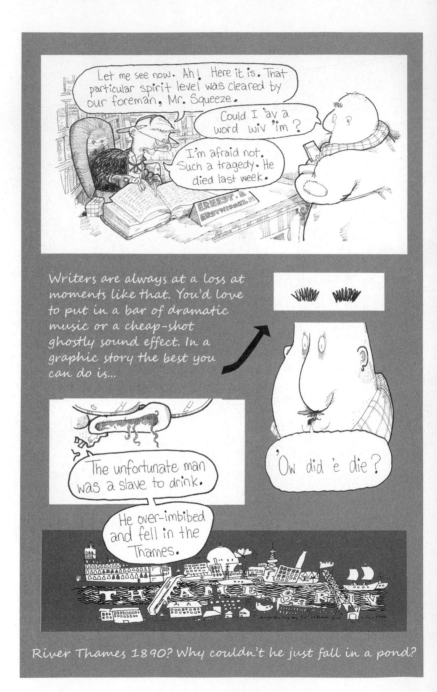

I mean, where was I actually going with this?
Where did I pick up this annoying habit of starting a
story without a clue where it was going to take me? It's
a sort of self-imposed dementia.

I'd painted myself into a corner
with a spirit level. There was no
logical reason why it would give a
false reading. I even contacted some
sad loser on a website for un-
attractive middle-aged physicists
and Eric told me you'd have to be
in a zero gravity environment for
it to fail.   Thank you, Eric.

It was January already
and I didn't have a
story for Laurie. But I
had a book to write. We
had bills to pay. I went
off to a friend's place in
the mountains. (We arty
people have friends with "places.") There I was lulled to
sleep by the bats massacring insects and woken by the
distant hum of deforestation. But that and a few casks
of cheap red worked for me somehow.

Back home I checked my Sherlock file. I thought the fairies might have finished the story while I was away.

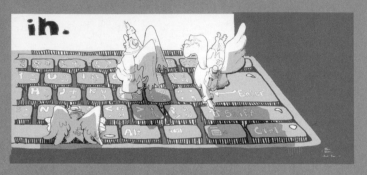

The bastards hadn't done a thing.

We were into February. Long rainless weeks. Hot as Hades. Sweat on the drawing board.

Gogo had bought a refrigerator the size of Buckingham Palace but still the two of us didn't fit inside. Not that we didn't try. The temp... Wait. That was it. It was all about temperature. Even though the bulb went out

when you shut the door, I saw the light right there in our fridge.

Yes, it was starting to get a bit wordy, but I had a lot of denouement to get through so I figured it was worth it.

N.B. This is the first recorded incidence of the use of a "wire" in police investigations, which means the producers of the show **The Wire** technically owe me a shipload of money in royalties.

THE Right Honourable Marquess of Salisbury hands commoner George Groombridge the princely sum of four shillings and threepence at a ceremony at the Houses of Parliament in Westminster yesterday.

And so there, dear Laurie, you have it. A little cheeky intrigue and a happy ending. But it was not the mystery that has plagued me since receiving your letter and the generous cheque for four dollars and twenty cents (the bank charged eighteen dollars to process it). The real bafflement is this. Although I did plan the story I've outlined here, even completed a number of sketches, I didn't get around to finishing it. Nor did I send it to you. So, you see, I don't really understand how you could have received it. All of the illustrations featuring my wife and me are still scattered around the studio floor. The rest are missing. It's my fault. I let my dogs run riot in there and they're a terribly undisciplined crowd.

The tail end.

Colin Cotterill is the author of the popular Dr. Siri mysteries set in the Lao People's Democratic Republic. He was born in England in the days before they started to keep records of such things. He lives on the Gulf of Thailand almost unnoticed among a pack of rescue dogs. He has absolutely no interest in Sherlock Holmes but will do almost anything for money.

Larry King was not harmed in the making of this story.

The Case of Death and Honey

Neil Gaiman

It was a mystery in those parts for years what had happened to the old white ghost man, the barbarian with his huge shoulder bag. There were some who supposed him to have been murdered, and, later, they dug up the floor of Old Gao's little shack high on the hillside, looking for treasure, but they found nothing but ash and fire-blackened tin trays.

This was after Old Gao himself had vanished, you understand, and before his son came back from Lijiang to take over the beehives on the hill.

This is the problem, *wrote Holmes in 1899:* ennui. And lack of interest. Or rather, it all becomes too easy. When the joy of solving crimes is the challenge, the possibility that you cannot, why then the crimes have something to hold your attention. But when each crime is soluble, and so easily soluble at that, why then there is no point in solving them.

Look: this man has been murdered. Well then, someone murdered him. He was murdered for one or more of a tiny handful of reasons: he inconvenienced someone, or he had something that someone wanted, or he had angered someone. Where is the challenge in that?

I would read in the dailies an account of a crime
that had the police baffled, and I would find that I had
solved it, in broad strokes if not in detail, before I had.
finished the article. Crime is too soluble. It dissolves.
Why call the police and tell them the answers to their
mysteries? I leave it, over and over again, as a challenge
for them, as it is no challenge for me.

I am only alive when I perceive a challenge.

The bees of the misty hills, hills so high that they were sometimes
called a mountain, were humming in the pale summer sun as
they moved from spring flower to spring flower on the slope.
Old Gao listened to them without pleasure. His cousin, in the
village across the valley, had many dozens of hives, all of them
already filling with honey, even this early in the year; also, the
honey was as white as snow-jade. Old Gao did not believe that
the white honey tasted any better than the yellow or light brown
honey that his own bees produced, although his bees produced
it in meagre quantities, but his cousin could sell his white honey
for twice what Old Gao could get for the best honey he had.

On his cousin's side of the hill, the bees were earnest, hardworking, golden brown workers, who brought pollen and nectar
back to the hives in enormous quantities. Old Gao's bees were
ill-tempered and black, shiny as bullets, who produced as much
honey as they needed to get through the winter and only a little
more: enough for Old Gao to sell from door to door, to his
fellow villagers, one small lump of honeycomb at a time. He
would charge more for the brood-comb, filled with bee larvae,
sweet-tasting morsels of protein, when he had brood-comb to
sell, which was rarely, for the bees were angry and sullen and
everything they did, they did as little as possible, including make
more bees, and Old Gao was always aware that each piece of
brood-comb he sold meant bees he would not have to make
honey for him to sell later in the year.

Old Gao was as sullen and as sharp as his bees. He had had a wife once, but she had died in childbirth. The son who had killed her lived for a week, then died himself. There would be nobody to say the funeral rites for Old Gao, no-one to clean his grave for festivals or to put offerings upon it. He would die unremembered, as unremarkable and as unremarked as his bees.

The old white stranger came over the mountains in late spring of that year, as soon as the roads were passable, with a huge brown bag strapped to his shoulders. Old Gao heard about him before he met him.

"There is a barbarian who is looking at bees," said his cousin.

Old Gao said nothing. He had gone to his cousin to buy a pailful of second-rate comb, damaged or uncapped and liable soon to spoil. He bought it cheaply to feed to his own bees, and if he sold some of it in his own village, no-one was any the wiser. The two men were drinking tea in Gao's cousin's hut on the hillside. From late spring, when the first honey started to flow, until first frost, Gao's cousin left his house in the village and went to live in the hut on the hillside, to live and to sleep beside his beehives, for fear of thieves. His wife and his children would take the honeycomb and the bottles of snow-white honey down the hill to sell.

Old Gao was not afraid of thieves. The shiny black bees of Old Gao's hives would have no mercy on anyone who disturbed them. He slept in his village, unless it was time to collect the honey.

"I will send him to you," said Gao's cousin. "Answer his questions, show him your bees, and he will pay you."

"He speaks our tongue?"

"His dialect is atrocious. He said he learned to speak from sailors, and they were mostly Cantonese. But he learns fast, although he is old."

Old Gao grunted, uninterested in sailors. It was late in the morning, and there was still four hours walking across the valley to his village, in the heat of the day. He finished his tea. His cousin drank finer tea than Old Gao had ever been able to afford.

He reached his hives while it was still light, put the majority of the uncapped honey into his weakest hives. He had eleven hives. His cousin had over a hundred. Old Gao was stung twice doing this, on the back of the hand and the back of the neck. He had been stung over a thousand times in his life. He could not have told you how many times. He barely noticed the stings of other bees, but the stings of his own black bees always hurt, even if they no longer swelled or burned.

The next day a boy came to Old Gao's house in the village, to tell him that there was someone—and that the someone was a giant foreigner—who was asking for him. Old Gao simply grunted. He walked across the village with the boy at his steady pace, until the boy ran ahead, and soon was lost to sight.

Old Gao found the stranger sitting drinking tea on the porch of the Widow Zhang's house. Old Gao had known the Widow Zhang's mother, fifty years ago. She had been a friend of his wife. Now she was long dead. He did not believe anyone who had known his wife still lived. The Widow Zhang fetched Old Gao tea, introduced him to the elderly barbarian, who had removed his bag and sat beside the small table.

They sipped their tea. The barbarian said, "I wish to see your bees."

Mycroft's death was the end of Empire, and no-one knew it but the two of us. He lay in that pale room, his only covering a thin white sheet, as if he were already becoming a ghost from the popular imagination, and needed only eye-holes in the sheet to finish the impression.

I had imagined that his illness might have wasted him away, but he seemed huger than ever, his fingers swollen into white suet sausages.

I said, "Good evening, Mycroft. Dr. Hopkins tells me you have two weeks to live, and stated that I was under no circumstances to inform you of this."

"The man's a dunderhead," said Mycroft, his breath coming in huge wheezes between the words. "I will not make it to Friday."

"Saturday at least," I said.

"You always were an optimist. No, Thursday evening and then I shall be nothing more than an exercise in practical geometry for Hopkins and the funeral directors at Snigsby and Malterson, who will have the challenge, given the narrowness of the doors and corridors, of getting my carcass out of this room and out of the building."

"I had wondered," I said. "Particularly given the staircase. But they will take out the window frame and lower you to the street like a grand piano."

Mycroft snorted at that. Then, "I am fifty-four years old, Sherlock. In my head is the British Government. Not the ballot and hustings nonsense, but the business of the thing. There is no-one else knows what the troop movements in the hills of Afghanistan have to do with the desolate shores of North Wales, no-one else who sees the whole picture. Can you imagine the mess that this lot and their children will make of Indian Independence?"

I had not previously given any thought to the matter. "Will India become independent?"

"Inevitably. In thirty years, at the outside. I have written several recent memoranda on the topic. As I have on so many other subjects. There are memoranda on the Russian Revolution—that'll be along within the decade, I'll wager—and on the German problem and... oh, so many others. Not that I expect them to be read or understood." Another wheeze. My brother's lungs rattled like the windows in an empty house. "You know, if I were to live, the British Empire might last another thousand years, bringing peace and improvement to the world."

In the past, especially when I was a boy, whenever I heard Mycroft make a grandiose pronouncement like that I would say something to bait him. But not now, not on his death-bed. And also I was certain that he was not speaking of the Empire as it was, a flawed and fallible construct of flawed and fallible people, but of a British Empire that existed only in his head, a glorious force for civilisation and universal prosperity.

I do not, and did not, believe in empires. But I believed in Mycroft.

Mycroft Holmes. Four-and-fifty years of age. He had seen in the new century but the Queen would still outlive him by several months. She was almost thirty years older than he was, and in every way a tough old bird. I wondered to myself whether this unfortunate end might have been avoided.

Mycroft said, "You are right, of course, Sherlock. Had I forced myself to exercise. Had I lived on bird-seed and cabbages instead of porterhouse steak. Had I taken up country dancing along with a wife and a puppy and in all other ways behaved contrary to my nature, I might have bought myself another dozen or so years. But what is that in the scheme of things? Little enough. And sooner or later, I would enter my dotage. No. I am of the opinion that it would take two hundred years to train a functioning Civil Service, let alone a secret service..."

I had said nothing.

The pale room had no decorations on the wall of any kind. None of Mycroft's citations. No illustrations, photographs, or paintings. I compared his austere digs to my own cluttered rooms in Baker Street and I wondered, not for the first time, at Mycroft's mind. He needed nothing on the outside, for it was all on the inside—everything he had seen, everything he had experienced, everything he had read. He could close his eyes and walk through the National Gallery, or browse the British Museum Reading Room—or, more likely, compare intelligence reports from the edge of the Empire with the price of wool in Wigan and the unemployment statistics in Hove, and then, from this and only this, order a man promoted or a traitor's quiet death.

Mycroft wheezed enormously, and then he said, "It is a crime, Sherlock."

"I beg your pardon?"

"A crime. It is a crime, my brother, as heinous and as monstrous as any of the penny-dreadful massacres you have investigated. A crime against the world, against nature, against order."

"I must confess, my dear fellow, that I do not entirely follow you. What is a crime?"

"My death," said Mycroft, "in the specific. And Death in general." He looked into my eyes. "I mean it," he said. "Now isn't that a crime worth investigating, Sherlock, old fellow? One that might keep your attention for longer than it will take you to establish that the poor fellow who used to conduct the brass band in Hyde Park was murdered by the third cornet using a preparation of strychnine."

"Arsenic," I corrected him, almost automatically.

"I think you will find," wheezed Mycroft, "that the arsenic, while present, had in fact fallen in flakes from the green-painted bandstand itself onto his supper. Symptoms of arsenical poison are a complete red-herring. No, it was strychnine that did for the poor fellow."

Mycroft said no more to me that day or ever. He breathed his last the following Thursday, late in the afternoon, and on the Friday the worthies of Snigsby and Malterson removed the casing from the window of the pale room and lowered my brother's remains into the street, like a grand piano.

His funeral service was attended by me, by my friend Watson, by our cousin Harriet and—in accordance with Mycroft's express wishes—by no-one else. The Civil Service, the Foreign Office, even the Diogenes Club—these institutions and their representatives were absent. Mycroft had been reclusive in life; he was to be equally as reclusive in death. So it was the three of us, and the parson, who had not known my brother, and had no conception that it was the more omniscient arm of the British Government itself that he was consigning to the grave.

Four burly men held fast to the ropes and lowered my brother's remains to their final resting place, and did, I daresay, their utmost not to curse at the weight of the thing. I tipped each of them half a crown.

Mycroft was dead at fifty-four, and, as they lowered him into his grave, in my imagination I could still hear his clipped, grey wheeze as he seemed to be saying, "Now *there* is a crime worth investigating."

The stranger's accent was not too bad, although his vocabulary seemed limited, but he seemed to be talking in the local dialect, or something near to it. He was a fast learner. Old Gao hawked and spat into the dust of the street. He said nothing. He did not wish to take the stranger up the hillside; he did not wish to disturb his bees. In Old Gao's experience, the less he bothered his bees, the better they did. And if they stung the barbarian, what then?

The stranger's hair was silver-white, and sparse; his nose, the first barbarian nose that Old Gao had seen, was huge and curved and put Old Gao in mind of the beak of an eagle; his skin was tanned the same colour as Old Gao's own, and was lined deeply. Old Gao was not certain that he could read a barbarian's face as he could read the face of a person, but he thought the man seemed most serious and, perhaps, unhappy.

"Why?"

"I study bees. Your brother tells me you have big black bees here. Unusual bees."

Old Gao shrugged. He did not correct the man on the relationship with his cousin.

The stranger asked Old Gao if he had eaten, and when Gao said that he had not the stranger asked the Widow Zhang to bring them soup and rice and whatever was good that she had in her kitchen, which turned out to be a stew of black tree-fungus and vegetables and tiny transparent river fish, little bigger than tadpoles. The two men ate in silence. When they had finished eating, the stranger said, "I would be honoured if you would show me your bees."

Old Gao said nothing, but the stranger paid the Widow Zhang well and he put his bag on his back. Then he waited, and, when Old Gao began to walk, the stranger followed him. He carried his bag as if it weighed nothing to him. He was strong for an old man, thought Old Gao, and wondered whether all such barbarians were so strong.

"Where are you from?"

"England," said the stranger.

Old Gao remembered his father telling him about a war with the English, over trade and over opium, but that was long ago.

They walked up the hillside, that was, perhaps, a mountainside. It was steep, and the hillside was too rocky to be cut into fields. Old Gao tested the stranger's pace, walking faster than usual, and the stranger kept up with him, with his pack on his back.

The stranger stopped several times, however. He stopped to examine flowers—the small white flowers that bloomed in early spring elsewhere in the valley, but in late spring here on the side of the hill. There was a bee on one of the flowers, and the stranger knelt and observed it. Then he reached into his pocket, produced a large magnifying glass and examined the bee through it, and made notes in a small pocket notebook, in an incomprehensible writing.

Old Gao had never seen a magnifying glass before, and he leaned in to look at the bee, so black and so strong and so very different from the bees elsewhere in that valley.

"One of your bees?"

"Yes," said Old Gao. "Or one like it."

"Then we shall let her find her own way home," said the stranger, and he did not disturb the bee, and he put away the magnifying glass.

The Croft
East Dene, Sussex

August 11th, 1922

My dear Watson,

I have taken our discussion of this afternoon to heart, considered it carefully, and am prepared to modify my previous opinions.

I am amenable to your publishing your account of the incidents of 1903, specifically of the final case before my retirement, under the following conditions.

In addition to the usual changes that you would make to disguise actual people and places, I would suggest that you replace the entire scenario we encountered (I speak of Professor Presbury's garden. I shall not write of it further here) with monkey glands, or a similar extract from the testes of an ape or lemur, sent by some foreign mystery-man. Perhaps the monkey-extract could have the effect of making Professor Presbury move like an ape—he could be some kind of "creeping man," perhaps?—or possibly make him able to clamber up the sides of buildings and up trees. I would suggest that he could grow a tail, but this might be too fanciful even for you, Watson, although no more fanciful than many of the rococo additions you have made in your histories to otherwise humdrum events in my life and work.

In addition, I have written the following speech, to be delivered by myself, at the end of your narrative. Please make certain that something much like this is there, in which I inveigh against living too long, and the foolish urges that push foolish people to do foolish things to prolong their foolish lives:

> There is a very real danger to humanity, if one could live for ever, if youth were simply there for the taking, that the material, the sensual, the worldly would all prolong their worthless lives. The spiritual would not avoid the call to something higher. It would be the survival of the least fit. What sort of cesspool may not our poor world become?

Something along those lines, I fancy, would set my mind at rest.

Let me see the finished article, please, before you submit it to be published.

I remain, old friend, your most obedient servant,

Sherlock Holmes

They reached Old Gao's bees late in the afternoon. The beehives were grey wooden boxes piled behind a structure so simple it could barely be called a shack. Four posts, a roof, and hangings of oiled cloth that served to keep out the worst of the spring rains and the summer storms. A small charcoal brazier served for warmth, if you placed a blanket over it and yourself, and to cook upon; a wooden pallet in the center of the structure, with an ancient ceramic pillow, served as a bed on the occasions that Old Gao slept up on the mountainside with the bees, particularly in the autumn, when he harvested most of the honey. There was little enough of it compared to the output of his cousin's hives, but it was enough that he would sometimes spend two or three days waiting for the comb that he had crushed and stirred into a slurry to drain through the cloth into the buckets and pots that he had carried up the mountainside. Finally he would melt the remainder, the sticky wax and bits of pollen and dirt and bee slurry, in a pot, to extract the beeswax, and he would give the sweet water back to the bees. Then he would carry the honey and the wax blocks down the hill to the village to sell.

He showed the barbarian stranger the eleven hives, watched impassively as the stranger put on a veil and opened a hive, examining first the bees, then the contents of a brood box, and finally the queen, through his magnifying glass. He showed no fear, no discomfort: in everything he did the stranger's movements were gentle and slow, and he was not stung, nor did he crush or hurt a single bee. This impressed Old Gao. He had assumed that barbarians were inscrutable, unreadable, mysterious creatures, but this man seemed overjoyed to have encountered Gao's bees. His eyes were shining.

Old Gao fired up the brazier, to boil some water. Long before the charcoal was hot, however, the stranger had removed from his bag a contraption of glass and metal. He had filled the upper half of it with water from the stream, lit a flame, and soon a kettleful of water was steaming and bubbling. Then the stranger took two tin mugs from his bag, and some green tea leaves wrapped in paper, and dropped the leaves into the mug, and poured on the water.

It was the finest tea that Old Gao had ever drunk: better by far than his cousin's tea. They drank it cross-legged on the floor.

"I would like to stay here for the summer, in this house," said the stranger.

"Here? This is not even a house," said Old Gao. "Stay down in the village. Widow Zhang has a room."

"I will stay here," said the stranger. "Also I would like to rent one of your beehives."

Old Gao had not laughed in years. There were those in the village who would have thought such a thing impossible. But still, he laughed then, a guffaw of surprise and amusement that seemed to have been jerked out of him.

"I am serious," said the stranger. He placed four silver coins on the ground between them. Old Gao had not seen where he got them from: three silver Mexican pesos, a coin that had become popular in China years before, and a large silver yuan. It was as much money as Old Gao might see in a year of selling honey. "For this money," said the stranger, "I would like someone to bring me food: every three days should suffice."

Old Gao said nothing. He finished his tea and stood up. He pushed through the oiled cloth to the clearing high on the hillside. He walked over to the eleven hives: each consisted of two brood boxes with one, two, three or, in one case, even four boxes above that. He took the stranger to the hive with four boxes above it, each box filled with frames of comb.

"This hive is yours," he said.

They were plant extracts. That was obvious. They worked, in their way, for a limited time, but they were also extremely poisonous. But watching poor Professor Presbury during those final days—his skin, his eyes, his gait—had convinced me that he had not been on entirely the wrong path.

I took his case of seeds, of pods, of roots, and of dried extracts and I thought. I pondered. I cogitated. I reflected. It was an intellectual problem, and could be solved, as my old maths tutor had always sought to demonstrate to me, by intellect.

They were plant extracts, and they were lethal.

Methods I used to render them non-lethal rendered them quite ineffective.

It was not a three pipe problem. I suspect it was something approaching a three hundred pipe problem before I hit upon an initial idea—a notion, perhaps—of a way of processing the plants that might allow them to be ingested by human beings.

It was not a line of investigation that could easily be followed in Baker Street. So it was, in the autumn of 1903, that I moved to Sussex, and spent the winter reading every book and pamphlet and monograph so far published, I fancy, upon the care and keeping of bees. And so it was that in early April of 1904, armed only with theoretical knowledge, I took delivery from a local farmer of my first package of bees.

I wonder, sometimes, that Watson did not suspect anything. Then again, Watson's glorious obtuseness has never ceased to surprise me, and sometimes, indeed, I had relied upon it. Still, he knew what I was like when I had no work to occupy my mind, no case to solve. He knew my lassitude, my black moods when I had no case to occupy me.

So how could he believe that I had truly retired? He knew my methods.

Indeed, Watson was there when I took receipt of my first bees. He watched, from a safe distance, as I poured the bees from the package into the empty, waiting hive, like slow, humming, gentle treacle.

He saw my excitement, and he saw nothing.

And the years passed, and we watched the Empire crumble, we watched the Government unable to govern, we watched those poor heroic boys sent to the trenches of Flanders to die, all these things confirmed me in my opinions. I was not doing the right thing. I was doing the only thing.

As my face grew unfamiliar, and my finger-joints swelled and ached (not so much as they might have done, though, which I attributed to the many bee-stings I had received in my first few years as an investigative apiarist) and as Watson, dear, brave, obtuse Watson, faded with time and paled and shrank, his skin becoming greyer, his mustache becoming the same shade of grey, my resolve to conclude my researches did not diminish. If anything, it increased.

So: my initial hypotheses were tested upon the South Downs, in an apiary of my own devising, each hive modelled upon Langstroth's. I do believe that I made every mistake that ever a novice beekeeper could or has ever made, and in addition, due to my investigations, an entire hiveful of mistakes that no beekeeper has ever made before, or shall, I trust, ever make again. "The Case of the Poisoned Beehive," Watson might have called many of them, although "The Mystery of the Transfixed Women's Institute" would have drawn more attention to my researches, had anyone been interested enough to investigate. (As it was, I chided Mrs Telford for simply taking a jar of honey from the shelves here without consulting me, and I ensured that, in the future, she was given several jars for her cooking from the more regular hives, and that honey from the experimental hives was locked away once it had been collected. I do not believe that this ever drew comment.)

I experimented with Dutch bees, with German bees and with Italians, with Carniolans and Caucasians. I regretted the loss of our British bees to blight and, even where they had survived, to interbreeding, although I found and worked with a small hive I purchased and grew up from a frame of brood and a queen cell, from an old Abbey in St. Albans, which seemed to me to be original British breeding stock.

I experimented for the best part of two decades, before I concluded that the bees that I sought, if they existed, were not to be found in England, and would not survive the distances they would need to travel to reach me by international parcel post. I needed to examine bees in India. I needed to travel perhaps farther afield than that.

I have a smattering of languages.

I had my flower-seeds, and my extracts and tinctures in syrup. I needed nothing more.

I packed them up, arranged for the cottage on the Downs to be cleaned and aired once a week, and for Master Wilkins—to whom I am afraid I had developed the habit of referring, to his obvious distress, as "Young Villikins"—to inspect the beehives, and to harvest and sell surplus honey in Eastbourne market, and to prepare the hives for winter.

I told them I did not know when I should be back.

I am an old man. Perhaps they did not expect me to return.

And, if this was indeed the case, they would, strictly speaking, have been right.

Old Gao was impressed, despite himself. He had lived his life among bees. Still, watching the stranger shake the bees from the boxes, with a practised flick of his wrist, so cleanly and so sharply that the black bees seemed more surprised than angered, and simply flew or crawled back into their hive, was remarkable. The stranger then stacked the boxes filled with comb on top of one of the weaker hives, so Old Gao would still have the honey from the hive the stranger was renting.

So it was that Old Gao gained a lodger.

Old Gao gave the Widow Zhang's granddaughter a few coins to take the stranger food three times a week—mostly rice and vegetables, along with an earthenware pot filled, when she left at least, with boiling soup.

Every ten days Old Gao would walk up the hill himself. He went initially to check on the hives, but soon discovered that under the stranger's care all eleven hives were thriving as they had never thrived before. And indeed, there was now a twelfth hive, from a captured swarm of the black bees the stranger had encountered while on a walk along the hill.

Old Gao brought wood, the next time he came up to the shack, and he and the stranger spent several afternoons wordlessly working together, making extra boxes to go on the hives, building frames to fill the boxes.

One evening the stranger told Old Gao that the frames they were making had been invented by an American, only seventy years before. This seemed like nonsense to Old Gao, who made frames as his father had, and as they did across the valley, and as, he was certain, his grandfather and his grandfather's grandfather had, but he said nothing.

He enjoyed the stranger's company. They made hives together, and Old Gao wished that the stranger was a younger man. Then he would stay there for a long time, and Old Gao would have someone to leave his beehives to, when he died. But they were two old men, nailing boxes together, with thin frosty hair and old faces, and neither of them would see another dozen winters.

Old Gao noticed that the stranger had planted a small, neat garden beside the hive that he had claimed as his own, which he had moved away from the rest of the hives. He had covered it with a net. He had also created a "back door" to the hive, so that the only bees that could reach the plants came from the hive that he was renting. Old Gao also observed that, beneath the netting, there were several trays filled with what appeared to be sugar solution of some kind, one coloured bright red, one green, one a startling blue, one yellow. He pointed to them, but all the stranger did was nod and smile.

The bees were lapping up the syrups, though, clustering and crowding on the sides of the tin dishes with their tongues down, eating until they could eat no more, and then returning to the hive.

The stranger had made sketches of Old Gao's bees. He showed the sketches to Old Gao, tried to explain the ways that Old Gao's bees differed from other honeybees, talked of ancient bees preserved in stone for millions of years, but here the stranger's Chinese failed him, and, truthfully, Old Gao was not interested. They were his bees, until he died, and after that, they were the bees of the mountainside. He had brought other bees here, but they had sickened and died, or been killed in raids by the black bees, who took their honey and left them to starve.

The last of these visits was in late summer. Old Gao went down the mountainside. He did not see the stranger again.

It is done.

It works. Already I feel a strange combination of triumph and of disappointment, as if of defeat, or of distant storm-clouds teasing at my senses.

It is strange to look at my hands and to see, not my hands as I know them, but the hands I remember from my younger days: knuckles unswollen, dark hairs, not snow-white, on the backs.

It was a quest that had defeated so many, a problem with no apparent solution. The first Emperor of China died and nearly destroyed his empire in pursuit of it, three thousand years ago, and all it took me was, what, twenty years?

I do not know if I did the right thing or not (although any "retirement" without such an occupation would have been, literally, maddening). I took the commission from Mycroft. I investigated the problem. I arrived, inevitably, at the solution.

Will I tell the world? I will not.

And yet, I have half a pot of dark brown honey remaining in my bag; a half a pot of honey that is worth more than nations. (I was tempted to write, *worth more than all the tea in China,* perhaps because of my current situation, but fear that even Watson would deride it as cliché.)

And speaking of Watson...

There is one thing left to do. My only remaining goal, and it is small enough. I shall make my way to Shanghai, and from there I shall take ship to Southampton, a half a world away.

And once I am there, I shall seek out Watson, if he still lives—and I fancy he does. It is irrational, I know, and yet I am certain that I would know, somehow, had Watson passed beyond the veil.

I shall buy theatrical makeup, disguise myself as an old man, so as not to startle him, and I shall invite my old friend over for tea.

There will be honey on buttered toast served for tea that afternoon, I fancy.

There were tales of a barbarian who passed through the village on his way east, but the people who told Old Gao this did not believe that it could have been the same man who had lived in Gao's shack. This one was young and proud, and his hair was dark. It was not the old man who had walked through those parts in the spring, although, one person told Gao, the bag was similar.

Old Gao walked up the mountainside to investigate, although he suspected what he would find before he got there.

The stranger was gone, and the stranger's bag.

There had been much burning, though. That was clear. Papers had been burnt—Old Gao recognised the edge of a drawing the stranger had made of one of his bees, but the rest of the papers were ash, or blackened beyond recognition, even had Old Gao been able to read barbarian writing. The papers were not the only things to have been burnt; parts of the hive that the stranger had rented were now only twisted ash; there were blackened, twisted strips of tin that might once have contained brightly coloured syrups.

The colour was added to the syrups, the stranger had told him once, so that he could tell them apart, although for what purpose Old Gao had never enquired.

He examined the shack like a detective, searching for a clue as to the stranger's nature or his whereabouts. On the ceramic pillow four silver coins had been left for him to find—two yuan and two pesos—and he put them away.

Behind the shack he found a heap of used slurry, with the last bees of the day still crawling upon it, tasting whatever sweetness was still on the surface of the still-sticky wax.

Old Gao thought long and hard before he gathered up the slurry, wrapped it loosely in cloth, and put it in a pot, which he filled with water. He heated the water on the brazier, but did not let it boil. Soon enough the wax floated to the surface, leaving the dead bees and the dirt and the pollen and the propolis inside the cloth.

He let it cool.

Then he walked outside, and he stared up at the moon. It was almost full.

He wondered how many villagers knew that his son had died as a baby. He remembered his wife, but her face was distant, and he had no portraits or photographs of her. He thought that there was nothing he was so suited for on the face of the earth as to keep the black, bulletlike bees on the side of this high, high hill. There was no other man who knew their temperament as he did.

The water had cooled. He lifted the now solid block of beeswax out of the water, placed it on the boards of the bed to finish cooling. He took the cloth filled with dirt and impurities out of the pot. And then, because he too was, in his way, a detective, and once you have eliminated the impossible whatever remains, however unlikely, must be the truth, he drank the sweet water in the pot. There is a lot of honey in slurry, after all, even after the majority of it has dripped through a cloth and been purified. The water tasted of honey, but not a honey that Gao had ever tasted before. It tasted of smoke, and metal, and strange flowers, and odd perfumes. It tasted, Gao thought, a little like sex.

He drank it all down, and then he slept, with his head on the ceramic pillow.

When he woke, he thought, he would decide how to deal with his cousin, who would expect to inherit the twelve hives on the hill when Old Gao went missing.

He would be an illegitimate son, perhaps, the young man who would return in the days to come. Or perhaps a son. Young Gao. Who would remember, now? It did not matter.

He would go to the city and then he would return, and he would keep the black bees on the side of the mountain for as long as days and circumstances would allow.

Neil Gaiman is the only author to have won both the Carnegie and Newbery Medals, for his novel *The Graveyard Book,* and to have won a Hugo Award for Best Short Story for his Sherlock Holmes/H. P. Lovecraft tale "A Study in Emerald." He first encountered Holmes at the age of ten, in the library of Ardingly College Junior School, and immediately added the Great Detective to the list of People He Wanted to Be When He Grew Up, a list that at that point probably included P. G. Wodehouse's Psmith and Michael Moorcock's Elric. He became a writer when he grew up, which is almost as good.

Gaiman was invested into the Baker Street Irregulars in 2005, under the name of The Devil's Foot.

The only information in the Sherlock Holmes Canon about Holmes's interest in bees may be found in the stories entitled "The Lion's Mane" and "His Last Bow." The latter, which takes place in 1914, mentions Holmes's "*magnum opus* of [his] latter years": *Practical Handbook of Bee Culture, with Some Observations upon the Segregation of the Queen.*

A Triumph of Logic

Gayle Lynds and John Sheldon

Linwood Boothby was catching a smoke outside the Franklin County courthouse. He'd cut down to one cigarette a day, midafternoon, to revive himself during jury trials. There was no courtroom work today, but he was indulging himself anyway.

"Hi, Judge." I stepped out onto the courthouse portico. "I heard a good one today."

Boothby raised his red, bushy eyebrows, which contrasted with his bald head and were his most distinctive facial feature.

"What do you call a Maine lawyer who doesn't know anything?" I asked.

"I don't know, Artie. What do you call a Maine lawyer who doesn't know anything?"

"Your Honor."

He let out something between a chuckle and a growl, inhaled his cigarette, then took it out of his mouth and studied it. "Artie, what do you call a Maine law clerk who's a wiseass?"

"I don't know, what?"

"Unemployed."

"Uh-uh." I raised my index finger. "Empty threat. You already fired me last week."

"Yeah, but it felt so good I wanted to do it again."

"Besides, your eminence, you need a vassal, a Dr. Watson if you will, both to preserve your record for history"—I did a small genuflection—"as well as to announce your visitors, such as the one awaiting you at this very moment, in your chambers above."

"Who?" He raised the cigarette to his lips again.

"Emmy Holcrofts."

Boothby looked at me in mid-puff, and the eyebrows shot up again, this time in surprise. Emmy was a court reporter, and court reporters were usually seen only during trials and hearings; they spent the rest of their professional lives cloistered, transcribing their notes.

Boothby looked longingly at his Pall Mall, snubbed it out in the cigarette receptacle, and followed me into the building.

"Hi, Judge Boothby."

As he mounted the stairs to his office ahead of me, Boothby looked up. Emmy Holcrofts was waiting for him in the hall. Compact, with a halo of gray curls, she wore trifocals on a softly lined face.

"Hi, Emmy. Go on in." He climbed the final two steps and followed her across the threshold.

Inside the room she turned. "Could Artie stay, too? I'm in a bind, and I'd be grateful if I could bounce some questions off both of you."

"Sure, if you don't mind sitting in a confined space with Frank Zappa." He pointed at me. Boothby loved prodding me about my nonlawyerly—my steadfastly, ardently nonlawyerly—appearance. I rolled my eyes, but when he motioned me in I went gladly, grateful for a reprieve from the law library.

"Grab a seat, Emmy," Boothby said. "What's up?"

Emmy sat on the brown leather couch, and I on a matching armchair.

"You probably know I'm Ina Lederer's executor." Emmy arranged her skirt.

Boothby had taken the other armchair against the adjoining wall. "I'm not surprised. I'm sorry, Emmy. You and she were close, weren't you?"

"Yes…" Staring down at her hands, she folded them in her lap. "She was my niece, and I've been inventorying her possessions…" She stopped, her eyes brimming with tears.

"Take your time," Boothby said gently. Emmy had been working with him for more than a decade.

"Thank you." She gave a weak smile. "Ina was a difficult child. In college she got into drugs, flunked out, and had nowhere to go—her parents were furious. I took her in, and a year later she'd cleaned up. But then she didn't have anything to do." She sighed. "She hadn't liked college, and I didn't want her flipping burgers because she was so bright. So I showed her the basics of my steno machine. That interested her, and I covered her expenses while she studied stenography. After she was certified, she applied to the court system and they took her. She was just twenty-four, and I thought she was on her way." She shook her head.

Boothby furrowed his forehead, eyebrows nearly meeting. "What do you think happened?" The newspapers had reported a suicide.

"I don't know." She scanned the walls blankly. "The police found a suicide note saying she'd let everybody down. When traces of cocaine were discovered in her system, they concluded she'd been depressed about her addiction."

He leaned forward. "What can we do?"

"Well, two things. First, I've found some of Ina's steno notes that may need to be transcribed. Is there anything you want quickly?"

Boothby considered. "Yes. A few weeks ago she recorded a discussion I had here, in chambers, about an agreement between the Feds and the state. It was with defense counsel and the persecutor." Boothby referred to the DA's prosecutors as the "persecutors" in jest, but also, I think, to remind them of what they weren't supposed to be. "The defendant's name was Doak. He agreed to cooperate with the DEA, and if they liked what he disclosed, they'd drop all federal charges and he'd plead to lesser state charges."

"Okay," she said, "that shouldn't take long. The second thing is, I found something the police don't know about: an account book and thirty-five hundred dollars cash. They were wrapped together in plastic and hidden in the bottom of a garbage can under the trash bag. The account book shows some big transactions, sometimes exceeding two thousand dollars. What do I do? That stuff suggests she might've been selling drugs, which is police business, but if I tell them, they may confiscate the cash as evidence. I'm administering the estate, so I'm supposed to protect its assets for the heirs—her two brothers—aren't I?"

Boothby and I exchanged uncertain glances.

Emmy continued: "If I inventory it and claim it for the estate in my report to the probate court, are the heirs benefiting from what might be her illegal activity? And am I an accomplice after the fact?" She looked at her hands, still clasped in her lap, and awaited an answer.

"Jeez." Boothby tugged at his left eyebrow. "You put me in a difficult position. Judges can't give legal advice, you know. You need a lawyer."

She nodded but said nothing.

He gazed upward and spoke at the ceiling. "On the other hand, it's okay if Artie and I brainify out loud"—"brainify": sometimes I think he wants to sound like an idiot—"even though you're sitting right here." He cocked his head and glanced at me conspiratorially.

I chuckled.

"So, thinking aloud, Artie, I'd say the police can't bring a case against Ina because she's dead. But maybe the greenbacks are evidence against someone else, especially if they're marked bills, and Emmy doesn't need an obstruction of justice charge. So she could put the bills in a safety deposit box and file with the probate court an inventory listing the money as an asset. That's what it is, after all. Artie?"

"Good so far," I said.

"And maybe I'd put the account book in the same safety deposit box. But before I did any of that, I'd photocopy the bills and the book for the police. That way nobody hid anything from anyone."

I nodded agreement, but Emmy didn't look comfortable.

"I don't want to get Ina's friends in trouble," she said. "She mentioned one friend in her diary a lot. Someone named Teenie, but Teenie also shows up in the account book. I can't betray the people Ina cared about."

"Her diary?" Boothby scratched his ear. "Think the cops need that, Artie?"

"Judge," I answered, maintaining the pretense, "if Teenie was really her friend she wouldn't be in the account book, right? Ina would be sharing whatever it was with her, not selling it."

"Makes sense," he answered.

"So it doesn't compromise a friendship if you make photocopies and give them to the police. At this point, I think it's CYA."

Boothby nodded. "And I'd preserve the original diary in the safety deposit box."

"Yup," I said.

"Okay." Boothby poked a finger at Emmy. "My clerk and I think you'd better get a lawyer—you can charge it to the estate. Notwithstanding you overheard us, you ain't suing us for malpractice 'cause we didn't give you any legal advice. All we told you is, get a lawyer."

"Thanks, Judge." She smiled briefly as she stood up. "I felt so alone. You've helped me a lot."

Boothby and I stood to shake her hand.

"We're here for you, Emmy," he told her. "Any time."

As her eyes became watery again, she turned quickly and walked out of the office.

Boothby considered me. "This young court reporter...Ina... I'd never noticed her." He took off his glasses and massaged his eyes. "She was like a piece of courtroom furniture to me—fingers attached to a steno machine. A life I never took interest in, Artie, until it was over."

The Depression-era ditty "Brother, Can You Spare a Dime?" was just audible over the hubbub. That and other paeans to poverty bespoke the theme of Judge Gibson Watts's "The Taxman Goeth" party, held annually on the first Saturday after April 15.

The Watts home was a 3,500-square-foot log building, sitting on fifteen acres with six hundred feet of shoreline on Muscongus Bay in Maine. It was built in the 1920s by a New York City physician who wanted to combine the New England experiences of a log home and a view of Maine's rocky coast. So he ordered a spruce log palace, appropriate for snow country in the northern woods and mountains, to be built overlooking the coastline, where it fit in like a Shinto temple along the Thames. The Watts family had bought it in the fifties, when Maine real estate was dirt cheap by their Baltimore standards and the Spruce Goose, as the locals called it, was even cheaper. Watts and his two sisters inherited it when their mother died in 1971; he bought them out soon thereafter and moved into it when he relocated to Maine from Maryland to practice law. A lifelong bachelor, Watts had the place to himself.

An eclectic group of the judge's friends had shown up, including other judges, lawyers, assorted court personnel, lobstermen, the proprietor of the local convenience store, and the chief of the Maine State Police (a former client). Those expecting tax refunds received happy face stickers to wear. Those experiencing "taxectomy" received tin cups with which to solicit charitable donations.

Boothby was filling his tin cup with cashews at the dining room table, and I was at the sideboard sampling the shrimp, when I heard someone rip off a couple of arpeggios on the piano across the hall. A semiskilled pianist, I knew great technique when I heard it. When the pianist started in on Chopin's D-flat nocturne I headed into the living room. The reprise section has a filigree that's beyond my skill, and I wanted to see it done up close.

I recognized the pianist as Julia Austrian, a Juilliard-trained concert pianist who had a home in nearby Damariscotta. I pulled up a chair behind her just as she approached the difficult passage: her right hand glided gracefully over the keyboard, her fingers touching the keys with an astonishing combination of speed, precision, and apparent ease.

"How do you *do* that?" I asked after she had finished.

She turned around and smiled. "Four hundred thousand hours of practice." We both laughed, and she added, "Are you a pianist?"

"I'm a *wish-I-could* pianist, but I see I should keep my day job. By the way, I'm Artie Morey." I extended my hand.

She shook it. "Julia Austrian, Artie. Since you're a pianist, let me ask you: did you notice anything in the left hand?"

I hesitated, unsure of what to say. "It was as smooth as maple syrup. I'd give my right arm if it made my left hand that silky."

"Thanks! That means I carried it off."

"Carried it off?"

"Before starting I noticed that a couple of the low notes were off key," she explained. "Probably brand-new strings—new strings stretch out of tune—so I had to substitute notes."

"You improvised on the fly?"

Austrian nodded. My jaw dropped in awe.

She shrugged and smiled. "The best thing I learned at Juilliard was how to fake it."

"*Juilliard* trains pianists to *fake*?"

"Sure. What do you do when you have a memory lapse? You can't just stop."

"That was wonderful, Julia." Judge Watts appeared beside us, smiling broadly, and handed her a glass of white wine. "Better than any concert we ever get around here."

Watts was a tall, wiry man with wide shoulders, a full head of curly gray hair, and a profile like Basil Rathbone's. He looked as if he'd been a basketball player—small forward, perhaps—and he was astonishingly smart. When he'd come onto the trial bench a year or so earlier nobody expected him to stay at that level for long. He had an almost magical intuition for law that enabled him to resolve legal issues as quickly as lawyers could state them. Other judges sought him out for help with difficult cases, and he came to be known as the Sherlock Holmes of the judiciary for more than his silhouette. It was said that if the entire Maine Supreme Court bench of seven justices died in a plane crash the governor could replace them all with Gibson Watts.

"Thanks, Judge." She pointed to the nine-foot Steinway grand. "I rarely find an instrument this superb in a private home. I had to try it."

"Glad you did!" Taciturn, even dour, around the courthouse—thinking too deeply to be bothered with civility—he was the opposite here, an enthusiastic and warm host.

"Do you play?" she asked him.

He chuckled. "Dumb fingers. I keep the piano tuned because it's too beautiful to ignore." He lifted his glass toward me. "Alas, Mr. Morey, I'd have brought you some wine too, but the King of Reversible Error is looking for you and prefers you not slur your words."

"Thanks, Judge," I replied. "A pleasure, Ms. Austrian."

"Thanks, Artie."

I crossed the hall and found King Boothby in the dining room at the salmon.

I approached semireverently. "Judge Watts delivered your summons."

He looked up as he was shoving the last of his salmon sandwich into his mouth. Holding his index finger in the air, he chewed for a moment and then gulped it down. "Emmy Holcrofts arrived a few minutes ago. She's agitated about her niece and wants to talk right away. I asked her to wait in the library. Would you like to join us?"

I followed Boothby to a small, book-lined room. A wood fire in the modest fieldstone fireplace made it cozy—an atmosphere to calm the nerves.

Emmy started to stand, but Boothby waved her back into her seat. "What's the matter, Emmy?"

He and I took chairs.

"I've been going through Ina's steno tapes to find her notes of the Doak case—the one you asked me to transcribe?" When he nodded, she continued. "I found them and was preparing a transcript when I got a visit from a federal drug enforcement investigator. She asked if I had information about Ina's relationship with Harold Doak—the same man. Doak had named Ina as a customer."

"Wait a minute," I interrupted. "Ina was the court reporter who took notes of a plea bargain, for her very own supplier?"

"And the Feds wanted to keep the plea bargain secret," Boothby added, "so neither Doak's suppliers nor his customers would know. Christ. Ina had to realize DEA agents would be on her doorstep soon. Maybe that explains her suicide."

"No, I think you're wrong," said Emmy. "I read her diary again. That's where she put her emotional entries—happy, sad, angry, all kinds of feelings. What the police are calling her 'suicide note' was on the tape in her steno machine. Why there and not in her diary? I spent the last two days reviewing all the tapes of all the hearings she attended for the last year. The only personal entry is that single note the police found."

"So that was unusual for her—but so is suicide," Boothby said. "She must have been distraught."

"I brought the police report." She reached into her large handbag, pulled out a document. "Here's her note. It says, 'I can't face my family anymore. They believed in me, and I betrayed them.' Ina wouldn't have said that. I was the only person she considered family, the only family member she'd mentioned in her journal for the past year. I'm one person, not 'them.' The only time she referred to family plural was this single entry on the steno tape—where she would never have put it."

"What about the brothers?" I asked.

"She wasn't close to them. They were lucky: the law designates them her heirs."

Boothby's eyebrows descended in a frown. "So you think someone else wrote the suicide note."

I scrooched forward on the couch. "Maybe it was written after Ina died, to make it look like a suicide?"

Eyebrows up, then down again, thinking.

"Someone who knew steno machines," I continued, "and felt safer typing the note than faking Ina's handwriting."

Boothby picked up the thread: "Assuming Ina'd been selling the stuff she got from Doak and told a customer about Doak's plea agreement, that customer wouldn't want Ina doing to him—or her—what Doak would likely do to Ina. Killing Ina prevents her from revealing anyone to the cops."

All this theorizing ignited my suspicion: "What else about Ina's death, Emmy, suggests murder?"

"Read the police report." She handed it to me. "They found her in the basement of her apartment building, hanging by a wire wrapped around her neck, the other end around a hook in a ceiling rafter. Near her was a stool, an aerosol can of cold-start ether, and a rag. The investigators concluded she strung herself up, then used the ether to anesthetize herself so she'd fall off the stool but not suffer while she was strangling to death." Emmy looked away. "This is so awful. Poor Ina."

It *was* awful, I thought, then pointed to the report. "Says here no signs of struggle. Suppose there were no signs of struggle because Ina was already unconscious when she was strung up?"

"No struggle because she trusted the other person and wasn't expecting a faceful of ether." Boothby cocked his right eyebrow up, pointed at me, and turned to Emmy. "Let's take a look at Ina's basement. Before suggesting the police got it wrong, let's see whether what we're brainifying about makes sense. Tomorrow afternoon?"

"And just what are you three desperadoes conspiring about here?" We all looked up to find Judge Watts leaning against the doorjamb and munching on some grapes, an eyebrow raised in mock suspicion.

"Hi, Gibson," said Boothby. "Great party! We're talking to Emmy here about Ina Lederer. Ina was Emmy's niece."

He turned to her. "I'm so sorry about what happened, Emmy. Losing a loved one to suicide is the worst kind of loss."

"I don't believe it was suicide," Emmy said.

Watts moved into the room and furrowed his brow. "What else could it be then—except…murder?"

"Bingo." Boothby nodded.

Watts looked incredulous. "Who'd want to murder her?"

Boothby shrugged. "No idea. We're just brainifying."

"Wow—murder," Watts said. "Linwood," he said to Boothby, "this is both horrifying and intriguing. I'd like to hear your, uh, brainifying when you have a chance—and when I don't have a party to conduct." He nodded toward the people in the adjoining room. "Got to go. Again, Emmy, my condolences."

After Watts left, Boothby stood and held up his glass. "Time to refuel. Emmy, you need to try some of Gibson's lobster dip. You too, Artie—let's mingle."

◇◇◇

Ina's apartment was on the ground floor of a four-story tenement in Lewiston, a dingy nineteenth-century mill town that had been dying for eighty years. Emmy let us in. Ina's place was neat, but dust on the furniture indicated no one had been there in a while.

She led us to the back of the apartment, then through a door and down steps to the basement. It was a large, open area with brick columns evenly spaced along the length of the room to support carrying timbers. Clotheslines drooped between the columns; a bicycle was chained to one of them; a stool stood next to another. A decrepit upright piano occupied what had probably been the coal bin.

Emmy showed us the hook, embedded in one of the joists, from which Ina was found hanging, and pointed out the stool that Ina was supposed to have used.

"How big was Ina?" Boothby asked Emmy.

"Five-three, a hundred and ten pounds maybe."

"So how would someone be able to lift her and hold her aloft long enough to hang her off that hook?" Boothby asked me.

"Had to be strong," I said, "so I'm guessing a man. Maybe he wrapped the wire around her neck, boosted her onto his shoulder, climbed onto the stool, wrapped the other end of the wire around the hook, and let her go."

"Next question: Why use a wire? Why not some of that clothesline?"

"Clothesline's fragile, might break. The police report says it was a piano wire, probably from that wrecked piano."

We walked over to it. Its keyboard resembled a mouthful of rotted teeth, and it lacked its upper and lower front panels. Several strings dangled free of their pins, and some were missing altogether.

Boothby studied it. "Using a piano wire supports the idea of suicide because the means of death is right here."

Emmy spoke up: "Ina's apartment is the only one in the building with direct access to the basement. That other door"—she pointed to the rear—"leads to a common stairway for the other apartments. Someone in Ina's apartment could get down here and back up without much risk of being seen."

Boothby nodded. "What's going to happen to her apartment?"

"I've got to sublet it. Ina's lease has another six months to run and doesn't have a clause that terminates it upon death. So if you're done, why don't I show you out? I need to clean it to get it ready."

◇◇◇

As we got into Boothby's vehicle of choice, a gray 1980s four-door Citroën—another of his iconoclasms—I said, "Judge, the wire didn't come from that piano."

"Why not?"

"I know that the longest bass string on an upright is about three feet. To do the job right—sorry—with a stool as short as the one we saw, you need something long enough to wrap around the hook, wrap around her neck, and still leave slack. Like a string from a grand piano."

"Okay, so?"

"Bear with me. What do you know about cocaine?"

"Between you and me and this gear shift, I did a line once when I was in the army. I felt great for an hour and instantly understood why it's so popular. And also why I should avoid it."

"Cocaine makes you feel like a million bucks, doesn't it? But besides dependence, overuse produces nosebleeds. Snorting too much burns out your nose tissue, which renders the blood vessels fragile."

"Another reason to avoid it. What's your point?"

"Judge Watts's law clerk told me the judge had been suffering nosebleeds. Recently one was bad enough he had to recess a jury trial for forty-five minutes."

Boothby hit the brakes. The driver behind us blared his horn angrily and swept around us. Boothby ignored him and narrowed his eyes at me: "You're calling Gibson Watts a cocaine addict?" Eyebrows down, he was incredulous. "More likely he's Clark Kent and suffering exposure to kryptonite."

"I'm not calling him anything, but please hear me out. He also has a grand piano. And some of its bass strings were recently replaced, or at least that's what Julia Austrian thought. The investigation report said Ina was hanged on a bass piano string."

Boothby was glowering at me, but at least he seemed to be listening.

"This is probably a coincidence," I continued, "but coincidences always get my antennae quivering. Suppose Judge Watts had been buying cocaine from Ina, and someone told him about Doak's plea bargain. He had to have been worried Ina would report him in exchange for a plea bargain, too."

Boothby was silent. Then he checked the outside mirror and resumed driving. "Watts knows about the plea bargain. I mentioned it at lunch the next day."

We drove in silence. I looked at him. Eyebrows down: trouble coming.

He stopped for a red light. "A couple of years ago I ran into one of Watts's law school classmates at a bar meeting in Vermont. He asked how 'Tini' Watts was doing. In law school they called him 'Martini,' a play on his name, Gibson. It also reflected his love affair with gin."

"T-i-n-i. As in T-e-e-n-i-e from the diary? Holy shit." I thought about it. "Are you going to tell the police?"

The light turned green, and he continued driving. "Gibson Watts is a friend of mine, and he's a wonderful judge. Report this and I'm jeopardizing his career—just try to get renominated to another judicial term after you've been suspected of drug use, let alone murder. Right now all we've got are some unconnected dots."

"Judge, let me find out who tunes Judge Watts's piano; perhaps the strings weren't changed, or if they were, they can be accounted for."

"Good idea. Meanwhile, we'd better interrupt Emmy's cleaning. Best to preserve any DNA evidence the forensics people might find. Suspecting suicide, they might not have scoured the place as thoroughly as they would if they were thinking murder." He made a sudden, swooping U-turn that would have earned him a ticket if any of Lewiston's finest had seen it.

A couple of days later I was standing at the sidewalk hot dog stand in front of the courthouse when Boothby came up to me and suggested a walk in the park. I slapped some mustard on my dog and followed him across the street and onto a bricked walkway leading to a large pond in the middle.

"I got your note," he said. "Fill me in."

"I located the person who tuned Judge Watts's piano. She replaced three bass strings a week before the party. She wanted to retune the piano after the strings had 'matured'—her term—and before the party, but didn't have a chance. She said those strings were about eight feet long. She left the old ones in Judge Watts's metal recycling receptacle."

I glanced at him. Eyebrows amidship: he was listening closely.

"According to the police report, one end of the wire that killed Ina had been cut," I continued. "The investigators found several bass strings on that old upright piano had been cut off, so that's where they thought the wire came from. By cutting the wire short you can disguise its origin."

We walked on until we reached the pond, where several Canada geese were gliding around. We stopped to admire them.

Finally he said, "Well, shit, piss, and corruption." A pause, followed by a sigh. "I've been doing some investigating too. Guess what Watts did before he went to law school."

"Other than college?"

Boothby rubbed his hands. "I called up that law school classmate of his I'd met in Vermont, and I lied." He shrugged, a small mea culpa. "I said I was preparing a roast for Watts and needed some dirt about his background." Brief pause. "Watts was a court reporter in Maryland. His college GPA hadn't been strong, but he wanted to become a lawyer so to get his nose into the legal community's tent he chose stenography. A few years later he applied to law school. I guess his experience in the courtroom overcame his college record."

"So Tini knew how to use a steno machine?"

"Yup."

So we had the Big Three: opportunity, means, and motive. Opportunity because Watts knew Ina and, if "Teenie" was the same person as "Tini," Ina considered him a friend. Means because of the piano wire and his steno experience. Motive because of the risk that Ina would turn state's evidence. If Watts had been using cocaine, it all fit together.

"What now?" I asked.

"Gibson called, inviting me over to discuss Ina. He says he's shocked to think she was murdered. I think I'll go. Want to come?"

"Me? Sounds like it ought to be private."

He turned to face me. "I'm being cautious: it's harder to, uh, 'silence' two of us than just one."

It was Saturday afternoon, and we were at Gibson Watts's front door. I rang the bell.

The door opened, and Watts stood there in his baggy day-off clothes. He greeted us with a warm "Welcome, guys."

"Hi, Martini!" Boothby sounded as enthusiastic as a kid at a circus. He moved forward to give Watts an energetic handshake.

Watts seemed startled, but pleasantly so. "Who hit you with the happy stick? And where'd you learn that nickname?"

"Friends in low places. Your reputation has finally caught up with you." Boothby was being as affable as possible.

Not me. The Glock Model 26 between my waistband and the small of my back reminded me of the potential downside of this meeting. Boothby wanted to keep it "at a personal and judicial level, in case we're wrong," but I didn't care about judicial levels. I was worried about getting "silenced." I'd spent some time in Baghdad before law school, and I'd learned not to go unarmed into what could be hostile territory. So I'd borrowed the pistol from an NRA-nut friend. I didn't have a license to carry it. I hadn't told Boothby.

Watts ushered us in and directed us to the same study where we'd met Emmy. All of us grabbed armchairs.

"Okay, Linwood, how come the tag team?" He pointed at me.

"We've been thinking about Ina. And we need your help. I want to squeeze your nose."

Watts looked as if he'd been hit with a water balloon. He closed his eyes tight and then shook his head once, violently, opened his eyes, and peered at Boothby. "You want to what?"

"Squeeze your nose. It's what cops do sometimes when they encounter a coke suspect."

"What the Christ have you been smoking?"

"Wrong question, Gibson. The question is, what have you been sniffing? We need to know you're not on cocaine."

"*Cocaine?*" Watts moved forward in his chair. "Are you fucking nuts?"

"Gibson, please listen. There are reasons to suspect you of murder."

Watts started to rise out of his chair.

"*Please* listen, *please* don't take offense." Boothby motioned him back into his seat. "We're here because we're *worried* about you, not suspicious."

Watts sat down but squinted at Boothby. His eyes were dark, and his face so tense that he looked ready to explode.

Boothby continued: "Ina was apparently dealing cocaine, and one of the names of her possible customers was Teenie—T-e-e-n-i-e. Ina died hanging from a bass piano string, just like one of those you had replaced. The old strings remained in your possession."

Watts leaned back in his chair, crossed his arms, and turned halfway to his left to look out a window. He said nothing.

"A supposed suicide note was found on a steno tape. You know how to use steno machines. And you've been suffering nosebleeds, a symptom of many things, including cocaine use."

Watts continued to stare out the window.

"Ina took down the plea agreement involving her own supplier, so she knew her days were numbered. You knew about that plea agreement. So what does all of this amount to? Nothing, I hope. Teenie could be someone else. I'm here because I'm both your friend and a judge. The Rules of Judicial Conduct say because I don't *know* you've done anything wrong, I don't have to report anything to anyone. The only person I've been talking to about this is Artie. The Rules say I'm supposed to 'take appropriate action,' so here I am."

His upper body still facing the window, Watts glared at Boothby. "You call accusing me of murder 'appropriate action'?"

"You bet." Boothby nodded vigorously. "I want to be wrong. I'm risking our friendship because I'm worried. If you're not using cocaine, I've misled myself and Artie, and I'll get on my knees and beg your forgiveness."

Watts looked at me for the first time, as icy a glare as I've ever experienced. He focused on Boothby again: "Ina was probably dealing to a court reporter acquaintance, or to someone who learned how to type a suicide note on a steno machine for the occasion. And Teenie as you spell it is a common nickname."

Boothby nodded. "You're absolutely right. So here's the next issue. Ina's apartment hasn't been vacuumed or swept since her death. If you're not clean, or if I'm unsure, I take what I have to the cops and they'll start checking it—and you—for DNA evidence."

Watts stared at Boothby. Boothby stared back. I looked from one to the other and back again. No one said anything. The tension was like ozone before a lightning strike: I could smell it.

Boothby stirred. "If you've been seriously snorting and I squeeze your nose—damn, squeeze your own nose—it'll hurt like hell and you'll get a nosebleed. If you haven't, you won't. Please help us both."

Watts looked out the window again, put his left elbow on the arm of the chair, and rested his chin in his palm. There was silence. The longer the silence lasted the more my suspicion grew.

Finally Watts gazed at Boothby. "You ain't squeezing my nose, Linwood." His voice rose. "Nobody's squeezing my nose. This whole conversation abuses my integrity, and nobody's abusing my person as well." His face got bright red. "You were just leaving, *weren't you?*" He spat the last two words.

Boothby seemed ready for it. "Not unless you physically throw me out. Maybe you're mad because I've offended a sensitive and innocent person, or maybe you're mad because I've cornered a less-than-innocent person. I need to know it's the former. Please, Gibson."

Watts jumped to his feet. "You're out, Boothby! Get out of here, and take your lackey with you!" he roared.

It was intimidating how he towered over us as he raged, but neither Boothby nor I moved. The arteries in his neck stood out, throbbing. He was breathing quickly and heavily, and trembling as he glared at Boothby, practically gasping for breath. A drop of blood slid from one nostril. His hand shot into his pocket and produced a handkerchief. More blood dripped from his nose. He wiped it and stared at the handkerchief, then at Boothby, then back at the handkerchief. A moment later his eyes seemed to get wet. He kept staring at the handkerchief. Tears slid down his cheeks, and blood flowed freely from his nostrils. He pressed the handkerchief to his nose and dropped back into his armchair, the handkerchief covering his face, shaking and weeping uncontrollably.

Boothby slowly got to his feet. He put his hand on his friend's shoulder. "Gibson, get a lawyer. Please." He motioned to me and I followed him out.

The next Tuesday afternoon I was in the law library thrilling at Maine's case law on easements by prescription when the court clerk told me Boothby wanted me to meet him in the park again. It took a while, but finally I found him by the pond. He looked grumpy, so I decided to try to lighten his mood.

"Hi, Judge." I pointed to the three Canada geese paddling across the pond. "You know how to tell a male Canada goose from a female Canada goose?"

"I don't know, Artie. How do you tell a male Canada goose from a female Canada goose?"

"Simple: the males are white and gray and black, whereas the females are black and gray and white."

Boothby raised his left eyebrow and looked at me, snorted with the tiniest smile, and shook his head.

"Artie," he said, "how the fuck did you ever pass the bar exam?"

Well, it worked, sort of. He watched the geese for a while, then pulled out his Pall Malls for his afternoon treat. His movements were unhurried, and he didn't say anything. Nor did I.

Finally: "I just learned—don't tell anyone—that Gibson Watts has taken leave to attend a four-week rehab program." He put a cigarette to his mouth and lit it.

I nodded. This would end Watts's judicial career and maybe bring him beyond the tipping point for reasonable doubt about murder.

"After dropping you off on Saturday," he said, "I called the State Police. I told their investigator everything we'd learned. And I've hardly gotten any sleep since." An inhale followed by a smoke ring. "What did you learn from this experience, Artie?"

"It's good to be suspicious of coincidences."

"Right. And it's good to exercise logic. Over the past few days you and I analyzed the evidence logically, so we probably solved the crime—in fact, an especially odious one because, if I may paraphrase Sherlock Holmes, when a judge goes wrong he's the worst of criminals. And we're just like Holmes, aren't we? We achieved a triumph of logic. And that's what we lawyers are trained for. So I should feel triumphant, shouldn't I? So why do I feel like dogshit?"

I couldn't resist; nobody was going to out-Conan-Doyle me: "Because," I said, "as Moriarty once told Holmes, the situation had become an impossible one. In other words, there was no satisfactory outcome."

"That's true." He flicked the ash off the end of his cigarette. "But that's not what's bothering me." Another inhale. "Now that we're in Sherlock Holmes mode, do you remember 'The Adventure of the Copper Beeches'?"

Well, he had me there. "No," I admitted.

"Then let me enlighten you with my favorite Holmesian quotation." He smiled at me unenthusiastically. "'Crime is common. Logic is rare. Therefore it is upon the logic rather than upon the crime that you should dwell.' What do you think of that, Artie?"

I didn't have a clue, so I shrugged.

"It's as fictitious as Holmes himself." He paused and looked toward the geese again. He was gathering himself.

"Ina was murdered, Artie. Murdered. The closest I'd ever been to murder was in the courtroom, where all I do is control the proceedings so the defendant gets a proper trial. A purely formal process, the less emotional the better. I'd never known someone who was murdered, let alone someone who did it, so I'd never experienced its horror personally. No triumph of logic, no intellectual grand slam, can tame my reaction to such hideousness. It can't lessen my outrage over Ina's death, or my sympathy for Emmy, or, for that matter, my anguish for Gibson, a great friend, and what he's become."

He turned to me. "So here's what I learned: that's how it *should* be. It's emotion that fulfills us, Artie, not intellect. Pure logic is sterile, an emotionless refuge for incomplete people. In the end, what's important isn't how capably we think, it's how capably we feel."

I realized something: "Sherlock Holmes was a cocaine addict, wasn't he?"

He stared at me for a moment. The eyebrows went up. "And a bachelor."

He dropped his cigarette on the ground and smushed it slowly with his shoe. When he'd finished he looked up and poked me in the arm. "Come on, I'll buy you lunch."

Longtime admirers of Sherlock Holmes and Dr. Watson, John Sheldon and Gayle Lynds are also partners in crime and life. They live together in rural Maine, where "A Triumph of Logic" is set. The story's hero, Judge Linwood Boothby, comes from John's experience as a Maine prosecutor, defense attorney, and judge, and a Visiting Scholar at the Harvard Law School. He's working on his first suspense novel featuring, of course, Judge Boothby and Artie Morey. The pianist in the story, Julia Austrian, is the heroine of Gayle's book *Mosaic*. Gayle is a *New York Times* bestselling spy thriller author. Her new novel is *The Book of Spies,* named one of the best thrillers of the year by *Library Journal.* She is cofounder (with David Morrell) of International Thriller Writers and is a member of the Association for Intelligence Officers.

Readers are invited to search this story for clues to a subplot: Dr. Watson has murdered Sherlock Holmes's love, Irene Adler, and his crime has been solved by the combined efforts of Sherlock's brother, Mycroft, and, of all people, Holmes's archenemy Moriarty.

The Last of
Sheila-Locke Holmes

Laura Lippman

Years later, when people tried to tease her about the summer
she turned eleven and opened her own detective agency, she
always changed the subject. People thought she was embarrassed because she wore a deerstalker cap with a sweatshirt and
utility belt and advertised her services under the name Sheila
Locke-Holmes, which was almost her real name anyway. She
was actually Sheila Locke-Weiner, but it was bad enough to be
that in real life. The only case she ever solved was the one about
her father's missing *Wall Street Journal* and she disbanded her
agency by summer's end.

Besides, it didn't begin with the deerstalker cap, despite what
her parents think they remember. She was already open for business when she found the cap, on her mother's side of the walk-in
closet, in a box full of odd things. Because her mother was Firmly
Against Clutter—a pronouncement she made often, usually to
Sheila's father, who was apparently on the side of clutter—this
unmarked box was particularly interesting to Sheila. It contained
the deerstalker cap, although she did not know to call it that; a
very faded orange T-shirt that said GO CLIMB A ROCK; a sky blue
wool cape with a red plaid lining; and a silver charm bracelet.

She took the box to her mother, who told Sheila that she really must learn to respect other people's privacy and property. "We talked about this. Remember, Sheila? You promised to do better."

"But I have to practice searching for things," Sheila said. "It's my job. May I have the T-shirt? It's cool, like the shirts people buy at Abercrombie, only even better because it's really old, not fake-old."

"Don't you want the cape, too? And the charm bracelet? I think those things are back in style as well."

Sheila maintained a polite silence. Her mother was not the kind of mother who was actually up-to-date on what was cool. She just thought she was. "I like the cap. It's like the one on that book that Daddy is always reading, the one he says he wants to work on if it ever becomes a film."

Her mother looked puzzled. "Sherlock Holmes?"

"No, the one about the stupid people who fought for the South in the Civil War."

"Stupid people?"

"The dunces."

"The dunces—oh, no, Sheila, that's not what the book is about. But, yes, the man in *A Confederacy of Dunces* wears a cap like this. And writes things down on Big Chief tablets, sort of like you've been doing."

Sheila could not let this pass. "I use black-and-white composition books like Harriet M. Welsch in *Harriet the Spy.*"

She took the cap, though, to be nice. Grown-ups thought they were always watching out for children's feelings, but Sheila believed it was the other way around just as often. Sheila was tender with her mother, who was sensitive in her own way, and indulgent of her father, who was dreamy and absentminded, usually lost inside whatever film he was editing. He had worked on some very famous films, but he worked in an office, no closer to the movie stars than Sheila was when she watched a movie on her computer, so no one at school thought what her father did was cool. Her mother was a lawyer, which definitely wasn't cool. It wasn't uncool. It just was.

Sheila sometimes went to her father's workplace, all the way downtown, on Canal Street. This usually happened on school holidays that her mother's law office didn't recognize as holidays or during the summer because of what her parents called child-care chaos. They had a lot of child-care chaos the summer that Sheila was eleven. On these days, Sheila and her father took the 1 train, which irritated her father because it was a local, but she liked all the extra stops. There were more people coming and going. She tried to make up a story about each person in the car. They tended to be sad stories.

Her father worked at a big Mac computer and it was always exciting—for the first half hour or so. Sheila would even start to think that maybe she would be a film editor. She enjoyed her father's lectures about the choices he had, how he sometimes had to find the film that the filmmaker failed to make, that it was like trying to cook a meal with only what was already in the pantry. But it was slow, tedious work. She eventually got bored, wandered to the lunchroom where the bagels were set out, or asked if there was a computer she could use, or played games on her father's phone. Most often, though, she pulled out a book, usually a mystery or something with magic.

"You're on a crime spree," her father joked. But she was not an indiscriminate reader of mystery books. She started with Encyclopedia Brown and tried very hard not to cheat by looking up the solutions in the back, but some of the clues were awfully small. (How was she supposed to know that Southerners called the Battle of Bull Run the Battle of Manassas?) She read books by Zilpha Keatley Snyder, which were sort of like mysteries, and *Harriet the Spy* and *The Long Secret,* the sequel, which she liked even better. Despite her deerstalker cap, she did not read Sherlock Holmes. Nor did she read Nancy Drew. Sheila *hated* Nancy Drew, who reminded her of a girl in her class and not just because she had red hair. Like Nancy Drew, Trista had two friends, Caitlin and Harmony, whose job seemed to be to advertise her wonderfulness. *Oh Trista,* they would moan, *you are so smart, you are so pretty, your clothes are the best.* They said this over and over again and somehow it all became true. When it wasn't, not in Sheila's opinion.

Sheila talked to her father about Trista and her friends because her father was interested in why people did the things they did, whereas her mother said such conversations were merely gossip, which she forbade, along with *Gossip Girl*. Her father said it was psychoanalysis and that gossip was fine, anyway, as long as it didn't become like the Gossip Game in *The Last of Sheila*, a film that he particularly liked. Sheila pretended to like it, too, because it seemed important to her father. He needed her to like *The Last of Sheila*, *Paths of Glory*, *McCabe & Mrs. Miller*, *The Magnificent Ambersons*, *Miller's Crossing*, and *Funny Bones*. So she did, and she never told him that *Funny Bones* was very scary for what was supposed to be a funny movie and that she didn't understand what anyone in *Miller's Crossing* was talking about, no matter how many times she watched it.

"It's like this Trista has her own PR firm," Sheila's father said.

"Puerto Rican?"

"What?"

"That's what they call the Sharks in *West Side Story*. PRs." Her father had shown her the film on television, telling her to look at the color of the sky as Tony walked through the alleys, singing of Maria. He was critical of the editing, although it had won an Oscar, according to the white-haired man, the one who talked after the movies on that channel. "Awards don't mean anything," her father told Sheila, yet his awards—none of them Oscars—were framed and hanging in his office.

"Oh, I meant public relations. You know, people who are hired to tell other people how great people are."

"Could I have someone like that? Instead of a babysitter? Could you hire someone to tell people I'm great?"

Her father laughed. But Sheila was serious. She had not had a good year in fifth grade and she was dreading sixth grade. She was not sure a vintage GO CLIMB A ROCK T-shirt could solve all her problems, although she hoped it would be a start. But how much easier it would be if someone would go to the school and tell everyone she was great. *Sheila the Great.* There was a book by that name, a Judy Blume, but it made her sad, because the Sheila in that book was so clearly not great.

However, Sheila did not realize how bad fifth grade had been until her parents received a call from the school, suggesting they come in for a conference before the new school year began. "Just to make sure we're all on the same page as far as Sheila's behavior is concerned." She knew this because she picked up the extension in her parents' bedroom and her father caught her.

"Eavesdroppers hear no good of themselves," he said.

"It's part of my job. I have to know things. That's how I found out what was happening to your newspaper. I heard the super complaining to the doorman that people were subscribing to newspapers and leaving them downstairs for days at a time, so he was just going to start throwing them away if people didn't come down and get them by nine."

"I'm down by nine."

Sheila gave her father a look. "Almost never. You leave for work at ten or eleven and, most nights, don't come home until after my bedtime."

He gave her a story by Saki, which apparently was related to what her mother drank from the little carafe at the sushi place. The story was about a cat, Tobermory, that learned to talk and told everyone's secrets and the people then plotted to poison him. They didn't get a chance—he was killed in a fight by another cat—but that didn't worry Sheila. She knew how to get around being poisoned. You just made sure that someone else tasted your food first. She also decided that if she ever was allowed to have a cat, she would name him Tobermory and call him Toby for short. She thought about changing the name of her stuffed white-and-gray tabby, which had been passed down to her by her mother, but it didn't seem right, changing someone's name when he was so old. Her mother was fifty, so her stuffed animals must be…almost fifty. Sheila had wanted to change her own name. Last year she had asked if she could be Sheila Locke instead of Locke-Weiner. She argued that a girl should have her mother's surname, that it was good for women's rights. Her mother said such a change would hurt her father's feelings, that he had managed to grow up with the same name and all Sheila had to do was remind people, politely, that it was pronounced *whiner.*

Like that was so much better.

After solving the case of her father's missing newspaper, Sheila felt she needed more work. She put up a small note, advertising her services, but the super scolded her and said such postings were not allowed in the hallways. Her family's building had lots of rules like that, almost more than school. For example, no delivery people were ever allowed past the lobby, which was part of the reason that all those newspapers ended up on a table and then got thrown away by the angry super.

People in the building were always stressing that this rule was very good for the kids because they could come and go throughout the building and their parents would know that they would never meet an outsider. But there weren't that many kids and Sheila wasn't friends with them anyway so she would have gladly traded that rule for having Chinese food brought right to the door with everybody already in pajamas. There was nothing cozier than eating Chinese food with her parents with everyone already in pajamas. But because someone had to go downstairs to fetch it, they never ended up doing it that way. Besides, they seldom ate dinner as a family because her father worked late. He said he couldn't help being a night owl. Sometimes her mother ate with Sheila; sometimes she drank a glass of wine while Sheila ate dinner by herself. They had a formal dining room, but it was rare for them to eat in there because it was so formal. They were not formal people, her father said. They all preferred the little breakfast bar in the kitchen, which was bright and cheerful.

But everyone else, guests and strangers, loved the dining room with its scary crimson walls and the chandelier that looked like something that might become a monster at night. *It's a beautiful apartment.* That's what everyone said, upon entering. *What a beautiful apartment.* They praised her parents' taste. They expressed envy for the bookshelves, for the tiny study that her parents shared, for the floors, which were parquet, which Sheila eventually figured out was not a type of margarine. But whenever her mother led someone down the hall with the bedrooms, she would say apologetically: "The bedrooms are kind of mean." Sheila felt this made their bedrooms sound much more exciting than they were. They were small and square with such limited closet space that the smallest one, in the middle, had been transformed into a walk-in closet/dressing room. Her father got one side, her mother got the other. Sheila remained stuck with the little stinky one in her room.

The summer she turned eleven, she began to spend a lot of time in the walk-in closet and that was how she found her mother's deerstalker cap.

"Were you popular?" she asked her mother, twirling the cap on her index finger. "When you were my age?"

"I was kind of in the middle. Not popular, but I had lots of friends."

"Were you pretty?" Her mother was one of the old mothers at her school and although there were quite a few old mothers, she was one of the old-old mothers.

"I didn't think so, but I was, actually. I had shiny hair and such a nice smile. When I see photographs of myself from that time, I could kick myself for not realizing how pretty I was. Don't make the same mistake, Sheila. Whatever age you are, you'll look back ten years and you would kill to look like that again."

"I don't want to look like I'm one years old. I was fat and I had no hair."

Her mother laughed. "Later, I mean. At thirty, a woman wants to look as she did at twenty, so on and so forth."

Sheila had shiny hair and she supposed her smile was nice, but that was not enough, not at her school. Things must have been simpler in her mother's times. Then again, she grew up in Ohio.

Sheila spent entire days in the closet and her babysitter didn't care. The summer babysitter was old, a woman who didn't want to go anywhere and had to visit the doctor a lot, which is why there was so much child-care chaos. Sheila found she could hear whatever her parents said in their bedroom, if she crept into the closet late at night after a bathroom run. They talked about her at times. It was neither good nor bad, so her father wasn't exactly right about eavesdroppers. Her parents were worried about school. They talked about bullies and clicks. Trista's name came up. Trista was a bully, for sure. She was the worst kind of bully, the kind that had other people do her bullying for her. Her hair was shiny, too. So shiny hair was part of being popular, but it wasn't the only thing that would make a person popular. In her composition book, Sheila began working on a list of things required for popularity and came up with:

1. Shiny hair
2. Nice smile (no braces. lip gloss?)
3. Good clothes
4. Being nice to most people but maybe mean to one person
5. To be continued

She continued to search the walk-in closet. Her father saved everything. Everything! Single cufflinks, keys to forgotten places and key rings with no keys, coasters, old business cards. He had a box of Sheila's baby clothes, nothing special, yet he kept them. It was embarrassing to see those stupid clothes, especially the Yankees onesie. Girls shouldn't wear baseball onesies.

But it was in her mother's jewelry box, the one that Sheila was never, ever supposed to touch, that Sheila found the heavy engraved card with her father's name and a woman's name and an address downtown, on Chambers Street. She did not know her father had been in business with a woman named Chloe Beezer. Sheila had never met Chloe Beezer, or heard her father speak of her. The card was pretty, cream-colored and on heavy paper, with a thin green line around their names. Beezer—what an ugly name. A person would have to be very pretty to survive such a name.

There was a photograph clipped to the back. Her father, with a mustache and longer hair, tilted his head toward a woman with blond hair. They were somewhere with palm trees, bright orange drinks in front of them, an orange sky behind them.

"Dad, who was Chloe Beezer?" she asked him on the 1 train, coming back from his office. It was the final week of her summer vacation and the train was hot and smelly.

"How do you know that name?" he asked her.

"I found a card, with her name on it and yours."

"Where?"

Why did she lie? It was instinctive. Instinctive lying was part of the reason that Sheila was in trouble at school. She took things. She lied about it. But how could one tell the truth about taking things? How could she explain to anyone that Trista's billfold, which had a pattern of gold swirls and caramel whorls that reminded Sheila of a blond brownie, had seemed magical to her. A *talisman,* a word she had found in books by E. Nesbit and Edward Eager, writers her father insisted were superior to J. K. Rowling. If she had a billfold like that, she would be powerful. And she was very considerate, which is probably why she got caught: she removed the money and the credit card and the other personal items and put them back in Trista's purse, taking only the billfold. Trista's family was rich-rich. A billfold meant nothing to her. She would have a new one in a month or two. Whereas Sheila's family was comfortable, according to her parents. Except in their dining room, which made them all uncomfortable.

She was not supposed to snoop. But she also was not supposed to go into her mother's jewelry box, which sat on the vanity that separated her father's cluttered side of the closet from her mother's neat, orderly side.

She decided to admit to a smaller crime.

"I found it in a box you had with cufflinks and other old stuff."

"You shouldn't be poking around in other people's things, Sheila."

"Why? Do you have secrets?"

"I have a reasonable expectation of privacy. Do you want me to go in your room and search through your things?"

"I wouldn't mind. I've hidden my composition book. You'll never find it." If there was a lesson to be learned from Harriet the

Spy, it was to maintain control over one's diary, not that Sheila's had anything juicy in it. "Who was Chloe Beezer?"

Her father sighed. "You know, I think, that I was married once before. Before your mother."

She did know that, in some vague way. It had just never been real to her.

"The card was something she made when we got married and moved in together. We sent it out to our friends. We didn't have a wedding, so we wanted our friends to know where we had set up house."

"Was she Beezer-Weiner?"

He laughed, as if this were a ridiculous question. "Chloe? No. No. She wanted no part of Weiner." He laughed again, but it was a different kind of laugh.

"Did she die?"

"No! What made you think that?"

"I don't know. Did you get divorced?"

"Yes."

"Why?"

"It's an odd thing, Sheila, but I don't really remember. We married quickly. Perhaps we didn't think it through. Are you ready for school next week? Don't we need to make a trip for school supplies?"

She knew her father was changing the subject. She let him.

But once at home, she had to know if her mother was aware of this extraordinary thing about her father. "Did you know Daddy was married before?" she asked her mother when she came home. "To someone named Chloe Beezer?"

"Yes," her mother said. "I did know that. You did, too. We told you, years ago."

"I might have known, but I guess I forgot."

Her mother looked at her father, who was reading his *Wall Street Journal* at the breakfast bar. Because he had to come home early with Sheila, they were going to have takeout from City Diner. "Why is this coming up now?"

Before Sheila could answer, her father said: "She found an old piece of paper in a box of my stuff. I told her she should respect our privacy more and she said she would. Right, Sheila?"

"Right," she said, although she didn't remember agreeing. "And a photograph. There was a photograph paper-clipped to it."

"Do you want sweet potato fries, Sheila?" her mother asked.

"Yes, with cinnamon sugar."

That night, as her mother put her to bed, Sheila was thinking about lying. She wasn't supposed to do it even when it made sense. But what about when someone else repeated one of her lies? Her father was the one who said she found the card in his boxes, but it had been in the jewelry box, which she was specifically forbidden to touch. Didn't her mother remember it was there? It was right on top, in clear view. She would see it tomorrow morning. Her mother went to that box every workday, pulling out golden chains and silver bangles. Her mother was very particular about her jewelry. She spent more time on selecting jewelry than she did on making up her face. "An old face needs an ornate frame," she said, laughing. It was an old face, even as mother's faces went. Sheila wished this wasn't so, but it was. She could see that her mother had been at least medium-pretty once, in the same way that she had been medium-popular. But she wasn't pretty now. It might help if she were. Trista's mother was pretty.

"Mom, I went into your jewelry box."

"I figured that out, Sheila. That's okay. It's good you're being honest about it with me. That's the first step. Telling the truth."

"Why did you have that card?"

"What?"

"The card, with the photograph."

"Oh, you know how hard it is to keep things in order sometimes."

Yes, on her father's side of the closet. But her mother's side was always neat, with shoe boxes with Polaroid pictures of the shoes inside and clothing hanging according to type and color. Everything was labeled and accounted for on her mother's side.

"Daddy thought it was in his boxes."

"It probably was."

"Do you snoop, too, Mom?"

She didn't answer right away. "I did. But it's wrong, Sheila. I don't do it anymore." She kissed her good night.

Two days later, Sheila disbanded Sheila Locke-Holmes. She left the deerstalker cap on a hook in her closet, put her almost-blank notebook down the trash chute, and took apart the utility belt that she had created in homage to Harriet the Spy. She told her mother that she would like to wear the charm bracelet, after all, that charm bracelets were popular again. She wore it to school the first day, along with her mother's T-shirt. Sixth grade was better than she thought it would be and she began to hope she might, one day, at least be medium-popular. Like her mother, she had shiny hair and a nice smile. Like her father, she was dreamy and absentminded, lost in her own world. There were worse ways to be.

Sheila's mother was not dreamy. She did not indulge conversations about why people did what they did. She did not stop movies and show Sheila the color of the sky or explain how Dr. Horrible could go down wearing one thing and rise up wearing another a second later. But she was sometimes right about things, as Sheila learned with each passing year. At thirty, Sheila would sigh with envy over her twenty-year-old face. At forty, she would look longingly back at thirty.

She would never yearn for that summer when she was eleven. Whenever someone brought up the time that she wore the deerstalker cap and started her own detective agency, she changed the subject but not because she was embarrassed. She could not bear to remember how sad her mother looked that night, when she confessed to snooping. She wanted to say to her mother: *He saves everything! It doesn't matter!* She wanted to ask her mother: *Why did you take the card? Did you want him to know you took it? Why did you put it somewhere you would have to see it every day?* She wanted to ask her father: *Why did you keep it? Do you miss Chloe Beezer? Aren't you happy that you married Mommy and had me? What was in those orange drinks?*

But all these things went unsaid. Which, to Sheila's way of thinking, was also a kind of lying, but the kind of lying of which grown-ups approved.

Laura Lippman purchased a deerstalker cap in London when she was fourteen and still owns it, although she will never be an expert in all things Sherlock Holmes and, in fact, made a really embarrassing error about Sir Arthur Conan Doyle's work in her Tess Monaghan series. A *New York Times* bestseller and winner of several awards for crime writing, past president of the Mystery Writers of America, she has published sixteen novels, a novella, and a collection of short stories. She lives in Baltimore and New Orleans.

The Adventure of the Concert Pianist

Margaret Maron

The bell rang at two o'clock precisely that early April afternoon and when my maid showed him into the parlour, my caller was, as I expected, Dr Watson. Although heavy mourning had somewhat gone out of style for men, he still wore a band of black velvet on the sleeve of his brown tweed jacket, which indicated to me that his grief for Mrs Watson had not fully abated despite the months that had passed.

"So good of you to come," I said.

"Not at all, Mrs Hudson." He handed Alice his hat and stick. "Indeed, I should have called upon you sooner. Your kind expression of sympathy upon my Mary's passing touched me immensely, and I—" He broke off and looked around the parlour with undisguised pleasure.

"So many changes in my life and yet nothing has changed here."

I smiled and did not correct him. Whilst he lodged here before his marriage, Dr Watson had taken tea with me several times. Mr Holmes had joined us here but once before his tragic end, yet I daresay *he* would have immediately noticed my new curtains. In most respects, a very noticing man, Mr Holmes.

Tea had been laid in anticipation of the visit, and when my guest was seated in the chair on the other side of the low table, I poured steaming cups for both of us and passed the scones, still warm from the oven.

"I suppose you have let his rooms to a new lodger?"

"Not as yet," I replied, offering him gooseberry jam.

"After all this time?" He was clearly surprised. "You have left your best rooms vacant for nearly three years?"

I nodded.

"Forgive my presumption, Mrs Hudson, but does this not represent a financial hardship?"

"Perhaps not as much as you may think, Doctor. Mr Holmes had paid through the end of his year before he left London. Moreover, after your marriage, he insisted on raising that rent to compensate for the damages."

"Damages?"

"Chemical burns on the carpet, dirty finger marks on the wallpaper from those street urchins who were up and down the staircase at least once a fortnight, and surely you have not forgotten how he used a pistol to inscribe the queen's initials in my beautiful oak overmantel?"

(To be quite honest, when I heard the shots, I was almost as upset as Mr Powell, a bookkeeper in the City, whose sitting room was directly overhead and who immediately gave notice.)

Smiling, the doctor spread jam onto a bite-sized piece of scone and assured me that he had not forgotten.

"I have twice written to Mr Mycroft Holmes to ask what should be done with his brother's personal effects. In response to my first letter, he came, looked at the mass of books and papers, and said he simply could not deal with it at the time. He claimed pressing affairs of government, but I suspect that a disinclination for physical exertion is the true reason he insisted I take his cheque for another year's rent."

"You say you wrote twice? Did he not reply the second time?"

"Indeed he did reply, Doctor. Another cheque for another year. I fear that he does not accept his brother's death and wishes everything to be left as it was in the event that Mr Holmes—*our* Mr Holmes—should ever return. I understand and I sympathise. I, too, mourn the loss, but turning my house into a memorial is more than I can bear. Mrs Jamison shivers every time she passes that door. You ask if this has been a financial hardship? No, but it has been an emotional hardship, sir."

Tears blurred my eyes and I fear my voice trembled.

Dr Watson patted my hand in manly consternation. "My dear Mrs Hudson! Shall I ring for your maid?"

"Please don't." I dabbed my eyes and apologised for my lack of control, but he waved my apology aside and made sure my cup still held tea, which he urged me to drink.

"You are quite right to be troubled. You should not be asked to continue this morbid arrangement. I confess that I, too, have had difficulty in accepting our friend's death, yet I have not been daily reminded of our loss as have you. Shall I speak to Mr Mycroft Holmes on your behalf?"

"Oh, Doctor!" I exclaimed. "If only you would! Surely he will listen to you, a man who held his brother in such esteem. I've had a new carpet laid and the overmantel repaired even though the cabinetmaker was hard-pressed to match the central panel. Were Mr Holmes's personal possessions removed, Alice and I could give the rooms a good cleaning and perhaps have a new lodger settled in by the first of May."

Assuring me he would call on Mr Mycroft Holmes the very next day, Dr Watson accepted a cream biscuit and the rest of the hour passed in pleasant reminiscences of the past.

"I do miss the adventuring," he said wistfully, when he rose to go. "I find that medicine is so much duller than detection that I have considered selling my practice and perhaps going to America."

I hardly knew what to say. We moved out into the vestibule, but before I could hand him his hat and cane, the bell rang long and loudly.

The fashionably dressed young woman who stood there with her hand still on the bell pull seemed startled to have the door opened so promptly.

I myself stared in surprise at the pale face beneath that pert straw boater. *"Elizabeth?"*

"Oh, Aunt, please help me! Mr Holmes—is he still with you? I must see him at once!"

Before I could gather my wits, she greeted my guest by name. "It's Dr Watson, isn't it? *Benissimo!* If you're still here, then surely Mr Holmes is, too? Someone wants to kill me."

"My dear girl!" Dr Watson gasped.

"Kill you?" I exclaimed.

When last I saw my niece, she was a child of twelve. My late brother had lived and worked in our native Edinburgh and while his widow, a woman of Italian parentage, settled his affairs there, she had sent Elizabeth to stay with me a month.

During that visit, Mr Holmes had several times required the services of his ragtag "Baker Street Irregulars," and Elizabeth had been so curious about their business with my lodger that even though he frightened her, she trailed them upstairs one evening and hid behind a chair to listen as they rendered their report. When he charged them with the task of following a certain lady, Elizabeth revealed herself and begged to be allowed to help.

The boys had sneered, but Mr Holmes considered her dainty dress and determined chin, then silenced them with a look. "You chaps have followed our quarry to a milliner's shop twice this past week, but we do not know what she does there nor to whom she speaks. This young lady can enter the shop without exciting suspicion. If your aunt will allow it, Miss Elizabeth, I myself will escort you to the shop's location and wait for you to come out."

I should not have agreed to such a plan for anyone except him, and Elizabeth carried it off admirably. Or so he said. I myself did not see the significance of the hats the lady had ordered, but Elizabeth's descriptions were enough to let him deduce that she planned a trip to Russia in the near future. With that information, Mr Holmes was able to bring the case to a satisfactory conclusion for his client.

Indeed, he was so pleased that he gave my niece half a crown and said he was sorry she could not remain in London to assist him should such a need ever arise again.

After my sister-in-law's return to Italy, I tried to keep in touch, but she was an indifferent correspondent. A year or two later, I received a letter that she planned to remarry. After that, nothing. My letters were returned unopened.

Now, suddenly, here was my niece, ten years older, a wedding band on her finger and fear in her eyes.

"You're not well," Dr Watson said, and indeed she was near swooning.

We helped her to the sofa in my parlour and I rang for Alice to bring smelling salts and a fresh pot of tea.

When she had somewhat recovered, Elizabeth explained that her mother had died six years earlier and that she had gone to live in Venice with her grandparents, who were itinerant musicians. She earned her keep by giving private English lessons. "My grandfather arranged for me to work with the opera company there, and I played piano for singers who were learning their roles. That's how I met William."

I took her hand in mine and touched the ring. "William is your husband? Is he English?"

She nodded. "William Breckenridge. He's a concert pianist and a composer as well. Perhaps you know his *Venetian Springtime*?"

I did not, but Dr Watson seemed impressed. "A suite of caprices, are they not? Mr Holmes had one of them transcribed for the violin. *The Bridge of Sighs*, if I'm not mistaken. By Jove! That's your husband?"

Elizabeth flushed with shy pride at his praise.

I was not deterred. "Surely he's not the one who wants to kill you?"

"No! Yes! Oh, Aunt, I can't be sure. That's why I hope Mr Holmes will help me."

Sadly, I had to tell her that the great detective was no more. "But what has happened to make you fear for your life?"

"This is William's first tour in England since our marriage two years ago. I hoped it would be a second honeymoon. Instead it's been a nightmare. He has become distant and almost cold to me. Normally, I wouldn't worry because he always withdraws into himself when he is composing and working out the musical problems he sets himself, but the difference this time is that I'm being poisoned."

I was shocked. "Poisoned? How?"

For a moment her old spirited nature flashed in her brown eyes. "If I knew that, do you not think I would avoid it? I can't even be sure he's the one doing it, yet who else could it be?"

She looked at us in despair.

"Tell us everything," Dr Watson said. "Perhaps we can help."

◇◇◇

"It began two days after we arrived in London," Elizabeth said. She spoke flawless English but an occasional word or phrase and a certain musical lilt in her inflections reflected her years in Italy. "William took rooms for us in a *pensione* where he has stayed before. It's popular with musicians. There's a grand piano he can use in the front parlour and it's near his copyist."

"Copyist?" I asked.

She nodded. "He met Mrs Manning on his first tour of England and has used her ever since. He sends her a manuscript and she returns it within the month. She's quick and accurate and quite reasonable. She even inserts his scribbled notations neatly. William makes such a mess of his practice scores that he likes to have a fresh set for his performances."

Dr Watson seemed surprised. "He doesn't play from memory?"

She smiled. "Of course he does, but he doesn't trust himself. Once he became so tangled in a Liszt concerto that he vowed never again to play in public without a score in front of him. I turn the pages for him and half the time he forgets to signal me to turn. If I did not follow carefully, he would be two pages ahead of me."

Dr Watson may have been interested in this musical digression, but I was not. "Please come to the point, Elizabeth," I said impatiently.

She sighed and complied.

Soon after settling into their lodgings, Mr Breckenridge had played at a reception for Lord P———.

"It is our custom to eat a light meal before a performance," Elizabeth said. "Nothing more than bread and butter and some consommé. Just the two of us alone so that William can approach the music in a serene state of mind. Afterwards, we have a late supper with some of the other musicians or with the patron who sponsored the concert.

"That evening, all was as usual, yet by the end of it, I found myself light-headed and short of breath. I ascribed it to our change of air and thought little of it, especially as I felt fine the next day. Two nights later, it happened again, and again I was better for the rest of the week. The pattern has continued. I am quite well until I share a light meal with him before he plays, then I become increasingly ill until I can barely get through a performance. Three nights ago, I could not rise from my chair and had to be helped from the stage. It was so bad I had to miss the last two performances. Only today was I well enough to seek Mr Holmes's help. Now you tell me I have come in vain."

She sank back on the sofa, defeated.

"Not necessarily, my dear," said Dr Watson. "I may lack his quick intelligence, but I learned much from close observation of his methods."

"And I have read all your published accounts of his remarkable deductions," I said. (I would not be so bold as to tell him that in one or two of those accounts Mr Holmes seemed to go around his elbow to reach his thumb whereas a woman would have gone directly across the palm, so to speak.) "Perhaps together we may help. Where do you take those light meals? Who prepares the food? Who serves it?"

We soon had a full account from her. Her maid brought up a tray to their rooms. As a rule, the tray held a small tureen of clear broth, a half loaf of bread and butter, and a pot of tea.

"Who serves?" asked Dr Watson as he made notes on a small pad he had taken from his pocket.

"I do," Elizabeth told him. "I dismiss the maid and ladle the soup from the tureen into identical bowls. I also cut and butter our bread. My husband pours the tea, then adds one lump of sugar to each cup, and a few drops of milk." She paused before continuing with a bitter look of shame. "It pains me to admit that when I asked him to fetch a handkerchief from our bedroom three nights ago, I switched our cups in case he should have slipped something into the tea without my seeing even though I had watched his every movement. That night, as I've told you, I was as sick as ever I have been. It was a long programme and I almost collapsed before it was finished."

Dr Watson looked up from his notes. "Your maid?"

"Maria was born in my grandparents' house. If she wishes me harm, why wait until we are in London? As for the manservant, Giorgio did resent me when William and I first married. A wife *does* bring change, does she not?"

"Indeed," Dr Watson murmured, and I felt he was remembering the changes his own marriage had wrought.

"He has since forgiven me, though, because he and Maria are to wed when we return to Venice. Nevertheless, my first suspicions fell there, yet how could either of them poison a tureen of soup, a loaf of bread, or a pot of tea without poisoning both of us? No, it has to be William. There's no one else. But how? And why?"

"Is there another woman?" I asked.

"No, Aunt. At least I don't think so. He's very handsome and many women have thrown themselves at him whether or not I am there, but I can honestly say he doesn't seem to notice. His family tell me that he was quite homely as a boy—all arms and gangly legs and interested only in his music. He still thinks of himself that way." A blush brought colour to her pale face. "I am the first woman to break through his reserve."

"Would he benefit by your death?" asked the doctor.

With a smile for me, Elizabeth shook her head. "As Aunt will tell you, sir, my father married for love, not money; and what money he did leave disappeared into her second marriage."

"When is your husband's next performance?"

"Tonight. We will sup together as usual and I will be there to assist him as long as I am able. It's a shorter programme than last time, so perhaps I can manage." She reached for her handbag. "I brought two passes. I hoped that you and Mr Holmes might agree to come and we could act as if the meeting were an accident."

"An excellent idea," I said briskly, plucking the tickets from her hand. I gave one to Dr Watson and retained the other for myself. "Even better would be if I joined you for your early meal."

She started to protest but I held up my hand to stop her. "While he may prefer to sup alone with you, I am your aunt whom you have not seen in years. We can go back to your lodgings together as if the accidental meeting occurred this afternoon."

"I *have* told William about you," she said slowly, "and we did plan to call on you during our stay here."

"Excellent," said Dr Watson. "Having met accidentally, it would be only natural that your aunt should wish to meet your husband immediately. I do not see how he can object and I doubt he will attempt anything with two pairs of eyes watching."

He questioned Elizabeth a second time about her exact symptoms, then asked if he might borrow the key to Mr Holmes's rooms. "I should like to consult his notes on poisons."

I handed it over most willingly.

At about six o'clock that very day, my niece and I arrived at a large and attractive house near the West End that had once been a nobleman's private residence. We entered to the sound of piano music and Elizabeth led me straight through the hall into a spacious room furnished with two pianos, a harpsichord, several music stands, and many small gilt chairs. Three of the chairs stood near the grand piano. A stout gentleman of middle age sat next to a younger woman. Their dress indicated wealth and taste. A second woman in a modest skirt and jacket with lilacs pinned to the collar of her shirtwaist occupied the chair slightly behind and to the left of the man who was playing so beautifully.

Upon seeing us enter, she rose and hastily gathered up the loose sheets of music on the piano.

Surprised, the pianist followed her eyes, then sprang to his feet. "Elizabeth! I was beginning to fear something had happened to you. You're not well enough to go out alone."

"Something *has* happened, William," she said. "This is my aunt whom I told you of, Mrs Hudson. We met in one of the shops and I insisted she come meet you at once."

"Splendid!"

Mr Breckenridge appeared to be eight or ten years older than Elizabeth. I was prepared for his handsome features, his height, and his long fingers; I was not prepared for the warmth of his smile and the genuine pleasure he seemed to take in meeting me, nor the pride with which he introduced my niece to the others.

"Sir Anthony Stockton, Lady Anne, allow me to present my wife and her aunt Mrs Hudson. Elizabeth, Sir Anthony wishes to commission a work to celebrate their wedding anniversary."

Although Sir Anthony said all the proper things, I noted that Lady Anne boldly looked my niece up and down and murmured, "Delighted, Mrs Breckenridge. You are a very lucky woman to have such a...*talented* husband."

Her smile gave a double meaning to the word *talented,* but the men seemed not to notice.

Elizabeth then introduced me to Mrs Sarah Manning, the copyist that she had so praised earlier. A soft-spoken woman of some thirty years, her manner was respectful and self-effacing. I later learned that she was the widow of a well-regarded piano teacher who now earned her living by turning drafts of manuscripts into finished scores and by providing fresh copies whenever needed. Lady Anne had been Mr Manning's student and the friendship had continued after his death.

As the Stocktons took their leave of Mr Breckenridge and he walked them to the door, Mrs Manning asked my niece, "Will you feel well enough to assist tonight?"

"I'm quite recovered now," Elizabeth said. "Thank you for taking my place these past two nights on such short notice." She gestured toward a portfolio that lay upon the piano. "Is that tonight's score?"

Mrs Manning nodded. "But Mr Breckenridge wanted me to make some small changes, so I'll bring it to the theatre."

Then she, too, took her leave and I went upstairs with Elizabeth and her husband. He seemed in exceptionally high spirits and soon explained the reason. "On our trip over, I suddenly realised that the coda of a new piece I've been working on captured the wrong mood and it has worried me immensely. This morning I finally saw what was needed."

"Is that what you were playing when we came in?" Elizabeth asked.

He frowned and did not answer.

"And why did Mrs Manning gather up the sheets and put them in her portfolio as if she did not wish me to see them?"

My new nephew, who had asked me to call him by his Christian name, turned to me as if to an old confidant and said, "Was she always this curious as a child, Aunt Hudson?"

I smiled and said nothing.

"Elizabeth has told me so much of her happy childhood in Scotland that I accepted an invitation to play in Edinburgh this summer."

"It will mark my first visit there since Father died," she said to me. "But, William, what has that to do with Mrs Manning's odd behaviour?"

"It's a Scottish rhapsody for you, my dearest. I planned to play it on our first evening there as your birthday surprise. Unfortunately, Lady Anne saw the draft I had left with Mrs Manning and immediately wanted it. It seems that Sir Anthony's fortune was built on Scottish wool and she thought it would be perfect for their grand anniversary celebration. They prevailed upon Mrs Manning to arrange today's meeting and begged me to play it for them. He offered me quite a handsome sum, but of course I refused."

"Oh, William!" said my niece, her face aglow with happiness.

◇◇◇

Shortly thereafter, her maid entered, bearing a tray that held a light meal for the three of us. After his earlier display of affection, I could not bring myself to believe that William Breckenridge would do anything to hurt her. Indeed, he told me of his concern for her health and made her promise she would consult a doctor should her dizziness return. Nevertheless, I watched his every movement but Elizabeth managed it so that his hands never came near her food or drink.

A carriage had been provided by the theatre management and upon our arrival, I saw Elizabeth draw from her pocket a small lozenge and discreetly put it in her mouth. Before we parted in the vestibule of the theatre, I managed to question her privately about it.

"When I first began to accompany singers back at La Fenice, my grandfather warned me to take extra care that my breath would never offend. As a result, I always take a piece of peppermint before a performance."

The odour of mint was quite distinct as I bent my ear to her lips. "Could that—?"

"No, dear Aunt, I threw away the drops I brought with me from Italy and purchased fresh ones here which I keep very close. They are much stronger than I prefer but they serve their purpose."

◇◇◇

When I slipped into my seat beside Dr Watson, I told him all that I had seen and observed. "Did you learn anything in your search of Mr Holmes's notes?"

"Indeed I did. From her symptoms—giddiness, headaches, and difficulty in breathing—I suspected cyanide poisoning and Holmes's notebook entries confirm it. Whatever the source, your niece must be ingesting very tiny amounts. A large dose would kill her instantly and would be quickly detected. It may be that the poisoner wishes to make it appear a natural illness."

As the lights went down, I drew his attention to a box overlooking the stage. "Sir Anthony and Lady Anne," I whispered. "I fear she has designs on Elizabeth's husband."

The first half of the program was devoted to a Beethoven string quartet. We remained in our seats during the interval and watched while Mrs Manning, in a charming yellow gown with a bouquet of primroses at her bosom, raised the piano lid, adjusted the bench, and placed sheets of music on the rack. A few minutes later, I saw her enter Sir Anthony's box and take a seat beside Lady Anne. According to the programme, the evening was to end with Schubert's "Trout" quintet.

I'm sure it was delightful. Certainly the audience applauded enthusiastically, as did Dr Watson, but all my attention was for Elizabeth, who sat in a straight chair behind and to the left of her husband and followed the notes on the pages before him. At regular intervals, she rose unobtrusively and, using her left hand so as not to obstruct his sight, she quickly turned a page, then sat down again.

Halfway through the music, I touched Dr Watson's sleeve and whispered, "Watch my niece."

A moment later, his eyes widened and I heard an almost inaudible "By Jove!"

It seemed to both of us that she grew steadily weaker through the playing of the concerto and after turning the last page, she quitted the stage with unsteady steps. As soon as the lights came up again, we hurried to the dressing room where we found Elizabeth lying back in a chair, her eyes closed and her mouth open as she laboured to breathe. Mr Breckenridge knelt beside her with a cold cloth in one hand and a glass of water in the other. Distraught, he looked up at me and said, "She's had another attack."

I quickly introduced Dr Watson, who took her pulse and said, "Can you hear me, Miss Elizabeth?"

She nodded weakly.

"Do you feel as if ice water is running through your veins?"

Her eyes flew open. "Yes! And my chest! It feels as if it's bound by iron bands."

"She needs fresh air," Dr Watson said. "Now."

My nephew gathered her up in his strong arms and strode down the hall through an outer door into an enclosed courtyard with a stone bench. He held her until her breathing slowed to normal and she could sit unaided.

William seemed more worried than ever and asked if Dr Watson could diagnose Elizabeth's illness.

Before he could answer, Sir Anthony, followed by Lady Anne and Mrs Manning, pushed through the small group of musicians and their friends who had gathered in concern. "I know an excellent doctor in Harley Street, Breckenridge. Allow me to send for him."

Elizabeth tried to protest, but even Dr Watson urged her to submit to a thorough examination. It was agreed that he would come to their rooms next morning and join Sir Anthony's doctor for a consultation.

With the immediate crisis past, we went back inside and talk turned to the mundane. William was warmly complimented on his performance and Dr Watson asked if he might borrow the score that Mrs Manning had collected from the piano rack. "I am no musician but there's a passage in the first movement that I should like to examine, if I may."

"Let me give you a fresh copy, sir," said Mrs Manning, who started to open a leather portfolio.

"No need," he assured her.

Despite her protests, he insisted. "This one will do nicely for my purpose. I'll return it when I come tomorrow morning."

Carriages were called for and Dr Watson escorted me back to Baker Street, where he retired to Mr Holmes's old rooms. I had the maid put fresh linens on one of the beds and sent up a supper tray. It was almost like old times.

Next morning, I was up and out at daybreak, yet I managed to be seated by my niece's side when Dr Watson and Sir Ernest Fowler, the noted physician, arrived at ten o'clock.

After a thorough examination, the two left the bedroom to confer.

"What is it?" William asked anxiously when they returned. "Will she recover?"

"Thanks to Dr Watson," Sir Ernest said. "Mrs Breckenridge, I'm told you suspect someone is trying to poison you?"

William looked thunderstruck when she nodded. "Poison?"

"Without Dr Watson's help, sir, your wife would surely have died by the end of the month."

"But how?" she cried.

"And who?" William demanded. "Why?"

"The how and the who I can tell you," said Dr Watson. "The why will have to come from the poisoner's own lips."

He drew the Schubert score from his bag, along with a small glass vial. The score was sadly the worse for wear. The upper corners had been clipped off.

"Last night, I soaked the corners in water, then added iron sulfate to the fusion." He held the glass vial up to the light. The liquid inside was a rich, dark blue. "Prussian blue," he said.

"A positive test for cyanide," Sir Ernest said approvingly. "Well done, Dr Watson!"

Elizabeth and William both seemed stunned. "Cyanide on the corners of the music?"

"You did not become ill from any food you ate," Dr Watson told her. "It came from the music, carried to your mouth on your own fingers. Each time you rose to turn a page for your husband, I observed that you touched your thumb and index finger to your tongue to moisten your fingers. The corners of the score had been painted with a thin film of cyanide. The bitterness you might have noticed was masked by the strong peppermint drops you habitually use before and during a concert."

"Mrs Manning!" William exclaimed. "Why?"

"That is something you can ask her yourself when the police have arrested her," said Dr Watson.

"She will not be there," I said quietly. "She has fled the country."

My niece was bewildered. "Aunt?"

"I did not think you and William would welcome the scandal of an arrest and a sensational trial, so I went to Mrs Manning this morning and found her just as she was leaving for Victoria Station. When Dr Watson insisted on taking the Schubert score, she realised that all was over and she sails for Canada this very evening," I said. "Mrs Manning confessed to me that she was much attracted to you when you first met her, William. You were kind to her and she felt the attraction was mutual. When you returned with a bride, she thought that if Elizabeth should sicken and die, you might turn your attention to her."

"Never!" he said sturdily.

"She realises now the hopelessness of that dream," I told them, "and she begged me to beseech your forgiveness."

The April day was unusually mild and after leaving my niece in the arms of her husband, Dr Watson and I decided to walk a few blocks before hailing a cab. He expostulated on my impulsive act, but I would not admit that I had been wrong to allow Mrs Manning to flee. Scandal had been averted, William's reputation would continue to grow, and Elizabeth was no longer in danger. What was to be gained by prosecuting that unhappy woman?

As we crossed the street to a cab stand near Piccadilly Circus, a newsboy was shouting the latest headlines of a mysterious death in Park Lane. After an evening of cards at the Bagatelle Club, a young nobleman had been shot dead inside a locked room.

"The very sort of puzzle that would have intrigued Holmes," Dr Watson sighed wistfully as he handed me into the hackney.

With a heart that was equally sad, I reminded him of his promise to speak to Mr Mycroft Holmes and he agreed to go that very day.

We parted at my doorstep and I fumbled in my handbag for my house key while a thousand bittersweet memories whirled through my head as I admitted to myself the true reason I had gone to warn Mrs Manning. I had seen the flash in her eye when

Lady Anne spoke so boldly to Elizabeth and I had felt a certain kinship. As a young widow, I too had once yearned for what I could not attain.

For what now could never be attained.

Alice met me in the vestibule. "A rather strange old gentleman has been waiting ever so long to see you," she whispered.

Through the open doorway, I saw an elderly deformed man with a curved back and old-fashioned white side-whiskers. Upon seeing me, he rose to his feet with unexpected ease, straightened his back, and gave a familiar smile.

And then I fainted.

Margaret Maron is the author of twenty-seven novels and two collections of short stories. Winner of several major American awards for mysteries, she has received the North Carolina Award for Literature, her native state's highest civilian honor. Her works are on the reading lists of various courses in contemporary Southern literature and have been translated into seventeen languages. She has served as national president of Sisters in Crime, the American Crime Writers League, and Mystery Writers of America. She lives with her husband on their century farm near Raleigh, North Carolina. Her brother received a collection of Sherlock Holmes stories one Christmas, but she was the one who read it cover to cover. Despite her upbringing as a daughter of the colloquial South, Maron was captivated by the formal language of nineteenth-century London.

Dr. Watson provides an account of the events that occurred shortly after Mrs. Hudson's fainting spell in "The Empty House," published in the *Strand* (1903) and collected in *The Return of Sherlock Holmes*.

The Shadow Not Cast

Lionel Chetwynd

The Rabbi sat in the main sanctuary of his synagogue and marveled at the understated beauty, a reminder of its nineteenth-century origin as Washington's first place of Jewish worship. It was now, late at night, he loved it most: soft indirect light rimming the high ceiling, the shimmering backlit curtain of the Ark and its sacred Torahs, the eternal flame flickering. He fixed his eyes on the deep blue stained-glass window whose Star of David had been with the synagogue from its very beginning more than a century and a half ago. Tears welled in his eyes. He buried his head in his hands.

Perhaps he heard the stranger enter at the rear of the sanctuary, but if so, he gave no indication, only his hunched shoulders betraying his weeping. The man proceeded down the center aisle, coming to a definite halt at the Rabbi's front pew. The Rabbi spoke without turning.

"You're not unexpected," he said, only then allowing his eyes to flicker to the stranger. At the sight of the visitor his eyes widened, his expression one of great shock. "You!" he half-whispered. "You came yourself!" The visitor said nothing. And so the Rabbi stood and walked to the aisle. "I considered your offer. But my mind is set. I must do as my conscience dictates. You might not understand."

The visitor showed no emotion. Abruptly, he reached out, grabbed the Rabbi, and spun him around—snapping his neck in a single motion, the crack of the spine echoing through the empty sanctuary.

Letting the Rabbi crumple to the floor, he strode to the Ark, opened it to reveal the Torahs dressed in fine silver breastplates and scroll handle sleeves. Taking a Hefty bag from his coat pocket he opened it roughly, and went swiftly and efficiently about collecting the silver.

Sergeant-Major Robert Jackson, his back to his students, stared out the seminar room window at the perfectly kept green expanse of the U.S. Army's Carlisle Barracks. He approved of the order, the regularity. Even so, he could not deny the familiar feeling welling up inside him: boredom. Not that he didn't like teaching at the Army War College; on the contrary, it was an honor to be here, where the Army boasted "tomorrow's senior leaders are trained." It was simply that he could only deal with so much theory. He was a soldier, and a good one, and so always listened for the sound of the guns. Fighting back the ennui, he turned to his class and looked out at the dozen or so captains, sprinkled with two or three lieutenants and one major. Ramrod straight, hair short, khaki uniform unwrinkled, razor-sharp creases, shoes spit-polished, it was impossible to know quite how old he was; perhaps fifty, but too fit to pigeonhole. He wore no ribbons on this day, only jump-master's wings above his left pocket, Canadian paratrooper wings above the right. On his left shoulder was the screaming eagle patch of the 101st Airborne and on his right the Army College insignia. Now, even as he crossed the short distance to the head of the table, he was every inch the soldier's soldier. A man who might be soft-spoken, but whose every word was authoritative.

"An officer in the field observing an enemy position applies five criteria: size, shape, shadow, color, and movement. These same elements should be used by a senior officer in any command situation where he is confronted by gaps in his knowledge." He picked up the remote control for the oversized television monitor on the wall. "You are now, let us say, majors of infantry. Use those five elements to call down artillery on an advancing enemy you know is there, but cannot see."

With a click of the remote, the monitor sprang to life. It showed a large wooded hillside, that seemed uniform, keeping whoever or whatever it concealed safe from sight. A lieutenant barked out, "Shape!" Jackson froze the frame and the lieutenant continued, "Upper left quadrant, eleven o'clock." The rest of the class studied the picture; sure enough, trees in that area seemed very boxy. Jackson restarted the image and almost immediately a tank emerged. He clicked again and the hillside imagery reset.

This time, a major called, "Color, lower left, seven o'clock!" Indeed, those trees were just a bit too green, and once the film restarted an artillery piece fired, revealing its camouflage. Jackson again reset and now the answers came quickly.

"Size! Top left, ten o'clock!" offered a triumphant lieutenant who had spotted a pine tree simply too perfect, exposed by a zoom as a radio tower.

The next reset, a captain offered, "Movement, midfield." A beat for them to realize the bushes there did move differently; quickly, insurgents emerged.

Jackson reset the image but no one had anything to offer. He let it run until, with a sigh, he stopped it. "Problem?" he asked. They seemed cowed, embarrassed—except for the class's only woman, an attractive captain of perhaps thirty, wearing the insignia of the Judge Advocate General's Corps. She made firm eye contact with Jackson.

"The fifth element is shadow, but this field is overcast, no shadows possible."

Jackson returned the steady eye contact. "Are you sure, Captain Snow?"

"As sure as I dare be, Sarn't-Major."

Jackson stood, returned to the window. It irritated him that she was in his class. He did not deceive himself by thinking it was an accident; she must have known she'd see him every day. Without turning, he answered with an authority intended to remind her who was in charge. "Shadow: verb, transitive. Middle English. From Old English *sceaduwe,* oblique case of *sceadu.* But it can be intransitive. Not the shadow you cast, Captain Snow, but the shadow you don't. Upper left, please, ten o'clock. That copse reflects nothing at all."

Still without turning, he clicked the remote and the frame zoomed into a comparatively dull patch of foliage, almost a matte finish. He let the zoom continue, finally revealing camouflage net disguising a command post. Another click and the image died. He turned and stared at her.

"Once again, Captain Snow, I remind you the good officer should always dare to be sure but not too sure. So, let us repeat the elements of observation."

His students almost shouted in perfect unison, "Size! Shape! Shadow! Color! Movement!" He was satisfied. Until the silence was broken. By Captain Maggie Snow.

"Sound!"

The sudden hushed silence left no doubt she had crossed a boundary, her classmates avoiding even looking at her. Flustered, it was clear she wished she could call it back. She looked down at the table, avoiding the ever-placid Jackson who simply smiled slightly.

"I beg your pardon, ma'am?"

Her words came with difficulty. "I, er, just thought…in the modern world…where electronic communications are part of the battlefield…we might add sound. You know…heavy electronics tend to drive birds away, send animal life to ground. A silent forest is probably a dangerous one." She waited for an awkward silence before adding uncomfortably, "Just a thought, Sarn't-Major."

"I shall ask the Army to consider your thought for a revised field manual, Captain. But not until you've all had your breakfast." He came stiffly to attention. "Gentlemen. Ma'am."

Relieved, they stood. He saluted smartly, waiting for their return salute before exiting and leaving Maggie to her classmates' unenvious eyes.

Zakaria was tired, and even though he knew he was fortunate to be employed as the synagogue's janitor, he had to work constantly at blocking out thoughts of where life had led him, and what might have been. America was fine but it wasn't home and he missed the smells and excitement of the Soukh. At least the job was easy, nobody bothered him, and it was not unusual for him to begin work this late in the midmorning. And there were those special benefits; they were what kept him on the job. Pushing them from his mind, he trudged to the sanctuary, mop and broom in hand, opened the door wearily, and entered.

Something was wrong; the Ark was open. A deep dread clutched his stomach. As he slowly walked toward it, he caught a whiff of the familiar and unwelcome smell of danger, menace— just as he saw the rabbi. Dropping his mop and broom, he ran to the crumpled body and knelt, checking for a neck pulse with the efficiency of a man who has done this many times before. He knew there would be no pulse to be found. Shaking his head from side to side in grief, he reached for his cell phone, but then stopped. A frown crossed his face. Nodding to himself, he pocketed his cell phone, stood, scooped up his cleaning utensils, and exited, closing the sanctuary doors behind him.

◇◇◇

Sergeant-Major Jackson was irritated. He had been pleasantly at ease in his favorite armchair, the *Meditations* of Marcus Aurelius open to a favorite passage, the single ice cube in the glass of Talisker Isle of Skye whisky almost dissolved to where he felt confident the proper aromas and textures were now released in this favored malt, his music system ready for *The Pipes and Drums of the Black Watch (Royal Highland Regiment) of Canada* to play "The Road to the Isles"—when his doorbell had roused him from his solitude. The invader was none other than Captain Maggie Snow, she of the certain answer to all questions. She had allegedly come to apologize for conduct unbecoming in the afternoon seminar and he had not the temerity to refuse an officer—any officer—entry. But she was a woman, and he therefore insisted the front door of his modest on-base cottage remain open throughout her stay, and they keep in its line of vision.

As she entered his spare, minimalist home, he became uncharacteristically self-conscious; the one personal item on display was a photograph. No ordinary thing, it was he and his late wife, Bonny, on holiday. With Maggie's parents. The two couples had been the best of friends, always together until the evil hand struck that dreadful afternoon. As quickly as that flooded his mind, he dismissed it, resolving to confront her with his suspicion she had joined his class only because of the personal connection. She began by explaining that her purpose for coming was to apologize. He shook his head.

"No. You came for absolution."

"If you prefer," she conceded.

"I cannot give you that."

"Why not?"

"Because you outrank me. You are an officer. Ma'am."

That stung her. "You once called me Maggie."

"And shall again. On family or personal occasions. I daresay this is neither."

When she asked why he so resented her, he replied he frankly doubted her motives for taking his class. JAG officers were lawyers, and while he might be a famed criminal investigator, this course was Field Command Training. As a lawyer, she would never hold a Line Command. So why take a course meant for true soldiers? She had countered that in the modern world officers did not command tactical engagement. Lawyers did.

He bitterly admitted to himself that, in this politically correct era he so despised, she was right. Division Commanders—*generals, for goodness' sake*—had to be sure operations complied with law as it *might* be applied in *civilian courts*! Idiocy! There was a Uniform Code of Military Justice, an excellent document that had kept the Army an honest force, not some third world street gang in uniforms, thank you very much!

But that, of course, reinforced her point. He felt obliged to listen a while longer.

Captain Eric Turner of the District of Columbia Metropolitan Police Department Homicide Division stood at the rear of the sanctuary soaking in the rich tapestry of color and symbolism, only to be accosted by his too-eager, relentlessly bright and cheerful assistant, Baxter.

"Didn't expect you, Cap'n. Seems a routine murder-robbery."

Turner wanted to scream *When did murder become routine?* but instead answered in his favored monotone. "It's not the crime, it's the venue. I'm fond of this building. Where's the deceased?"

Baxter led him to the body, cheerfully reporting the medical examiner was delayed in traffic but would arrive any moment. Turner had no sooner set eyes upon the twisted, slumped corpse than a familiar voice grated on his nerves.

"So, it's true. You do have a dead rabbi."

Turner sighed, turned to face his opposite number at the FBI regional. "Yeah, it sure looks like a corpse, Hamstein. But the rabbi part would be speculation. In either event, what's it matter to you?"

FBI Special Agent Hamstein's grin dripped cool superiority. "Well, the dear departed was a cleric of interest to us."

"Then I give you jurisdiction. With quiet joy."

"Don't know if I want it. Depends on whether it really is connected to the other murder."

"Other murder?" Turner hated to be outfoxed by the FBI. The District was his turf, he should know first.

"Mmmm." Hamstein grinned. "Across town. A real stumper. They're connected. I know how, but have no idea why."

Turner understood. "So if I take this and fail, you become the white knight riding in to save the day. Might as well hand it over to you immediately."

Hamstein's grin evaporated. "It's only going to come back to you. Because I'm stumped. Fact is, I can only think of one man who might—might—understand it."

"And you can't call him unless you federalize it. Take jurisdiction."

Hamstein nodded.

◇◇◇

Still in view of the open door, the Sergeant-Major was attempt-ing—without much luck—to explain to Maggie why she would never make a good officer without hands-on, in-the-field experi-ence. JAGs were desk jockeys. Necessary, of course, but dwellers in a land of theory. She, of course, maintained she was more than capable of understanding the field without that experience. And then the phone rang.

Jackson listened for a moment as he stared at Maggie. "Be delighted to be of service, Captain. I can be there in an hour. But...would you object if I brought an apprentice associate with me? Good. See you soon."

He clicked off his cell phone, smiled tightly at Maggie. He would finally make his point. "If you're free, we can put the value of field experience to the test."

"As an 'apprentice associate,'" she asked, her horror at the title plain.

"Yes. A generous bit of nomenclature, I'll agree. Let's see if you can merit it."

She paused only a moment before following him out the door.

The officious uniformed policeman held his hand up as Jackson and Snow approached, assuming that would stop them. It did not. Jackson simply shook the man's hand and entered the crime scene, a spare, sparse apartment in the quickly gentrifying area of Columbia Heights.

"Hey! You can't go in there!"

"We were invited," Jackson threw over his shoulder.

"Who by?"

Jackson stopped, turned, and faced the fresh-faced patrolman. "I believe that's 'By whom?'"

Before it escalated further, both Hamstein and Turner appeared.

"By me," they said in unison. Maggie sensed that Jackson enjoyed the attention and the attempt by both to curry favor.

"Meet my apprentice assistant: Snow, Margaret, Cap'n, JAG."

He strolled in, looked carefully around, addressed Maggie. "Notice the decor. High-tech, one might say. Hence charmless. One bookcase, only technical manuals and financial renderings. A bed. A finely equipped computer corner, replete with all the bells and whistles. And a corpse, male, white, thirties, who might seem to have fallen asleep at his monster computer save for the neat bullet hole in the middle of his forehead oozing a small amount of blood."

"The mortal remains of Gerry Rivers." Before Hamstein could continue, Jackson quickly inserted, "A financial reporter, no doubt."

Turner rolled his eyes. "And we know this because?"

"The bookcase. The only nontechnical editions are financial. Macroeconomics to judge by the titles. If they were micro, he might be a trader. But as it is, he must earn his living—modest, this home suggests—as a correspondent on such things. But why would that interest you, Special Agent?"

"Because last night a Rabbi Burman was also murdered. One we've had our eyes on regarding the movement of funds from here to organizations in the Middle East."

"Some of whom begin and end their meetings with 'Death to America'?"

"Now how in hell do you know that from what's here?" Hamstein sputtered.

"At times, Special Agent, a cigar is simply a cigar." Hamstein didn't get it. Jackson continued patiently, "Well, if he was supporting the Israeli Boy Scouts you'd hardly be concerned, now would you?" Then, to save Hamstein further embarrassment, he quickly added, "And I suppose the rabbi was dispatched by a sharp neck snap."

"How on earth—?" Turner sputtered.

"Because that would be the cause of death of our computer fiend, here. Yes, yes, I know it appears to be an execution, one shot to the forehead, but that would have produced much more blood. And it wouldn't have left his neck in that curious position."

"Yes," one of them mumbled. "We'd figured that out. Waiting for the ME to confirm."

"What else can you tell me of this man?"

"Found this just inches from his hand." Turner offered him a cell phone turned to the call log.

Jackson studied it. "Only five calls in four days. One number repeats."

"Ran a check," said Hamstein. "None other than Gorgi Pelachi."

The Sergeant-Major ran that over in his mind. Pelachi was a very powerful man, far up the food chain and something of a man of mystery. Emerging from the collapse of the Soviet Union as one of the most powerful oligarchs, he had a fortune that beggared the imagination. The source of the wealth was shrouded; some said he was a KGB general who amassed it in bribes, others that he'd profited under the Communist regime by fencing property confiscated from "enemies of the state" before they were shipped east of the Urals—Siberia. Others claimed both. But he had burst onto the scene with a spectacular hedge in Spanish currency that brought down their central bank—a trick he'd repeat on the emerging new states of Central Europe. Perhaps because of the rumors and innuendo, he shied away from the limelight. And that would include minor financial writers.

"Can you get me in to see him?" Jackson requested.

Hamstein cringed. "I'd rather not. Tick him off and he can go way over my boss's boss's head."

"I'll be polite. On my honor."

Hamstein nodded in resignation. "I'll see what I can do. Unless you can solve this on the spot."

Jackson admonished, "That, as well you know, would require at least a shred to go on."

Turner handed him a small Ziploc bag. In it was a business card: RABBI ELIEZAR BURMAN—EXECUTIVE DIRECTOR, THE RECONCILIATION PROJECT. Jackson turned it over. On the other side there was a neat column of citations:

ZEPHANIAH:	CHAPS. 3–4
EXODUS:	1:4
LEVITICUS:	4:9
JONAH:	2:3

As Jackson returned it to Turner, the detective assured him, "We've got our best men working on it now. Top scholars."

Jackson shook his head. "They'll find nothing. These citations are random." He approached the computer. "May we?"

Turner offered him a pair of latex gloves. "Knock yourself out." Jackson indicated the gloves should be given to Maggie.

Surprised, she took them. "What am I looking for?" she asked.

"Size, shape, shadow, color, movement," he replied.

She puzzled, finally shaking her head, stumped. "Not size… nor shadow…" She turned to him. "Could it be shape?"

"Last chance," he admonished her. "The shadow not cast. Look at the quotes. Study the room."

She knew this was the moment she would rise to his trust or be banished. She took her time, studied the room carefully. The shadow not cast. Intransitive. And then she spied a slight opening, a glimmer of light. She dashed to the computer, brought up "History," entered "Leviticus."

"Why that one?" he asked.

"Because Leviticus can have only one meaning. Unlike Exodus, Jonah, or even the proper name, Zephaniah. It would be used only in a Bible search." She hit "Return." A nanosecond and the screen reported NO RECENT SEARCHES FOR LEVITICUS.

"Okay," groused Hamstein. "What did we lesser mortals miss?"

"Predictably, the obvious. Maggie?"

The officer in her emerged. "Look around, gentlemen. No books, let alone a Bible. And no Web searches for one. So the biblical connection is lateral, not direct."

"Besides," added Jackson drily, "if you knew your scripture, you'd know these were random."

He sat at the desk, took a fresh piece of paper, and, never taking his eyes off the list, quickly filled the new sheet with a column, never looking, almost an autowriter. First, was Zephaniah: chaps. 3–4. Jackson counted three letters in, entered *p* and then the fourth letter, *h*. He moved quickly to Exodus: 1:4, producing *e* and *d*, then *i* and *s* from Leviticus: 4:9, and finally *o* and *n* from Jonah: 2:3. Jackson stared at the result: P-H-E-D-I-S-O-N.

The others gathered around him, leaned over his shoulder.

"Almost something," murmured Hamstein. "A name?"

"Unlikely," replied Jackson. "The consonant blend of *ph,* derived from the Vedic, carried into English by Hellenistic—" He stopped, smiled. "Of course! Zephaniah—a minor prophet, but a very interesting one, by the way—is presented with a dash rather than a colon as are the others." He struck out the *ph* with a single line, replaced it with *f.* F-E-D-I-S-O-N.

Turner was exultant. "Brilliant!" He snapped at Baxter, "Get on this. Check for an F. Edison. Every database."

"I'm also on it!" said Hamstein, already heading for the door.

The Sergeant-Major called after them: "I may wish to investigate further."

Turner's words faded as he hurried away. "Baxter! Give him—them—whatever they want!" And Jackson and Maggie were alone save for the police security.

"That *was* brilliant," conceded Maggie. "Once they find this Mr. Edison—" She stopped, added carefully, "If, in fact, that *is* the name of someone involved."

"I see you're beginning to learn already." He smiled as he strolled out in leisurely fashion. Maggie followed.

"Ah, yes. Detective Baxter told us to expect you."

Sergeant-Major Jackson turned his steady gaze from the still-open Ark to a pleasantly plump woman trying to smile despite a redness in her eyes that betrayed recent lengthy weeping.

"I'm Freyda Simon. Rabbi Burman's assistant." She also stared at the Ark. "This is a terrible thing."

"It certainly is. You have our heartfelt condolences." He indicated the Ark. "May I?"

"Of course. Whatever you need. But...if you don't mind, I'll wait for you in the office. At the end of the hall."

"By all means." As she turned to go, he added, "And the custodian? A Mr. Zakaria?"

"I'll have him join us."

Jackson and Maggie approached the Ark. The six Torah scrolls were undisturbed, though all but two had been stripped of their silver; the two remaining breastplates, both of striking modern design, glittered in the overhead light. The Sergeant-Major stood very still, only his eyes moving, wandering over everything. Then he noticed a tiny gleam on the carpet. He knelt, examined it: a small shred of heavy-duty brown plastic. He pocketed it, stood, smiled at Maggie.

"Our miscreant made serious errors. At least two. Can you spot any?" She stared, thought hard. But then, resigned, she shook her head. He nodded. "Don't be hard on yourself. They're small errors—important, but small. Only years in the field would sensitize you to their obviousness. Come. We are close to important facts."

She had to half-run to keep up with his fast stride to the office. It was small, neat despite piles of papers and books, and already crowded with both Freyda and Zakaria waiting.

Freyda handed him photographs of the stolen silver. "Perhaps this can help?"

"No doubt," he replied.

"Zakaria, can we provide the gentleman with an envelope?"

The janitor nodded, found one on a shelf, and in this small office needed only to stretch his arm out to offer it to Jackson. As he did so, something caught the Sergeant-Major's eye: the sleeve of the man's coveralls had naturally run up his extended arm, exposing his wrist. Seeing Jackson's quick reaction, Zakaria quickly moved to pull the sleeve down.

Jackson smiled. "You would be the custodian, I expect."

"Yes, yes. Zakaria is how I am called."

"Ah. Captain Turner informs me you're of Lebanese extraction."

"Oh, yes. But Christian, Maronite Christian."

Jackson thrust his hand out. "Sergeant-Major Robert Jackson."

Zakaria squirmed uncomfortably. But realizing the others in the room were watching him, he reached out to shake Jackson's hand, trying to keep his arm bent at the elbow. Jackson grasped the calloused workingman's hand, shook it vigorously while pulling it toward him—and bending it ever so slightly. Jackson glanced down; only he could see it: a small tattoo of a blue Maltese cross. As if it had gone unnoticed, he turned back to Freyda.

"Ma'am. If I may. Precisely what is the Reconciliation Project?"

"Ah. The RP was Rabbi Burman's passion, his life's work. We fund schools in the Middle East, nonsectarian schools, schools where Moslem, Arab, and Jewish Israeli children can learn together, side by side, come to know one another. We already have six throughout the Holy Land. We had hoped to double that this year. But now…" She trailed off in despair.

Jackson smiled encouragingly. "Surely, the work need not end. If not six new schools, then perhaps two. Or even one."

"Unlikely. Funding has come slowly. Rabbi Burman was working on a major gift, very large, enough to get it done. But it hadn't closed."

"And now you suspect the donor will demur?"

"Couldn't say. He or she was to remain anonymous until the papers were signed. I have no idea who he or she might be. Nobody does."

"A pity. But perhaps in time he—or she—will step forward. But your other donors? All on the public record?"

"As the law requires. Though let me save you endless bureaucratic research. I have prepared this for you." She handed him a computer printout headed *Schedule of Donors*. "If I can be of any help, all my numbers are there. So many numbers nowadays."

"Thank you," said Jackson, gently adding, "*Shabbat shalom.*"

She smiled gratefully. "And the peace of the Sabbath be with you."

He turned to Zakaria, still smiling warmly. "*Ma'rah'bone.*"

The janitor immediately replied reflexively, "*Ma'rah'obtain—*" then tried to swallow the words.

But too late. Jackson was gone, Maggie hurrying to catch up.

Freyda was feeling better. "Such a nice man," she said. "And speaking both Hebrew and Arabic."

"Yes. A nice man indeed," said Zakaria before quickly leaving.

Once on the street, Maggie was again racing to keep up, her curiosity piqued.

"What was all that about?" she asked. "Something happened in there, didn't it?"

"I should say so. It bodes well that you noticed."

"Yes, but noticed what, Sarn't-Major?"

"Probably the first break in this case." She waited for more but her cell phone vibration demanded she glance at the text. She looked up, surprised. "Special Agent Hamstein. Contacting me?"

"Yes." Jackson nodded. "I gave him your number. Those things irritate me. What's he have to say?"

"That we have a meeting."

The offices of Pelachi Enterprises Worldwide (Pty) were remarkably modest given that they housed one of the world's three richest men, a mysterious figure best known for funding all manner of social and political organizations; indeed, there were those who warned darkly of an attempt to subvert American democracy and install a one-world government. But the smiling, avuncular man with the twinkling eyes and the boyish mop of largely gray hair now seated across from the Sergeant-Major seemed anything but menacing. His office was sparse, no "wall of fame" boasting photographs of Pelachi with the famous and powerful he counted as friends; in fact, the room was bereft of virtually all personal markers. The refreshment offered was tap water—"Sustainable water use is everyone's obligation," he had explained—aerated by his own little machine.

Jackson had watched carefully when he asked the man, first, whether he knew Gerry Rivers—which, after a moment's memory retrieval, Pelachi said he did, but only slightly—and second, was he aware the man was dead? He apparently was not and seemed untroubled by the news. How about Rabbi Burman? Again, he had paused to search his memory, only to draw a blank.

"I can't place him. But his death is nonetheless lamentable."

"Indeed," agreed Jackson. "But tell me, if you would be so kind, whatever you can about the journalist Gerry Rivers."

"Not much to tell, really. A financial writer for one of the news services—Bloomberg, MarketWatch, Reuters, one of those. He'd call me regularly as the interest rate announcement from the Fed would approach. Wanted my prediction. Tomorrow is the quarterly announcement. It made sense he would telephone me."

"So you weren't friends or anything of that nature?"

"Goodness, no! Frankly, I didn't like the man. Bit of a blowhard, not very bright, and hiding behind that ridiculous mustache. But, as I say, tomorrow's announcement loomed."

Jackson could see Maggie was eager to ask a question. His nod to her was barely perceptible. She jumped in.

"If you so disliked him, why did you grant him interviews?"

Pelachi took a moment to admire Maggie, then offered his most charming smile. "Because he always announced my soothsaying—on the Web—moments before the announcement. And I was always correct. Helped feed the myth."

Jackson smiled. "Your candor is disarming, Mr. Pelachi."

"Candor is who I am, Sergeant-Major." He smiled as he stood, a signal the interview was over. Jackson complied, and in moments, he and Maggie were back on the sidewalk at Fourteenth and L.

She looked to him. "Nothing much new there. Or was there?"

"There may have been a great deal. But time is short. So we shall be forced to split up. Not only because the operation is now time-critical, but also I believe you've shown sufficient progress to warrant command of your own reconnaissance patrol."

He handed her the donor list. "Somewhere in there is a donor. Someone unlike the others. He—or she—will have given twice, three times at most, always at the same time of the month. The sums will have increased slightly. But it will have an oddity. I need the dates of the transactions."

Dismayed, she held the thick file up, leafed the pages. "There's hundreds of names here. Maybe thousands. How do I—?"

But he was already striding across the street, slowing just long enough to toss over his shoulder, "If you're a good field officer, you'll find the right shortcut. Just remember: size, shape, shadow, color, movement." Then he turned back. "It might be a familiar name."

"Should I check on how they're doing finding Mr. Edison?"

"Don't bother! They're wasting their time!"

And on that enigmatic certainty, he disappeared, melding into the midday crowds.

◇◇◇

Sergeant-Major Jackson knew when he was being deceived, and there was no doubt about this one. He had spent over an hour with Gerry Rivers's immediate superior at the wire service, the rather bookish Will Diamond—thick glasses, male pattern baldness and an annoying habit of incessantly clicking his retractable ballpoint pen. *Click-click.*

"So is it fair to say Mr. Rivers was a beat reporter, your man at the Fed?"

Click-click. "Fair? Who knows what's fair nowadays, eh, Warrant Officer?"

"Perhaps you might try?"

Click-click. "Rivers didn't really have a beat. He kinda floated. But he did do the Fed announcements. Exclusively, you might say."

"Because he excelled at that analysis?"

Click-click. "Not really. He was pretty average. To be honest about it, he was a pushy pain in the ass. I tried to can him once."

Jackson waited for more, but all he got was *Click-click.* The man was obtuse. "Tried?"

Click-click. "Yeah. But upstairs said no. Keep him where he is for now, they said. Temporary, they said. Three, almost four years ago."

"Did they explain why?" Jackson asked, steeling his nerves for the noise of the ballpoint. But none came—and Jackson wondered if the noise, or the silence, was deliberately intended to throw him off. He stared at Diamond.

"Nah. I figured he had photographs of the publisher."

"I see. One last thing, if you would indulge me: Rabbi Eliezar Burman? Were you acquainted with the gentleman?"

Click-click. "Nah. But he's a big deal in the Jewish community so I guess our paths must've crossed. But I wouldn't claim to know him."

"To your knowledge, would the late Mr. Rivers have done so?"

Jackson took it as unease that the answer came quickly, even before the clicking started, the two mingling. "Can't [*click*] imagine that." *Click.*

Trying to forget the sound of the clicking pen had slowed Jackson's afternoon work, and by the time he was done touring various government offices collecting the information he needed, it was twilight in the white canyons of the District's federal buildings. But he had learned a little about Rivers and his employers, enough to perhaps make a difference if his suspicions began to show validity.

But now darkness was closing as he strode down near-empty G Street in Washington's Southeast quadrant, his sharp, military-time footfalls echoing off the buildings, some empty and derelict, others timidly showing small yellow lamps. As he moved, he kept his senses sharp, not missing the shadows that seemed alive, or the infrequent darting silhouette ahead. As he turned into Ninth Street, he knew he was entering a world that, particularly at night, was inhospitable to strangers, particularly one such as himself. About midway down the block he could sense the two men following him. Ignoring the urge—if there was any—to walk faster, he held his pace until, after a few moments, he could hear the faint sound of music from an otherwise apparently deserted town house on his left.

He turned in quickly, rapped sharply on the door. After a moment a small sliding door opened to reveal the face of a burly African American who exuded not a trace of warmth.

"It's the Sarn't-Major," Jackson said softly, noting the footsteps following him had stopped. The opaque face was quickly obscured by the man's huge hand directing a flashlight beam into Jackson's face. The soldier did not blink. The African American beamed.

"It sure as hell *is* you!" The door swung open and Jackson stepped inside. Once the door was properly closed and locked, the huge bouncer embraced the Sergeant-Major warmly. "Been too damned long, Sarn't-Major."

Jackson smiled true appreciation at the warmth. "It has that, Sergeant."

"Your man's in the back. He'll be happy for the sight of you."

Jackson strode through the large anteroom, a bar-cum-club, its walls completely covered with photographs of soldiers, many taken in Vietnam but even more from Iraq and Afghanistan. The ceiling was a tapestry of military shoulder patches, captured enemy flags—and pinups of beautiful women in various stages of undress. As he strode to the back, he received respectful nods and smiles from nearly all of the select group of African American men, some seated at tables, talking, laughing, sipping beer; others gathered around a huge flat-screen television with the Wizards-Lakers game; others just fixed on the Al Green ballad from the antique jukebox. He returned every one with direct eye contact, a nod, and a smile. He reached a curtain at the rear, pulled it aside, and knocked a rhythmic code on the door it concealed. Almost instantly, it swung open to admit Jackson, quickly closing behind him.

It took a moment for his eyes to adjust to the dimmer lighting; it was a semi-office with two muscular men occupying chairs in opposite corners, as if for protection. The slim, attractive black man behind the desk was already on his feet and coming around the desk, a huge smile on his face. Jackson couldn't help but beam as broadly as he ever had.

"P.K.! Good to see you, brother. How are you?"

"All the better for laying eyes on you, blood." The use of the most intimate term of familiarity in a Vietnam-era black soldier's vocabulary was not lost on the Sergeant-Major. He embraced P.K. and then they sat in armchairs away from the desk.

P.K. turned to one of his guards. "Whisky for an honored guest. The good stuff." The man crossed to the desk and P.K. settled his eyes on Jackson. "How's the struggle, Bob?"

"Better than it was, not as good as it could be."

"Telling me my own story."

The guard put down two glasses and a bottle of twenty-five-year-old Oban from the famed Western Highlands. "And the ice." The man scurried off. "So what misfortune brought me the good luck of entertaining you?"

Jackson grinned. "Do I only show up when I need help?"

P.K. laughed. "I reckon! This is no resort area. I wouldn't pay a visit myself except as I needed. Besides, we're proud to be your irregular troops, Bob. You've never been on the wrong side. So what's up?"

Jackson reached inside his shirt, withdrew the envelope with the photographs of the stolen silver Torah dressings.

P.K. studied them. "Heard they robbed the synagogue over at Sixth and I. This the loot?"

Jackson nodded. "One police theory is it's a random robbery, common in the neighborhood. In which case, the silver should already be in the hands of a fence. And no doubt you'd know about it."

"I would. But I don't. Besides, the bad guys who work that turf wouldn't touch this. They're pros and they'd know better."

"You think so?"

"I'd bet on it. They don't hit churches or synagogues. And this building is both."

"It is." Jackson nodded. "Originally a synagogue, then when the Jews moved to the suburbs, an AME church."

P.K. grinned. "And the benefits of upward mobility march on: now the AMEs are gone to the suburbs and the Jews are back. All life's a circle."

The guard returned with a glass of ice. P.K. poured two glasses of whisky, dropped a single ice cube in each. He looked up at Jackson. "One minute to release the aroma and texture?"

The Sergeant-Major nodded. "You always were a good soldier."

They raised their glasses. "Here's tae uys," said P.K.

"T'ose lak uys," Jackson replied. Then both murmured "…to absent friends…" and drank.

"Will you keep your ears open?"

P.K. nodded reassuringly. "I'll put the word out."

They sipped some more. Jackson frowned as if the next question had just occurred to him. "The men who work that area? Any of them skilled in a one-move neck-snap?"

P.K. pondered that for a moment then shook his head. "No. That's black ops. Brit SAS, KGB, SEALs. Those guys would never sink as low as knocking off a synagogue."

Jackson nodded; as usual, P.K. made perfect sense.

The Sergeant-Major was reluctant to acknowledge the feeling he experienced as Maggie reported on her recce patrol. But it was inescapable: he was pleased. She had exceeded his expectation. She was recounting her efforts, and whether or not she'd had useful results, her methodology met his rigorous standards. His mind was wandering. He interrupted her. "I lost the chain. Go back three sentences."

She coughed, tried to remember what she'd said, went back. "So I just kept looking at it, hoping something would jump out—like the hillside in the training film. But the longer I stared, the less anything stood out. I kept thinking about the five markers, but they didn't seem to apply. Names don't move, they don't have color. But then it struck me: philanthropy has a shadow. It involves money. Money always leaves a trail, shadows, if you will. It has observable consequences, if only to accountants and auditors. So I started running numbers, and something leapt out: two donations, the first a modest ten thousand, the second a more extravagant quarter of a million. The Reconciliation Project showed them both as anonymous. But when I compared the private listing to their government report, they were shown as received from a 501c(3)—a charitable institution passing money along to another cause. So I researched the donor and identified it. As you predicted, a familiar name—"

He interrupted quickly. "The Zakaria Fund?"

Maggie tried to hide her surprise. "The Zakaria Foundation, actually. But you have the concept."

"And no doubt the address was the janitor's home." She nodded. "And were the dates the fifteenth of the month or the thirtieth?"

"One of each," she answered, a little disappointed he was so far ahead of her.

"The question is, then: who financed our janitor? Terrorists? Criminals?"

"And is he the murderer?"

Jackson looked at her; here was a test. "All indications point in his direction, do they not?"

"Every single one. Which begs the question: can there be too many shadows?"

What he now felt was pride. His mentee was learning very quickly. "We shall have to find out. Come."

Keeping in plain view of the open front door, he led her to his computer. "I'm not as proficient as you, I daresay, with this machinery. So I would ask you to find the website listing donations, compare them until you find one of those 501 things you mentioned making identical donations on the same days. Are your two samples enough to produce results?"

"To get started, yes. But not on this. There's a program on the base IT that could do it in less than an hour. But it's for official use only."

"Then we shall vouchsafe our officialness." He picked up his almost quaint land-line telephone, tapped in a number.

Turner was irritated at having to drive over an hour to simply gain access to an army computer. But he had to be present while this woman—not a bad looker when he paid attention—ran endless regressional analyses on numbers and charities. It reminded him how nowadays the government knew everything, which meant any nerd with a keyboard could accomplish in minutes what old-time cops like himself had once done by hand, their knowledge and experience prerequisites to success. But now…

He checked his watch; still time to catch the playoff game if this Maggie person could find what Jackson wanted. The man could be a strain on your nerves, but he was never wrong and Turner needed this case off his desk. He'd hoped he'd find the Edison guy, but when he left, Baxter was down to just three Franks, two Freds, and a Francis and Turner's gut told him none of them would pan out.

Maggie's exultant shout of "Jackpot!" sharply interrupted his reverie. Instantly, he and Jackson were looking over her shoulder. "Here's the link to the so-called anonymous donor!"

She hit a key and a Web homepage floated onto her screen: THE JUPITER PROJECT. A FUND TO HELP THOSE SEEKING A HARMONIOUS SOCIETY. There were literally hundreds of recipients listed. The Reconciliation Project was among them. She turned to look up at Turner. "Isn't Pelachi connected to that?"

"Probably." He shrugged. "But his money is everywhere in that world. Probably a coincidence." He turned to Jackson. "Wouldn't you say, Sarn't-Major?"

"Not knowing that world, I must demur. However, I believe I can provide that answer tomorrow morning. If—and only if— you meet me exactly where I say at precisely oh-eight-twenty-five hours. With the following people in tow." He scribbled some names on a Post-it, handed it to Turner, hurried to leave.

"Where the hell are you running this time of night?"

"If we are to put this matter to rest tomorrow as I've described, there is pressing business to which I must attend."

And before more could be demanded, he was gone from sight.

Maggie, Turner, and those he had rounded up—Hamstein, Freyda, Zakaria, and Will Diamond, the last clearly irritable at having been pulled away—waited patiently in the coffee shop on L Street. The wall clock read 8:24. Diamond fulminated.

"You said he'd meet us at eight twenty-five, and I have no time to waste—" but he stopped short as, simultaneously, the wall clock slid to 8:25 and Sergeant-Major Jackson opened the front door, striding directly toward them, surveying the group.

"Well done, Captain Turner. I see we're all here." Then, indicating Diamond, "Captain, Special Agent, I see you've met the late Gerry Rivers's employer."

"Employer? Hardly," Diamond snapped. "I'm just his boss. His employer is a man much wealthier than I could ever dream of being."

"Point taken. Then let's get on the march. Our destination is one and one-half blocks away."

Maggie got it immediately. "Pelachi's office?"

He smiled. She definitely had promise.

At first, they had been denied access to Pelachi's inner sanctum. But under unrelenting pressure from Jackson, Hamstein had waved his badge about, backed by Turner's, and eventually they'd been led upstairs, Hamstein muttering to Jackson as they went, "This better pan out or my job is on the line, Bob." He hardly ever used the familiar with the Sergeant-Major, but he needed to emphasize how serious it was to pressure Pelachi. It was not lost on Jackson.

Once in the office, Pelachi wasted no time berating each and every one. "This is a great inconvenience! It had damned well be important!" he thundered, the grandfatherly Pelachi apparently swallowed whole by a harsh and hard-bitten businessman.

"As you wish, sir." By now, they were all seated, save for the two policemen at the door and Jackson at the window. Jackson was ready.

"Our nation's capital has been witness to two ghastly murders in the span of a few hours." He eyed them carefully, one at a time; then, "And the murderer—for one person was responsible for both killings—is in this room. With us. Now."

Pelachi bristled. "I appreciate your refined sense of theatrics. But could you please just divulge who it is and let the rest of us get on with our lives?"

Jackson ignored the remark, continued, "The critical question: was any one person connected to both deceased?"

Turner couldn't contain his curiosity. "No one here. Not as I can see?"

"Really?" He walked slowly to Diamond, who twitched nervously. He stared at the editor. "You knew them both, didn't you?"

"No! That's ridicul—" He stopped, nodded his head woodenly. "Yes. Yes, I did."

Jackson hovered over him more closely. "Precisely. Rivers worked for you. And, although it was well hidden, that boss's boss to whom you referred earlier was none other than Mr. Pelachi."

Diamond nodded. Jackson pressed harder. "And that was why you always issued Mr. Pelachi's predictions. Rivers was merely a message boy."

"Yes! I never denied knowing Rivers!" Diamond snapped defensively. "But the rabbi?"

Jackson betrayed a little irritation. "Have you forgotten your donation to the Reconciliation Project? Because the government hasn't. Your name appears on the donor list on file."

"*You're* that Mr. Diamond?" exclaimed Freyda.

"All right! I knew them both! But I didn't kill anyone!"

Jackson stared at him for so long, it became unbearable. "Perhaps. We shall see, shall we not?" Jackson turned to Freyda. "And you?"

"*Me?* Kill someone? I'm a vegetarian. A total vegan!"

"But you knew something was wrong. And you knew it involved..." he turned quickly to Zakaria "...our loyal custodian. A Lebanese?"

"Yes, yes, sir. But—"

"No. Not Lebanese. Egyptian. Coptic, I believe."

Zakaria hung his head, held up his arm to reveal the small Maltese cross tattoo. "This gave me away, yes?"

"That and your accent. When we exchanged farewells, your Arabic was Egyptian. Significantly different from the Levantine dialect of Lebanon."

Zakaria was crestfallen. "You are a very clever man. Clever enough to know it was not me who took lives, who has blood on his hands."

"I don't know if I am. But let us review what we know: a rabbi is murdered, his synagogue looted—but not by a regular felon. How do we know this? First, because the stolen silver has not appeared on the underworld market after nearly seventy-two hours."

"Hmmph," snorted Diamond. "Makes sense. The thieves could simply be waiting for it to blow over."

"Thank you for revealing your ignorance of the ordinary criminal. Run-of-the-mill thieves are in chronic need of folding money. And they know the longer they cling to their booty, the likelier the authorities will find them. So, the rule is, get rid of it. Quickly. To a fence who can buy it for a steal—pun intended—and afford to hold on to it until the coast, as they say, is clear. And we," he added, indicating Turner and Hamstein, "are assured the purloined items have not surfaced. Anywhere."

He looked at them, each in turn, seeking a telltale quiver or blink the criminal might now show; but nothing. So he continued, "But this was a person with knowledge of his swag. He left the more modern, easily available Torah dressings but scooped up all the antiques, the survivors of the Holocaust, the ancient gems from tsarist Russia. Is he a collector? A dealer in stolen antiquities? Perhaps. But not a common, ignorant street thief who steals for quick money." He paused. "From this, we can be sure he is a man who can, for now at least, live within his means."

"That applies to everyone here, surely." Pelachi was fidgety.

"But why kill the rabbi? An accident? Perhaps. But a man of means could wait until he was certain the synagogue was deserted." Jackson stood still, his voice taking on gravitas. "A more likely explanation: the purpose of the criminal's visit was the murder. The silver theft was simply a distraction."

"But who would kill such a good man?" lamented Freyda.

"What if it was precisely because he was a good man? One whose passion was to create peace." Then, more darkly, Jackson continued, "And perhaps that passion made him vulnerable."

Turner could no longer contain himself. "To who?"

"Whom," corrected the Sergeant-Major. "To someone who needed a command and control infrastructure. A very particular network. One that could move money in ways the authorities could never find. If you will, a transaction that casts no shadow." His eyes fell on Pelachi. "Such a man would either be wealthy—" and then, turning to both Diamond and Zakaria equally "—or represent interests that were." He paused. "But why would such a person murder the rabbi? I actually puzzled over that for some time. But the good Mr. Diamond pointed me in the right direction."

"*Me?*" exclaimed the editor, nervously biting his lip. "What did I say? I'm nothing to do with this!"

"Then why so anxious, so—if I may—guilty?" The man had no answer. Jackson twitched a smile. "No worries. Yours was a passing remark. You speculated Rivers's security came from having photographs of the grand and powerful. Which led me to wonder: what if, playing on the rabbi's passion, our conspirator induced him to accept large donations, as anonymously as possible, to fund his vital and important work, on the understanding a significant portion would be returned secretly?"

"Money laundering!" Hamstein was beginning to enjoy it. Another quick cracking of a high-profile case. Good on the record.

"Precisely. The rabbi had a perfect end use—an organization in a very tricky part of the world, where records are sparse, and there's a history of soaking up huge sums of money never to be seen again."

Maggie was puzzled. "That would make it easy to arrange receiving the funds. But it wouldn't conceal a kickback. That would require a local receiver…" She trailed off as she involuntarily turned to Zakaria.

Jackson crossed slowly to Zakaria. "And that man, or woman, would need a motive—other than money, because he had to be incredibly low profile." He was now standing over the poor janitor, who trembled like a Colorado aspen. Jackson grabbed his arm, raised it so all could see the tattoo. "A very special mark. The mark Coptic Christians accept to profess their loyalty to their Church." Before the janitor could object, Jackson continued sternly, "A Church suffering a genocide at the hands of Muslim extremists the length and breadth of Egypt. There is a desperate need for money to save those who wish to leave: bribes, visas, travel allowances." He turned to the others. "Who, under those circumstances, would not be prone to helping what was presented as an innocent desire to spread peace?"

"I had no choice! I felt God had sent me the opportunity! Now…" Zakaria broke down in tears.

Jackson put a comforting hand on the weeping man's shoulder. He turned to Pelachi and stared.

The Russian slammed his fist on the desk. "This is an outrage! I will have your job *and* your pension. Now get out! OUT!"

Jackson looked at Hamstein. It was up to him now. He squirmed for a moment but then shook his head at Pelachi.

"Not for the moment, sir. I'd appreciate it if you could sit for a few more moments. Though I also think, this time, our colleague has jumped the shark."

Pelachi, unsure of the meaning of that, slowly subsided into his seat. Quickly calm, he smiled graciously. "By all means continue. The story is fascinating—especially since I, of all people, have no need of another's infrastructure. I could virtually rule the world if I wished."

"Certainly that part of it which is for sale," agreed Jackson. "But what of that which is not? Money derived from great secrets, vast sums, all feloniously obtained, all a threat even to our national security? Those proceeds would have to be hidden. Hence a foreign structure with which one arm of your empire had a slim, tangential connection? Your philanthropic arm, perhaps. Hence, the rabbi."

If Pelachi was nervous, he now had it well concealed. "How fascinating. I'll need to hear all your story before speaking with your superiors. So, please, do go on."

"Thank you. Now, the problem was, once the rabbi was involved, he had, in Mr. Diamond's imagery, photographs. Should his better angels reassert their grip on his spirit, or should he simply become frightened, the engineer of the plot would be threatened. Existentially. It would be his life—or Eliezar Burman's."

"I see," cooed the Russian. "But you miss one thing: from where would such vast sums of money be derived?"

"Ah. At last we come to the elusive Mr. F. Edison. Except the code was not a name. It was a message: FED IS ON. Rivers was signaling his partner in crime that conditions were ripe to anticipate the Federal Reserve's interest rate and skim millions—even billions—of dollars from the market in the hours before the actual announcement. I have no doubt when Mr. Hamstein's FBI lab finishes with Gerry Rivers's computer, they will discover he had developed a program to crack the Federal Reserve computers and read the announcement as soon as it was ready on the website—*sometimes hours before it was released to the general public.*"

Hamstein whistled under his breath. "Insider trading. Bigger even than anything Giuliani busted."

Turner nodded. "And don't forget the biggest money-laundering rap ever!"

Pelachi was finally betraying serious nervousness: nostrils flaring, ears back, jaw clenching.

The Sergeant-Major pressed the offensive home. "It had worked twice before. Dry runs. This was to be the killing. It would corner the market. All that was needed was for Rivers to find the posting code. Late in the evening, he found it. He was poised to read the announcement in time for sheer havoc. He sent the word to his master: Fed is on. That meant he would find the memo. But that master, Mr. Pelachi, would not know the contents until he read Rivers's article online—the one in which he would give your always correct prediction. Except, my guess is, this time he'd make you incorrect so while others followed your advice, you could crash everything else. It's also my guess it was why he was kept in his job despite obvious reasons for his dismissal. Easy to arrange when the company that owned the wire service that employed him was part of your impossibly complex empire." Before Pelachi could object, Jackson explained, "A fact I discovered after a long afternoon scouring government records. My, but yours is an opaque empire. It almost eluded me."

"Then why am I not on the phone this very minute placing orders?"

"Because neither you nor Rivers expected any man to put his conscience ahead of vast sums of money. When the good rabbi realized he could no longer aid and abet your crime, this particular caper had to be delayed until another infrastructure could be identified. In the meantime, the rabbi had to go. And you could trust no one else with the job. By the same token, you realized Rivers himself was a threat. And that all you needed was his program. No doubt you downloaded his files after snapping his neck. It was simply eliminating the middleman. Good business to your way of thinking."

Pelachi was near the breaking point. "You go too far! You're crossing the line of your own destruction!"

"Not once the FBI scours your computers."

For the first time, Pelachi showed fear. Panic. He urgently appealed to the policemen. "Honestly! Do you really believe I would be prowling the streets late at night? That I would kill a man with my bare hands? I'm an old man!"

"Come, come. You know as well as I the means of murder used requires not strength but skill. Anyone trained—as you, I am quite sure, were—in the craft of the KGB could easily dispatch a man several times his strength."

It was too much for Freyda. She loosed an involuntary yelp and broke down in wrenching sobs. Maggie immediately dashed to her, embracing her, offering comfort. Suddenly the mood changed from one of interest to something highly charged with great anxiety.

Pelachi leapt on it, challenged Hamstein.

"Look at this! This is an atrocity. Charge me or leave." He turned to Jackson contemptuously. "You can prove none of this, sir!"

The Sergeant-Major waited for Freyda to calm, then replied crisply, "Yes. I suppose one might dismiss it all as pure speculative fantasy. But there is the matter of the eyewitness."

Both policemen were startled. This was the first they had heard of it. Pelachi gulped. Hard. But he stayed on the offensive. "Ridiculous! You can produce no such eyewitness."

"In fact, sir, I daresay he's outside your door at this very instant." Jackson nodded at Turner who, though puzzled, opened the door. And a familiar figure entered. The two officers were startled.

"P.K.! What the hell are you doing here? I thought you were legit nowadays!"

The confident P.K. of the prior evening was now carefully disguised with the scattered manner of a street person. "Oh, I am, Cap'n, Special Agent. Honest as the day is long. But there's this girl, see, oh, such a delight, but you know how—"

"Get on with it, man!" Pelachi was red in the face.

"Well…" P.K. drawled on, feigning a slowness of wit that in no way deceived those who knew him but certainly had Pelachi's attention. "…my girl lives down near that synagogue. I was going home about two in the morning. When I saw a man run from the synagogue. He was carrying a stuffed Hefty bag." He looked directly at Pelachi. "Yeah, that's the guy."

"Insane! You're all finished! Careers over! Now get out!"

But Jackson held his ground. "Are you sure, Mr. P.K.?"

"Certain. He'd stopped under a street lamp. I saw him plain, I did."

"Why would he stop?"

"Well, sir, the Hefty bag had split. And a big slab of silver was falling out."

"You see! A lie! The bag never bro—" Even as the words tumbled from his mouth, Pelachi knew he had been tricked. P.K.'s ruse had exposed him. It was over. He turned to the window, perhaps to jump. But Jackson blocked his path. Pelachi turned to the door. Hamstein and Turner were waiting for him.

He backed off, began to circle, Jackson following at a discreet distance. Pelachi reached inside his jacket—and out came a 9 mm Beretta.

"Keep away," he warned. "And no one will be hurt," he promised. He edged toward the door, Jackson keeping pace. Across the room, P.K. also shifted his position, unnoticed by the Russian pointing his Beretta at the policemen, who quickly deserted the door to keep out of his path. He glanced down, seeking the doorknob. It was the only instant he lowered his guard. But it was all that was needed.

With a fearsome war cry, Jackson dove toward Pelachi, who, terrified by the sound and furious movement, dodged to the side—and directly into the arms of P.K., who had been moving in concert with Jackson and was now perfectly positioned to chop at the fugitive's gun hand.

The pistol flew high in the air. Pelachi dived to catch it.

And would have, had not Maggie dived lightning-fast for it, scooping it out of the air a hairbreadth from Pelachi's grasp.

In a moment, it was over. This man, so powerful only moments ago, was suddenly just another pathetic criminal about to take his perp walk.

As they turned to lead him away, Turner looked at Hamstein. "Your bust or mine?"

"Joint operation?" Hamstein suggested.

"Works for me."

Pelachi was in shock. He hissed at Jackson, "You'll regret this! I will make you pay!"

Jackson smiled. "In our next life, perhaps. You'll be spending the rest of this one in Leavenworth."

Pelachi's scream of anger receded as Turner and Hamstein led him off.

◇◇◇

Sergeant-Major Jackson rarely entertained, but now, in his modest home, surrounded by his colleagues, he felt, well, almost happy, a sensation he had almost forgotten. They had just arrived and were going about the unexpectedly difficult task of getting settled. Jackson had few chairs, but while the conversation flowed he found one or two from the little dining area and a camp stool and deck chair from the neat front closet.

Well," Hamstein confessed, "I said there was only one man who could figure this out and I was right."

"*We* were right," grumbled Turner. "But bringing in P.K. that way was a huge risk. Could've tainted the case if we'd known about it."

"Which," said P.K., "is why it remained between Sergeant-Major Jackson and myself."

"But what if he hadn't fallen for it?" Maggie knew Jackson had the answer and wanted him to have his moment. He saw that and offered what was almost a smile of gratitude. But he dismissed her thought.

"Once he said Hefty bag—correct to the very brand—Pelachi would know the jig was up."

"Yeah," remembered Hamstein. "I wondered about that. How'd you know he had a Hefty bag?"

Jackson's hand reached into the pocket where he had placed the shining bit of plastic found near the Ark, withdrew the shred, held it up. "A very particular polymer base, patented by a particular company. It had to be their product."

"What will happen to Zakaria?" Maggie worried.

Hamstein shrugged. "Don't sweat it. He'll get immunity for his testimony."

Finally everyone was comfortably seated. Jackson rubbed his hands.

"Well. Can I offer you some cheer? Perhaps a little *uisge beatha*?"

They clearly had no idea what he meant. Except for Maggie. "Scottish Gaelic—Erse, if you prefer—for 'water of life.' Corrupted into English as 'whisky.'"

The men gazed at her in mixed admiration and intimidation.

Hamstein glanced at Turner, murmured, "They belong together."

They all burst into laughter, punctuated by P.K.'s cry of "Bring it on!"

Maggie agreed. "Bring it on, indeed. My father always said you had the world's greatest collection of whisky!"

"You knew her father?" the others all asked more or less at once.

For a moment it seemed Sergeant-Major Jackson might answer. But then he thought better. He turned sternly to Maggie.

"I'm quite certain you're mistaken, ma'am. I expect he said I had a collection…" He turned to a cupboard in the built-in TV shelving, threw its door open, adding, "of the world's greatest whiskies!"

There were but four bottles on display: two single malts, a Talisker from the Isle of Skye, and an Oban from the eponymous Western Highland glen that gave it life. Only one blend, Justerini & Brooks. And a bottle of Bell's, the daily "wee dram afore ye go" of the Glasgow working people. With a flourish, Sergeant-Major Jackson swept his hand to the display.

"There, good friends, is all you ever need to know about the water of life! Maggie, choose for us all!"

"Oban," she said softly.

He gazed at her warmly. "An excellent choice. Like father, like daughter."

And the celebration began.

After leaving school—not of his own volition—at fifteen, Lionel Chetwynd formed the ambition to become as comprehensively clever as Sherlock Holmes; that way, he reasoned, he could quit the factory and sleep in late like his hero. He has not, as yet, succeeded. In the interim he has occupied himself with more than forty feature motion picture and long-form television credits and has written, produced, and directed more than twenty-one documentaries. He has received both Oscar and Emmy nominations; six Writers Guild of America nominations, including an award; the New York Film Festival Gold Medal; two Christophers; two George Washington Freedom Medals; and six Telly Awards. In 2001, he was appointed to the President's Committee on the Arts and the Humanities. He is a recipient of the John Singleton Copley Medal from the National Portrait Gallery, the Smithsonian Institution. Lionel is married to actress Gloria Carlin and lives in Southern California, where they exult in their four grandchildren.

The Eyak Interpreter

A KATE SHUGAK SHORT STORY

Dana Stabenow

A Park Rat's Blog

[Note to my twenty-seven Park Rat followers, who think reading along is such a hoot. This blog is a yearlong assignment for Mrs. Doogan in my honors English class. Don't screw with my grade by being trolls in the comments. I can delete you, you know.]

Tuesday, October 25th, by Johnny

We're not in the Park anymore, Toto.

I hate dentists. I floss and brush and all that stuff every day, I don't know why I had to have a cavity. I hate Kate, too. She's never had a cavity in her whole life. Makes me want to hold her down and force-feed her a five-pound bag of sugar.

Although this dentist she took me to in Anchorage, Dorman, was okay, even if he was way too tan to be an Alaskan. He likes Kate, I can tell, but then every man she's ever met likes her. Except maybe all the ones she put in jail, and sometimes I'm not so sure about them. Except if she's never had a cavity I don't know why she needs her own dentist. She sure was awful quick to get us on a plane when I got my toothache.

<u>Here's</u> the grossest picture I could find of a cavity on the Internet. Mine was a lot smaller.

So here we are in Anchorage, staying at Dad's town house on Westchester Lagoon. Kate and Mutt are out for a walk on the <u>Coastal Trail</u>. There's nothing on television and I don't want to go anywhere until I don't drool when I talk. Disgusting. So I'm sitting here writing a post for my twenty-seven followers (Bobby, you better not read this one over Park Air like you did the one about counting caribou with Ruthe Bauman. She didn't speak to me for a week). We'd be on a plane back to the Park right now if the weather hadn't socked in behind us. Van texted me that it's blowing snow and fog and Mrs. Doogan strung a rope from the front door to the bullrail so everyone could feel their way to their vehicles. I checked the National Weather Service website and the forecast is for more of the same for the next day and maybe two.

I'd still rather be there than here. Too many people in Anchorage, going too fast in too many cars.

So would Kate, and Mutt. We've been weathered in in Anchorage before and they both get antsy and cranky and snappish. Mutt I can understand, but Kate doesn't want to go to the movies or shopping or out to eat, she just keeps looking east, trying to get a bead on what's coming next out of the Gulf, and if it's flyable.

Okay, a few minutes later, they're back and Kate got a call (she actually answered her cell phone!) and we're going to go see somebody. Later…

Comments

   Bobby says, "Too late, kid."

   Ruthe says, "I'm still not speaking to you."

   Van says, "Miss you, babe."

   Katya says, "johnny bring me a unclmilton moon form toyzrus"

   Katya says, "mom says please"

   Mrs. Doogan says, "Good narrative flow, Johnny, if a little elliptical on occasion. Topic sentences aren't

*mandatory in journal form, but you do want the
reader to be able to follow the thread of the story.
Resist the parenthetical phrase, too. For a moment
there in the fifth paragraph I thought you were in
Anchorage with Ruthe, not Kate."*

Tuesday, October 25th, that evening, by Johnny

We have a case, and I get to help!

Well, I get to go along, anyway.

We went downtown to this old restaurant on Fifth Avenue, the Club Paris, and met this old fart named Max. He's a retired state trooper (here's the Alaska State Trooper website) and I mean really retired, he's so wrinkled he looks like he shrunk in the wash and then got left in the dryer for a week. He's kind of feeble, walks with a cane, but he's even smarter than Kate and he sure can put away the martinis. The waitress, a total babe named Brenda, calls him by his first name and she never lets his glass get more than half empty before she's got a refill on the table. Brenda gave Kate a funny look when Kate ordered a Diet 7UP. Real women drink martinis, I guess.

Best steak sandwich I ever ate. About halfway through it Max said, "Heard a weird story last week. Grandson of an old flying buddy from Red Run."

"Red Run?" Kate said.

Max nodded. "I know, last village on the Kanuyaq before you hit the Gulf. Why I thought to tell you about it."

"What's his name?"

"He's a Totemoff."

"Which one?"

"Gilbert."

Kate forked up a big hunk of New York strip and chewed with her eyes closed for a minute. She swallowed and opened her eyes and said, "Chief Evan's grandson."

Max nodded.

"What's his story?"

"He got kidnapped."

Kate actually stopped chewing. "What?"

Max nodded. I felt cold air on the back of my neck as the door opened and Mutt's ears went up. "But I'll let him tell you the story himself. Gilbert, you know Kate Shugak."

Gilbert Totemoff was short and stocky with dark hair that had been cut under a bowl and big brown eyes like a cow's. His Carhartt's looked like they'd started life going over the Chilkoot Pass in 1898, and he smelled like woodsmoke and gasoline and tanned moosehide. His voice was so low I had to lean forward to hear him. He had a little bit of an accent, too, sounded like one of the aunties when they're going all Native in front of a gussuk they don't like. Village raised, for sure.

Max was right. Totemoff's story was a weird one.

He had come to town on a Costco run the week after the permanent fund dividend came out from the state (http:// www.pfd.state.ak.us/), the same week as the Alaska Federation of Natives convention (http://www.nativefederation.org/con-vention/index.php). He took his pickup on the fast ferry from Cordova, where he lived in the winter, to Whittier and then drove up to Anchorage.

"I met up with some cousins from Tatitlek and we went down to AFN and spent the afternoon there. That night we went to the Snow Ball to check out our old girlfriends."

Kate grinned, Max laughed, and Totemoff blushed. "But there wasn't much going on, so my cousin Philip said we should go somewhere else."

"Where else?" Kate said.

Gilbert wouldn't look at her. He mumbled something.

"Where?" Kate said.

He still wouldn't look at her. "The Bush Company."

Again he shut up. This time I think he was more embarrassed at telling a woman he'd gone to a strip club, especially a Native woman, especially a Native woman who was his elder. Brenda came over and gave us the fishy eye but Max winked at her and she went off and brought him back another martini. His third. Might have been his fourth.

Totemoff said that he and his cousins had a lot to drink, and between that and the lap dances they had their PFDs spent before midnight. Totemoff didn't say all this, of course, but you can read a lot into a Native silence.

They were just about to leave when these two guys they knew showed up.

"What two guys?" Kate said.

"They were at the convention," Totemoff said. "Not Natives, but hanging around the craft fair. One of them said he was looking for an ivory cribbage board for his mother. We got to talking, they asked us what tribe we were, and they seemed interested when we told them Eyak."

So the two guys sat down at their table at the Bush Company and offered to buy them a round. One round turned into two and maybe more. Totemoff didn't know what time it was when he got up to go to the john. When he stepped out of the door, somebody hit him, hard, a couple of times, and while he was trying to get his knees back up under him they threw a blanket or a bag or something over his head and carried him outside and tossed him in the back of a car.

"I was in and out," he said. "Felt kind of sick. Maybe we drove for fifteen minutes. Maybe longer. Next thing, the car stops and they pull me out and toss me in the back of an airplane."

"What kind of airplane?" I said. Totemoff stopped talking again. Kate frowned at me, Max said, "Shut up, kid," and even Mutt gave me a dirty look. I could feel my ears turning red, and we had to wait until Totemoff started talking again.

"We flew about an hour," he said. "I think. My head was hurting pretty bad and I barfed all over the inside of the blanket. They cussed me out and one of them hit me again and then I was out of it until we landed. They pulled me out of the plane and walked me into a cabin and pulled off the blanket. It was the two white guys from the convention who showed up at the bar."

The cabin was one room, built of logs. "Looked pretty old," Totemoff said. "The wind was whistling through the holes where the chink had fallen out." There was a woodstove, the table a plywood sheet laid on a pair of sawhorses, some mismatched dining chairs, and a cot in one corner.

On the cot was an old man. A very old Native man, bruised and emaciated.

The whole time Totemoff was telling his story, Kate sat without moving a muscle, staring at her plate. I've seen her do this before. It's a Native thing that you don't look directly at the person speaking to you, but it's like she's listening with every cell of her body.

The old man was tied to the bed. The younger of the two kidnappers brought a chair and the older man forced Totemoff down on it. "Ask him if he'll sign the papers," the older one said.

"I didn't know what he meant," Totemoff said. "I was confused, so I didn't say anything. He hit me, knocked me off the chair. When my ears stopped ringing, I heard the old man say something. In Eyak."

Kate seemed to sigh, and sat back a little in her chair.

"They got me back in the chair and the young one hit me this time," Totemoff said. "'Tell him to sign the papers,' he said."

He was silent again for a while. "I was afraid," he said. "They wanted me to talk to the old man in Eyak. But they don't know that there're no Eyak speakers left. When my grandmother died, the language died with her. I know what it sounds like, but I don't have more than a couple cuss words."

Eyak, Kate told me later, was an Alaska Native language from east of Cordova and west of Yakutat. The Tlingits crowded it out from the south and the Athabascans from the north and the Aleuts from the west, and Kate says after the whites took over, the elders wanted the kids to learn English so they wouldn't be at a disadvantage when they grew up. When the kids got sent away to the BIA (http://en.wikipedia.org/wiki/Bureau of Indian Affairs) schools in Sitka and Outside, they could even be beaten for talking anything but English. So most of the Eyak speakers are gone, except maybe a few elders.

Like the old man in the cabin.

"They brought me a long way, used up a lot of gas getting me there," Totemoff said. "If they found out I couldn't speak Eyak, I was afraid they would kill me."

He was quiet again. I was getting used to his silences. They had a rhythm to them, he'd get so many words out, and then stop for a while like he was recharging. The tougher the story got, the more his grammar deteriorated. "The old man figured it out before they did. He started making signs when they're not looking. I think maybe he spoke English just fine. From the way he looked at them sometimes.

"When they hit me I'd say the few words I knew. Wet snow. Dry snow. Snow drift. Bear. Wolf. Fish. Beaver. Titty."

I don't think he meant to say that last word because his face got red again.

"I mixed them up and changed the way I said them so they would think I was saying whole sentences. They made me tell him, over and over again, to sign the papers. The younger man pulled out a bunch of papers and waved them at him. The elder, I think he was pretending to be weaker than he really was, he'd just shake his head and moan." Totemoff smiled for the first time. "What words he said that I understood, I'm pretty sure my mom would have washed my mouth out for using." He shrugged. "But they don't know the difference."

Another silence. "I was there for a day and a night, I think. They had the windows covered up. It was a long time." He paused. "Once when the younger man was outside and the older man was feeding the stove, the elder, he whispered something to me."

We waited. Again, Kate didn't move a muscle. I'm not sure if me and Max and Mutt even registered on her peripheral vision, she was concentrating so hard on every word Totemoff said.

"I was hungry and thirsty and hungover, so I'm not sure, but it sounded like he said, 'Tell Myra I said no.'"

He was quiet for a long time then.

"I think I must have passed out, because the next thing I knew I was on a bench in front of the convention center and the guy from the Community Patrol was trying to wake me up and get me into the van to take me to the Brother Francis Shelter. There was a cop there, too. I tried to tell him what happened, but I guess he figured I was drunk and he wouldn't listen."

Kate didn't say anything but I wouldn't be that cop for a million dollars.

"I stayed at the shelter for a couple of days, until I felt better. I didn't know what to do. And then I remembered my dad's friend Max."

For the first time he looked directly at Kate. "I'm worried about the elder."

He sat back in his chair. He was done talking.

Max waited a minute before he drained his fifth—or maybe his sixth—martini and cleared his throat. "Victoria's got me up to my ears in a security overhaul," he said, looking at Kate. "My life ain't my own anymore, thanks to you, or I'd look into this myself. When I heard you were in town, I thought you might take it on."

Kate looked at me. "We're weathered out of the Park for the next day or two anyway. Might as well." She turned to Totemoff. "I have to ask you some questions, Gilbert. No right or wrong here, okay? Take your time, tell me as much as you can remember." Totemoff nodded without looking up.

"When you took off in the airplane. Was it on pavement, or on gravel?"

"Gravel."

"Could you hear any other planes?"

He started rubbing his legs and he still wouldn't look at any of us, but he nodded.

"What kind of planes? Small planes? Jets?"

"Both," he said.

"Jets? Like they were close by?"

"Real close," he said.

Kate nodded. "Do you have an idea of what kind of plane they put you in?"

"Sounded like a Cessna," he said. "They were both sitting up front. Maybe a 172. But maybe a 170."

"Okay. What about a description of the two strangers? What did they look like?"

"They were white."

"Young? Your age? Or old? Like Max?"

"Old," Totemoff said. "Like you."

Max laughed. Well, it was more like a cackle. Kate ignored him. "Tall? Or short?"

Totemoff shrugged. "Little taller than me, maybe." He was about five foot six.

"Fat or thin?"

Totemoff shrugged again. "The older guy was kind of bony. The younger guy had all the muscle."

"Hair long or short? What color?"

"Old guy never took his cap off, but he looked gray around the ears. Young guy was blond, lots of hair scraggling down the back of his neck."

"How did they talk? Southern, like somebody from Tecks-ass, yawl? Or northern, like somebody from Bahstan? Or, I don't know, like Sylvester Stallone, dem and deese and dose?"

Totemoff shook his head. "Just white."

Kate nodded. Not once did she seem impatient or irritated. "How were they dressed?"

"Jeans. Boots. Jackets. Baseball hats."

"Hats?" Kate said. "Anything on them? A logo, like for Chevron, or the Seattle Seahawks?"

Totemoff thought. "The young guy's hat had an Anchorage Aces logo on it."

"Anchorage Aces?" Kate said.

"Local semi-pro hockey team," Max said.

"You didn't know the elder?" Kate said to Totemoff, who shook his head. "Not that many Eyaks left," she said. "You sure?"

Totemoff shook his head again. "Never saw him around Cordova. He doesn't come from Red Run. Never saw him in Anchorage."

The only three places Gilbert Totemoff has been in his life, I bet. That's one more than a lot of people who live in the Bush.

"Know anyone named Myra?"

Totemoff shook his head again. "No."

"How much longer are you in town?"

"Saturday. It's the soonest I could get a space on the fast ferry back to Cordova."

"Got a phone number?"

Totemoff produced a cell phone.

"All right," Kate said, getting to her feet. "We'll be in touch."

Comments

> Bobby says, "Auntie Balasha was my on-air guest on *Park Air* this morning. She's going downriver tomorrow to teach a quilting class in Chulyin. She says an Eyak family used to live there and she'll ask around for Myras."
>
> Katya says, "did you get it yet"
>
> Katya says, "mom says please"
>
> Mrs. Doogan says, "Watch out for run-on sentences, as for example in paragraph 19. Remember the compound clause rule for commas. This may seem nitpicky to you, but if your followers can't trust your punctuation (or spelling, or grammar), why should they trust anything you say?"
>
> Van says, "Mrs. Doogan has been reading your blog out loud in class. Can you tell?"
>
> Van says, "Wait a minute. A total babe named Brenda?"
>
> Bernie says, "Busted."

Wednesday, October 26th, by Johnny

Kate was making breakfast in the kitchen by the time I got downstairs. I had my computer and I was writing the previous post. "What are you writing?" she said, so I told her.

"Can I see?" she said.

"No," I said.

She laughed. "Anything in there that isn't about Vanessa?"

I could feel my face get red. "There's lots of stuff that isn't about Van. I wrote about the caribou count I did with Ruthe up on the Gruening last year. You know, on our second try." I hesitated. "I wrote about Old Sam."

She was standing at the stove with her back to me, but she kind of stopped with the spatula in her hand. "You did?"

"Yeah. I don't want to forget him."

The spatula started moving again. "Good."

"And I write about your cases."

This time she looked over her shoulder. "What?"

"I write about your cases." I shrugged. "As much as I know about them, anyway."

One of her eyebrows went up. "You write about yesterday?"

I nodded.

"Huh." She turned back to the stove and started piling French toast and link sausages on two plates. "Okay, Dr. Watson. What do you think?"

Kinda cool that she asked, so I did a recap while we ate breakfast. When I was done she said, "So? What do we do first?"

"Uh," I said. "Go to <u>Merrill</u>, talk to the air traffic controllers?"

"What kind of surface did they take off on?"

"Gravel. Oh. Merrill's paved. *Birchwood? Campbell Air strip?*"

"What did Totemoff hear when they were stuffing him into the plane?"

"Oh. Jet engines, real close. So, *Stevens International.*"

She pointed a finger at me. "Ding, ding, ding. Lake Hood airstrip. What do we ask when we get to the tower?"

"About small plane takeoffs that night. It was late, there can't have been that many."

"Good. But first we get out a map."

"Why?"

"Totemoff said he thought it was a 170 or a 172. If I remember right, a 172 cruises at about a hundred and forty miles per hour. He said he thought they'd been in the air about an hour. He'd been drinking and they'd been thumping on him so he isn't the most reliable witness, but we can at least make a stab at figuring out where they took him within that radius."

We got the map out.

The thing about Alaska is that there's a dirt strip pretty much everywhere you look (Atlas Aviation has a good page on aviation facilities in Alaska), over three thousand of them, Jim says, and most of them unmaintained. First thing a gold miner does is hack one out of the scrub spruce so he can get in and out. Somebody's building a cabin or a lodge, same thing. And then there's the natural resource companies, they put in airstrips long enough to take a Herc carrying a drilling rig or a commercial gold dredge. When they're done digging or drilling it's not like they can roll it up and take it with them, so when the oil or gas company is gone the hunters and the fishermen and the backpackers start using it as a staging area.

That's good news if you're in the air and you've got trouble and you need to put her down. It's not so good if you're trying to figure out where one small plane went late one October night. There are literally hundreds of possibilities. We narrowed it down some, but not much. "If you were going to eliminate a few more of these, how would you go about it?" Kate said.

I didn't know.

"Where's Totemoff from?"

"Red Run," I said.

"Where are his cousins from? The ones he met at the AFN convention?"

"Tatitlek. Oh. Oh! Plus the guys who kidnapped him needed an Eyak speaker to talk to the elder. So, Prince William Sound? But isn't it too far for a 172?"

She smiled. I guess I did look kind of excited. But it was kind of cool, brainstorming a backtrail that way. "Maybe you'd need a bigger plane to get that far that fast, but remember Totemoff was only guessing. What about Myra?"

"Myra? Oh, you mean when the elder told him to tell Myra he said no?" Kate nodded. "You want us to look for her, too?"

She laughed. "Don't sound so downhearted. I admit, if we were trying to find somebody from <u>Shaktoolik</u>, we'd have a problem. But if Myra is from <u>Tatitlek</u>, or <u>Chenega</u>, or even <u>Whittier</u> or <u>Seward</u> or <u>Valdez</u>, we've got an ace in the hole. Four of them, in fact."

And then Bobby posted that comment on yesterday's post, about Auntie Balasha going to Chulyin. I told Kate.

She laughed. "See?"

Comments

> *AuntieVi says, "Bobby makes me wirte this pretty cool ridealong."*
>
> *MiketheMan says, "Dude, cool that you're putting in all the links so I don't have to google any for my own blog. Mrs. D. will never know."*
>
> *RangerDan says, [Comment deleted by author.]*
>
> *RangerDan says, "What mother-effing moron gets himself kidnapped out of the Bush Company by anybody but one of the dancers?"*
>
> *RangerDan says, "Hey, when you finally get your asses back to the Park, could you and Kate stop by the NPS Anchorage office on your way to Merrill and pick up a box of the new Park maps for me? It's been sitting there for two months while they try to figure out where Niniltna is."*
>
> *RangerDan says, "Is the Girdwood strip gravel or paved? Lots of anonymous little cabins tucked away in the mountains there."*
>
> *Mrs. Doogan says, "You write, When they're done drilling it's not like they can roll it up and take it with them...Roll up what? The drilling rig or the air strip? I know, the context makes it clear, but you need to pay more attention to your pronouns. And, Michael Abraham Moonin, Mrs. D. most certainly does know."*

Wednesday, October 26th, 12 P.M., by Johnny

We went out to Stevens International and talked to the guys in the tower. (Really cool up there, lots going on, planes in the air everywhere you look, passenger 737s and cargo 747s almost nonstop in and out of <u>Stevens International</u>, F-22 squadrons training at <u>Elmendorf</u>, hunters coming and going from <u>Lake Hood</u>, not to mention all the wannabe pilots doing touch-and-goes at Merrill. (<u>Here</u>'s a story on <u>AlaskaDispatch.com</u> about somebody ground-looping a Super Cub on the Lake Hood strip yesterday. Like Jim says, that's what happens when you learn on a <u>tricycle</u> and then buy a <u>taildragger</u>. Lucky nobody died.) They told me to come back in the summer to see it when it's really hopping. Later Kate said they are always looking for new controllers, it's a tough job and they burn out fast. I believe it.)

Anyway, the plane. Whoever was flying it didn't file a flight plan (I know what Dad would have said about that) but the tower had the <u>tail numbers</u>. We tracked down the owner and he says he doesn't know anything about the flight and that he was home asleep when it took off. Now his plane is gone. He sounded really pissed off, and said he was going to have a conversation with "those f****** airport rentacops." He lives with his wife and two kids and everybody was home in bed at the time. Kate checked with Brendan, the guy's had like one ticket for speeding in his whole life, so I think she kind of believes him. As much as Kate ever believes anybody.

2 P.M.—Got a text from Van, who got a text from Bobby, who heard from Auntie B on the marine band, who says there was a Myra Gordaoff born in <u>Cordova</u> nineteen years ago. I checked, she's on Facebook. Her profile says she graduated from Cordova High, that she's working for the <u>AC</u>, and that she's in a relationship. One of her friends tagged her in a photo at a party, she's sitting on some guy's lap. He looks white, but you can't see his face because he's got a ball cap pulled down over his eyes.

The ball cap has an <u>Anchorage Aces</u> logo on it.

She hasn't posted anything for a week and there are messages from three friends wondering where she disappeared to. I e-mailed all of them on Facebook.

7 P.M.—Heard back from one of Myra's friends, a woman named Louise. She says Myra is engaged to be married to some guy named Chris, a cheechako who moved to Alaska last summer. He came to Cordova with a pal of his, an older man who is maybe a relative, she didn't know for sure, both of them looking for jobs on a fishing boat.

Louise also says that Myra's grandfather, Herman Gordaoff, is a big noise in the local Native community, one of the last surviving elders. Myra is his only grandchild, and besides both of them being shareholders in the local Native Association, Herman has a lot of money and property, including a twenty-eight-hundred-square-foot home on the slough, twenty-five acres out Hartney Bay road, a couple of gold mines, and a vacation cabin at Boswell Bay, not to mention a fifty-foot salmon seiner and a fishing permit whose area includes the Kanuyaq River flats, which even I know is probably the most lucrative permit a fisherman can own in the state. I asked Louise if Herman spoke English. She said yes. She was kind of mifty about it.

I told Kate. She looked grim. "I don't know what's worse," she said, "living with 'No dogs or Natives allowed' signs in the store windows fifty years ago, or Native women being preyed on today because they've got a big fat quarterly shareholder dividend coming in."

"You think this Chris guy wants to marry Myra so he can get his hands on her money?"

"I think he wants to marry Myra so he can get her hands on her grandfather's money," Kate said. "I'll bet they came to Alaska with the intention of finding a female shareholder they could live off of. They nosed around, zeroed in on the Gordaoffs, and either followed Herman out to his cabin or kidnapped him and took him there. Herman was smart enough to play dumb, pretend he couldn't speak English, figured to buy himself a little time so maybe he could make a break for it.

"So Chris and his buddy went to AFN looking for Eyak speakers, found Gilbert, kidnapped him, and took him to the cabin. When that didn't work, they took him back to Anchorage and dumped him off."

"What about Herman Gordaoff?"

Kate was already dialing her cell phone.

Comments

> Mrs. Doogan says, "Who asked you to come back to the tower, the air traffic controllers or the people who crashed in the Super Cub? Who doesn't have a record, Brendan or the plane's owner? Who does Kate believe, Brendan or the plane's owner? Who didn't know, Myra or Louise? Spend a little time matching your nouns and verbs before you hit 'Post.' Also, employing parentheses within parentheses requires more care and caution than you show here. I understand that the blog format is a conversational one, but can you imagine being allowed to get all that out in a conversation? And being understood?"

Thursday, October 27th, by Johnny [Reblog]

(http://www.thecordovatimes.com/) BODY OF EYAK ELDER FOUND—Acting on information received from Alaska private investigator E. I. "Kate" Shugak, authorities discovered the body of Herman Obadaiah Gordaoff at a remote cabin on his gold claim on Cheneganak Creek in Prince William Sound. Evidence at the scene indicated that Gordaoff had been physically assaulted and that he had been dead for some time before his body was found. The Alaska State Troopers say that the investigation is ongoing.

Comments

Friday, October 28th, by Johnny

We went home by way of Cordova. We met up with Myra Gordaoff at the Cordova House, who had been out at her grandfather's cabin at Boswell Bay. She's a quiet, pretty girl with a lot of black hair who seems younger than nineteen. We told her what we think happened.

She was, I don't know, kind of frozen. She wouldn't believe us about the boyfriend, but she did say she didn't like his friend, Fred. She said Fred was a pilot, that he was older than Chris, and that they had both come to Alaska this summer, looking for work. She said that she and Chris had gone out to Boswell Bay to spend the weekend, and then Fred flew out to pick him up because he said he had a line on a couple of high-paying jobs in Prudhoe Bay. Chris told Myra he'd be right back and to wait for him. When he didn't show up, she hitched a ride back to Cordova with a fisherman named Hank and his daughter, Annie.

I remember once Jim telling me that the worst part of being a state trooper was having to inform the victim's family. "You never know how they're going to react," he said.

You sure don't.

Comments
   Mrs. Doogan says, [Comment deleted by author.]
   Katya says, "I got my Mr. moon"
   Katya says, "mom says thanks JOhnny!!!!@!"

Thursday, December 5th, by Johnny [Reblog]

(www.ADN.com, 10am) USCG CALLS OFF SEARCH—The U.S. Coast Guard has called off the search for a small airplane missing since the end of October. The pilot, Frederick Berdoll, age 41, of Anchorage and his passenger, Christopher Mason, 37, also of Anchorage, took off in Berdoll's Cessna 172 from Cordova, where Mason was visiting his fiancée, Myra Gordaoff.

Rescuers, including response teams from Kulis Air National Guard Base and the Civil Air Patrol, searched for weeks but found neither debris nor any sign of either Berdoll or Mason. Since much of the flight plan was over the Sound, it is assumed that the plane must have gone down in the water. "Currents and tides in Prince William Sound are pretty powerful," NWS meteorologist Jim Kemper said. "That plane is probably halfway to Hawaii by now."

The day after the plane failed to arrive at Lake Hood as scheduled, Myra Gordaoff said, "I waved them off from the Cordova airport. They should have been back in Anchorage later that afternoon. I watched until they were out of sight and I'm no pilot but the plane seemed okay to me."

(www.adn.com, 4:13pm update) The disappearance of Berdoll and Mason took an odd twist when this afternoon a spokesman for the Alaska State Troopers reported that the Cessna 172 in which the two men were flying was revealed to have been stolen from Lake Hood airstrip the week before it disappeared. The aircraft was registered to Matthew Liedholm of Airport Heights, who said he had been notified of its theft by the police. "Kinda wonder what I'm getting for my tiedown fee," Liedholm said. He also said that to his knowledge he had never met either of the missing men.

Comments

> George says, "Lots of easy ways to screw with an airplane engine so it don't get where it's supposed to go. Hell, sugar in the gas tank. Don't have to be an A&P to figger that."
>
> Jim says, "No wreckage, no evidence. No evidence, no case."
>
> Bobby says, "Revenge is a dish best served cold."
>
> Mrs. Doogan says, "Libel: a written statement in which a plaintiff in certain courts sets forth the cause of action or the relief sought. (www.merriam-webster. com)"
>
> RangerDan says, [Comment deleted by author.]
>
> Bernie says, [Comment deleted by author.]
>
> Bobby says, "Wimps."

Dana Stabenow was born in Anchorage and raised on a seventy-five-foot fish tender in the Gulf of Alaska. She knew there was a warmer, drier job out there somewhere and found it in writing. Her first science fiction novel, *Second Star,* sank without a trace; her first crime fiction novel, *A Cold Day for Murder,* won an Edgar Award; her first thriller, *Blindfold Game,* hit the *New York Times* bestseller list; and her twenty-eighth novel and nineteenth Kate Shugak novel, *Restless in the Grave,* comes out in February 2012. Stabenow currently lives in Alaska. Her long, intimate relationship with Sherlock Holmes began when she got to the Ds of the Seldovia Public Library when she was ten years old. She only hopes Mary Russell doesn't find out.

An eerily similar adventure is recounted by Dr. Watson in "The Adventure of the Greek Interpreter," which was first published in *The Strand Magazine* in 1893, and can be found in *The Memoirs of Sherlock Holmes.*

The Case That Holmes Lost

Charles Todd

John Whitman rose as the door to his office opened and an energetic man, his face lined with worry, walked in.

"Sir Arthur," he said, offering his hand.

Sir Arthur Conan Doyle took it in a firm grip, saying, "Thank you for seeing me so quickly, John. It's rather urgent." Taking the chair across from his solicitor's desk, he went on, "Holmes has got himself into a great deal of trouble."

Hiding a smile, Whitman said, "Indeed."

"Yes," Conan Doyle replied testily. "He's being sued."

"Sued! Are you quite serious?"

"I don't joke about such matters, I assure you."

"But Holmes—I beg your pardon for saying this—but he's your creation. I can understand that someone might sue you. It's not that unusual for an author to be sued. Plagiarism, for one thing; libel for another. Infringement of rights. But no one sues his chief character."

"Yes, well, there's a first time for everything. It's a frivolous suit. I want it dismissed."

Whitman reached for a sheaf of paper and his pen. "Let's begin at the beginning. Why is Holmes being sued?"

"Smith—my editor—wanted a new story, and I wrote one for him. It was loosely based on something that happened while

I was in Edinburgh, studying medicine. Of course I changed the setting from Scotland to London, and I changed names. The result was a very different case, and well suited to Holmes. There is absolutely no reason why anyone should have uncovered the source of the plot."

"And what has become of this story? Have you turned it over to your editor?"

"As soon as it was finished. Three days later I was informed that someone intended to sue Holmes."

"How did this someone come to know of the existence of your manuscript?"

"There is the crux of the problem, you see. He couldn't have. Only two people had read the story. I was one, of course, and my editor was the other."

"How did you send this manuscript to him?"

Conan Doyle smiled. "A question worthy of Holmes. By private messenger. But from the time the manuscript left my hands to the time it was delivered was no more than three quarters of an hour. Hardly time to read the story, much less make a copy of it for anyone."

"Had you told anyone else you were writing this particular story?"

"No, no. That would have defeated my purpose in changing the details."

"Will you tell me a little about this case?"

Conan Doyle hesitated, then said, "Yes, of course. You must know what it is about, if you are to shut down this ridiculous business before it becomes public knowledge."

He got up and walked to the window, gazing down into the busy street below.

"You see, Scottish law isn't quite the same as English law. In addition to the usual verdict of guilty or not guilty, there is a third possibility: not proven. It is sometimes a limbo, where one is neither exonerated nor convicted. There have been a few famous cases where this verdict became a millstone around the neck of the accused."

"As a solicitor, I'm aware of this difference," Whitman said dryly.

Conan Doyle glanced over his shoulder. "Yes, of course, how stupid of me." He went back to his study of the street.

"A man was accused of murder. He was, in fact, a colleague of mine, although he was five years older and already in private practice. It was said that William—I shan't give you his surname, unless you must have it—that William had become enamored of one of his patients. That much is quite true. According to later accounts she refused his advances, reminding him that she was in fact a happily married woman. Still, he was clearly obsessed with her, and in the end, he convinced himself—so it was claimed—that his chances would be improved if she found herself a widow. And so he set about devising the means by which to accomplish this."

"He intended to murder her husband?" Whitman asked, shocked.

"Sadly, the police insist that he did just that. I should like to think that I'm a good enough judge of character to believe otherwise. The William I thought I knew could have wished with all his heart that this woman was free, but that's vastly different from deciding to act on such a wish."

Whitman could hear the ambivalence in Conan Doyle's voice. As if duty compelled him to profess faith in a friend, but later events made him begin to doubt his own judgment.

"What means would he have employed? If he had decided to act?"

"In the medical profession there are a number of drugs that can be used for the good of a patient—but in the hands of an unscrupulous person, they can also be used to kill. All that is required, then, is an opportunity to employ one of these drugs. And in due course, the victim—the husband—was dispatched. Or simply died, depending on whether you believe William or the case against him. Oddly enough, the grieving widow found William a pillar of strength during the year that followed, and increasingly leaned on him during the long months of probate.

This of course gave William hope, and he even began to think about proposing marriage as soon as a decent period of mourning ended. When he did declare himself, the lovely widow asked for twenty-four hours in which to consider her answer. The next morning, instead of learning his fate, he was taken up by the police on a charge of murder."

"Upon what evidence?" Whitman asked. "After a year's time?"

"The widow had been reminded that William had made advances while her husband was still alive."

"Reminded by whom? Do you know?"

"By her maid," Conan Doyle said. "She was in fact one of the witnesses against William."

"And who reminded her maid?" Whitman asked, curious.

"I don't believe anyone did. It appeared that she'd never cared for William and persuaded her mistress that he'd not behaved properly while the victim was still alive. William denied that he had done any such thing or had spoken out of turn while the lady was still married. At any rate, the case came to trial. But the jury wasn't satisfied that the police had discovered the method of killing the husband. Suspicion was one thing. However, the postmortem had shown no particular cause of death—a healthy man of thirty-seven seldom drops dead without some underlying condition, but there was nothing. And you must know there is no universal test for poison. Those that the coroner did make, given the unusual circumstances, were negative, and at the time of death, no suspicion fell on William or anyone else. Still, with the widow's finger now pointing at him, the police were willing to reconsider the matter."

"I can see why this case interested you."

"Indeed. William's counsel argued that William had not gained in any way from the man's death, that his proposal was the result of propinquity, not premeditation. The eventual verdict was not proven, and William was set free. Meanwhile, the widow finally made her choice, and it wasn't William. Even more painful was the fact that she chose a friend of his. Still, the damage to his reputation had been done, and William never practiced medicine again."

"But of course, Holmes didn't leave it there."

Conan Doyle came back to his chair and sat down. "No, no, how could he? The fact is, he discovered that William—he's called Hamilton in the story—had been the victim of a clever plot. This trial took place in an English courtroom, you understand, where of course poor William was found guilty. The truth was, the now-wealthy widow and the friend she later married had devised a plan to rid themselves of her husband. First she had let William believe that she could care for him. Second, she had used a poison, so as to point directly to William, the medical man. The only problem was that in their ignorance of such matters, the plotters chose a West African poison so obscure it couldn't be traced. Rather than one that William might have selected from his medical bag, you see. But there was other evidence, manufactured but sound enough for conviction."

"Why West Africa?"

"I was there for a time, you know. And in my story, so was the man the widow eventually marries. At any rate, this conniving widow had encouraged Holmes's client, William, from the start, leading him to believe she cared for him. The poor man had no chance against such a devious pair. Yet it looked very dark for him, the date of execution having been set. Just the sort of hopeless case that would appeal to Holmes. There's the matter of obscure poisons as well. Holmes has always prided himself on his knowledge of that subject. And William's plea to Holmes to look into his plight interested Dr. Watson as well, of course, since there was a physician involved. 'First do no harm,' the oath admonishes. What's more, Watson had served in India and had some little understanding of the unique properties of many plants that we in England aren't acquainted with."

Intrigued, John Whitman asked, "And how did Holmes solve this case?"

"The final clue comes when Holmes bluffs the widow by telling her that since she is wealthier than her new husband, she should beware. And he shows her an empty envelope that Mycroft has given him from Foreign Office correspondence, posted from Africa but with the address removed—Holmes knows something about inks, as you recall—and replaced with that of her husband's place of business. And Holmes wonders aloud if the man has sent for more of the same poison. The letter here is missing, you understand, but she believes Holmes when he tells her that this envelope was found in the dustbin at her London house. She dissolves into tears and confesses—she thinks to save her own life—how her new husband came up with and carried out this wicked scheme."

"Have you considered—there may be more truth in your work of fiction than someone could safely ignore? And not necessarily in Scotland."

"Yes, that's always possible. But the question remains: how did anyone come to know that I was writing such a story, and what's more, that it was finished? This happened in Edinburgh more than a quarter of a century ago. And William is dead. Did I tell you that? He took his own life in a bout of severe depression some years after the trial. That's why I felt safe in using the facts of the case in my story."

"Then I find it interesting that someone has chosen to sue Sherlock Holmes and not Sir Arthur Conan Doyle."

"Well, I'm glad you find it interesting," Conan Doyle snapped irritably. "How do they expect to bring Holmes into a court-room, I ask you!"

"Perhaps it has nothing to do with Holmes or a suit against him. Perhaps someone wishes to see you settle this case out of court. For instance, with an offer of money."

"I shall do no such thing. And what about this short story? Am I to allow my editor to publish it? Or am I to abandon it like an unwanted child? Smith will not be happy with me, I can tell you, if I withdraw it. He has already scheduled its publication, and is poised to announce a new Holmes to readers in the next issue of *The Strand Magazine*."

"That will have to be dealt with. At the moment, I think we should have a conversation with the solicitor representing your adversary."

"To call him an adversary is to give him status. Moriarty was an adversary. Irene Adler was an adversary. Whoever is plaguing me with this suit is nothing of the sort."

Whitman smiled. "Yes, I take your point. Who is the solicitor?"

"A man called Baines. He has chambers in London on Ironmonger Lane. Rather an unprepossessing address. As you would expect of someone willing to be involved in such a frivolous business."

"I'll call on him tomorrow. Meanwhile, I advise you to think no more about it."

But Conan Doyle wasn't satisfied. "I should like to know how the manuscript fell into the hands of these people."

"Have you had anyone in to work on drains? To look for dry rot or worm in the attics? Anyone who could have had access to your study?"

"By God. There was a chimney sweep last week."

"The same one you have employed before this?"

"How should I know? Their faces are always black with soot. But there was no reason—until now, at any rate—to suspect he was anything other than what he claimed to be. I don't deal with such matters, but I saw him walking to the service door as I left one morning."

"Ah. Was the manuscript accessible? Could he have read it?"

"I suppose he could. But if he had no idea I was writing such a story—and no one did—how could he have known to look for it?"

"Perhaps any story would have done. You are a famous author, after all. It isn't out of the realm of possibility that you'd be currently at work on a Holmes case."

Conan Doyle hesitated. "I did inquire of a friend in Edinburgh to discover what had become of the principals in the real case. I was told the clever widow and her new husband left for

Canada shortly after William's suicide. But Fergus MacTaggart is utterly trustworthy. He and William and I were close at one time. MacTaggart remained William's friend when everyone else turned his back."

"Everyone appears to be trustworthy, until we've been shown otherwise."

"Yes, well, it's easier to write about devious people than it is to search for them in one's own life."

With that he left. Whitman looked down at his notes. Would Conan Doyle's editor wish to publish a short story that was the center of controversy? If it increased circulation, probably. But if it led to questions about the story itself, would Herbert Smith shy away from it? And was that the reason behind this suit? Holmes had a brilliant track record as a consulting detective. Had he stumbled on a truth that someone wished to keep out of the public eye?

That seemed to be the crux of the case. A settlement that included an agreement to withdraw the story from publication would prove the point.

But the question was, who would benefit from withdrawing the story? That remained to be seen.

The next morning Whitman went to call on Ronald Baines.

His chambers were in the first floor of Number 12 Iron-monger Lane. The door was paneled mahogany, with a brass plate affixed to it. Whitman opened it to find a well-furnished waiting room. A clerk came in as soon as Whitman was about to take a seat.

"Do you have an appointment, sir?" the man asked, peering at Whitman over the top of his glasses.

Whitman identified himself and the reason for his visit.

The clerk said, "I'll see if Mr. Baines is free." He went away and Whitman took a chair by the window, watching clouds scuttle across the city, promising a change in the fine weather London had been enjoying.

The clerk finally reappeared and informed Whitman that Mr. Baines would see him, but only for ten minutes, as he was expecting another client at eleven o'clock. He led Whitman down a passage where gilt-framed hunting prints were hung. The room at the end of the passage was spacious and occupied a corner of the building. A French Empire desk took pride of place, and behind it a large, florid man rose to hold out his hand.

"Good morning," he said affably. "I don't believe we've had the pleasure of meeting before this."

"Thank you for seeing me," Whitman replied. "I've come about the suit pending against Sherlock Holmes."

Baines indicated a chair. "Ah, yes. Indeed."

"I'm astonished, to put it mildly, that you would take on such a frivolous matter."

"Hardly frivolous. My client had considered suing Sir Arthur, but the problem isn't the author, the problem is his character. Mr. Holmes has taken on an unusual case and solved it with his usual skill. It is that skill which is the problem. My client feels that in solving the mystery at hand, he has put my client in jeopardy of his livelihood."

"I must say, I don't see how that's possible. Mr. Holmes is a fictional character. Do you tell me that your client is also fictional?"

There was a flash of anger in Ronald Baines's eyes. "I can assure you that he is quite real. As it happens, his wife died recently, and he has been occupying himself in writing a book concerning a certain murder case in Scotland many years ago. It is currently under consideration by a publishing house. If Mr. Holmes solves it before the manuscript has been sold, who will be interested in it? When Mr. Holmes has taken the wind out of its sails, so to speak."

"I don't see that there's a problem. One is nonfiction, and the other fiction. How do they overlap?"

Baines said, "Mr. Holmes is a name most everyone in Britain recognizes. Indeed, he's considered the premier consulting detective in the world; his popularity is undeniable. And he is about to steal my client's livelihood."

"I should like to know how your client discovered that such a story was being written by Sir Arthur. As far as I'm aware, only two people knew the contents of that particular case."

"Let us say that a friend felt he should be made aware of Conan Doyle's intentions."

"And all your client wishes is to see the story withdrawn from publication? No monetary damages? No other requirements to be satisfied before the suit is withdrawn?"

"My client is not a mercenary man. He merely wishes to have the story withdrawn, so as to protect his own work. And a promise, of course, from your client, that he will never speak of this story again. Surely this is not a difficult decision. Sir Arthur is a very clever writer; he can easily invent another case in place of this one."

"I should like to know the name of your client."

"Ah. I'm afraid I can't answer that. He has asked for anonymity. Adverse publicity will also do him considerable harm, you see. He has a right to see his work in print and successful. And judged on its own merit. How can that be, if there are comparisons with Holmes at every turn? That will be brought up, do you see, in every review, and speculation will grow over the way Holmes solved the murder. Sir Arthur is an author; he will surely appreciate the problem."

"Sir Arthur has changed the facts in the case."

"But not sufficiently, sad to say."

It was clear that Baines had given all the information that he was willing to divulge.

Still, Whitman persisted. "Will he step out of the shadows, your client, if Sir Arthur agrees to the withdrawal of the story? After all, you have the advantage of us. We don't know who we're dealing with."

"I think he will not."

"Then I shall have to consult my client to see how he feels about your demands."

"Not demands. A request, merely. From one author to another."

Whitman left shortly thereafter, unsatisfied. He sent word to his own client, and that afternoon Conan Doyle arrived at his chambers. After telling him what had transpired at Baines's office, Whitman asked, "How do you feel about withdrawing your story?"

"This client forgets that Holmes is also my own livelihood. If someone else is writing a book on the events I used for Holmes's case, then he should have contacted me personally and asked that I withdraw it until such time as his book is published. I'd have taken his request under consideration—even if I don't feel I have stepped on his toes in any way. Call it professional courtesy."

"But not knowing you personally, he couldn't have counted on your good will. Or professional courtesy."

"True." Conan Doyle sighed. "I can see his dilemma. But I'm still angry over this suit."

"Do you know of anyone who could have a reason either to write his own version of events or to question yours?"

"No one. In fact, yesterday afternoon I went to speak to a friend of mine. I asked if she could identify the forces set against me. She said the dead are no threat to me."

"You visited a *seer*?" Whitman was taken aback.

"I thought it wise," Conan Doyle replied defensively. "After all, if this person lives in the shadows, I have a right to seek him out in any way I can."

"I must remind you that the seer's advice is all very well and good—but a dead man cannot bring suit in an English courtroom. My suggestion, as your legal adviser, is to let this suit proceed and see then who comes out of those shadows."

"At what expense to my story?"

"I don't know. You must answer that. Is the story so important?"

"I think Holmes was particularly clever in this one. I should hate to lose it. And it isn't the story of William—well, of *that* William. It was a starting point only. The rest is Holmes. I've had a very uneasy relationship with him, my creation or not, as you well know. But I cannot spite him."

"What about the widow and her new husband? Your story isn't complimentary toward them. After all, they were never tried—if your conclusions are correct, they may be at some risk, if the police see fit to reopen the case. And Canada is not that far away."

"How would they have discovered what I was doing? And they would be foolish to raise objections. To do so would only draw attention to them."

"Baines told me that his client had recently lost his wife. That could very well mean that this is the widow's husband, returned to England or Scotland to live."

"I can believe in a jealous author before—" Conan Doyle stopped in midsentence, and then asked, "His client's wife died recently, you say?"

"Yes. It was the reason his client turned to writing—a way of managing his grief."

Conan Doyle frowned. "MacTaggart." He got up and began to pace the floor. "He has just lost his own wife. Confound it, I thought he was reliable. I hadn't counted on grief turning his mind. It's the only explanation for his behavior."

Whitman answered carefully. "Where does his loyalty lie, I wonder? Either he betrayed you to someone—"

"It's the only solution. Not the sweep. MacTaggart."

"—or he himself has something to fear from your story. How would Holmes see this?"

Conan Doyle stopped his pacing, sat down, and stared at his solicitor. "In my story," he said slowly, "Holmes faults the man who conducted the postmortem. He believed that he'd muddled the case."

Whitman said nothing.

As he examined the past, Conan Doyle's eyes went to the framed photograph of the king above Whitman's head.

"Damn it. There's no book being written, is there? Holmes saw it from the beginning! I took his remarks to Watson to mean that the man didn't know enough about poisons. But it wasn't that, was it? In the Scottish case, *MacTaggart* did the postmortem. And he shouldn't have, don't you see? At the time, I believed he was just the man to find out how Moira's husband had died. Good God, we all knew that MacTaggart had been one of Moira MacGregor's suitors before she was married. We never dreamed he still cared for her. I'd suspected William Scott had been infatuated with her. I wasn't surprised when he was in and out of her house after her husband's death, helping her with the funeral arrangements and the will. The family doctor and all that. MacTaggart was there nearly as often, and we put it down to kindness."

"And no one wondered at this?"

"We never gave it a thought. He must have been the first to realize that Moira was favoring William. He was there to see it for himself. If he'd killed the husband only to watch another man usurp his place, it would explain everything. What's more, it could very well have been MacTaggart who put a word in the maid's ear after William proposed. Who better?"

"Who, indeed," Whitman agreed. "He could hardly speak against William Scott himself. The widow wouldn't have listened. Was he a persuasive man? Could he have managed that?"

"MacTaggart? Not persuasive, precisely. But his reputation for rectitude and honesty was well known. The maid would have taken to heart any such concern on his part. And he could have thought himself safe in blaming William, because he'd already declared that no poison had been found in the victim's body. Well, of course it hadn't—he himself had seen to that. Fortunately for William, that was also what led to the verdict of not proven. MacTaggart was *jealous* of William. The man he claimed was his dearest *friend.*" Conan Doyle surged to his feet. "And now he wants Holmes silenced. Because Holmes could raise questions about the case."

"Legally it makes sense. If he had brought suit against you, we would have had to know his name. By attacking your creation, he could remain anonymous."

"By God, I'll have his liver for this."

He was already on his way to the door. Turning, he said to his solicitor, "My fame counts for something. Thanks to Holmes, although sometimes it galls me to say it. I'm about to ask the Home Office to exhume William Scott's body. He hanged himself in the stairwell of his home. But did he? Was this suicide MacTaggart's final act of revenge against William?"

"The Home Office—" John Whitman began.

"I know. They have no authority in Scotland. But you see, William Scott went to live in Northumberland after the trial. Driven out of Edinburgh by the verdict of not proven. And so he died in England. I'll give you any odds you like that it was murder. The trial was not punishment enough. MacTaggart wanted poor William hounded to his grave. And I call myself a writer of detective fiction. *It happened under my nose, and I didn't see it.*"

"You did," Whitman pointed out. "You let Holmes solve it for you. Still, if MacTaggart is convicted in England for William Scott's murder, that won't clear Scott's name."

"Indeed it will. I'll see to that. Perhaps not in a Scottish court, but in the court of public opinion."

"What will you do about the story now?"

"Destroy it. Write something else. If I'm to be involved in William's redemption, I want Holmes out of it. I don't want that case clouding what I'm about to do."

"Is that fair to Holmes?" Whitman asked. "I've yet to read the story, but I can see it was brilliant detection. As well as true."

"You will never read it," Conan Doyle replied grimly. "As you said, I created Holmes. I tried once to destroy him and failed. But I can take this case away from him. I can do that."

And he was gone, slamming the door behind him.

"Charles Todd" is the mother and son team of Charles and Caroline Todd. They are the authors of thirteen Ian Rutledge novels, two Bess Crawford novels, *The Murder Stone,* and many short stories. Their latest Rutledge is *A Lonely Death* (Morrow, January 2011) and the new Bess Crawford title is *A Bitter Truth* (Morrow, August 2011). "Charles Todd" is a *New York Times* bestselling author, and they have received nominations for the

Edgar, Anthony, John Creasey, and Indie Awards, and won the Deadly Pleasures Mystery Magazine–Barry Award. They live on the East Coast of the United States.

Caroline's fourth-grade teacher promised to read to her class the last twenty minutes of each day if they were good and worked hard. Fortunately, the teacher loved Sherlock Holmes and didn't think him too mature for nine-year-olds. Caroline admits to owing her not only for the multiplication tables and long division but for opening a new world of adventure and mystery that was just as valuable. As an "innocent young lad," Charles met Sherlock Holmes through Dr. Watson as read to him before bedtime by his mother. He went off to sleep dreaming of redheaded speckled-banded stick figures from Bohemia.

Although the events recorded in this story are not dated, it clearly takes place after 1905, when King Edward was on the throne and Sir Arthur had accepted a knighthood. From 1903 to 1927, tales of Holmes continued to appear sporadically in *The Strand Magazine,* under the steady editorial hand of Herbert Greenhough Smith.

The Imitator

Jan Burke

A summer storm caused us to cancel our plans to ride to the river and spend a lazy day fishing. By one o'clock, we had tired of billiards, cards, and chess. We had adjourned to the upstairs library, where I got no further in a letter to my sister than "Dear Sarah,…"

For his part, Slye stood at one of the long windows, staring out toward the woods beyond the back lawn. The rain had let up, but the day was still misty, so I doubted he could see much.

Not much that was actually there, in any case.

I had been more anxious about him a few hours earlier. The first thunderclap had me watching him with concern. He noted my scrutiny with a wry smile, and turned his back to me. I kept watching. Although I saw a certain rigidity in his spine and shoulders, he did not seem unsettled to the degree I might once have expected, and I began to cherish hope that he might, after all, be able to return to the city at some point in time. Seven months had passed from the time of the incident that had encouraged his family to urge him to retire to the country. He had asked me to come with him, an invitation I had happily accepted.

Some men returned from the Great War whole of body and mind. Slye and I, while thankful (on our good days) to have survived, were not undamaged. My scars were plainly visible, but his had not made themselves known—to others, at least—until nearly a year after we had returned. Slye would, I thought, soon fit back into society. The methods espoused by Dr. Rivers of England for the treatment of what some call "shell shock" were doing him a great deal of good.

I had just decided not to interrupt Slye's brooding silence when his excellent butler, Digby, quietly entered the room.

"Excuse me, sir. The younger Mr. Hanslow—Mr. Aloysius Hanslow—"

Digby got no further—Wishy Hanslow dodged past him, disheveled and a little damp.

Hanslow wore his usual outfit—clothing of another decade, another continent, another man. Slye had once explained to me that long before Hanslow became a devoted reader of Sir Arthur Conan Doyle's books, Wishy had found an 1891 copy of the *Strand* among the stacks of periodicals his father hoarded— which perhaps had planted the seed that later blossomed into his present mania for all things Sherlockian. Hanslow had been particularly taken with one of Sidney Paget's drawings from "The Boscombe Valley Mystery," and two years ago his tailor and hatter had been charged with re-creating Sherlock Holmes's long coat and deerstalker. Judging by the condition of these articles of clothing, Hanslow seemed not to have seen the drawings in which Holmes carried an umbrella.

"No need to announce me, Digby!" Hanslow said now. "No need! All family here!"

"Indeed?" Digby said in an arctic tone.

"Of course! I think of Bunny as a brother!"

"Now, Wishy," Slye said, as Digby frowned, "stop trying to irritate Digby. You and I are friends, and as such, far more likely to get along than I do with my brothers." He turned to Digby. "Thank you, Digby."

"Sir, he would not let me take his hat and coat," Digby said, looking anxiously at the carpet.

"No, I don't suppose he would," Slye said. "But we'll be leaving soon, I'm sure, so no need to worry."

"Don't know why you keep him around," Wishy said as soon as the butler left. "If I had to look at that mug of his seven days a week, I'd be a nerve case, too. Sure that's not your problem?"

I couldn't help but stiffen. Slye observed this, smiled at me, then said, "Do you suppose Wishy is on to something, Max?"

Hanslow turned, only just then noticing my presence. He winced and moved his gaze to a point somewhere over my left shoulder. "Oh, didn't realize you were in the room, Dr. Tyndale." He didn't sound pleased. The feeling was mutual.

"No, Wishy isn't on to anything," I said, answering Slye. "What would you do without Digby?"

"True," Slye said. "He is indispensable to what passes for my happiness. Now, Wishy, what brings you out on this dreary day?"

"Crime, Bunny! Crime. I need your help! Lord, I wish you'd get a telephone!"

"I find them unrestful."

"You have one in the city!"

"Yes, but the city is already unrestful, so I don't notice it as much there."

"Well, never mind that. Will you come with me to Holder's Crossing?"

"What has occurred at Holder's Crossing?"

"The colonel's gone missing—looks like foul play."

"Not Colonel Harris?" Slye said, looking troubled.

"Yes. Sheriff Anderson called and particularly asked me to lend a hand. Mentioned you, too, Bunny. Must have my Watson with me. And—er, you can come along as well, Dr. Tyndale, if you'd like."

"We'd be delighted to help in any way possible," Slye said. "Wouldn't we, Max?"

This was by no means the first time we had accompanied Wishy on such an expedition. I had given up trying to persuade Slye that we were only encouraging Hanslow to embrace his delusion that he was an American Sherlock Holmes. Bunny rightly pointed out that Wishy would never claim to be as great as his hero. "Of course not!" I said. "My dear Slye, the gap between the intelligence of the two is nearly as wide as the ocean that separates them!"

"Oh no," Slye said in his calm way. "Wishy isn't at all stupid."

I kept my tongue behind my teeth. Sometimes, friends must agree—even if silently—to disagree.

Wishy Hanslow had a second obsession—automobiles. I have been told that he razed his former stables and built a structure that houses no fewer than ten of them. It was easier to abide this infatuation. As a result of it, we rode in comfort in his chauffeured Pierce-Arrow Series 51 limousine to Holder's Crossing. On the way, I asked him why he had been out in the storm.

"Oh, you've noticed my clothing is a bit damp! Very observant. I was coming back from driving myself to a separate case—"

"I told you I would have driven you, sir!" the chauffeur said.

"Yes, well, now I wish I had listened to you. Thing is, bad roads, had a flat, and had just managed to change the tire when the rain started."

Slye asked him about that case, which involved finding a missing dog, detective work that apparently fell within Wishy's capabilities. Somehow in the telling of his tale, he seemed to grow more accustomed to my scarred face, actually looking me in the eye when he answered my questions.

When Slye asked what he knew about the case at Holder's Crossing, though, he blushed and admitted that he knew very little. Sheriff Anderson had called and stated that Colonel Harris had gone missing. "Said there was reason to suspect foul play, but that he would explain everything in detail if I would be so good as to bring you along."

"How kind of him to mention me," Slye said.

"I've asked him to ensure that nothing is disturbed until we get there. He promised he would do his best."

"You know this missing gentleman?" I asked.

"Oh yes. He must be in his seventies now. I haven't seen him in years, though."

He briefly fell into one of his moods, but Wishy's incessant chatter seemed to distract him, for by the time we arrived at Colonel Harris's estate, he was looking mildly amused.

The estate lay three miles or so beyond Holder's Crossing. We took a winding, mostly paved, relatively wide road up a wooded slope, passing a few narrow farm lanes here and there, before suddenly coming upon a clearing. A large two-story home stood at the end of a sweeping drive. The house was not as large as Slye's, nor even Hanslow's, but there could be no doubt that this was the home of a wealthy man. The grounds, although not extensive, were well kept. A service road led to a horse barn and other outbuildings, but no other houses were within sight. The home's situation, placed as it was within the woods, gave one a sense of peacefulness and privacy.

A Model T was parked in the drive. It was splattered with so much mud that the grime nearly obscured the sheriff's department's markings on its doors. The vehicle was dwarfed by the far less muddied yellow Rolls-Royce parked next to it, a gorgeous machine that drew a sigh from Wishy. "A forty/fifty," he said. "Silver Ghost. Six cylinders and quiet as a whisper."

"The colonel's?" I asked.

"Oh, I doubt that very much," Hanslow said. "He's something of a pinchpenny."

"Still getting around by horse and buggy?"

"No, he sold off his horses five years ago, on his seventieth birthday."

He fell silent, and suddenly looked so sad, I couldn't help but feel both pity and curiosity. I was about to ask him what was wrong, when Slye said, "Wishy is an expert on automobiles, and a walking catalog of his neighbors' vehicles. What does the colonel drive, Aloysius?"

"Model T Center Door Sedan—1915, I believe," he answered, perking up. "Thank you, Bunny. I'm flattered you've noticed.

I have a scheme in mind about the individual identification of automobiles, but I haven't quite worked out all the details."

"License plates do that, don't they?" I asked.

"Oh, no. Not at all. Easy to switch them. Now what I have in mind involves something like the engine casting number—"

I was spared a lecture on his automotive identification scheme when the chauffeur opened his car door before ours, causing Wishy to remonstrate with him, and to switch his attention to the topic of automotive etiquette, and his strong view that his passengers should have been allowed to exit first.

◇◇◇

The colonel's elderly butler, Rawls, knew my companions—I noticed he did not attempt to relieve Wishy of his deerstalker. He looked pale and shaken, but maintained a dignified pace as he guided us to a parlor on the first floor. Sheriff Anderson, a stout man of sixty with luxuriant mustachios, stood by the fireplace, studying a small notebook. He looked up as we were announced and smiled. "Aloysius, thank you for coming! And you've brought Mr. Slye and Dr. Tyndale! Excellent!"

"Is this some sort of jest?"

We turned toward the speaker—a frowning, elegantly dressed young blonde, who lounged carelessly in a large chair at the opposite end of the room. She flinched when she beheld my beauty, and quickly busied herself with taking a cigarette from a gold case and fitting it into an ebony holder.

She was not alone. A pale, sandy-haired gentleman, whose clothes were equally fine, stood just behind her. He blushed when our eyes met, then moved to light her cigarette.

"You own the Rolls-Royce Silver Ghost parked in the drive," Hanslow said with some reverence, removing his hat in the lady's presence.

She lifted her brows and addressed the sheriff. "Is this play actor supposed to find my uncle?"

"Allow me to introduce Colonel Harris's niece and nephew, the children of his youngest sister," Sheriff Anderson said coldly. "Miss Alice Simms and Mr. Anthony Simms."

Anthony Simms came forward and shook hands with each of us as the sheriff named us. He had an athletic build and a firm grip, but his palms were damp.

Alice stayed where she was.

"Mr. Simms works in an office," Hanslow began. "He rushed here today from work. Note the smudge of ink on his vest—"

"Are you certain that's ink, Aloysius?" Slye asked.

Hanslow held up a large magnifying glass and bent closer to Simms.

"Now, see here!" Simms protested. "I don't know what you're blathering about but I don't care to be—"

Wishy straightened and said with resignation, "No, might not be. But it is a smudge. And it's improperly buttoned."

Simms peered down at his vest in dismay and hastened to correct the buttoning problem.

"I thought you said they were here to help," Alice said to the sheriff. "I really don't think an itemized list of my brother's sartorial mishaps is what we were hoping for."

Sheriff Anderson ignored her and invited us to take seats near the fire, then began to tell us about the case. "At six this morning, Colonel Harris, an early riser, had breakfast with his son."

"His so-called son," Alice interrupted.

"If you please, Miss Alice!" the sheriff snapped.

She sighed dramatically, then fell silent.

"I should explain," the sheriff said, "that the colonel had only recently been reunited with his son. It seems that during the colonel's service in the previous war—er, well—I should say, the war with Spain."

"Ah, yes," Slye said. "The 'splendid little war.' He fought in Cuba."

"Yes," the sheriff said. "Not a Rough Rider, but with the regular army. A major at that time, then promoted again not long before he left the military. He had been in the cavalry since the Civil War."

"Bunny and I used to love to listen to his war stories," Wishy said.

"When we were children, yes," Slye said. "But you were going to tell us about his son?"

"Yes, of course," the sheriff said. "The colonel has outlived his two sisters, his only siblings, but to the surprise of their offspring, he recently revealed that while he was in Cuba, he married an American woman whose family had been living in Havana for some years."

Alice said, "Oh, no. We've known about the marriage for years. It was Uncle's Tragic Love Story. At the ripe old age of fifty-three, he fell head over heels for his nurse—a dark-haired woman thirty years his junior—while he was delirious with yellow fever. Typical silly old man, wasn't he? He recovered and was shipped back before he could make arrangements for her to join him. But here's the thing—according to my uncle, she died there. I remember Mama saying it was for the best, or we would have been mortified by the spectacle he would have made of himself. For my own part, I thought it was good to know the old dickens had had a bit of fun."

"The colonel didn't quite look at it in that way," the sheriff said repressively. "He thought the woman he loved had died. Turns out, she didn't. That is, not at that time. She gave birth to a son, and continued to live in Cuba until she died two years ago."

"Never contacting her husband—her *wealthy* husband—during those twenty years!" Alice said.

"Nor bothering to divorce him," the sheriff said. "And he didn't make any effort to go down there and find her, now did he? Perhaps that hurt her. I don't know. In any case, according to her son, she decided she didn't want to leave Cuba or her family. She told him his father had died of yellow fever. We have no opportunity to ask her what her motives were, and it hardly matters now. As for the colonel's wealth, her own family is extremely wealthy—wealthier than the colonel, by what the colonel told me. They own a sugar plantation."

Alice subsided.

"Anyway," the sheriff went on, "Robert—his son—was told on his twenty-first birthday that his father the soldier had not died of the fever, as Robert had long believed, but was alive and well. He was given some papers that helped him to track down the colonel—no difficult thing, after all. He came up here last year, and the colonel was delighted to meet him. Welcomed him into his home, couldn't have been prouder."

"Look, we came over here several times to try to get to know Robert," Anthony said. "Welcome him into the family, all that. We just became convinced he was a con man taking advantage of our uncle."

Anderson turned to give a hard stare to the Simmses. "He told me himself that he had no doubt that Robert was his son, but that his nephews and niece weren't taking it too well."

"Nephews?" Wishy said. "Plural?" He looked around as if expecting to find another of the colonel's relatives hiding behind a chair.

"My men are still looking for Carlton Wedge, his other nephew."

"Carlton Wedge!" Wishy said. "Now I look at you, Mr. Simms, I see a family resemblance—no insult intended. You could knock me over with a feather. Never knew he and the old man were related!"

"Well, Uncle really hasn't been part of our lives until recent years," Alice said. "Our mother and Carlton's were much younger than the colonel. He was their half brother—after his mother died, our grandfather married a much younger woman."

"Apples not falling far from trees," Slye murmured to me.

"My uncle was a grown man, out west fighting Indians when his sisters were born," Alice went on. "He was hardly ever home. So the family has never been what one might call close-knit. But in the last five years or so, my uncle has been doing his best to change that."

"Carlton Wedge," Wishy repeated. "Can't think how one would find him. Gambled away the homestead years ago."

"Before the Volstead Act," Slye said, "one would merely have to ask which bar was doing the most business. Now I suppose it will be necessary to search for him in speakeasies."

"As we mentioned to the sheriff," Alice said, "Carlton also drives a Model T."

"No help. So do tens of millions of other Americans." He turned to the sheriff. "Where is Robert Harris? Er—I assume the newly found son is using the colonel's surname?"

"Yes. As for where he is—he is in Mercy Hospital, fighting for his life."

This announcement drew astonished gasps from Hanslow and me, but Slye only said, "As fascinating as these family histories are, I see we have interrupted you too often. Would you please give us the tale from the beginning?"

"Yes, certainly. As I said, the colonel and his son, Robert, had breakfast at six this morning, then spent time together in the colonel's study. Rawls believes they were going over some business papers—apparently the colonel has been including Robert in more and more of his business dealings. The phone rang at eight, and the colonel answered it himself, as is his custom. Then both gentlemen hurried from the house without telling any of the servants where they were bound. They left in the colonel's Model T.

"Shortly before nine o'clock, the housekeeper looked out from one of the upstairs windows. Though it was raining, she caught a glimpse of the colonel's car returning, coming up the road through the woods. She made her way downstairs, to tell the cook that the gentlemen would soon be back, and might want something to eat. But the gentlemen did not enter the house."

He paused, then said, "She is getting on in years, and visibility was limited, so perhaps she was mistaken about the vehicle, because a short time later, Mr. Simms and his sister arrived. They tell me their uncle had asked them to come here, to speak to them about Carlton."

"Carlton had called him in a drunken rage," Alice said. "Threatened him. Said he was convinced Robert was a fraud, pretending to be someone he couldn't possibly be." She looked pointedly toward Wishy, who was busily writing notes. Hearing her pause, he looked up. She smiled at him in the way a shark might smile at a sardine, then said to Slye, "I hasten to add that Uncle wasn't in the least afraid of Carlton—in fact, he's rather fond of him. But he thought it was time to have the dear boy committed to a sanitarium."

"Sheriff Anderson," Slye said, "have you asked Rawls about this threatening call?"

"Yes. He confirms that the colonel not only received a call from Mr. Wedge yesterday, but that two days earlier, Mr. Wedge, while in an inebriated condition, attempted to visit him. The colonel barred him from the house, told him to sleep it off in the horse barn, and, according to Rawls, added that he'd better not show his face around here again until he'd gained some sense. But he also added that the colonel was embarrassed about Mr. Wedge, and never discussed him with the staff."

"Mr. Simms, did you know of this drunken visit?"

Anthony Simms glanced at his sister, then shook his head. "No. Shocking."

"He mentioned it to me," Alice said. "Sorry, darling," she said to Anthony. "I should have told you."

"Interesting," Slye said. "But we are interrupting again. Sheriff, please do continue."

The sheriff consulted his notes. "Shortly after the Simmses arrived, a delivery truck from the village grocer drove up to the back of the house. Normally the boy would have been here early in the morning, but the storm made him decide to make deliveries to his customers who lived on less well maintained roads before those lanes became impassable. He had been delayed all the same, and a lucky thing that turned out to be. The housekeeper, certain that she had seen the colonel's car, wondered if he might have had a flat tire, or some other problem. The young man told her he had seen the Rolls, some distance ahead of him, but not the colonel's Model T. But he promised the housekeeper that he'd keep an eye out on his way back to the village.

"The storm eased about then, and so as the delivery boy made his return trip, he looked down each of the lanes as he passed them. At the fourth such lane, he was greeted with a startling sight—young Mr. Harris, his face covered in blood, lying next to a car.

"The boy hurried down the lane, thinking there had been a terrible accident, but the car appeared to be undamaged. He hardly gave it more than a glance, though, because when he got out of the truck and knelt next to Robert Harris, he saw that the colonel's son had been shot.

"I'll say this for the lad—he had presence of mind. He looked around quickly, and seeing no sign of the colonel or anyone else, put Mr. Harris into his truck and drove as fast as he could toward the village—smart enough to figure out that the doctor would be there, rather than wasting time taking the wounded man back up here, where they'd only have to wait for the doctor to come up. The doctor did the best he could for him, then drove him to Mercy Hospital over in Tarrington."

"They've an excellent man there," I said. "Dr. Charles Smith. We served together overseas. He'll know what to do for such injuries."

"I'm glad to hear that—that's the very man who's caring for him. I've also got two of my deputies there to guard him, and to see if he can tell them anything once the doctor permits them to question him."

He rubbed a hand over his forehead, as if to clear his thoughts.

"So while Robert Harris was being cared for by the medical men, I was called, and the boy took me back to the lane. I was quite anxious to find the colonel, of course. Unfortunately, although his car is there, he's nowhere nearby."

"May I take a look at it?" Wishy asked.

"Yes, I hope you will, because I must say there's something—" He glanced at the Simmses and said, "We can discuss all this along the way."

He rang for Rawls, and asked him to fetch his deputies up from the kitchen, where they had been offered hot coffee and sandwiches.

"Are we to be kept prisoner here, then?" asked Alice.

"It's best for now if you wait here, under guard. I would hate to see any further harm come to any member of your family."

"For our own protection, then?"

"That, and because I feel certain I'll have more questions for you."

"Can I at least stroll around the gardens now that the sun is out?"

The sheriff hesitated, glancing at Slye, who gave the slightest shake of his head. "No, miss," the sheriff said, "I can't risk it. You'll stay in this room, please, and if you have need, there's a lavatory just across the hall. Should you need anything else, food or drink, just ring for Rawls and I'm sure he'll bring it to you."

She pouted, but clearly saw she'd not win him over. Anthony tried to argue that they should at least be given the run of their own uncle's house, but the sheriff, I was quickly learning, was a man who could assert his will when necessary.

The trip to the lane where the car was still parked was brief but productive. Wishy wouldn't hear of taking the Pierce-Arrow down the narrow muddy track, so we cautiously made our way on foot. Fortunately, the summer sun had been out for a little while, so at least we weren't making the trip in the rain.

The sheriff's deputies posted there had made good use of their time, one staying with the car while three others searched the woods. "No sign of the colonel yet, sir," the one at the car reported. "Though it seems obvious that poor young gentleman crawled out to the lane after being shot. We followed your orders and didn't touch the car. Any idea when the fingerprint man will be here?"

"Any time now."

I saw that Hanslow, when in his element, was not the idiot I had assumed him to be. He could not be dissuaded from mimicking what he believed to be Sherlock Holmes's manner of investigating, making use of the magnifying glass, muttering to himself, and frowning a great deal. Slye several times had to point out that there was more than one way to interpret the tire tracks and boot marks Wishy observed in the mud. But these were mere preliminaries.

When Aloysius Hanslow stopped playing at being the Great Detective and really looked at the vehicle mired in the lane, he did what none of the rest of us could do—and with a degree of confidence that transformed him. Some part of my brain registered this transformation, but not for long, for the shock of his pronouncement dislodged all other thought.

"Dear me, Bunny!" he said. "This isn't the colonel's car!"

Slye had an arrested look, as I'm sure we all did. Then he smiled and said, "Tell us how you know."

I couldn't completely follow all that followed, but I could grasp that some sort of difference in radiators and other features of the machine itself were nothing compared to what one could learn simply by looking at—and smelling, through a window that was not quite closed—the interior of the automobile. "Bunny, this car was not owned by a man of the colonel's disposition!"

He was right. The car was strewn with wads of paper, bits of tinfoil wrappers, and empty bottles. It stank of cheap gin and emitted other unsavory odors of unmistakable but unnamable origins. I thought of the neat, well-kept home I had just been in and knew Wishy was absolutely correct.

"Carlton's?" Slye asked.

Wishy surprised me by considering the question carefully as he put on a pair of gloves. "I believe so. Sheriff, you said you'll have a fingerprint man up here soon?"

"Yes, he's on his way. But Aloysius, you know that Carlton's fingerprints on his own car, if it is his car—"

"Certainly—of no use. But if the fingerprints of the colonel and Mr. Robert Harris are on the inside of the vehicle—"

"I don't think anyone other than a driver has recently occupied this vehicle," Slye said, peering in through a side window. "The seats are covered with too much detritus. At the very least, those wads of paper would have been crushed and flattened. I suspect if you are brave enough to look through them, you will find evidence that this is indeed Carlton's Model T. In fact, I can see several envelopes addressed to him lying on the backseat." He stepped away from the car. "Wishy, could a Rolls-Royce be driven down this lane?"

"Not without damage to the paint. That's why we left my car on the paved road."

"The grocery truck?"

"It's a Model T truck. No wider than this car."

"Confound it," the sheriff said, "this only raises more questions! If this is Carlton's car, then what happened to the colonel's car? And if no passenger sat in this car, how did Mr. Robert Harris come to be here?"

"Sheriff," Slye said, "our answers are undoubtedly at the house. I'd like to return there as quickly as possible. Also, I'm afraid Carlton Wedge may be in some danger."

"My men are looking for him, I assure you. I intend to try to get the Simmses to be more forthcoming about his recent whereabouts."

With this we had to be satisfied.

Once back at the colonel's house, the sheriff went into the study to use the telephone, while Wishy, given specific instructions by Slye, walked toward the Silver Ghost. I followed Slye into the kitchen, where I frightened a young maid into giving a little scream. I begged the cook not to carry out her threat to beat some sense into the girl. Slye asked if Rawls and the housekeeper could be brought there without alerting the Simmses to the fact, which the maid readily agreed to.

Slye questioned these two worthies about the arrival of the Simmses, thanked them, and strode outdoors. He stood gazing toward the outbuildings. Wishy hurried up to us. "You were right, Bunny. The floorboards are filthy. A shame, to muddy a car like that!"

"I suspect they were rather rushed." He paused, then said in one of the gentlest voices I had ever heard him use, "I'm afraid I must next look into the horse barn, Wishy."

"Oh," Wishy said, turning pale.

"Would you like to search the other outbuildings, while Max helps me there? Or report your findings to the sheriff?"

"I'll search the other buildings, if that's quite all right."

"Most helpful," Slye said.

"Good, then."

We walked together toward the outbuildings. Hanslow studiously avoided looking at the horse barn. Before we had drawn very close to it, he said, "I'll meet you back at the house, then. But if you should need me—you know I'll come, Bunny."

Slye put a hand on his shoulder. "Never a doubt of it, Wishy."

Hanslow looked at me, for what was probably the longest period of time he had ever gazed directly at my face, then said to Slye, "You can tell him about her if you'd like. Understanding sort of fellow, Max."

"Yes, he is. Thank you, Wishy. See you in a bit."

"Oh—ah, Bunny, what am I looking for?"

"You might come across a gun, muddy clothing, or some other important clue."

"Right!" He marched off with renewed purpose.

Slye said nothing more until Wishy was out of earshot, then smiled at me. "You've had an honor bestowed on you, Max."

"So I gather," I said, watching his friend head for the building farthest away from the horse barn.

"When I left for the war, Wishy was the best horseman in the county. Raised and trained thoroughbreds, won races. He was too big to be a jockey, of course, but he loved few things on earth more than to take a fast horse for a gallop in a meadow.

"Unlike the colonel's family, the Hanslows are close-knit, and Aloysius was an especially devoted brother. Adored his little sister. Gwendolyn. Five years his junior and bidding fair to become a beauty. Gwen was easy to adore. She was vivacious, smart, and if, like her brother, she was a chatterbox whose enthusiasm sometimes outpaced good sense, she was also, like her brother, generous and sweet-natured. She worshipped him."

He fell silent, his face set in lines of grief. He didn't speak again until we were nearly to the stable doors.

"Wishy saw it happen. One moment he was enjoying a pleasant spring afternoon, turning back toward the stable, when Gwen came racing toward him on a horse. She gave a great whoop, called out, 'Look at me, big brother!' and fell—for reasons no one has been able to explain to Wishy's satisfaction—breaking her neck. She was dead before he reached her.

"He didn't blame the horse, and even refused his father's demand that the animal be put down. But he sold all his horses, and razed his stables. A few months later, he became an automobile enthusiast.

"He experienced one other change. Wishy's mother told me that her son has been dressing like Sherlock Holmes—or his notion of Holmes—since shortly after his sister died. Her theory is that the idea of being like Holmes, able to solve mysteries, to explain the inexplicable, to see the small clue that has gone overlooked, makes Wishy more comfortable in a world that has battered him with its random misfortunes and senseless sorrows."

"You know, Slye," I said after a moment, "where we were, one couldn't help but think of the lost dreams and desires of fallen comrades, the theft from the world of their potential. But I think we sometimes forgot that even before the influenza pandemic, here at home there were losses that were no less bitter for being faced one by one."

"No." He sighed. "But we must go forward, even with these hitches in our gaits. Let's see what we can do for the colonel."

He pulled the stable doors open. There was straw strewn about in the center aisle, in a building that had not housed horses for five years.

"From Carlton's night of sleeping off a binge?"

"No, someone trying to cover up parallel tracks of mud, unless I miss my guess," Slye said.

The car was in the fourth stall down, the one nearest the ladder into the hayloft. I thought we might need Hanslow to verify that it was the colonel's Model T—and I supposed we'd have to take it out of the stables to do that—but there was no doubt in either of our minds that we had found the missing automobile. Slye bent to examine something on the floor of the stall, while I moved closer to the car.

"Slye, there are bloodstains on the backseat!"

He didn't answer, and when I looked back at him he was standing stock-still, his face drained of all color, a look of abject terror on his face.

I damned myself three times over for not thinking of the effect—the cumulative effect!—this day's events might have on his mind.

"Boniface Slye," I said, quietly but firmly. "You are here with me."

He blinked, swallowed hard, reached a trembling hand up to his head, then held it up to me, palm out.

There was blood on his fingers.

"Slye!" I cried. "But how…"

He looked up, and as he did, a drop of blood fell on his face. He looked back at me, and said in a faint voice, "Is it real, Max? Or am I imagining that it is raining blood again?"

"It's real, only—not what you're thinking, Slye! The hayloft!"

He seemed to come back to himself then, and we raced up the ladder. We found the colonel—alive, awake, and mad as fire, but in a seriously weakened condition. "Do what you can for him," Slye said as I worked to remove the gag from the colonel's mouth. "I'll fetch your medical bag from the car."

"Robert!" the colonel croaked. "Help him."

"He's being cared for, sir," I said, taking his blindfold off and looking at his head wound. To my relief, it appeared that it had clotted, then reopened—perhaps as he stirred awake. Still, the bloodstain on the floor of the hayloft was large enough to be worrisome.

"Untie me so that I can kill that damned bitch and her brother!"

"I'll untie you, but you must try to lie quietly. Sheriff Anderson is here, and he hasn't let your niece and nephew move an inch since he arrived."

"Ah. Good man, Anderson." He studied me a moment and said, "What the hell happened to your face?"

"Ruined by the same thing that ruined your manners."

He gave a crack of laughter, and was still overcome by mirth when Slye brought my kit up a few minutes later. Slye raised his brows.

"Hysteria," I said.

"A lot of that going around," he said, which set the colonel off again.

Eventually we had him cleaned up, stitched up, and comfortably ensconced in his bed. He had refused to go to the hospital, even when I tempted him with the idea of being closer to his son. "I'm not going to be able to do a damn thing for him there today, while I can still help Anderson here. If I go to that blasted hospital, they'll drug me sure as hell, and you know it."

Sheriff Anderson got a statement from him, and told us that Carlton had been located.

"It was a plan that might have worked," Slye said to the group assembled in the parlor. Sheriff Anderson, Carlton Wedge, the Simmses (now each handcuffed and under the eye of a burly deputy), Wishy, and I had been joined by the colonel, as tough an old bird as I ever care to meet. "You owe your life to your housekeeper and a grocery boy, Colonel Harris."

"We were never going to kill our uncle!" Anthony protested, even as his sister told him to shut up.

"I may not have every detail just right, but I believe I can come close enough," Slye said. "Last night, Anthony met Carlton and easily tempted Carlton to drive him to an abandoned barn where Anthony had hidden a few bottles of gin. Carlton, unaware that the drinks poured into his tumbler were spiked, woke up many hours later, wondering who had tied him up, and with no clear recollection of the previous evening's events. He was able to free himself, and was found by the sheriff's deputies as he wandered down the road to the village, thinking he must have left his car there.

"Carlton will be shocked, I'm sure, to learn that dear old cousin Anthony was setting him up to be falsely accused of murder.

"The Simmses planned to lure Robert Harris and Colonel Harris to a small lane on a seldom-traveled road. They knew the regular schedule of the household from previous recent visits. Rawls, the housekeeper, the cook—all recall finding the two of you being extraordinarily curious about their routines. The delivery boy from the village came by in the early morning. So matters would be taken care of a little later in the morning—not too late, or Carlton might awaken or be found away from the place where he was supposed to be committing a crime.

"What did they tell you when they called this morning, Colonel?"

"Alice told me that they had met Carlton in the village and told him I wanted to send him to an asylum. Said he'd gone off his head and was going to kill himself on one of the abandoned lanes."

"What!" Carlton said.

"It was an important part of the plan that the colonel be lured away from the road, to lessen the chance of something felonious being seen by inconvenient witnesses who might come driving up the hill. So Carlton's Model T was taken to the end of the lane. And Alice waited with the Rolls to keep an eye on things."

"Not quite," said the colonel. "She was there to point the way, and hurry us along by exclaiming that Anthony had run down the lane to try to intervene. But she got into my car with us, and rode with us to where Anthony was lying in wait for us. It had started to rain by then, quite hard."

"Which might, I suppose, have been seen as an aid to their plan: kill the colonel and his heir, make it appear that Carlton was the guilty party, and sit back and inherit. They needed to be sure that the bodies would be found—missing persons cases are hell on probate—so they would leave Carlton's car to point the way. The rain would make it seem that Carlton's vehicle got stuck in the mud."

"It did get stuck!" Anthony said. "And we didn't know how the old bastard had left his will, so we weren't going to kill him until we were sure."

"Anthony! Shut up!" Alice screamed at him.

"Oh, I was supposed to believe that Carlton clubbed me from behind while you two stood and watched? There must be a passel of nincompoops on your father's side of the family."

"All sorts of things went wrong, didn't they?" Wishy said. "Robert didn't stay to help you, sir?"

"Robert's no fool. I'm sure he knows that if a man finds himself unarmed and outnumbered, he must put some distance between himself and the attacking force!"

"So Anthony shot him in the back," I said. "And in the head, though fortunately that bullet merely grazed him. I've talked to Dr. Smith, and he assures me Robert will recover. You, on the other hand, Anthony, are doubtless going to the electric chair."

"No! No! I have no gun. It was Alice! And it's no use telling me to shut up, Alice, because I won't!"

"What happened after she shot him?" Slye asked.

"It was miserable out there, but I trussed up the colonel while Alice tried to hunt down Robert. Then she came running back, says there's no time to lose, the delivery boy is coming up the hill—she told me to put the colonel in his car and hide it in the horse barn, and wait there for her. She went tearing off, then took the Rolls up the road at lightning pace. I waited until the delivery boy went past, then took the car up along the service road out to the barn. We knew the servants would be busy talking to the lad on the other side of the house, getting the village gossip, and wouldn't see us. And I did just as she asked—even carried the old bugger up into the hayloft, and that wasn't easy, I tell you!

"I really thought we might pull it off. She had even thought to bring a change of clothes for each of us, so that by the time we went into the house, we didn't look so disheveled or damp."

"But the Rolls is designed to be noticed," Slye said, "and was noticed by the delivery boy, which made the staff wonder why it took so long for you to enter the house. Not only that, the housekeeper caught sight of the colonel's car, and wondered what was keeping him."

"You got the floorboard of the Rolls muddy!" Wishy said, as if this was the worst offense of all.

"Must I listen to this fake Holmes?" Alice shouted.

The room fell silent. Then Slye said, "Yes, for it would do you good. He has an excellent head and a genuine heart, both of which you lack."

◇◇◇

Carlton Wedge, as it turned out, felt himself to be at rock bottom, and was eager to take the colonel up on his offer to undergo treatment for alcoholism. We helped them find a facility worthy of their patronage.

Dr. Smith began driving out to Slye's place, asking me to consult with him on some of his cases. I find the work interesting, but not as interesting as helping Slye to recover, and with the little problems that come his way.

Aloysius Hanslow still dresses like Holmes and invites us to come with him whenever Sheriff Anderson calls. Wishy has stopped flinching when he looks at me.

Slye continues to improve, although those moments in the colonel's horse barn caused a minor setback. He talks of returning to the city, which he was never wont to do before now.

For the time being we are in the country, where old men tell young boys of war, and some of us who've seen it hope it never comes again, knowing it always will.

Jan Burke is the author of fourteen books, including *Bones,* which won the Edgar for Best Novel, *Disturbance,* and *The Messenger.* Her novels have appeared on the *USA Today* and *New York Times* bestseller lists and have been published internationally. She is also an award-winning short-story writer.

In college a boyfriend urged her to read *The Hound of the Baskervilles,* which soon led to the purchase of the entire Canon. Though she ultimately came to her senses about the value of the boyfriend, Burke's admiration of Sherlock Holmes only grew over the years, and she believes the respect for the power of physical evidence in Conan Doyle's writing not only influenced her own writing, but also laid the groundwork for her later advocacy for the improvement of public forensic science. In 2006, Burke founded the Crime Lab Project, a nonprofit organization supporting public forensic laboratories throughout the United States.

A Spot of Detection

Jacqueline Winspear

The boy was ill. He knew he was ill, and the fact that the school matron had sent him home—and Matron rarely sent anyone home—meant his demise could be imminent. The spots on his chest itched, worse than the itch caused by crushed rosehips when Weston—the sniveling rat, Weston—pushed a handful down the back of his collar. This morning he'd scratched and itched throughout Latin and into Algebra. And then after lunch the itch went from his chest to his legs, and then began to be apparent above the collar of his cornflower-blue-and-black uniform blazer. He'd wheezed and coughed well into Geography, and finally laid his head on the desk as if begging for mercy. But at least that was better than home, where there would be only his mother, Aunt Ethel, and his grandmother for company, with the occasional visit from his ill-tempered Uncle Ernest, who only ever talked about money and how much the family was costing him. He sighed and the sigh made him cough again. It was a long walk from school to the house and no one had offered to accompany him; he was, after all, expected to act like an Englishman, and the stiff upper lip—even one with a giant teasing spot on it—was not permitted to wobble. Once home, his mother would send him to bed and that would be that. The school would not let him rest though; work would be sent in a brown paper parcel for him to complete from his sickbed. He was second to last in his class to come down with measles, so he knew what to expect.

The sweat beaded across his forehead and trickled in rivulets from his neck down the gully that was his spine. Not long to go now, he thought. He rubbed his eyes, which were running as much as his nose, and he swayed a little, trembling with fever. As he lingered on Margaret Street trying to garner fortitude for the last half-mile, raised voices seemed to ricochet past his aching ears. At first he thought he had experienced some sort of hallucination. He cupped an ear and listened. Yes, he had definitely heard some level of discord, and the point of origin of the fracas appeared to be the upper floor of one of the three-story terraced houses that flanked his route. He shook his head to clear a mind befuddled by blocked sinuses. The voices, coming from somewhere above and to the left of him, were raised again, and now, as he looked up, squinting in an endeavor to ascertain the source of the row, he saw the shadows of a man and a woman silhouetted at the window of an adjacent house. One of them had raised a hand, but as the fever made everything around him seem disjointed, he was not sure if the hand belonged to the man or the woman, or whether it was simply something that floated in the air. Then the voices reached a crescendo.

"You are nothing but a philanderer, a thief, and a...a...a thoroughly nasty piece of work. I wish I had never met you."

"And that, madam, is a sure case of the pot calling the kettle black!"

"Don't you 'madam' me, you lout!"

The boy crinkled his eyes and pushed back his woolen school cap. It itched across his forehead. Silly, these English school caps—and at his age. Tiredness seeped through his being like waves at the seashore, and it made him think of the ocean; cool, cool water lapping over him, and how it might feel as it washed across his hot, sticky skin. Itch-itch-itch, scratch-scratch-scratch. Then there was a scream. A scream so loud, he thought everyone must hear. But there was no one else on the street to be alarmed, though at that very moment a brand-new shining motorcar bumped and blasted its way toward him, barely allowing margin for a costermonger's horse and cart. That's when he thought he heard a gunshot. *Crack! Crack!* it went, into the air. Then it was gone, and there was no more screaming and yelling. And no more shadows.

"Fell down right in front of me, he did, missus. Luck'ly, he knew where he lived, told me the address right off when I asked him— mind you, I had to shake him a bit. Looks like he's got a touch of the measles. Nasty, them measles. Had 'em when I was a lad."

The coster helped the boy across the threshold, whereupon the mother took charge, her manner of speaking causing the man to look up as she pressed a few pennies into his hand.

"Long way from home, aren't you, missus?"

"This is our home now, sir. Thank you for assisting my son—now I must get him to bed."

She closed the door, and at once she and the boy's aunt— there was no father present—helped him upstairs to his room at the front of the house. Having removed his school uniform, they laid him out on the bed, washed him with warm water and carbolic soap, and daubed the livid rash with calamine lotion before sending for the doctor. The boy remembered little of this, though he could, when he was on the mend, remember trying to press the point that he thought someone had been shot on Margaret Street. His words served only to convince the women of the severity of his fever, and the dangers inherent in a bout of childhood measles, which, they thought, would never have come to pass had mother and son remained in America. This was the 1900s now, after all, and London seemed a backward place to an immigrant from across the Atlantic, even though there was family here to help. It was to be some days before the illness became a source of boredom for the boy and a slight nuisance for the mother and aunt.

"He's on the mend, but I do wish he'd stop going on about hearing a gunshot on Margaret Street. The coster said he saw him collapse after the motorcar backfired and the horse shied, so of course it must have sounded like a shot from a gun to a sick boy."

The aunt had returned from a walk to the shops, ready for the mother's complaint. "This might feed his appetite for murder, Florence." She placed a brown-paper-wrapped book on the table.

"*The Boys' Sherlock Holmes?*" said the mother, her eyebrows raised just a little. "I'm not sure the masters at school would approve, and he has a mountain of prep to finish—he mustn't slip behind, you know."

"He's a good pupil, so a little something light might be just what the doctor ordered—and I think the nurse trumps the teachers in the management of convalescence."

"Hmmm," said the boy's mother. "I'll take it up with his tea."

◇◇◇

Turning the pages proved to be a problem, given the white cotton gloves his mother insisted adorn his hands so that if he attempted to scratch the spots, which were becoming even more itchy and crusty as they dried out, he would not break the skin. The calamine lotion helped to a degree—already his mother had sent out the maid for two more bottles—and he'd been encouraged to take a hot bath with a copious amount of Epsom salts added to the water, but still he'd taken off the gloves in a moment of frustration and scratched his forehead so much it bled. He licked a gloved finger and fumbled the page until it turned.

Without doubt, the adventures of Sherlock Holmes offered some respite from the Elizabethan authors he'd been studying, though he enjoyed the rhythm of the more ancient English employed by Shakespeare, Sir Philip Sidney, and Christopher Marlowe. He liked Sidney above all, having considered himself something of a poet; indeed the boy had made a vow to have his work published by the time he came of age. He could readily imagine himself lingering in an oak-lined study at Penshurst Place in Kent, where Sidney penned sweet rhyming letters to his love. It was said there was no more noble character than Sidney, in his day, and the boy thought that in itself was something to aspire to, for he wanted to be considered a noble Englishman. The endearing thing about Sidney was that he wrote about love, and the boy rather liked the idea of writing romantic verse; it appealed to him. He brought his attention back to Sherlock Holmes, though as thoughts danced and wove in his mind, he began thinking, again, about what he had seen and heard as he'd walked home from school with a raging fever. Was it his imagination? Had he really heard the altercation between the man and the woman—the lovers, as he now considered them to be? He suspected that, had Holmes been on the street, he would have uttered the words, "The game's afoot!"

There's a point, as sickness leaves but before a return to good health can be claimed, that a young male, in particular, will become bored and may resort to mischief to entertain himself in the long hours of convalescence. The discomfort of healing skin did not help matters for the boy, but the itch was now one of attention, of a desire for something more exciting in the day than his mother's footfall on the stairs as she brought a tray with breakfast, luncheon, tea, or supper. She assumed he read, wrote, or slept when alone, and to a point this was true. But now he wanted to move his limbs. And he wanted to indulge his curiosity.

A thought occurred to the boy when he had come to the end of *A Study in Scarlet,* so he took up his notebook and pencil, and began to turn the pages. He reread a snippet here, a sentence there. He copied whole paragraphs, and then tried to index them into some sort of order. According to the book, which included a serviceable biography of Sir Arthur Conan Doyle, together with a few pages on the man who had inspired the character of Sherlock Holmes, the detective could solve a crime in three days. *Three days.* Today was Tuesday, so if he dedicated Wednesday, Thursday, and Friday to the case—he now considered his experience a "case"—he would have all the answers he needed by the week's end. It was crucial that the fledgling idea must work in the allotted time, for the doctor decreed that he could get up from his bed and remain downstairs on Saturday and Sunday, ready to return to school on Monday next. *Three days.*

He consulted the book again. Holmes had instructed Watson—the boy rather liked Watson; he seemed warmer, more affable than the cold, calculating Holmes—that it was important to engage in reasoning backward and analytically. He wasn't sure how he could put such a process into practice with regard to his case, but he began to write down everything he remembered, backward from the time he arrived home from school. This was somewhat tricky, as he had been brought part of the way in the back of a coster's cart, among an array of wilting vegetables. The cabbage had been particularly pungent. Of essence, he realized, as he read on, was Holmes's dictate that the detective must examine on foot the property where the crime was committed. The boy began to scheme.

His mother and aunt walked after lunch each day, a peram-bulation that would extend for several hours, so having left the house at, say, one o'clock, they would return no later than four, when it was time for tea. During that time his grandmother would nod off in her chair, and be, to all intents and purposes, dead to the world. Since he had taken to his sickbed, his mother had called up the stairs as she left, then brought him a cup of tea and two plain oatmeal biscuits upon her return. Sometimes his aunt would come to his room, too, and together they would discuss his schoolwork, or an item in the newspaper of national import, and as they left, his aunt would be heard to say, "He's such a sensitive boy, isn't he?" or something of that order.

He decided to leave the house as soon as they had departed following luncheon on Wednesday, but he must be certain to return by teatime. Three days, three hours each day. Holmes would indubitably be able to find a solution in such a period of time—why couldn't he?

Tools were gathered with some stealth. Sherlock Holmes always had at least a tape measure and a magnifying glass, and these items were procured with ease—the former taken from his mother's sewing basket, and the latter from his grandmother's bedside table. And it was clear that he needed a disguise—not least to conceal the livid spots dotting his face. Cosmetic powder on his aunt's dressing table worked admirably, and soon it seemed as if he had been afflicted by no more than the odd pimple considered normal on a boy of his age. Having gathered everything he needed according to the practices of Sherlock Holmes, the boy sat on his bed and caught his breath. In truth he felt just a little dizzy, and droplets of perspiration had formed on the pale fluff above his lip. He reached for a glass of water, quenched his thirst, and slipped into bed again.

"See you later, dear. We'll be back by teatime." His mother's voice echoed up into the stairwell.

"Bye," replied the boy.

He waited until the door closed and he'd given the women enough time to walk to the end of the road, then pulled back the covers, leapt out of bed, and as an afterthought, shoved a pillow between the sheets so that it seemed as if he were there, but asleep. "The game's definitely afoot," he whispered, as he crept past the drawing room, where the sleeping grandmother snored and smacked her lips.

It took a good twenty minutes at not a very good pace to reach Margaret Street. Think backward, thought the boy. He referred to his notes—that morning he had recorded everything he could remember from the time he left school to the time he arrived home on the fateful day. Closing his eyes, he recalled the motorcar approaching, and the horse taking umbrage. Yes! It clipped the fence as it shied. The boy took out the magnifying glass and began to walk very slowly along the fence that ran the entire length of the terrace. There it was—though in truth, he could see the broken wood with his naked eye; there was no real need for magnification. Several slats were missing, and it was evident that the occupant of the house had pulled away the broken pieces and laid them to one side in the garden.

"What're you looking at?" The voice came from an open door. A woman, wearing a floral pinafore over a gray woolen dress, stood before him. As a rule he would not have noticed much about her, but now he could see that she had bunions on both feet—why else would she cut into her slippers at the joint of the big toe? She had been reading the newspaper, likely by the window—which had enabled her to see him inspecting her broken fence—because her fingertips were black. She might also be a widow, for a house of this size would not warrant a house-keeper or cook, so if she were married, she should be peeling potatoes or some such thing, not reading the newspapers. It was clear to see that this woman pleased herself. The fact that the wood had been left in a pile and the fence not mended also suggested a woman alone, for surely any man worth his salt would have done something about the gaping hole by now.

"I was just wondering about your fence. I assume that's where the motorcar caused the coster's horse to shy."

"You saw that, did you, lad?"

"Not really, madam. I was taken ill in the street, but I heard the noise, and I heard the coster, who kindly took me home, telling my mother about the disturbance."

"Disturbance? I'd like to find the blighter what did that to my fence; too right I would. I'd give him a disturbance if I knew where to find him. And if you come across him, you come and tell me about it."

"Yes, Mrs...."

"Tingley. Mrs. Tingley. Mr. Tingley passed away last year, otherwise that there hole would have been put right by now."

"Were you not at home when the event took place, Mrs. Tingley?"

The woman shook her head. "The one day a week I go to the church hall for a game of whist. All the ladies on the street go, so it's quiet around here—otherwise the blighter wouldn't've got away with it."

"Ahhh, I see," said the boy. "Well, good day to you, Mrs. Tingley."

He walked on, stopping after a few paces to make a note in his book. He could have walked and penned at the same time, but if he did so, he might miss a detail. A good consulting detective would not miss a detail.

Holmes was a stickler for the measuring and counting of strides to ascertain the height of a man. Though at this stage the boy had no reason to do so, the idea of taking account of his pace, and then logging the details in his notebook appealed to him in case something could be deduced that might be of use as the plot thickened. Trusting he wouldn't be seen, he went back to Mrs. Tingley's house and, using the broken fence as a starting point, he stepped out, hopefully toward the house from which he had heard the argument and the gunshot. Frankly, he really didn't know what he might discover in the pacing, but he was sure it would come in handy. He stopped to glance back every three strides. Yes, it was just about...here. He looked up at the terraced house. Was this the one? He tried to remember the day, to recall his feelings, then he began to feel a bit sick. He swallowed and wished he'd brought a flask of water with him, for his mouth had gone from moist to dry. But the sensation gave him an idea. He walked along the path, keeping his eyes peeled in case he saw a footprint in the soil, or something hidden in the hydrangeas. Nothing. He knocked at the door and waited.

Two locks were drawn back, and the door opened only to the extent that five inches of chain would allow.

"What d'yer want?"

"I am sorry to disturb you, madam, but I wonder—I have just recovered from a sickness and feel quite unwell. Might you have a cup of water?"

The boy thought the woman had recently enjoyed some sort of hairdressing experiment that caused small curls to form all over the scalp, so clearly she wasn't short of a shilling or two. Her eyes, though, revealed a person who might be a good deal more accommodating than one might believe at first blush. She was older, he thought, than the woman he'd seen silhouetted at the window—much older, for this woman before him was of an age somewhere between his mother and grandmother. And it occurred to the boy that she might be scared.

"You do look a bit peaky. Wait here, I'll get you the water." The woman closed the door, opening it again after three minutes had passed. Leaving the door on the chain, she handed a cup of water out to him.

"Thank you, madam." He drank the entire contents without taking a breath.

"You was thirsty, that you were." Now the woman was smiling.

The boy handed back the cup.

"Madam, do forgive me, but as a gentleman, I must ask—do you have cause to fear? You appear very cautious, as if you are expecting an unwanted visitor."

She shook her head. "No, not at all. Not at all." She pressed her face toward the open door, as if to see along the street, though the chain prevented a good look.

"Are you waiting for someone?"

The woman sighed. "You look like a good boy."

"My mother says as much, though she may have some bias."

"You at the College?"

He nodded and hoped she would not ask why he was not in uniform.

"It's that lodger of mine. Well, lodger as was. Not any more. No rent equals no board or lodging in this establishment. I lay down my rules when they come, and if the rent's not paid, then they get chucked out. Bloke hadn't been here long, but I had to give him his marching orders because I hardly saw the color of his money. He left sharpish enough, and without paying me a farthing of his arrears. You can't be too careful though; you never know if they're going to come back and give you a fourpenny-one and leave you with a black eye."

"Was he not a good man?"

"Oh, he was all right, I suppose. But he kept late hours, on top of the arrears, and he brought back women."

The boy blushed. "Did he?"

The woman looked up the street again without answering, then announced that this would never do, and she couldn't stand there talking all day. The boy consulted his watch and realized that he couldn't stand there either—for his mother and aunt would return to the house before him if he didn't cut along.

Florence and Ethel checked his homework after tea, and then read together—passing Sherlock Holmes from one to the other as they made their way through *The Sign of the Four.* The boy was fast coming to the conclusion that Holmes was not as interesting as he considered himself to be; then he remembered that the man was a fiction and probably didn't think of himself at all. But the detective's adventures inspired him, and he planned another excursion on the morrow, when he would go to the house on Margaret Street again. It occurred to him that, in the meantime, he must discover the name of the nearest detective inspector. He may not have a Lestrade waiting in the wings, but he was beginning to believe he was on to something—a murder, perhaps—and he would need a trusted policeman to apprehend the perpetrator of the crime. Alone in his room, the boy recalled details of the overheard argument and gunshot, and feared that the lodger at the house in Margaret Street was a criminal to be reckoned with.

"Back at four, dear!"

The front door closed behind the two women, and the grandmother could be heard padding along to her chair in the drawing room, the one by the window where a warming shaft of sunlight soothed her bones as if she were an old dog. The boy rose from his bed fully clothed, shoved the pillow under the covers, and set off on his quest for truth. It was day two of his investigation, and he had much to accomplish. He stopped at the bakery and bought four jam tarts, then went on his way again.

"Madam!" He smiled as the woman opened the door and peered at him over the chain. "You were so very kind yesterday, I thought I should repay you with a small treat. Do you like jam tarts?"

Her eyes lit up. "I most certainly do."

He held out the bag, and she wavered as she reached to take it from the boy. "I thought you looked like a nice sort of boy yesterday. Would you like to come in for a cup of tea?"

Indeed he would.

Mrs. Richmond—she had revealed her name as he followed her along the passageway—busied herself in the kitchen. It was a kitchen not unlike the one at the house in Auckland Road where he lived with his mother, aunt, and grandmother, though the kitchen at home was more spacious and better appointed. In Mrs. Richmond's kitchen a kettle boiled on a black cast-iron range, above which various towels and cloths were hung over a wooden clothes airer. A vase of paper flowers, now faded and brown, had been set in the center of a wooden table that was bowed in the middle from, he thought, many decades of use. Mrs. Richmond laid out two chipped cups and a plate with the jam tarts, and poured tea from a brown pot. She put milk and sugar in his cup without first asking.

"Do you live alone, apart from lodgers, Mrs. Richmond?"

The woman nodded. "Since I lost my Jim in the first Transvaal war. He was out there at the beginning. Regular army."

"I'm sorry."

"What're you sorry for?" She reached for a jam tart. "Weren't your fault. And I get a bit of a pension, just a few pennies, but it helps. We never had any children, and Jim was a good one for putting something away, so I'm not for the workhouse yet."

They sat in silence for a moment, then the boy spoke again. "I was wondering, after we spoke yesterday, if the room was still available. A friend of my mother is at this very moment looking for accommodation, and I thought it might be serendipitous that I was so taken with thirst yesterday, and in knocking at your door discovered you had a room to let."

"What with all the trouble that last lodger caused me, I only take gentlewomen of good standing now—no men." She looked at him as if weighing up his social station.

"I would imagine your mother's a fine woman, and any friend of hers would be cut from the same cloth."

"Might I see the room, so that I can best describe it to my mother's friend?"

The woman sighed. "I suppose it wouldn't do any harm."

She took a key from a hook on the wall above the sink, and motioned toward the passageway along which he had walked to the kitchen from the front door. As they reached the staircase, the woman leaned on the banister and sighed.

"Young man, I'm not as nippy on those stairs as I was, and I don't feel like running up and down more than once or twice a day. Here's the key. It's the room at the front; the door's directly behind you when you get to the landing. Don't be more than five minutes, or I'll think you're a thief."

The boy laughed, if somewhat nervously. "Can't imagine my struggling downstairs with a chest of drawers, Mrs. Richmond."

"I can." She gave him the key and ambled back toward the kitchen.

◇◇◇

The boy could not believe his good fortune. Having made his way up twenty steps to the landing, he unlocked the door to the front bedroom. He was about to walk in and begin his investigation, when he stopped. Holmes would perhaps linger, he would consider the room. He would clear his mind. After all, didn't he tell Watson that most people allow too much clutter to invade the clear processes of deduction? A large sash window at the front of the house needed a good clean, that was the first thing he noticed. Dust motes hung in the sunlight, which also served to draw attention to smears across the panes. He took out the magnifying glass in anticipation. The walls were clad in anaglypta, known for its sanitary properties and ease of cleaning, though it appeared that they had received only a cursory wipe of late, decorated as they were with tidemarks of nicotine.

A bed—wide enough for two, he noted—was set against the wall in such a way that anyone languishing there would be able to look out if the curtains were drawn back. A green-tiled washstand stood adjacent to the wall on the right, with a bowl and ewer atop the marble. A single grayish white cloth was hung on the towel rail. A fireplace directly opposite had been laid with newspaper and kindling, and a scuttle filled with coal placed alongside. Next to the bed, a dressing table supported a goodly layer of dust and in a recess in the wall neighbouring the fireplace stood a wardrobe of plain oak. The carpet had seen better days, but had been swept, though he recognized another hallmark of less than vigilant housekeeping—there were dust balls under the cast-iron bed. He stepped into the room and went straight to the window and looked out onto the street. This was the room. This was where something untoward—perhaps a murder—had taken place.

The problem was that there was precious little else for him to use as evidence. With the glass in hand he inspected the walls, the bed, under the bed, in the wardrobe, in every drawer of the dressing table, along the windowsill, under the windowsill, in the folds of the curtains. Nothing to suggest a murder. He was perplexed. The villain was clearly well versed in his trade, and a crafty sort. He would have to question Mrs. Richmond to a greater degree, perhaps tomorrow. As he completed his notes and made his way downstairs, he had the distinct feeling that he had missed something, but he could not imagine what it might be.

Mrs. Richmond took the key and returned it to the hook above the sink.

"I will definitely tell my mother about the room. I think it might do very well, though I might be late with the news, as the lady in question could already have secured accommodation."

"Well, if she comes, you just remember to tell her to remind me who sent her. There'll be a special consideration for a friend."

"Thank you, Mrs. Richmond." He looked at the clock on the mantelpiece above the stove. "Oh dear, I must be on my way."

◇◇◇

Having bowed to Mrs. Richmond, the boy ran all the way back to his home in Auckland Road, and having washed the powder from his face and hidden the magnifying glass and tape measure under the bed, he was betwixt the covers looking suitably flushed and feverish by the time his mother came in with tea and two oatmeal biscuits. Taking stock of his countenance, she sent the maid out to summon the doctor. This case of measles appeared to be taking quite a toll.

The following day, the aunt and mother decided that they would remain out for only one hour rather than take their customary long walk for good health. The boy sighed. There was precious little to be done in one hour, so it appeared the only course of action would be to alert the police to his suspicions before all necessary evidence was to hand. Such a leap of faith would be unacceptable to Sherlock Holmes, who would have had all the facts—no suppositions, no ifs, no buts—to hand before calling upon Lestrade. He could imagine Holmes chastising him: *You need more data!*

"Back in an hour, my dear—we're going out now," the mother called from the bottom of the stairs.

Within ten minutes the boy was closing the front door with as much stealth as possible, and was soon on his way to visit the Upper Norwood constabulary. A police sergeant was on duty at the desk as he entered, though it was the latest edition of the *Daily News* that claimed his attention, and not the doings of the local criminal element.

"Yes, young sir, what can I do for you today? Lost your dog?"

"I would like to see the detective inspector on duty, if I may."

The sergeant's eyes grew wider, and he grinned. "Oh you would, would you, sonny? Our Detective Inspector Stickley is a very busy man, so I'm assuming your purpose is genuine."

The boy straightened his shoulders. "I am here to report what I believe to be a *genuine* murder, witnessed by myself a week ago. I have been in my sickbed since then, however, I would like to see Detective Inspector Stickley as a matter of some urgency."

"Right you are. Sit yourself down over there, you're looking a bit peaky, if you don't mind my saying so."

The police sergeant left the desk, making his way along the corridor, where he entered the inner sanctum via wood-framed glass doors. The boy—who was now very hot and flushed—seated himself on the dark wooden bench. Soon the sergeant returned.

"This way, son."

The boy was slightly disappointed in Detective Inspector Stickley. He had hoped for a ferret-featured Lestrade, who would be suitably impressed by the findings of a new and potentially important consulting detective. This man was tall, checked his pocket watch as he entered the room, and seemed to treat the visitor as if he were the day's light entertainment.

"Right then, tell me what makes you think someone's been murdered on my patch."

The boy took a deep breath and recounted the story from the time he was sent home from school. And though he did not mention Holmes, the detective inspector appeared to have a sixth sense.

"Been reading a bit of old Sherlock, have we, son?"

The boy blushed but feigned ignorance. "Sherlock? I beg your pardon, sir, but I do not know what you mean."

"I thought all boys read Sherlock Holmes." He sighed. "Anyway, I'll do this for you. I'll go round and see your Mrs. Richmond, and I'll take a gander at the front bedroom, and we'll see if what you say gives us cause for concern. We've had a bit of trouble on that road in the past fortnight, what with reckless drivers of motorcars and what have you."

"Thank you, Detective Inspector Stickley."

The detective stood up and put his arm on the boy's shoulder as he guided him along the corridor.

"Thought about policing when you leave school, son?"

The boy turned to the man; the thought had never occurred to him. "Well, I thought I might like to study law at university, but my uncle has suggested the civil service examinations."

The policeman raised his eyebrows, but said little else, except to ask the sergeant if they had the young man's correct particulars on file.

Now the boy was more concerned with catching up with Algebra, Latin, and the Elizabethans than the mystery that had occupied the worst days of his sickness. He read a little Mark Twain and William Makepeace Thackeray—both favorite authors—and on Sunday morning skimmed through *The Adventure of the Noble Bachelor* for good measure. Clearly the police had not investigated the crime he'd witnessed, or perhaps they had not considered him man enough to keep him informed of their progress. Then, on Sunday afternoon while napping in his room, he was woken by voices at the front door. Though he had been allowed up since the day before, weakness left in the wake of the bout of measles—and his secret excursions—had sent him to his bed with fatigue. The doctor had already decreed that he could not return to school for another three days at least. Upon hearing an exchange between his mother and a man whose voice sounded familiar, the boy left his bed and made his way onto the landing to eavesdrop.

"A message for your son, madam—would you tell him that Detective Inspector Stickley called?"

"Oh dear, is there some sort of trouble?"

"Not at all, madam. He was most helpful in the matter of an investigation. Most helpful."

Clearly Stickley wasn't alone, for the boy heard another man begin to chuckle.

"Please inform him that we have completed our inquiries, and we would like him to have this as a mark of our gratitude for his sharp skills of observation."

The boy leaned around the wooden banister and could see his mother take an envelope from the man. She was flustered and—fortunately, he thought—simply thanked the man and bid him good-bye. The boy rushed back to bed and closed his eyes.

He heard the bedroom door open, and his mother's quiet breathing as she watched her sleeping son. Later she conducted her own investigation, and the boy managed to persuade her that he had only left the house once, to inform the police of the gunshots he'd heard on the day he came home from school sick with measles. She scolded him, but as he opened the envelope, she admitted she was proud of him.

"What does the letter say?"

The boy frowned. "The inspector thanked me for reporting what I saw on Margaret Street, and he says he hopes we enjoy ourselves." He held four tickets in his hand. "They're for Alexandra Palace on Wednesday."

The mother took the tickets. "It looks like a music hall comedy troupe. Let's see if you're well enough, shall we? It's quite a way across London, you know."

◇◇◇

The boy made sure he was well enough by Wednesday evening and, together with the women of the house, set off for Alexandra Palace in his uncle's motorcar. In an uncharacteristic offer of generosity, Ernest had provided a chauffeur to take his mother, sisters, and nephew to Alexandra Palace and bring them home again.

The family thoroughly enjoyed the music hall acts, from the songs to the slapstick. Then, close to the end of the show, the scenery was changed again to stage a drawing room in a grand house. A man and a woman took to the boards, and began a farcical exchange, whereby the man defended himself, with great aplomb, from verbal attack by the woman. The audience cheered and called out, and soon the man was turning to the crowd to ask for their support. More cheers, more calling, as men took the actor's side, and women called out in favor of the actress. And as the back and forth went on, so the boy began to slide down in his seat, covering his face with his hands. It would not take the mind of a consulting detective to predict the outcome. It was elementary. Voices on the stage were raised again.

"You are nothing but a philanderer, a thief, and a...a...a thoroughly nasty piece of work. I wish I had never met you."

"And that, madam, is a sure case of the pot calling the kettle black!"

"Don't you 'madam' me, you lout!"

The audience erupted again, as the man brandished a gun and fired into the air. The boy blushed, as his mother turned to him and smiled.

"Oh, Ray," she whispered in his ear. "I wish I had not doubted you—you were right all along. You did hear a gunshot."

The following morning, on his way to school, the boy called at the police station to see Detective Inspector Stickley, knowing that an English gentleman would offer an apology where one was required, and take a goodly bite of humble pie.

"No apologies needed, son." Stickley paused, regarding the boy. "But a bit of advice. *Deeper questioning.* You should have asked a few more questions about the lodger; you might have discovered that he was an actor and the troupe were moving on to Alexandra Palace after a run at the Empire down the road—and like many of his ilk, he tried to slip out without paying his rent. And the bloke was only practicing his lines for a new act with the girl who was playing opposite him—mind you, he shouldn't have broken the rule about women in his room. And if you'd've looked up, son, you would have seen a nasty black mark where the blank gunpowder wad hit the ceiling."

The boy left the police station and went on his way. Clearly detection was not for him. It was time to put all thoughts of Holmes, his silly backward thinking and his pacing, his magnifying glass and his tape measure behind him. He preferred poetry anyway.

◇◇◇

Mr. Hose, the English master, stood at the blackboard, chalk in hand. He regarded his class. For the first time in weeks, all were present. The outbreak of measles had swept through Dulwich College—a noted school for well-bred boys—like the plague.

His lessons would be a source of pleasure again, especially as his favorite pupil had returned and was well enough, if not yet hearty.

"Chandler, glad to see you in class again. I trust you have kept up with the Elizabethans?"

The boy stood up to answer, as was customary. "Yes, sir."

"Good. Now, if you would be so kind, do tell the class which of the learned gentlemen you chose as subject for your essay."

"Philip Marlowe, sir."

The class snickered.

"Still measled, are we, Chandler?"

"Sorry, sir. I meant to say, Sir Philip Sidney, sir."

"Didn't care for Marlowe, Chandler?"

The boy shook his head. "I rather prefer Sidney's verse, sir."

Hose nodded. "Yes, something of a poet, aren't we, Chandler? Great things are expected of you in that field of endeavor, young man. Well then, read on, if you will."

The boy cleared his throat, scratched the remains of a spot on his cheek, and proceeded to read his essay to the assembled class. He took his seat again, and following a discussion, it was time for another boy to read. Hose called upon Weston. Rotten Weston.

"I've chosen Philip Marlowe, sir." He looked across at Chandler and grinned. "Oh—oh dear, oops, I mean Christopher Marlowe."

The class laughed.

"That's enough! Indeed, more than enough of your particular strain of humor, Weston. A joke's only a true joke the first time. Now, what sort of Faustian pact have you made with the gods of true literature?"

Chandler, the boy who had, in his own estimation, made rather a hash of detection, even though he had been tutored at home by the esteemed Sir Arthur Conan Doyle, cast his eyes down to his notebook and doodled a name in the margin. *Philip Marlowe.* He wondered about the name, and after a while thought it might one day provide a good nom de plume for the man of verse he aspired to become. He suspected it might prove useful in time.

Jacqueline Winspear—author of the award-winning *New York Times* and national bestselling novels featuring ex–World War I nurse turned psychologist and investigator Maisie Dobbs—is a UK native but has made California her home for more than twenty years. Sherlock Holmes first came to her serious attention when portrayed by Jeremy Brett—on whom she admits having had a bit of a crush—in the critically acclaimed Granada Television series.

Raymond Chandler, acclaimed mystery novelist and screenwriter, creator of the iconic detective Philip Marlowe, was born in Illinois in 1888 but moved to London in 1900 with his mother. He attended a local school in Upper Norwood and after attending public school at Dulwich College, London, he became a naturalized British citizen and entered the civil service. In 1912, he moved to Los Angeles, where (with brief periods of absence) he resided for the rest of his life.

A Study in Sherlock: Afterword

Laurie R. King and Leslie S. Klinger

The following is a transcript of a conversation conducted via Twitter between Leslie S. Klinger (whose Twitter address is **@lklinger**) and Mary Russell (**@mary_russell**) in the fall of 2011. Klinger is the editor of *The New Annotated Sherlock Holmes*. Russell is a theologian and investigator, who married Mr. Sherlock Holmes in 1921 (*The Beekeeper's Apprentice*, et cetera).

(Les Klinger) @mary_russell Am editing w/LRKing "stories inspired by SH" & wd love an interview w/him or you. OK 4 LRK 2 giv me yr contact info?

(Mary Russell) @lklinger No, my literary agent Ms King does not have permission to give you my private contact information.

(LK) @mary_russell But wouldn't u prefer to talk in private?

(MR) @lklinger "Private" conversations undergo changes in the mind of the interviewer. I prefer that such exchanges be on public record.

(LK) @mary_russell U want me 2 interview u on Twitter?

(MR) @lklinger I do not wish you to interview me at all, but clearly that is not an option.

(LK) @mary_russell We could call it a Twinterview.

(MR) @lklinger Mr Klinger, if you wish my participation, I must ask that you refrain from whimsy. And excessive abbreviations.

(LK) @mary_russell Sorry, Ms Russell. Okay, no whimsy, & I'll keep the questions suitable for all eyes.

(MR) @lklinger I should hope so. And I prefer "Miss." Now, may we proceed with this conversation? I have an experiment awaiting me.

(LK) @mary_russell First, how does Mr Holmes feel about having inspired the creativity of more than a century of crime writers?

(MR) @lklinger My husband does not care to discuss his feelings.

(LK) @mary_russell OK, how do YOU feel re his having inspired 100 yrs of crime writers? People other than (sorry must make this 2 Tweets)

(LK) @mary_russell—than Dr Watson were telling Holmes stories even as the originals were coming out. Why do u think they felt that urge?

(MR) @lklinger They admired Holmes. They wished to speculate about him. So they made up stories.

(LK) @mary_russell That's it? Just a desire for more?

(MR) @lklinger Nicholas Meyer (your friend?) claimed that Dr Watson was such a great writer, others saw the stories as a challenge.

(LK) @mary_russell But NM was explaining why he wrote his books & doesn't speak for others. I'm not even sure I believe his excuse.

(MR) @lklinger I said claimed. I met Meyer when he was young. I think he wrote them through frustration with a mere 60 published tales.

(LK) @mary_russell Does it bother u that writers make up fictions about your husband? Some of their stories are pretty outrageous.

(MR) @lklinger I was young when I realised that since Holmes was seen as fictional, by contagion I would be so viewed as well.

(MR) @lklinger Thus I have lived a long life with one foot in the real world and the other in the world of being perceived as a fiction.

(MR) @lklinger My own literary agent, Laurie King, claims that it is necessary to categorise my memoirs—mine!—as novels.

(MR) @lklinger And since I expect that you will now ask how that makes me "feel," I will admit that the sensation of being fictional is—

(MR) @lklinger—is indeed peculiar. What our—Holmes's and my—friend Neil Gaiman calls the sensation of being "the idea of a person."

(LK) @mary_russell Neil is one of those contributing to this current volume—which we're calling A Study in Sherlock.

(MR) @lklinger I grasp the reference to the initial Conan Doyle story, but this assumption of first-name familiarity jars, a bit.

(LK) @mary_russell Publishers, you know? This is the modern world. & you are after all American.

(MR) @lklinger Half American, and I retain very little of the accent, or attitudes.

(LK) @mary_russell Back 2 the questions. How did Dr Watson react? Some stories came out while his were still appearing in The Strand.

(MR) @lklinger Uncle John had many shouting matches down the telephone with Sir Arthur, demanding solicitors be hired. To no avail.

(LK) @mary_russell Well, we know what Shakespeare thought should be done with lawyers.

(MR) @lklinger That may be a bit drastic. Some of my best friends have lawyer relatives.

(LK) @mary_russell And, um, I'm a lawyer. At least during the day.

(MR) @lklinger I know you are a lawyer, Mr Klinger. That was my feeble attempt at humor. We are also very aware of your New Annotated

(MR) @lklinger—Annotated Sherlock Holmes. An excellent attempt at scholarship, which will do until Holmes's own notes are published.

(LK) @mary_russell May I ask when that will be?

(MR) @lklinger No need to worry, Mr Klinger, it will be several more years.

(LK) @mary_russell Right. So Dr W was upset, but not Holmes?

(MR) @lklinger Holmes learned long ago to leave the shouting to Dr Watson. He finds it best to stay aloof of the literary world.

(LK) @mary_russell Some stories in this collection are less about Holmes than about people affected by Dr W's stories. Do you approve?

(MR) @lklinger One might as well approve of breathing air, as of people falling under the spell of Sherlock Holmes, even secondhand.

(LK) @mary_russell So you do understand the appeal of the Sherlock Holmes stories over the ages?

(MR) @lklinger My dear young man, of course I understand their pull. I was captivated by the stories long before I met the man.

(LK) @mary_russell Speaking of captivation, may I ask about your relationship with Mr Holmes?

(MR) @lklinger No. Oh dear, Mr Klinger, ominous noises from the laboratory require my immediate attention. Good luck with your book.

(LK) @mary_russell Just another couple of questions, Miss Russell. May I ask, what is Mr Holmes doing these days?

(LK) @mary_russell Miss Russell?

(LK) @mary_russell Thank you, Miss Russell.

To receive a free catalog of Poisoned Pen Press titles, please contact us in one of the following ways:

Phone: 1-800-421-3976
Facsimile: 1-480-949-1707
Email: info@poisonedpenpress.com
Website: www.poisonedpenpress.com

Poisoned Pen Press
6962 E. First Ave. Ste 103
Scottsdale, AZ 85251